THE VINYL DETECTIVE

ATTACK AND DECAY

Also by Andrew Cartmel and available from Titan Books

Written in Dead Wax
The Run-Out Groove
Victory Disc
Flip Back
Low Action

THE VINYL DETECTIVE

ATTACK AND DECAY

ANDREW CARTMEL

TITAN BOOKS

The Vinyl Detective: Attack and Decay
Print edition ISBN: 9781789098969
E-book edition ISBN: 9781789098976

Published by Titan Books
A division of Titan Publishing Group Ltd.
144 Southwark Street, London SE1 0UP

First Titan edition: June 2022
10 9 8 7 6 5 4 3 2 1

A CIP catalogue record for this title is available from the British Library.

Printed and bound by CPI Group (UK) Ltd, Croydon, CR0 4YY.

For Alasdair Shanks, aka the Dude.

1: BAD TATTOO

"Someone is watching our house."

Nevada had just been out to do the recycling—mostly wine bottles, it has to be said—and was now standing between the Quad speakers, pretty much in the sweet spot, in fact, in front of the sofa where I was sitting with our friend Jordon Tinkler and one of our indolent wastrel cats.

"Is it that creepy corpse-faced motherfucker?" said Tinkler.

"I imagine it must be," said Nevada, "judging by the felicity of your description."

"Yeah, I noticed him, too."

"Well, thank you so much for alerting us."

"Oh, so now I'm supposed to be in charge of security around here?"

I was about to disrupt this bickering with a pressing enquiry about what exactly a corpse-faced motherfucker might look like, when the doorbell rang. I went and let Agatha in.

Our friend, Agatha DuBois-Kanes. Also known as Clean Head.

She came into the sitting room and settled into an armchair. She had the look of a woman who would be entirely relaxed if she suddenly discovered that a sharp-clawed obligate carnivore was hiding under her chair and might begin attacking her toes at any moment.

Which was just as well.

Perhaps with that in mind, she stretched her long legs in front of her. Out of obligate carnivore reach.

Tinkler couldn't keep his eyes off those legs, and you could hardly blame him. They were clad in dove-grey leggings, as tight and shiny as though they'd been sprayed on.

"Did you happen to notice someone watching the house?" I said.

Agatha looked up at me, perhaps a little startled. "Someone is watching your place?"

"A creepy-looking corpse-faced motherfucker," said Tinkler. "Standing out there, staring creepily like this." He made a blankly bug-eyed and fixedly gazing face which actually *was* fairly creepy.

"He could have been creepily staring at any of the buildings along here," I said. "Not necessarily our place."

Beside me on the sofa, Turk—short for Turquoise—stirred. She was lying on her side with her back luxuriantly arched and her paws stretched out to rest companionably against my leg, as though arrested in the spring and stride of the hunt. Now, perhaps in response to the tension in my voice, she allowed her sharp little claws to emerge briefly, pressing emphatically into me, maybe in readiness for that hunt.

Or perhaps just to remind me who was boss.

"No," said Tinkler. "Definitely your charming domicile that he's focused on. With obsessive interest, some might say."

"I'm sorry. I didn't notice anyone out there," said Agatha.

"You would have noticed this motherfucker," said Tinkler. "He's creepy and corpse-faced."

"Well, shouldn't we do something about him?" said Agatha. "If he is out there?"

To my surprise, Nevada shook her head. "No. He'll probably just go away."

"He'll probably just go away," I said.

Nevada had wandered over to the table where she was taking a cork out of a wine bottle. "And if he doesn't, there's nothing coming through that door that I can't handle."

"So much potential there for innuendo," said Tinkler. "Where to start?"

Just then, under Nevada's ministrations, the cork came out of the bottle with a ripely plosive *pop* that made me jump.

"Well, I want to get a look at this guy," I said, repressing the wave of anger that came from being startled. I was definitely on edge. The notion of a malevolent cadaverous onlooker tends to do that to me. "And maybe take a photo of him." Experience had taught me to err on the side of caution in these matters.

Nevada looked at me with approval and smiled. "That's a good idea."

At that moment the doorbell rang and our third dinner guest arrived. A new friend of ours called Saxon Ghost. Of course, he hadn't been born with a name like that. He'd created it himself in tribute to two great record producers who had been his heroes, back when he'd been an aspiring record producer himself. Unfortunately, he'd fucked it up—he'd got one of the names wrong—but, like a bad tattoo, he owned it.

Saxon Ghost was in many ways the opposite of Agatha—he was white, male, short, stout—but they shared one attribute. His scalp was as closely shaved as hers. Maybe he'd shaved it especially for us this evening.

Maybe she had, too.

As with Tinkler, Saxon Ghost had brought some records with him in a smart canvas shoulder bag the colour of damp sand, with dark tan leather trim, purpose-built for carrying LPs. A possession which I immediately coveted. As, apparently, did Tinkler.

"Is that your Original Peter?" he said, referring to the luggage brand. "Or are you just pleased to see us?"

Saxon gave this more of an indulgent chuckle than it merited. "Yeah, this model is called the Utrecht Record Hunter, I think."

Tinkler already had his phone out, looking it up. "Apparently its capacious gusset allows it to take more in than you can usually expect to fit." He was in full innuendo mode, grinning at Agatha.

"I'm not even listening," she said.

"It's lovely," said Nevada, who always had an eye for a stylish accessory. She glanced at me. "I think I know what I'm getting someone for his birthday."

"Costs over two hundred quid," said Tinkler. "Sorry to be pouring cold water, but I thought you ought to know."

Nevada was indeed a little taken aback. "Well, maybe if some funds flood in…"

Funds in our household came from Nevada's sales of vintage fashion items—i.e. second-hand clothes—and my sales of rare vinyl. Flooding in was not what they were currently doing.

"I might be able to help you with that," said Saxon Ghost.

"In that case, allow me to pour you a very generous glass of a very good wine," said Nevada.

Saxon chuckled and, while Nevada poured the wine in the kitchen, he opened his record bag. The Utrecht Record Hunter had apparently not been exploited to its full capacious extent—he took out a modest handful of albums.

As with the LPs Tinkler had brought, these were all Decca pressings.

Unlike Tinkler, however, Saxon's selection consisted of Stravinsky with a bit of Rimsky-Korsakov thrown in for variety.

Saxon Ghost didn't look like a man who listened to a lot of classical music. Indeed, his background was in producing punk rock. But nowadays he was a devotee of French and Russian symphonists of the late nineteenth to mid-twentieth century.

Whereas Tinkler had brought over a trio of albums by some sixties beat combo called the Rolling Stones.

The thing about Decca was that they had pretty much invented high-fidelity sound recording, at least on this side of the Atlantic, and had routinely created audiophile landmarks of the classical repertoire. It just so happened that the Stones had also been recording for this same label at the height of their powers.

What's more, there were a handful of British jazz masterpieces, like Tubby Hayes's early LPs, which had been recorded by Decca on their Tempo subsidiary in the 1950s and 1960s.

Indeed, I had a couple of these lined up for us to listen to later. First, though, we were playing the Stones' *Their Satanic Majesties Request*. Nevada looked at the lenticular cover. "I gave you a copy of this," she said. "I brought one back for you from America."

"That's right," said Tinkler. "Variant US copy. Thank you very much. This, however, is the British *original*." He held up the record. It was one of the rare examples of a Decca stereo pressing with a green label. Tinkler put it on the Garrard.

It sounded so good I almost forgot to worry about the guy watching the house.

Sometimes record companies compressed pop songs so they would sound better on cheap radios, but when Decca made these albums they were basically turning out Rolls-Royces. They didn't know how to do anything else.

Tinkler was busy showing Agatha the inner sleeve. The original inner sleeve, of course. "See the 'red smoke' design? A deliberate riposte to the red 'Fool' inner sleeve of *Sergeant Pepper*. That's a Beatles album."

"Of course it's a Beatles album," said Agatha. "*I'm* not a fool."

"I am, though, ma'am. Your humble fool. At your service."

"Now," said Nevada, leaning over and refilling Saxon Ghost's glass, "I believe you said something about money, money, money."

"Right." Saxon nodded and set his wine aside. Time for business. "Okay, so how much do you know about black metal or death metal?"

"I know enough not to listen to it," I said.

"Tut-tut," said Tinkler censoriously. "Very narrow-minded. And surely those are two quite different subgenres?"

"I'm just not as much of a headbanger as you," I said.

"Or, to put it differently, you're less of a headbanger than me."

Before I could ask Tinkler in what way he imagined this was putting it differently, the doorbell rang, announcing the arrival of our fourth and final guest that evening. Sydney Reasoner was a tall young woman who was employed as a camera operator. We had first met her on Halig Island when she was working for Stinky Stanmer, but we didn't hold that against her.

She was currently dating Saxon Ghost despite, to paraphrase Tinkler, being twice his height and half his age. After the flurry of greetings and much pouring of drinks, Saxon said, "Where were we?"

"We got as far as you asking us about death metal," I said.

He nodded. "That's right. I know this guy who runs a small but very lucrative record label." I could see Nevada start to glow at the word *lucrative*. "Specialises in hard rock music of the Nordic variety. His name is Owen Winter. Except Owen and Winter are both spelled with a 'Y'. Owyn Wynter."

"It's okay," I said. "We're friends with Erik Make Loud. We understand the principle of stupid rock music names."

"Of course you do. I was forgetting."

"And you think Mr Wynter might have a job for me."

"I do. That I do, mate. And it could involve an all-expenses-paid trip to Sweden."

"A trip to Sweden," said Nevada.

"I'll come along too," said Agatha, instantly. "It's about time for a road trip. What does the Tingler think?"

"My god," said Tinkler. "The Tingler is tingling. In fact, that sound you hear is me coming... Can I amend that to arriving? Arriving at the airport with you guys. All of us together. Going to Sweden together. Arriving there at the airport to join you. Road trip!"

"Road trip," concurred Agatha.

"Can I high-five you?" said Tinkler.

"No."

Saxon Ghost leaned forward. His small blue eyes were suddenly solemn. "There's one thing I want you to know," he said. He sounded very serious.

"Okay."

"Some of these death metal people were truly into some weird shit. They called them church burners."

"Is that because they..."

"Supposedly. Anyway, some of them were—and for all I know still *are*—genuinely dangerous." He looked at us. "You guys are my friends..."

"You're our friend, too," said Nevada warmly. And it wasn't just the wine talking.

"So, I don't want to send you into peril."

"Don't worry," said Nevada.

Beside her, Agatha nodded seriously in firm agreement. "We can handle ourselves."

"Can I watch it while you handle yourselves?" said Tinkler, adding thoughtfully, "I think I've settled on that line of innuendo."

"All right," said Saxon Ghost. "Just be careful, okay?" He glanced at his phone. "I've sent you Owyn's number and you can take it from there. Like I said, he's not short of a few bob. So don't undercharge him."

"Don't worry," said Nevada. "We won't."

Even though we hadn't even taken the job yet, Saxon's warning had unsettled me.

So, after supper I insisted that Nevada and I go out and look for the corpse-faced watcher.

There was no one there.

2: CORPSE-FACED MOTHERFUCKER

A few nights later I was returning from Putney where I'd spent several fruitful hours scouring the charity shops.

Normally this was an activity Nevada and I would have undertaken together, but Agatha was taking some time off work and she and Nevada had gone out for a girls' day— just the two of them. Their plan was to eat lunch at a pub in Richmond, their visit topped and tailed by a finely calibrated pillage of the local charity shops in pursuit of high fashion at low, low prices.

Not to be outdone, Tinkler had also decided to take a day off work—this never required much inciting—and invited me for a *boys'* day out, commencing with lunch at his place on Putney Hill, followed by a thorough perusal of every crate of vinyl in every charity shop in the vicinity.

Lunch at Tinkler's had consisted mostly, but to my surprise not entirely, of high-end takeaway delivered to his door. The surprising bit was that he had decided to try to do some cooking himself. In fact, he attempted to replicate one of my recipes—the parsnips with olive oil, maple syrup and herb glaze.

Tinkler volunteering to do anything resembling work in the kitchen would normally have set alarm bells ringing. But it seemed his obsession with Agatha, and with getting laid in general, had entered a new phase: he'd decided that the solution to all his problems was cooking for girls.

"Not just cooking for them, you understand. But cooking tasty, appealing, hip and *appealingly hip* cuisine. Think of it as the culinary equivalent of the rabat solo on Yusef Lateef's *Eastern Sounds*. Oh, and easy. Whatever recipes you give me must be easy. Above all else, on god's mercy, easy."

So I had started him off with the parsnips, which really was a very easy recipe. Gleaned off the back of a bag of those noble root vegetables, purchased at a local supermarket, if memory serves.

Tinkler hadn't had any maple syrup on hand, so he'd substituted honey. But despite this he actually managed to bake the parsnips to the correct golden brown, admittedly with my frequently solicited help and supervision, and the honey had provided a fine substitute. The parsnips had proved to be a pleasant addition to the lunch. Indeed, one of the highlights.

After eating the food and drinking the bottle of wine Nevada had thoughtfully provided for us—"It's that Viognier-Chardonnay blend, not a world beater, but fresh and tasty and you'll be eating spicy food anyway, right? It's always spicy food at the Tingler's"—we hit the charity shops.

My best find of the afternoon proved to be a bunch of Joni Mitchell albums, Japanese pressings, from the period when that certified genius had been working with some of the finest jazz musicians on the West Coast. They were in immaculate shape and I had no doubt that I could find a buyer for them at a healthy mark-up: the sort of mark-up that Nevada would approve of.

"You aren't tempted to keep them for yourself?" said Tinkler. "The vinyl is high purity and the pressings themselves…"

"Got to love that precision manufacturing."

"Right."

"But how can it ever be as faithful to the original sound as an original pressing?" I held up the Joni Mitchell albums. They made an agreeably weighty stack. "In this case, probably originating at some record plant in Santa Monica."

Tinkler chuckled. "I was the one who told you that. I was the first one to promulgate the thesis of the original pressing."

"You may well be telling the truth, my friend," I said. "Don't let it become a habit."

"No chance of that."

We shook hands and went our separate ways off into this late grey afternoon on Putney Hill. I caught the bus back home. Our estate is also on a hill, and there are a number of routes back there from a variety of bus stops. I tend to choose the one that takes me home through maximum greenery, including a patch of what you might almost call urban woodland.

This is where I found myself with the sun starting to set and the smoky grey afternoon transforming under the rich coppery light of evening. There was a strange quality to this copper glow spreading all around me—it added to an odd sense of stillness, as though the weather was about to change.

And, weirdly for this time of day, I found I was quite alone. I couldn't see another human being.

I did, however, see a cat. Turk came sneaking out of the foliage and began to accompany me on the walk home. Well, *accompany* is an exaggeration. She would dart ahead of me, wait for me to catch up, then dart ahead again.

And then she disappeared completely.

So I found myself walking alone once more—indeed, now even more emphatically alone, having been abandoned by my trusty cat.

I had left the patch of woodland behind and was now moving through our estate. A remote section that Nevada liked to describe as: "A location from *A Clockwork Orange* now covered with moss." Or, for purposes of brevity, "moss-covered *Clockwork Orange*".

It was a kind of modernist courtyard with a large oak tree at the centre. The sun was setting. In that last smouldering late light, the oak towered over the square. An inky shadow detached itself from the upper branches and flapped down towards me, swooping low over the strange statues.

A crow.

It landed in a thick, shiny green hedge just ahead of me and turned its head to observe me. Its eyes were quite unusual. But what really set this crow apart was its beak.

Through an accident, whether genetic or physical, the two halves of the beak met and overlapped. They made me think of the blades on an open pair of scissors.

I looked on the crow with a surge of sympathy. It must be hard getting on in life with a beak like that. The crow looked back at me calmly, seemingly aware of my sympathy but indifferent to it. Then he rose up, a shadow come to life, and flapped vigorously away.

I turned to watch this strange and somehow noble creature fly off, to lose its tiny blackness in the vast blackness of the night sky.

That was when I saw him.

He was dark as the crow, dressed all in black. His face was dead white but with bold black patches around his eyes, suggestive of the hollow sockets of a corpse. The alternative comparison, with a panda, did not occur at the time; even if it had, I doubt that it would have proved helpful or amusing.

I wasn't in any mood to be amused. Frankly, I was a little alarmed.

And that alarm was in no way diminished by the top hat.

Although it *was* tempered by an annoyed reflection that my beloved and my best friend had both neglected to warn me about that little detail. You'd think they could have at least mentioned the hat.

It was a black silk top hat, worn slightly askew, like a precarious stove pipe that might spew smoke at any moment.

We were staring at each other, myself and this apparition. It was a taut and progressively tightening moment. We stared at each other for what seemed like a long time.

In fact, time seemed to be slowing down. My heartbeat was thunderous in my ears, but steady and measured. The corpse-faced clown in the top hat stared at me and stared at me and didn't move. The moment stretched on and on, to the point that it began to seem quite possible, indeed quite likely, that it would never actually end.

Then a deeply affronted animal cry resounded off the mossy stone walls.

It was the unique sound of Turk voicing her displeasure.

I turned towards her cry, but she was nowhere to be seen. I looked back at the—

But he was gone.

Perhaps not unexpectedly, I very much kept my eyes open and maintained a vigilant watch on the remainder of my journey home. But I didn't see him again.

Turk, however, rejoined me a split second before I opened the garden gate. She waited while I held it open for her—despite the fact that, when she chose to, she could and did slither under it with ease—and then she ran inside. As soon as the door was securely locked behind us, I phoned Nevada. "I saw the corpse-faced motherfucker," I said.

"When? Just now?"

"Yes. You should have warned me about the top hat."

"What? He was wearing a *top hat*?"

"And you didn't say anything about a crow…"

"A crow? What crow? You mean a bird?"

"Yes."

"Are you feeling all right, dear?"

"No, actually. You know what, I don't feel that great." The room swum gently around me. "I think Tinkler has drugged me."

"The bastard. *Again*."

"I think so. Let me call you back later."

"Okay. I am coming home. Right home, right away."

"Okay." I hung up and dialled Tinkler's number. To his credit, he answered without delay and didn't dissemble. "It's a really mellow hit, isn't it?"

"Tinkler, that honey you used on the parsnips…"

"I was wondering when you'd notice!"

"It was the jar that Nevada's mother gave you."

"Well, not the exact jar. As you might imagine, I've gone through quite a number of jars since then."

"But it's the Hashish Honey."

"You do understand that hashish is a misnomer, inserted for meretricious reasons of alluring alliteration? It's actually *cannabis* honey. But what's in a name. Isn't it a zany high?"

"You should have warned me."

"I wasn't thinking. I didn't realise. I just used that honey for the recipe, not realising it was the doped honey. But I guess I should have surmised as much, given that it's the only kind of honey I ever have in my kitchen. Really mellow high, isn't it?"

"Not when you run into the corpse-faced—"

"Good old Corpse Face. Hang on, just a minute, I'm getting a text from Nevada. What is this? Something about a top hat? You're kidding! He was sporting a top hat this time?"

"I'll talk to you later, Tinkler."

"Later."

Even as I hung up, a key turned in the front door and Nevada stepped inside. "I've done a sweep of the estate," she said. "There's no sign of Corpse Face."

"Well, good," I said. Nevada was taking off her coat.

"Are you still high?" she said.

"Oh, yeah."

She took off her shoes and then continued taking off her clothes. "Would you like to come along to the bedroom?"

"Yes," I said. "Yes, I would."

3: OFFICIALLY NIGHT

Tinkler was over at our place for supper a few nights later when we saw our corpse-faced friend again.

His presence—Corpse Face's—was announced by Turk crashing through the cat flap, closely followed by our other cat Fanny, both fleeing into the safety of the house, clearly spooked by something. Nevada glanced out the kitchen window and then came through to the sitting room, abundant thunder brewing in those big blue eyes.

"I am a tolerant woman."

"Yes, you are, you certainly are," said Tinkler hastily.

"I am willing to put up with a certain amount of creepy corpse-faced motherfuckery."

"Of course you are. Very commendable. We're all tolerant people. We encourage tolerance. We frown on intolerance."

"But when they start scaring our cats, that's where I draw the line." Nevada looked at me. "Do you want to help me nail this bastard?"

"Of course," I said.

Nevada went into our bedroom and came back with an elegant green rucksack slung over her shoulder.

"What's that?" said Tinkler.

"My go-bag," said Nevada.

"And what, pray tell, constitutes a go-bag?"

"Well, in this case it's a highly fashionable Made Galli rucksack in forest green. I've also got the black one, but oddly enough the green is better for remaining unseen in low light conditions."

"Keep those fashion nuggets coming," said Tinkler. "I take it dinner won't be happening any time soon."

"I think it's chiefly because the bronze fittings are less reflective than the copper ones."

"So far, so snoozeworthy."

"Is *this* snoozeworthy?" Nevada unzipped the bag and drew out a Taser.

"I'm disappointed it isn't pink like your last one," said Tinkler. "Shocking pink. Get it? *Shocking*."

"We bought it for the same knockdown price as the shocking pink one," said Nevada, who liked her bargains. She turned to me, holding up the Taser. "So, are we going to nail this bastard? This cat-scaring bastard!"

"We are," I said.

"Can I stay here in safety and hide?" said Tinkler.

"Hard to imagine you doing anything else, old buddy."

"Well, hide and also listen to your admittedly fairly good hi-fi," said Tinkler to me. "I could entertain your cats, too."

"Okay," I said. "But don't touch supper. Those baked mushrooms will keep just fine for hours."

"Hours," said Tinkler with sudden concern. "Are you likely to be gone for hours?"

"No, all I'm saying is that the mushrooms will keep just fine. They will only need a little warming up when we get back from—"

"Seeking to perpetrate an act of vigilante violence on a corpse-faced interloper."

"We are not perpetrating anything," said Nevada, tucking the Taser back into her natty green rucksack and zipping it shut. "This is just for eventualities."

"Eventualities, I see. Is it all right if I at least eat some bread while you're gone?"

"Just don't eat the whole loaf. Don't spoil your appetite."

"Have vigilante fun."

"He was standing over here," said Nevada, "when he scared our cats." She pointed left, and we went out of our front gate and turned that way. We went past Ginnie and Sue's house, past the dense patch of vegetation on the corner where Fanny liked to lurk and periodically spring out at us, past the ramp down to the lower level of the estate where the central boiler room had once existed, and out into the street that looped around between our estate and the walled perimeter of the Abbey.

"You said you saw him hanging around moss-covered *Clockwork Orange*?"

"Yes," I said. And that was in the opposite direction to the way we were heading now.

Then we saw him. "There he is," whispered Nevada, gripping my arm.

And, as if he'd heard her whisper, Corpse Face turned to look at us.

I was glad to see that he was still wearing his top hat, to confirm that I hadn't imagined it.

But he'd added a dapper black ribbon to the hat, a long silk ribbon that trailed down at the back. When he turned to the light, I saw that the ribbon also served to fasten a flower to the hat. Some kind of all-black flower, that is. It looked like a rose.

A black rose. But of course.

Since his clothing was also all black and clung close to his body, it was difficult to make out any detail. Perhaps a close-fitting business suit…?

Corpse-faced motherfucker in a business suit?

Well, why not?

He turned away from us in a prompt but calm and orderly fashion, and strode off down the street, across the pavement and up a walkway into the estate.

We hurried after him.

As we followed him into the enclosed walkway, we couldn't see him, but we could hear the echo of his boots. He was wearing pointy-toed black boots with high Cuban heels. Of course he was.

And he was making pretty good time in them.

We pursued him, his heels tapping, down a white stone staircase with a blue steel handrail which led out into an open area, where it converged with a retrofitted wheelchair ramp that curved down from the right.

To our left was another enclosed walkway, this one made of chocolate-brown brick set in concrete. It was into this that Corpse Face was walking briskly, but still quite calmly. Certainly with no sense of panic.

We followed him through the walkway, closing in on him inexorably.

His boot heels echoed clearly all around us, the sound staying briskly ahead of us, as steady and as stable as a metronome.

At the far end of the walkway was daylight—well, *evening* light—and we saw Corpse Face impose his dark silhouette on this fading glow as he reached the end and turned left.

We turned left a second later, following him.

We found ourselves in a part of the estate I couldn't recall venturing into before, a sort of rectangular canyon of brown brick. It was abruptly cooler in this artificial canyon—chilly, in fact—and I found myself suddenly shivering.

On three sides of us were dwellings with cheery lights coming on in their kitchens as families began to serve dinner. The lights swelled out into generously sized gardens in front of these flats.

I call them flats, but they were more like compact town houses, with another level on top of them. Like at my place, the ones on the ground level all had big front gardens, in which a commendable amount of greenery thrived, giving this concrete canyon something of the feel of a natural, wild place rather than somewhere boringly tamed and urban.

But I would have appreciated the boringly tamed and urban just now.

Because when we emerged from the enclosed walkway, close on the heels—the Cuban heels—of Corpse Face, he was abruptly nowhere to be seen.

He was, however, still to be *heard*.

Specifically the sharp clip of his boot heels, marching away from us at the same efficient, measured pace. Ghostly footsteps marched past a wall of cypress trees on our left. Light spilled out of the kitchen windows, turning the trees into lime-green beacons in the dim evening light.

We *heard* his boots walking past the pale green trees.

But we couldn't see him.

I looked at Nevada. "Can you see him?"

"No. But I can hear him. Can you hear him too?"

"Yes, he's walking along there."

"Past those cedars…?"

"Yes."

Nevada and I looked at each other. The footsteps continued, drawing away from us, maintaining their brisk, forthright pace.

But we couldn't see him.

I told myself there had to be a rational explanation, but nonetheless I felt a cold thrill go through me.

The disembodied footsteps stopped. They had reached the end of the row of cedars and now there was silence. Several moments passed.

And then Corpse Face appeared.

Standing at the end of the row of trees. He waved to us, grinning.

I felt as if the ground had suddenly dropped out from under me. "How the hell did he do that?" I said. He had vanished and then reappeared again, as if rendered temporarily invisible.

Corpse Face lifted his top hat and tipped it at us in salute. Revealed by the removal of the hat, his hair was long and—wait for it—dead black.

"I don't know," said Nevada. "But he's not getting away with scaring our cats."

We moved forwards, towards him.

Instantly, he was gone again.

There was a pause. And then his footsteps resumed, the emphatic tapping of those boot heels moving along now in a new direction, some distance ahead of us, but equally invisible.

We could hear him clearly moving past another row of gardens. We could see those gardens, but we couldn't see *him*. Then the footsteps changed direction. Now they were to our right but coming towards us, getting louder, echoing clearly in this concrete canyon as they inexorably approached.

Nevada and I were looking at each other. It was the eeriest of sensations. We could hear the motherfucker, but we couldn't see him.

Then, suddenly, we *could* see him.

He was moving up the curving white concrete of the wheelchair ramp. His already impressive pace seemed to be, if anything, increasing. Before he disappeared entirely, we set off after him.

The curvature of the ramp was such that we didn't glimpse him again until he was emerging from it, back up onto street level.

And then we saw the direction he was heading.

Beside me, I heard Nevada suck in her breath. We had both come to the realisation at the same time. "He's doubling back," said Nevada.

"He's heading for our house," I said.

The streetlights came on around us as we broke into a run. It was suddenly, officially night.

To our right was the dark bulk of the Abbey with its comfortingly high wall shielding it. To our left, concealed by its own modest wall, was our back garden.

And, as we drew nearer, we could hear someone moving around inside.

We ran to the gate and flung it open.

Tinkler was there, eating, with his feet propped up on one of our all-weather outdoor tables. He was seated on the all-weather garden sofa and making use of another one of the outdoor tables to fully enjoy a plate of food, a glass of wine, a spliff and his tablet with the vivid hues of what might well have been some shameless pornography flashing on it, shining brightly in the twilight garden.

He also had both our cats at his feet.

Tinkler looked up in surprise as we came in through the gate, frozen in the act of lifting a sandwich to his mouth. It was a very characteristic act.

The cats yawned. Or rather Fanny yawned and Turk couldn't be bothered. Our arrival held no surprises for them. With their keen feline hearing they had both, unlike the startled Tinkler, heard us coming from a long way off.

Nevada and I came into the garden. I was still straining to listen for the distinctive rapping of those Cuban heels, but all around us was silence.

"I hope you don't mind," said Tinkler. "I'm eating the supper you prepared in the much easier sandwich format."

"Tinkler. The baked mushrooms…"

"I had to eat them. You've been gone for hours."

"We've been gone for less than seven minutes."

"Really? It felt like *forever*. What happened with Corpse Face?"

"He… slipped away from us."

Somewhere out in the night, a fox yelped.

"Get your feet off that table, Tinkler," snarled Nevada. It has to be said, my darling was a trifle on edge.

"Well, excuse me," said Tinkler, nevertheless removing his feet from the garden furniture with commendable alacrity.

"It's not a fucking *footstool*."

"All right, all right. So touchy…"

Nevada retrieved control of herself. "I don't mean to be uncivil, Tinkler."

"Of course not."

"It's just that this corpse-faced motherfucker is leading us a merry dance."

"Doesn't sound so merry."

"It isn't," I said. "Not least because he has given us the strong impression that he can disappear."

"Disappear? As in…"

"Become invisible."

"Well, that's not good."

* * *

We left Tinkler and our cats as we'd found them, closed the garden gate behind us, and circled around to the other side of our house. I knew that we wouldn't find Corpse Face there. He would have pulled another one of his patented disappearing acts.

But I was wrong.

Lo and behold, there he was.

Standing politely enough outside our front gate, though also peering with apparently unabashed voyeurism through the various shrubs Nevada had planted in a vain attempt to screen our house, directly into our kitchen window.

The kitchen had the look of an abandoned stage set. The big oval glass casserole dish that had contained the baked mushrooms was on display on top of the stove, with most of its contents pillaged and gone. Stuffed into Tinkler's face. Normally this would have occasioned some knee-jerk outrage at his greed, selfishness and general poor behaviour. At the moment, we had other things on our mind.

Corpse Face turned to look at us as though we'd been expected and, what's more, we were irritatingly late.

Then he turned and strode away.

It was not at all like he was fleeing from us. It was like he was a fitness instructor—admittedly a weird-looking fitness instructor entirely dressed in black—and we were incompetent stragglers in his class—admittedly a small and angry class—who needed to pull ourselves together and catch up. And he was certainly not going to slow down for us.

Instead, he moved at an athletic and progressively increasing clip, loping off across the estate, moving at a speed that in other circumstances and from another individual might have been impressive, even admirable.

From Corpse Face, it was just plain annoying.

It rapidly became clear that he was heading towards the place where I'd first seen him—and seen his herald, the crow with the twisted beak.

We pursued Corpse Face's swift-moving thin black figure, descended a staircase to a lower level and suddenly there we were, in moss-covered *Clockwork Orange*. The oak tree loomed over us as we descended the stairs, cutting off the luminous underbelly of the clouds in turn reflecting the lights of the city sprawled around us.

As with the concrete canyon where we'd earlier pursued Corpse Face, there were generously sized gardens on three sides of us. But there the resemblance ended. Instead of lemon-scented cypress trees, glowing like elegant beacons in the darkness, the disembodied tapping of Corpse Face's Cuban heels now advanced briskly among heaps of rubbish, discarded furniture, unrecycled recycling and a mouldering mattress with the words *Nothing Really Mattress* spray-painted on it in large red letters.

Also, dormant and defunct barbecues, ditto bicycles, and many an abandoned, unloved and rain-sodden toy.

Nevada and I looked at each other. Even my beloved's resolve seemed to weaken a little at this point. *Here we go again*, we both thought.

The footsteps of our nemesis continued, not fleeing, but making firm, invisible and uncompromising progress past the gardens full of garbage.

We listened to the distinctive ringing of those boot heels connecting with the concrete: assertive, ineluctable, invisible.

Then, suddenly, there was another invisible sound…

A door opening. Right beside us. We turned and looked at the nearest flat: indeed, the one right beside us. Unhappily, its door wasn't open. It was very firmly closed. And the dark windows suggested an empty property.

But we had heard what we had heard. Nevada and I looked at each other. Then, from the phantom open door beside us, we heard the voices of two young women, invisible but apparently standing right next to us, and the following deathless exchange ensued:

"She's not really a blonde, you know. I mean, the actual actress who plays her. She is actually a brunette."

"I know, I've seen her."

"It's a bit of a shock to discover that the Mother of Dragons isn't a natural blonde."

"I know, but I'd still give her one."

Nevada and I looked at each other again.

Then we looked up.

Above us, on top of the row of ground floor flats, was a row of upstairs flats with a walkway in front of them. And on that walkway, immediately above us, were two young women, one of them unlocking a bicycle and the other looking on, arms folded, as they discussed the shagability of Daenerys Targaryen.

Beyond them, at the far end of the walkway, we could see good ol' Corpse Face.

He was now above the position where his footsteps had ceased, at the end of the row of gardens. He'd stopped and currently had his foot up on the low concrete wall of the walkway, revealing a shocking red sock.

He had unzipped his boots and removed them.

Now he lowered his red-socked foot and scooted off, disappearing soundlessly into the stairwell of the walkway. A moment later, after a now familiar pause which was no doubt necessitated by putting his boots back on and zipping them back up, he appeared and waved to us. Then he disappeared back into the stairwell.

Now we knew what was going on, we went up the stairs at our end and pursued him. Much good it did us. When he realised that we were on to him, he actually did flee. And he ran like an Olympic sprinter.

I have no idea how he could run in boots with heels like that, but he did.

We followed him down the stairs, past the oak tree, out of the square, down past the row of garages. There we watched him run like hell, his shadow stretching then reversing as he ran past the floodlights of the playing field. He was drawing inexorably away from us.

By the time we reached Beverley Brook, he was gone.

"So that's how he kept disappearing," said Tinkler.

"Yes."

"He was running around on the upstairs walkways?"

"Yes."

Tinkler chortled.

"Why are you amused?" said Nevada.

Tinkler was doing his idiot yokel face. "He was using one of those new-fangled *staircase* things. It enabled him to *go upwards*. You ain't seen nothing like it. They only have them in the big cities, amongst them urban elites."

I could see Nevada in danger of getting seriously angry. But Tinkler was on a roll and he just kept going.

"There's people in the air above us! We don't get that where we come from…" He paused and thankfully dropped the yokel schtick. "But we *do* get that where we come from." He wagged an accusing finger at us. "Or rather where *you* come from. You've got one of those walkways right above this place. You live under one."

"It's a matter of sound perception," I said.

Tinkler wiped the obnoxious glee off his face. He might even have been genuinely interested now.

"Sound perception? How so?"

"Well, as you have noticed, this place does have a walkway above it, but it faces out into open space."

"So, nothing to reflect the sound." For a buffoon, he was often surprisingly quick-witted.

"Right," I said. "So when people are moving along on the upstairs walkway here you hardly hear them."

Nevada was nodding now, her anger faded, caught up in the problem as we discussed how both the concrete canyon and moss-covered *Clockwork Orange* were effectively courtyards. "In contrast to us here, they're almost completely surrounded with stone walls, and as a consequence there's this acoustic trick."

"Curse those acoustic tricks. You mean the acoustic reflectivity of the built environment in those places conspired to create an auditory illusion?"

"Yes."

"And Corpse Face exploited it."

"Judging by the fact that he took his noisy footwear off when he crept up the stairs, he knew exactly what he was doing."

"You know what that means?" said Tinkler.

"That he's a very annoying corpse-faced motherfucker," said Nevada.

Tinkler shook his head. "This guy knows about acoustics."

4: NO BLOOD

"Saxon Ghost is very emphatic that you are the man for this job and, having done some research on you, I dare say I agree with him." Owyn Wynter smiled and nodded, affably enough, at me and then Nevada. And then his gaze returned, a trifle nervously, to his hand.

Which Fanny was holding between her paws.

Owyn Wynter seemed like a nice guy, so much so that one was almost tempted to forgive him for the spelling of his name.

There was more to forgive, however. His record company was called White Raven Records.

"Except it's spelled Whyte Ravyn Records," I'd told Nevada. "With a 'y' in White and a 'y' in Raven."

"Of course it is."

"But that, at least, is for a fairly good reason."

"Can there be such a thing?"

The fairly good reason, as Owyn Wynter himself explained to us in some detail, was that, after they came up with the name, they found out there already was a White Raven Records—conventional spelling—in Poland.

Owyn had come over to our house for dinner on a warm and windy Thursday evening. I had diced shallots and garlic, steamed three kinds of beans—petit-pois, broad beans and fine beans, all sweet and green—then gently cooked them all in olive oil, with added lemon juice, lemon zest and fresh dill. For her part, Nevada had agonised over whether to serve up our best Rhône red, or our second best, and ended up popping the corks on both.

She was a little nervous because she'd built up this meeting in her expectations and now it suddenly was upon us. While we'd issued the invitation soon after Saxon had given us Owyn's number, it had taken a little while for our diaries to synchronise. Or at least, for Owyn Wynter's busy diary to synchronise with our somewhat less busy one.

"Whyte Ravyn Records," he'd said almost as soon as he was through the door, insisting on giving us both a business card. I suppose it was less rude than playing favourites and only giving a card to one of us. "We used to call it Right Raving Records. Because we used to party so hard." He announced this with the smoothness of a much-repeated anecdote, and Nevada laughed dutifully.

It was hard to imagine Owyn Wynter ever partying hard. It was much easier to imagine him taking care to remain hydrated on his mountain bike during a bracing ride to the gym. He had short blond hair, an affable, open face and he was athletic in a casual, laidback way. As I say, he seemed like a nice guy. Even the cats took a shine to him.

At least, Fanny did. She'd permitted our visitor to stroke her and enjoyed the attention considerably; so much so that, when he tried to withdraw his hand, she did what Nevada calls "her little trick".

Owyn Wynter looked at us. He was definitely getting a little nervous now. "How long does she usually…"

"Oh, not long. She generally lets go after a couple of minutes."

"A couple of minutes, I see."

"The important thing," said Nevada, "is not to suddenly pull your hand away, because then things could get messy."

"Messy, I see."

"I mean, right now she has her claws sunk into your hand, but they are so fantastically sharp, and sunk in with such precision and surgical skill, they won't leave a trace."

"Won't leave a trace. I see," said Owyn Wynter. "Surgical skill." He didn't sound entirely convinced.

"There won't even be any blood," said Nevada.

"No blood."

"She's normally very good. She'd never hurt anyone. She doesn't even hurt mice when she brings them in. It's just that, if you're stroking her and you stop stroking her before she feels she's had her full complement of stroking…"

"She grabs your hand and sinks her claws in and holds it there," said Owyn Wynter, in an admirably clear and brief summary.

"Yes."

Suddenly tiring of her game, Fanny released her grip and let the poor human being go free. The poor human being stared at his hand. "My god. You were right. She didn't leave a trace."

"You see?" said Nevada, with something very like pride in her voice.

"You can just see the *faintest* mark where her claws went in."

"That will fade quickly."

"And it hardly hurts at all," said Owyn Wynter gamely, squeezing his hand briefly but comfortingly under his armpit. "Now where was I?"

"You were being poured a glass of very nice wine." Nevada filled his glass. She was outwardly relaxed, but I knew her well enough to sense her enormous relief that the wayward behaviour of a nefarious family pet hadn't deep-sixed our chance of a major payday.

She even gave Fanny a quick caress, running her hand along the supple length of her tail.

"You were just saying he's the right man for the job." Nevada looked at me. It was a look that combined affection and warmth with an unspoken but nonetheless firmly worded request for me not to fuck up what was, despite the excellent food and wine and light-hearted instance of guest-mutilation inflicted by our beloved cat, basically a job interview.

"That's right." Owyn Wynter nodded decisively. "I don't know how much Saxon told you about me…"

He did mention that we shouldn't undercharge you, both Nevada and I were thinking, but instead I said, "Not much, apart from saying you ran a record label."

"I do. We predominantly use streaming, of course. But we also manufacture in physical formats. The sale of these is a comparatively small part of our turnover, although vinyl is a growth area." He looked at me. "In fact, in future, as we continue to expand, I foresee a possible role for you. In supervising the quality control of our vinyl releases. We need someone who understands vinyl and its challenges, and who has good ears."

Nevada's own ears pricked up at this—the prospect of a potentially long-term, potentially lucrative gig. She looked at me. I tried to look back at her with the expression of a man who hadn't already decided that no gig could be sufficiently lucrative to tempt him to listen to Owyn Wynter's kind of music on a long-term basis.

"Anyway, the record label is valuable not just in itself but crucially because it gives us a relationship with the artists. The groups. We get to know them, and they come to trust us. They hire us to arrange their gigs and tours, including some very substantial concerts at big venues."

"That must be so exciting," said Nevada in her best hostess, keep-the-conversation-rolling mode.

"It is. But we're not here to talk about that." He fixed me with his clear-eyed gaze. "Do you know what demonic metal is?"

I said, "I assume it's heavy metal with a lot of pretentious references to demons. Plus gothic typography, of course."

He laughed. "It's *exactly* that. Have you ever heard of the Storm Dream Troopers?"

"Sorry, no."

"For short, just called the Troopers. They were arguably the greatest demonic metal band. Two blokes, two birds." For a moment I thought he meant literally birds—and an angular scissor-beaked crow flapped through my memories on its wide black wings. But then I realised that when he said *birds* he meant *women*. "They were going out. And then they got married. Two couples. They looked great visually. One blond couple, one dark. Like a sort of death metal Abba."

Perhaps to my discredit, this did indeed help me to visualise what the Storm Dream Troopers might look like. It was not a great look.

"Anyway, these guys were Sweden's most extreme demonic metal band. And their album, *Attack and Decay*, is exceptionally rare because it was banned by the Church."

"Can they do that in Sweden?"

"Not really. Probably not anywhere, probably not even in Russia. But what they *can* do, the good people of the Church, is buy up every copy and destroy it. Which is pretty much what they did."

"And you want me to find you a copy," I said.

Owyn Wynter shook his head. "No, I've already found a copy."

Nevada and I looked at each other.

"Well, that makes a refreshing change," she said.

"In fact, I have found a copy of the *even more rare* audiophile 180-gram version. I mean, this is seriously rare. A member of the band was having supper with me the other night. Patrik Nordenfalk." He said this as if he was dropping an important name. "We had dinner together and he told me even *he* doesn't have a copy."

"But you do," said Nevada succinctly.

"Yes," said Owyn Wynter. He had a happy glow in his eye which, I have to admit, as a fellow fanatic, I could all too easily recognise.

"But if you've already got a copy…" I said.

"Well, I haven't actually *got* it," he conceded a trifle ruefully. "I have secured a copy for purchase but I have yet to physically acquire it. Which is where you come in."

"You want us to collect the record for you?" I said.

"And effect payment?" said Nevada. "Make sure it's secure?" Clearly, my honeypie's mind, with its keen aptitude for mayhem, was racing ahead: already weighing up scenarios and potential opportunities for profit.

"All that, yes, please, thank you," said Owyn Wynter. He looked me in the eye. The record-collecting fanatic's gleam had gone and now he was all business. "But most of all, I want you to listen to the record and make sure it's the real thing."

I sighed inwardly because I knew Nevada was not going to be tickled at me looking a gift horse in the mouth, but somebody had to ask the obvious question.

"Why don't you go and pick it up yourself?" I hadn't underestimated my beloved's reaction. Her blue eyes flashed hot with disbelief at this faux pas.

Owyn was unfazed. "Too busy at work. I simply don't have the time. And someone needs to listen to it, listen to it properly, check it out."

Given that this really wasn't my kind of music, I had very few qualms about persisting with another obvious question. "Surely you need to check it out yourself?" Those hot blue eyes had switched to giving me a *My office, now* look. But I persisted. "Wouldn't that be better?"

"Frankly, no," said Owyn Wynter. He turned to Nevada. Her reaction to my obfuscation apparently hadn't gone unnoticed. "I trust his ears better than I trust my own." He said this simply and almost humbly.

"Well, so you should," said Nevada, suddenly both gratified and mollified. She looked at me. I was instantly out of the doghouse, which was a relief because I'm fundamentally a cat person.

"He has very good ears," she said. "He has the *best* ears."

Owyn Wynter seemed gratifyingly disinclined to contradict her. Instead, he nodded and said, "The thing is, Magnus, the guy who is selling this record, says it's in perfect condition. And he's charging me a considerable premium for the privilege of acquiring it in such superb shape. So that's one of the things I want you to do over there—"

"Over there?" said Nevada quickly.

"Over in Sweden."

"Sweden?" said Nevada happily. No doubt the words *foreign jaunt* and *all expenses paid* were dancing in her lively mind.

"Sweden, yes."

"Excellent," said Nevada. "Just checking. When Saxon outlined this caper to us, he did say it might involve a subsidised excursion to beautiful, beautiful Sweden."

"Saxon is absolutely right. I want you go over there, on a subsidised excursion, listen to this record on my behalf and determine if it is indeed the real thing, and indeed in perfect condition, before I pay this Magnus fellow what many might deem a considerable fortune for it."

"Darling," said Nevada, turning to me. "Isn't that lovely? We really are going to get paid to go to Sweden."

"Beautiful, beautiful Sweden."

"Yes. Just so you can listen to a record."

"It is demonic metal," I said. "Don't forget that. We'll be earning every penny."

Owyn chuckled. "Yes, don't forget that. And in case you're wondering, Magnus has very firmly said that he won't ship it over, for us to listen to here," he nodded at my beloved record player which currently had an equally beloved cat asleep in front of it, comfortably sprawled between the Quads. Fanny had apparently exhausted herself savaging our guest's hand earlier. "So you have to go over there."

"So we *have* to go to Sweden," said Nevada. "That is such a shame."

We all laughed, but there was something nagging, small but ceaseless, at the back of my mind. "I kind of hate to bring this up, but Saxon said this job might be dangerous."

"No, darling," chuckled Nevada, taking my hand. "At most he *implied* that it might be dangerous."

Owyn Wynter shrugged. "I don't know why he said that."

"*Implied* that," corrected Nevada.

"Some of these bands are quite eccentric, admittedly…"

"You said this record had been suppressed by the Church."

"Well, they bought up every copy they could find. And presumably destroyed them all, which is one reason it is so sought after."

"And why did they do that?" I said. "Suppress it?"

"Oh, some nonsense about demonic influences corrupting young people. That sort of thing."

"Sounds like a great record."

"No, it is, seriously it is," said Owyn. A happy little note came into his voice when he discussed this venerated piece of vinyl. "It's a very early and very pure example of demonic metal. A great, great classic record. But I still don't see why Saxon would think that you guys just going over there and evaluating and picking up a copy for me should represent any kind of danger to you."

"Well, I guess we were all a little on edge," I said, my mind going back to that evening when Saxon Ghost had come over to dinner, and indeed to a couple of subsequent occasions.

"Why?" said Owyn Wynter. "Was there a reason for you to be on edge? Good name for a band, by the way. On Edge. I wonder if anyone has used it?"

As he considered the possibility of looking this up on his phone, then dismissed it out of fear of being rude, Nevada and I looked at each other. And then, between the two of us, we proceeded to give Owyn a detailed description of the corpse-faced motherfucker and an account of his peregrinations.

Owyn listened patiently and with considerable attention.

Then, when we'd concluded, he immediately said, "Oh, that's Jaunty."

"Jaunty?"

"And he was in full makeup, was he?"

"You *know* this guy?"

Owyn Wynter nodded. "Why yes. He works for me."

"So this corpse-faced creepy motherfucker who has been hanging around our house is *working for you*?" said Nevada.

"And his name is Jaunty?" I said.

"It's short for Jonathan. He's my accountant."

"Your accountant."

"Well, financial comptroller, actually. He is a big fan of the music, hence his appearance. And, you see, he knows about this transaction I'm planning, the purchase of this copy of *Attack and Decay*. And since I'm both paying for the record and paying you for your services—" he looked at me and Nevada, "—through the company, Jaunty has to sign off on any significant capital expenditure. So, he was just doing what he regarded as his due diligence."

"Due diligence?"

"Yes."

"By standing outside our house at strange hours and staring at us?"

"He's eccentric, but he's a superb accountant. And he's harmless."

"Harmless?"

"Well, mostly harmless."

I repressed the urge to make a gag about the number 42, by way of riposte.

"Well, you scared the shit out of us with your corpse-faced motherfucker of an accountant," said Nevada.

"I am sorry about that. I do hope it won't mean you will refuse the job."

"No, but it does mean we expect you to pay for our friends to come along with us."

5: GOTHENBURG

"I hope they haven't lost my trunk," said Tinkler.

"Your trunk?" said Agatha.

"Or damaged it. Heaven forfend. My precious, precious trunk."

"You have a trunk?" said Nevada.

"I checked it in before you guys got here." We were all sitting in the departure lounge where we'd agreed to rendezvous, waiting for our flight. "Magnificent antique travel trunk with all the features. It's not only brass banded, it's bentwood bound."

"*You're* bentwood bound," said Agatha. She was in the seat beside Tinkler; Nevada and I sat opposite them. Through a glass wall beside us we could see down into the concourse of the airport, boiling with activity.

"I'll take that as a compliment. It's pale blue with elegant black trim. Lined with silk. Leather handles. It evokes the golden age of travel when no gentleman of any consequence would go abroad without a full range of accoutrements in a big fuck-off fancy trunk. To hell with your suitcase on wheels or your over-the-shoulder carry-on bag."

"This thing must be huge," said Nevada. Then she winced and said, "No obvious wisecracks, please."

"Concerning your no doubt miniature-size penis," added Agatha.

"Hey, I'm just glad we're talking about my penis at all," said Tinkler. "And I prefer to refer to it as 'fun size', by the way. But, concerning my magnificent antique travel trunk—bought for a snip, the bozo auctioning it must have been heartbroken—it is indeed huge. Why else do you think I arranged to have it dispatched to the airport separately?" His voice was not devoid of smugness on this last point. "Now," he added, "what is this godforsaken Swedish place we're going to? What's it called again? Troll's Diseased Appendage?"

"What are you raving about now, Tinkler?" said Agatha.

"This place we're going, the name of the town, it translates as Troll's Hideously Diseased Cock or something."

"It does *not*," said Nevada. "It translates as Troll's *Shoe*."

"Oh, well, that's much more lovely. Troll's Shoe."

"*Trollesko*, in Swedish. It's about a two-hour drive from Gothenburg."

"And Gothenburg is…?"

"A thousand-year-old bastion of culture," I said. "With a great university and a really great symphony orchestra."

"And it also happens to be the place we're flying into," said Nevada. "Didn't you even glance at your travel itinerary, Tinkler? At your tickets?"

"I like to be surprised," he said. "By the way, what have you done about your cats while you're gallivanting in Sweden? Have you just abandoned them to starve?"

"Fat chance of that," said Nevada. "I suspect my mother will be overfeeding them even now."

"That's right," said Tinkler. "Your mother. It's all coming back to me now. And if I understand this correctly, she had to get someone to cat-sit *her* cats while she relocates to London to cat-sit *your* cats."

Penny did indeed have two cats of her own. The rather mysterious Spirit and the highly gregarious Almodóvar, who as a kitten had been saved from a grisly fate.

"Yes."

"That makes lots of sense." Tinkler actually did have us here. For once. It was slightly ludicrous. But, instead of proceeding to rub our noses in it, Tinkler changed tack. "Do you know what I am going to be doing a lot of during our holiday in Sweden?"

"We don't know and we don't want to know."

"*Reading*," said Tinkler. "Starting with…" he named the latest Scandi noir sensation that had surmounted the bestseller lists.

"By a remarkable coincidence," said Agatha, "that happens to be exactly the same book that I'm reading."

"Is that so?" said Tinkler. "That really is a remarkable coincidence."

"And I happened to mention as much on my blog."

"Well, thanks to this remarkable coincidence we'll be able to compare notes. About this fascinating book. In fact,

I'll get it out now." Tinkler began digging in his carry-on bag. Gradually his face fell, and the digging became frantic.

"Forget to pack the book, Tinkler?"

"Oh shit. It's in my trunk. With all the others."

"All the others? The other what?"

"Books," said Tinkler.

"Books?"

"No need to sound so surprised," said Tinkler. "In fact, the contents of my trunk are mostly books."

"Your trunk is full of books."

"Crime books. Of the Scandinavian persuasion."

"A trunk full of crime fiction."

"Scandinavian crime fiction. Hold your horses. Does Iceland count? I think I have more than one brooding Icelandic detective in there."

"How many books did you bring with you, Tinkler?"

"A lot."

"How many?"

"Quite a lot. Like I say, a trunk full."

"In god's name, why?"

"To read, obviously."

"Tinkler, we're only going to be gone a week. Not even that."

"You'll be surprised how many I manage to read," said Tinkler.

"Yes, I will be surprised," said Nevada. She looked at me. "And before you ask why the sudden interest in Scandinavian crime fiction, it's because this fine young lady—" she indicated Agatha, "—has been writing all about it on her stylish new blog."

Nevada showed me the home page on her phone. *Clean Head's Crime Scene—personal musings about crime fiction in paperback*. The recent posts had all been devoted to Scandinavian crime novels, which did indeed explain Tinkler's sudden fascination with the genre.

I scrolled further down the page and was impressed when I saw the number of readers Agatha had, and I said as much. "Oh, they're probably all bots," said Tinkler.

"Not all of them," said Agatha. "At least one of them isn't a bot. And we're meeting him there in…"

"Troll's Cock," said Tinkler.

"Troll's Shoe," said Nevada. "Trollesko."

"Yes, he lives there," said Agatha. "When I announced on the blog that I was going to Sweden, he got in touch and asked if he could do an interview with me for the local newspaper."

"The *Troll's Cock Times*?" said Tinkler.

Agatha ignored him. "Apparently he's not only a fellow enthusiast and collector, he's a crime novelist himself. Which is kind of cool."

We all agreed it was kind of cool.

Something a lot less cool happened when I looked through the glass wall of the departure lounge, down on the surging activity of the main airport concourse, and suddenly thought I saw, striding through the crowds among the gaudy glitter of the shops, a familiar figure.

Then he was gone.

Nevada immediately knew something was wrong. "What is it?"

"Stinky. I think I saw Stinky Stanmer."

It was irrational, but I half expected to see Stinky on our plane. Maybe in the next seat. However, this most loathsome of scenarios did not arise; as far as we could determine, our flight was entirely Stanmer-free. Nevertheless, we didn't fully drop our guard until we reached Gothenburg airport and were waiting to collect our luggage from the slowly circulating carousel.

When there was still no sign of him there, we began to relax.

"He could have been heading anywhere," said Agatha. "After all, it was Heathrow. It's a big place. There are lots of flights to lots of destinations. He could have been going anywhere."

"He's probably never even heard of Troll's Schlong," agreed Tinkler.

"You're going to have to dial down the troll penis jokes," said Nevada. "We are soon going to be in the presence of people who actually live in Trollesko, who probably won't be amused by your brand of humour being deployed at the expense of their beloved home town."

"You said it was a two-hour drive to this place. That's at least two more hours of troll appendage jokes, surely. We'll need them to divert ourselves on the long, hard drive."

"Our driver on that long, hard drive is himself from Trollesko."

"You mean he lives in Troll's Cock?"

"No more of those jokes, Tinkler. We'll be seeing Magnus in a minute."

"Hold on, I thought Magnus was the guy selling the record."

"He is. He's also picking us up and giving us a ride."

"To Troll's Priapic Adjunct?"

"Stop it."

It was at that same baggage carousel in Gothenburg that we first realised the magnitude of Tinkler's crime. When it finally appeared on the endlessly rotating black rubber surface, quite possibly having killed several baggage handlers along the way, his much-discussed trunk did indeed prove to be an elegant item suitable for an Edwardian dandy, its sky-blue colour contrasting agreeably with the gleaming lacquered black wooden trim.

But the thing was *massive*.

And it was a heavy bastard, as I learned when I helped Tinkler wrestle it off the carousel and onto a luggage trolley. Apparently he hadn't been kidding when he said it was full of books.

"It's as solid as a coffin," said Nevada, inspecting the behemoth.

"A pale blue coffin full of books," said Agatha.

"With natty black trim," said Nevada

"Don't forget the leather handles," said Tinkler

Once we got it loaded on the trolley, he happily pushed

it to the arrivals area. A rare sighting of Tinkler pitching in and doing his share, or indeed partaking of any form of physical activity.

Despite Gothenburg's stature as an international city of culture, its airport was charmingly like that of a small town— an impression that was reinforced when we went outside into the cold bright afternoon to search for Magnus in the car park.

Sleet was coming down and there was a sharp chill in the air as we walked between buses and crossed over the pick-up and drop-off lanes, heading towards a modestly sized parking area.

A skinny, grinning figure in a bright orange puffer jacket approached us, waving. "Hello, I'm Magnus. Welcome, let me help you with that stuff."

"We've got a lot of luggage," I said.

"Oh, it's fine." He flapped a hand in a *no problem* gesture. Magnus Fernholm was a thin guy with a bland amiable face, an upturned snub nose and hair dyed a bright lemon yellow. His natural colouring, judging by his well-tended moustache, was nearer ginger. He grinned at us, his breath foggy on the chill air. "It's fine."

"As a matter of fact, one of us has a very large piece of luggage," said Nevada.

"No problem."

"That's right," said Tinkler. "I've brought this baby." He swivelled the trolley out from behind us to reveal the full expanse of the sky-blue sarcophagus.

Magnus had been grinning. Now that grin faltered somewhat.

"This baby," repeated Tinkler. He rapped the trunk cheerfully, which responded with a very solid wooden sound.

"No problem," repeated Magnus, no longer sounding entirely cheerful, or indeed entirely truthful. "Luckily I have come in an SUV, otherwise your friend here would have been in trouble."

"Oh, our friend here is always in trouble."

6: THE BURNING CAR

Magnus's SUV turned out to be a scruffy silver van with a transparent green strip at the top of the windscreen with the words *Obi Van Kenobi* printed in white. It may not have been original, but it *was* oddly reassuring to know that our driver was a nerd.

The van was clean on the inside, and commendably comfortable and spacious, even after most of the luggage area had been swallowed up by Tinkler's trunk. Magnus seemed to be relaxed and proficient behind the wheel, which was just as well because Agatha had been known to order unreliable drivers to pull up at the side of the road and make them swap seats with her.

We drove out of the airport car park, took a couple of turns, and then were suddenly in thick pine forests. We emerged from the woodland and drove in sweeping curves along jutting shoulders of rock in the hillside. Above us the jagged surfaces of grey stone gave way to green slopes and more forest.

We followed the winding road through another strip of woodland. Not pine this time, but deciduous trees in autumn colours. We took in the gorgeous spectacle before it disappeared, all too soon, behind us. We were now following the road along a craggy slope, a wall of rock like a cliff face beside us. But it wasn't a natural cliff. Its unnatural regularity indicated that it had been dynamited out of the rock. That past act of violence against this landscape seemed somehow echoed by the inky smoke we suddenly saw billowing into the sky ahead of us.

We rounded a curve. Fat clouds of black smoke poured up into the high clear sky, and at their source, a bright orange mass of flames which revealed itself to be a car, burning fiercely at the side of the road.

A man in a ribbed black and yellow puffer jacket, evidently the erstwhile driver of the car, was standing at a considerable distance from the blaze, talking on his phone, a small pile of his belongings at his side. We drove slowly past. The car was just a blackened metal skeleton, lying flat on its belly on the road, its tyres melted, entirely clothed in flame, heat pouring off it.

As we passed by, I could feel that tremendous heat radiating at us through the side of our own car, passing effortlessly through our closed door and window.

"Poor bastard," said Agatha.

"I wonder if they managed to get out," said Magnus, keeping his eyes fixed on the road ahead, as if to force away the possibility of any similar fate for us through sheer concentration.

"Yes," I said. "He's fine."

Indeed, the stranded driver seemed mostly bored, pissed off and not as grateful to be alive as one might have expected. He was a heavy-set man whose paunch made him seem pear shaped. His face was mostly chin, but it wasn't a strong face. It seemed to me a petulantly disappointed face.

We had driven past him and I was looking back. The man caught my eye, his gaze roving away and then coming quickly back to me. He gave us the strangest look as we drove past. But then he and the burning car were gone—we went around a curve and all we could see was an oily black coil of smoke flowing up into the high blue sky over the forest, marking the scene of the late automotive conflagration.

Soon the terrain changed again and we were bowling along across flat farmland.

Magnus turned and smiled back at us. "Look around here," he said. "All this area was part of the ocean bed." It was perhaps a standard tour-guide spiel that he gave people. If so, I doubt it had ever received a reception quite like this one.

We had all fallen very silent.

"Is something the matter?" said Magnus. "Did I say something wrong?"

"*We* were almost part of the ocean bed," said Tinkler nostalgically and we all laughed.

I tried to spare Magnus his bafflement. "He's right. But it's a long story."

I remembered sitting in another car, within sight of the holy island, as the sea came racing in at all sides. The others were all thinking the same, I'm sure. It was an eerie moment, a flash of group telepathy.

"That's a point," said Nevada. "At least we would have been *together*." She took my hand.

"That's right," said Tinkler, reaching out his own hand to take Agatha's.

She slapped it away. "I doubt that you and I would have been together. I would have been swimming strongly in the direction of safety and you would have been, essentially, ballast."

"But very lovable ballast."

"Anyway," said Magnus, eager to wrap this up, "that's one reason the soil is so fertile and so suitable for farming. It used to be ocean bed."

We were about half an hour away from our destination when two things happened. Tinkler began to talk incessantly about lunch. That wasn't unusual.

Sadly, it also wasn't unusual, or at least as unusual as we would have liked, when Agatha suddenly leaned towards us and said, "I think we're being followed."

"Why are you whispering?" said Tinkler.

"I'm not whispering. I'm speaking in a low voice. So as not to spook our driver."

Nevada was looking out the window, all business. "Who is it?"

"Mercedes-Benz S-Class. Nice car. I delivered one to the airport the other day. This one's black. Keeps hanging back and then hurrying forward when they think they might lose sight of us."

Nevada nodded and watched the traffic for a while. Then she nodded again and said, "You're right. Complete amateurs."

"Somebody is following us?" said Tinkler.

"Yes."

"And they're complete amateurs?"

"Yes," said Agatha. "Very clumsy about the whole thing."

"Then my money is on Jaunty," said Tinkler. "The corpse-faced motherfucker."

"Why?" said Nevada.

"Because the last time you had a security alert, it was him."

"We're calling it a security alert now?" I said.

"Why would he be following us?" said Nevada.

"Why was he watching your house?"

"Due diligence," I said.

"Did he really turn out to be an accountant?" said Tinkler.

"Financial comptroller," I said.

"In any case, a really boring person to be following us."

"If it's him," said Nevada.

"I'm confident it is," said Tinkler. "And there's no argument that he's really boring."

"Mostly harmless," I said.

"You see, the boyfriend agrees with me," said Tinkler.

"On matters vinyl," I said. "And not much else." I was far from convinced by Tinkler's Bizarro World logic in this instance. The revelation that we were being followed, despite the fact that it was by a nice car and the womenfolk seemed very relaxed about the whole thing, had set a hot sweat crawling over me.

"On matters vinyl and much else besides," said Tinkler. "Anyway, let's return to the more pressing topic of *lunch*." He said this last word loud enough to catch the attention of our driver.

"Well," said Magnus, "we can certainly get you something to eat. As soon we drop your stuff off at the hotel."

"No," said Tinkler firmly. "No, I think we definitely need to stop before we get into Trollesko."

Nevada and Agatha and I looked at each other in astonishment.

"In fact, I've found a place on the outskirts of Trollesko," said Tinkler, getting the name right again, just to rub it in. "Here." He leaned forward and showed Magnus his phone. Magnus studied it for what seemed like a long time as Tinkler smiled and smiled.

"I'm not sure it's appropriate," said Magnus finally.

"Not appropriate? Nonsense. I researched it online. Their pizzas get rave reviews."

"The pizzas are very good," Magnus conceded, after a reluctant pause.

"So, let's go there," said Tinkler. "Otherwise my stomach's going to start rumbling and no one wants that."

"Okay," said Magnus, rather grimly, I thought. "We will stop there for lunch."

* * *

"What's this about us having to be club members, Tinkler?"

"Oh, all that's just a formality. I simply had to join—just me, and I did that online—and now you guys can come in as my guests. I signed you in. It's all very straightforward."

"What's this about exemptions from hygiene laws?"

"Oh, it will all be fine," said Tinkler. "That's just red tape."

Tinkler's discovery was called the Red Iron Inn and its presence was announced by a fat slab of red wooden door hanging at the side of the road with that named carved on it in pale letters. The inn itself was located beside a tarmac parking lot, in what looked like a small office building occupying the site of what had apparently, not too long ago, been a large barn. I realised that it was a barn door serving as the sign hanging by the roadside.

Tinkler led us confidently through the deserted reception area of what might have been a small and particularly dull law firm, then down a brightly lit steel staircase into a less brightly lit basement.

The restaurant looked okay. It was styled in the manner of a 1950s American diner, with a lot of chrome. Most of all, it felt solid and secure—there was something comforting about being underground—and we were the only customers, so my paranoia about our follower in the black Mercedes began to ebb away.

Our waitress was a very pretty young woman with an impressive number of piercings. She led us to a large circular table, chrome legs and ebony top, got us seated in the chrome chairs and went off to get menus for us. We looked around.

The place was colourful and cheerful and perhaps even a little hip thanks to the engagingly crazy pop art murals on the walls, which Tinkler confidently identified as being from a certain 1960s French comic book. "You used to be a comic book nut, Tinkler?" said Agatha.

"Oh yes."

"But then you swapped your comic collecting obsession for a record collecting obsession?"

"Yes. I found the true faith."

The waitress brought the menus. It turned out that not only were the pizzas recommended here, they were the only thing they served. So we ordered pizzas. They all had two-word names like Viking Spirit, North Storm, Red Aura, Green Aura, Northern Light, First Snow, Wild Night, Fool's Delight, Green Man, Green Lady, Friendly Fire and, perhaps inevitably, Troll's Shoe.

"No Troll's Cock, then," said Tinkler.

"Tinkler—"

"I promised not to say anything in front of Magnus, but since he's chosen to remain in Obi Van Kenobi and sulk, I think I'm allowed free rein."

It was true that Magnus had declined to join us, saying he preferred to wait in his SUV. He'd seem genuinely a little conflicted, though. Clearly the pizzas tempted him.

They certainly tempted us. Tinkler ordered Viking Spirit, which came with a shot of vodka infused with garlic, and had fat golden brown cloves of roasted garlic dotted across a soft white cushion of melted mozzarella, decorated with wilted green strands of rocket and bright red spots of sliced baby tomatoes.

Friendly Fire, my choice, came with Ghost Pepper chili-infused extra virgin olive oil to drizzle on the buffalo mozzarella and sliced green and red peppers. I drizzled with care.

Green Lady, which Agatha had selected, was a vegetarian feast. And Nevada's Red Aura had a smoky tomato sauce with a bite of paprika in it, and came with a glass of red wine which Nevada sipped cautiously and then pronounced drinkable. And duly proceeded to drink.

To our surprise and relief, everything was excellent. Including the service. Our waitress cleared our plates away with alacrity when we'd finished. As Tinkler handed his plate to her, he said, "If I order a second pizza, will that interfere with anything?"

"No, of course not, sir. What would you like?"

"Fool's Delight."

"Good choice. Will the rest of the table remain clear?"

"Yes," said Tinkler.

"Then we'll complete your order, sir."

"Thank you."

As soon as she was gone, we all started upbraiding Tinkler for having a second pizza. Most of us had been unable to finish the first one. But we all agreed a pizza named Fool's Delight had been a good choice for him. Certainly, when it arrived and man met pizza, it seemed a match made in heaven.

As Tinkler commenced to tuck in, we saw the first signs of life other than our waitress since we'd arrived. In fact, despite his focus on his food, it was Tinkler who spotted him. "Hey, dig Creepy Elvis."

This was a characteristically unerring description of a short, portly man in a white safari suit with, yes, an Elvis Presley-style quiff in his gleaming and unconvincingly black hair. The flared white trousers of the safari suit were a little too short for him, revealing green high-top sneakers and green socks with black polka dots on them.

The compelling nature of this apparition may explain why we didn't immediately notice that someone else had also appeared. A young woman. She was petite but buxom, with long blonde hair, and was rather oddly dressed in a full-length silk dressing gown with grey and pink birds on it.

Her face had a kind of cartoon-critter cuteness, with big eyes, high cheekbones, and a sort of Slavic cast to her features. She came over to our table, and we thought for a moment she was going to sit down with us. But, to our astonishment, instead she *stood* on one of the unoccupied chairs and gamely scrambled up on to the circular tabletop.

She ended up in front of Tinkler, just about maintaining her dignity as she did so. Tinkler, it has to be said, was suspiciously unsurprised to see her. The silky dressing gown came off rather rapidly; I found myself thinking it must be cold up there on that gleaming black tabletop for someone wearing so little clothing.

Music began to boom out of a speaker hidden somewhere in a dark recess of the ceiling. I didn't recognise the tune, but then I didn't recognise much about what was now happening in this putative pizza joint.

The girl who was wearing so little had begun making a series of movements which smoothly transformed into a low-level dance, and she continued to dance directly in front of Tinkler as he ate.

The dancing, which was impressively proficient, was curtailed as the music came to a crescendo, the girl knelt in front of Tinkler and then briskly scooted around so her bottom was pointing at him, her legs akimbo, the toes of her bright red high-heeled shoes angled slightly off the tabletop. To avoid discomfort, I surmised.

Then she reached behind herself and hooked her index finger around the scant white gossamer line of the G-string between the cheeks of her pale and curvaceous bottom. She pulled the G-string aside, while with the other hand she spread her buttocks.

Tinkler watched avidly while continuing to shovel down the pizza with apparent gusto and appreciation. There was the sound of two chrome chairs abruptly scraping back on the stone floor. Nevada and Agatha gave the spectacle one final glance before walking out.

I followed them, admittedly with a small but real pang of regret. But I knew what was good for me.

I don't think Tinkler even noticed us leave, hypnotised as he was by the spectacle of nubile flesh gyrating in front of him.

We went back up the steel staircase and out into the cold late afternoon daylight. Magnus was standing outside his van in the parking lot. As soon as he saw us, he straightened up, like a dog glad to see its owner at last. He hurried over to join us, a smile appearing on his face. Apparently he was gratified by the disapproval which he could so clearly read on our own faces. Well, the faces of Nevada and Agatha.

ATTACK AND DECAY

I did my best to look disapproving, too.

Magnus shook his head as we walked with him back to the van. "I hope you don't think that place is typical of Sweden."

I said, "I don't think it's typical of anywhere."

We were just getting into the van when Tinkler came trotting out to join us. He scrambled into the vehicle as if he was worried we'd leave without him. I think Agatha might have done just that, but luckily Magnus was at the wheel.

"Thanks for leaving me stuck with the tip," said Tinkler.

"Presumably you inserted it in the designated place," said Nevada. "Jesus, Tinkler. No wonder we had to sign a special waiver about hygiene laws."

"Oh, now."

"Tinkler, you're disgusting," said Agatha. "You were happily chowing down while that girl was waving her anus in your face."

"Do you think they're missing a trick by not having a pizza called Anus Face?" said Tinkler.

7: TROLL'S SHOE

Trollesko was a small town on a lake. A river which fed into the lake flowed alongside us as we approached the town; a railway line ran parallel on the other side, as though in competition. Indeed, railroad and river would once have been in competition. Trollesko was a port town and goods would have come down the river before the railroad was built.

As we approached the centre of town, we saw a wide, white and rather elegant stone bridge. Magnus drove across it. The river flashed by on either side, gleaming lazily with late afternoon light.

Now the distant cool green smudge of the lake was to our left, just visible through a freight train terminus and, beyond that, a harbour area with the shadowy angular shape of cranes rising above it.

The downtown section of Trollesko spread open in front of us. "Wow," said Tinkler. "Clean, orderly streets, check."

He'd been doing this more or less since we'd landed at

Gothenburg, every time we encountered something that struck him as archetypically Scandinavian.

Magnus had perked up now that he was reaching the end of his long drive. "All right, okay guys. Now, first I will drop you all off at the hotel and you can check in and leave your stuff and chill out for a little while and then I will come back and pick you up." He glanced at me. "And I'll take you to the house where you'll be doing the listening. It belongs to a friend. Christer Vingqvist. Actually, friend isn't probably quite the right word."

"What is the right word?"

"I don't know. Acquaintance. Fellow audiophile. Christer has a pretty good system at his place. You'll certainly be able to listen to the record to an adequate degree of clarity to hear for yourself that it's in near-mint condition."

"Don't you have a hi-fi system of your own, Magnus?" said Tinkler.

Magnus instantly bristled at this. Tinkler had fallen into disfavour with him straight out of the gate, when he'd revealed his trunk. So to speak. Our chum's transgressions had only been compounded by the strip club pizza stunt.

So, it was with a perhaps justifiable note of annoyance in his voice that Magnus now said, "Of course I have a hi-fi system of my own. Rather better than Christer's. Christer is a Bang & Olufsen obsessive, you see."

My ears pricked up at this. There was, frankly, more than one piece of Bang & Olufsen kit that I coveted. But Tinkler was less impressed. He said, "Then why don't we just listen to the record at your place, Magnus?"

"Because I am the party selling the record. Who knows, maybe if you listen to it on *my* system, I might have done something to the system to somehow make the record sound better than it actually is."

Nevada had been leaning forward and listening with increasing interest to this précis of a potential swindle. She looked at me now. "Is that possible?"

"I suppose you could remove clicks from a scratched record," I said. "Marantz invented a domestic piece of hi-fi equipment that did exactly that."

"Did it digitally," said Tinkler. "It processed the analogue signal and made it digital and removed the clicks and then fed it back out again, now and forever contaminated by its digital conversion. When I suggest it might be wrong to treat the poor little innocent signal like that, I can see my analogue friend here agrees with me."

"I do," I said.

"Anyway, I will take you to Christer's house," said Magnus. "It's near the hotel. I will drive you over there the first time but after that you can walk there whenever you want, to use his listening room. He will give you a set of keys and you can come and go as you like, to listen to the record. However, please," he gave an insincere little chuckle, "please do not leave town with the record before full and proper payment has been made."

"Of course not," I said.

"And when I take you to his house, Christer has asked if he can also do the interview."

"What interview?"

"My interview," said Agatha. "Christer Vingqvist is not only an audiophile, he's a lover of crime fiction."

"Oh, so this is the guy from the newspaper, the *Troll*—" Tinkler caught himself just in time, "—the *Troll Shoe Times.*" With an unnecessarily heavy emphasis on the 'shoe', I thought.

"Yes, yes, he does do some journalism for the local paper," said Magnus, almost as if he was reluctant to concede the point.

"He's also a crime novelist in his own right," said Agatha. "Which is kind of cool."

Magnus chuckled, and this time it was genuine mirth. "Yes, indeed, he's published a novel all right. Unless I'm mistaken, there's a copy of it there in the glove compartment."

I had a look, and he was correct. There was a paperback book jammed in the glove compartment amongst the other junk, which included everything from a miniature chess set with Pokémon character pieces to a Union Jack asthma inhaler, and even, in a break with glove compartment tradition, some gloves. I fished the book out.

It took me a moment to discern that its cover image was a splash of blood on snow. It was hard to recognise because the image was squeezed so small under the title of the book, *Cold Angel, Dead Angel*. The title was itself fighting for space with the author's excessively large name above it. Larger even than the title. But there was still room for some boastful marketing text on a strapline. *Another terrifying adventure for Penumbra Snow*.

Penumbra Snow was apparently the name of Christer

Vingqvist's heroine—better known as Miss Snow. As on the back cover, where it declared…

Miss Snow is hot!

Now she investigates an unspeakably hideous crime in her most deadly case yet…

I looked for a list of other titles, but as far as I could tell this was her *only* case yet. There were certainly some glowing quotes, though, from people I'd never heard of, praising the book to the heavens. "Who are all these quotes from?" I said.

"Church officials," said Magnus.

"Church officials?"

"Yes, Christer is a deacon. A vocational deacon, actually. Here is your hotel."

We pulled into a street lined with tall, handsome old residential houses with large gardens, looking across at an equally long stretch of park. The park was full of trees in autumn colours, with a bandstand at its centre.

"These houses all used to belong to senior doctors," said Magnus. "We're quite near the hospital here. It's a major hospital. It serves the whole surrounding area and employs a lot of people locally. Christer works there, for example." Magnus pulled up. Our hotel was directly opposite the bandstand in the park.

We got out, stretched and began to unload our luggage, which was a pretty straightforward procedure until we got to Tinkler's trunk.

Finally, myself, Magnus and, it has to be said, Tinkler, faced the thing with glum resignation and started hauling it out of the van and towards the hotel.

The hotel was an elegant three-storey nineteenth-century construction in white wood with green trim and a green shingled, gabled roof. It was crowned with a black cast-iron widow's walk, and had a big circular skylight set into the green shingles on one side. Perched on top of the roof was a black cast-iron weathervane with a rooster on it.

Basically, it was the haunted house from a kids' book, but in much better repair.

We dragged the trunk across some pavement, across the lawn, along the flagstone path and up the stairs to the front door. There we rested, panting, while Magnus punched in some numbers on a keypad—which was the only thing about the house so far that didn't scream nineteenth century.

"I'll give you guys the door code," said Magnus, his breathing slowly returning to normal. "Or you can find a note of it with your keys."

The graceful front door had narrow panels of stained glass set in it. We opened it to reveal the peaceful polished wood of the hotel foyer. Nevada and Agatha went inside while us boys lifted the trunk and began to wrestle with it on the final stage of its long, long journey.

We tottered into the spacious, airy foyer—really just the front hall of a house. A very nice and quite large house. A staircase—all-natural gleaming wood—rose up in front of us, leading towards the dimly lit upper floors. I peered up through the shadows and saw the skylight letting in a pale slice of light.

To our immediate left was an alcove with a cloakroom and a toilet. To the right, an open doorway revealed a large, deserted and shadowy breakfast room full of small tables, chairs currently upturned on them, legs forlornly in the air.

Ahead and to the left was a short corridor, evidently leading to some of the guest rooms. To the right was a closed door with a sign beside it saying that the hotel office, kitchen and staff area lay beyond. The walls and floors were polished natural wood, as were the door frames. Everything looked gleaming and clean and inviting.

Directly in front of us was a wide wooden lectern that apparently served as a reception desk. There was no one behind it, indeed, no one to be seen anywhere. Magnus moved to the lectern and picked up three small bright red envelopes. He handed these out. One for Nevada and me, one each for Agatha and Tinkler. We opened the envelopes to find physical keys for our rooms and a slip of paper with the front door code and the wi-fi password printed on it, along with a chirpy message of greeting. And our room numbers. We compared these.

"It seems we're all upstairs," I said.

Magnus looked glumly at Tinkler's trunk.

"Almost there," said Tinkler cheerily. The girls sensibly went ahead up to the rooms and left us to our battle with the sky-blue behemoth.

Getting it up the steep wooden staircase was a task only slight less tricky than pyramid construction involving large slabs of stone hewn from a distant quarry.

We got it up to the first landing, halfway to the next floor, when Magnus decided he'd had enough. "I'm afraid I'll have to let you guys take it up the rest of the way. I need to get home and do a few things before I come back and collect you."

"What, you're just going to *leave* it here?" said Tinkler. He sounded scandalised. "But it's blocking the stairway." Tinkler the Samaritan. When had such a thing ever troubled him before?

"Well, perhaps we can get it up on this table," said Magnus. There was a small but luckily very solid-looking oak table at the rear of the landing with a vase of fresh flowers on it. Magnus moved the vase, the pink blossoms of the flowers nodding in agitation, and we grunted and struggled and got the blue behemoth up on the table. It was too small to accommodate the trunk lying flat, so we stood it on its end.

Once we got it up there it looked none too stable, but I was too exhausted to move it any further.

Meanwhile, Tinkler was already blithely heading up to his room and Magnus was making good his escape, back down the stairs and out through the stained-glass front door.

8: UNION JACK MINI

"Tinkler," said Nevada, "you can't leave your trunk there. It will topple over and fall down the stairs and fucking kill someone."

"You paint such a graphic picture."

"Get that trunk up the stairs. To your room."

"Yes, yes," said Tinkler tetchily, while making no discernible move to do so. Indeed, he continued walking with the rest of us *down* the stairs, then across the lobby and to the front door, where we gathered in a loose group, waiting for our ride to arrive.

Agatha was shaking her head. "Having successfully got his gigantic trunk full of crime fiction—"

"Scandi crime fiction," said Nevada.

"Right, having got his beloved trunk full of Scandi crime fiction all the way to Scandinavia, our Tinkler seems to have lost all interest in it."

"His tiny brain is too full of stripper," proposed Nevada,

finally stinging Tinkler to the extent that he shifted his attention from his phone to her.

"Please. She has a name: Ida."

"You spoke to her, did you?"

"Of course. We had a chat. Naturally."

"Naturally. After your 'table dance'."

"She's a very nice girl. Friendly and highly intelligent. Vivacious."

"If only we'd had a little more time," said Nevada. "She could have given you a vivacious lap dance."

"Exactly my point, perhaps."

The foyer of this hotel was unlike that of any other hotel I'd ever been in, both pleasantly and eccentrically so. I stared up into the shadowy recesses of the high ceiling.

The skylight, canted at an angle from this vantage, narrowed from a circle to an ellipse. That pale ellipse, way up there, looked strangely suggestive of a grey eye staring gravely down at us, from its own vantage deep in shadow.

Indeed, darkness seemed to flow down from it, shrouding the staircase and only beginning to give way to the incursions of visible light on the landing above us—where the cheerful and, as Nevada had lately pointed out, potentially lethal pale blue shape of Tinkler's trunk thrust up out of a pool of shadows.

Below that, recessed lighting illuminated the check-in lectern and the various doorways around us. The four of us were in the best-lit spot, with the overhead light supplemented by the daylight falling through the narrow stained-glass panels of the front door.

All around us, though, was deep shadow.

"Why don't they put on more lights?" said Nevada.

I shrugged. "Saving energy?"

"If the Addams Family were Swedish and they ran a hotel," opined Tinkler, "this would be it."

"Ran it in an absentee capacity," said Agatha, looking around at the apparently deserted building.

"Are you ready for your interview, Miss DuBois-Kanes?" said Nevada.

"Fairly ready."

"Have you read his novel so you can gush about it sycophantically to him?" said Tinkler.

"Of course not," snapped Agatha. Then, perhaps realising that Tinkler had successfully baited her, she added calmly, "But I have *started* to read it. I'll have it finished tomorrow."

"How is it?" said Nevada.

"Too soon to say," said Agatha in a tone of voice that suggested it wasn't.

"What's Miss Snow like?" said Tinkler.

"Is she hot?" I said.

"She's an autistic savant. And an albino."

"Autistic savant," said Tinkler. "Check. Albino, check."

"And she is a genius and a scientist. Guess what she's studying?"

"What is she studying?" said Nevada.

"The link between albinism and being an autistic savant."

"Naturally."

"But she gets sidetracked into investigating a crime. A murder, of course."

"Of course."

"How does she get sidetracked?" I said.

"She's working in her laboratory late one night—she has a laboratory in a mansion on a lonely mountain—working hard on finding a link between the condition of albinism and—"

"The condition of being autistic and the condition of being a savant," said Nevada.

"Right," said Agatha.

"So it's a cluster of conditions?" said Tinkler.

"Right, so she's investigating this cluster of conditions in her laboratory, as I mentioned, in a mansion on a lonely mountain late one night, and suddenly somebody drops a dead body through the skylight."

There was a pause.

Then we all looked up, involuntarily but in perfect unison, at the grave pale eye above us. It gazed unblinkingly down.

Nobody was dropping a dead body through *our* skylight, fortunately. At least, not at that moment. We all looked down again, at each other, somewhat sheepishly. Some of our number giggled nervously. I might have been among them.

Tinkler cleared his throat, trying to cover his giggle, which—it has be said—had sounded particularly unmanly.

"I too have begun to read about Miss Snow."

"What?" said Agatha.

"You sound surprised."

"I think what my friend means," said Nevada, "is that it seems a little odd that, with a trunk full of books, full of the cream of Scandi crime fiction, you've resorted to reading… what's it called?"

"*Cold Angel, Dead Angel*," I said.

"Where did you even get a copy?" said Agatha. "I took the one from the car."

"Well, not from my trunk, I can tell you that. That thing's balanced on a knife edge, that's for sure. When it goes, it's going to go just like an avalanche. Except, instead of an avalanche, it will be one big trunk falling down the stairs."

"Right, that does it," said Nevada, turning away from the front door. "I want that trunk upstairs *now*." She realised Agatha was giving her a droll look. It was Nevada's turn to have been successfully baited by Tinkler.

"There's a bookcase upstairs," said Tinkler, gesturing loftily towards the next floor, full of helpful explanations now that he'd productively got someone riled. "In the little lounge outside our rooms. And have you seen the rooms? Big four-poster beds. Definite bondage opportunities."

"Are there a lot of books?" said Agatha, connoisseur of rare paperbacks and not above pilfering a hotel library. "In the little lounge?"

"In the little lounge library? Just a few titles. But they do include *two* copies of *Cold Angel, Dead Angel*," said Tinkler. "Have you skipped to the grisly murder yet? Sorry, I meant read carefully and with full attention as far as the grisly murder yet."

"No but you clearly have. Skipped to it."

"No, I skipped *past* it, looking for sex scenes. And being singularly disappointed so far, I must say."

"Have you begun to form an opinion as to the work's literary merits?" I said.

"Too little sex. None at all, in fact. Which is way too little."

At this point further book chat was curtailed by the arrival of our ride. A tallish shadow loomed beyond the art nouveau flowers on the stained glass. The shadow hunched to one side, busily punching the entry code. Then the door swung open to reveal Magnus, beaming at us. He stood aside to introduce a red-haired Valkyrie of a woman: his wife, Emma.

Emma was tall and broad shouldered. Which made it even odder than it might have been that she was dressed like a parody of a Japanese schoolgirl.

It was only later that I would realise she was actually dressed as a parody of an *English* schoolgirl. Though the Harry Potter badge on the blazer should have been a giveaway.

Tinkler immediately took Magnus aside, leaving the Valkyrie schoolgirl stranded with us. We all stood around awkwardly for a moment before she said, "All right?"

The way Emma uttered the greeting, she sounded for all the world like one of the urchins from our estate in London.

"When Magnus said we were coming over here to pick you lot up," she said, "I was well chuffed. We haven't been in these ends for yonks, innit?"

Magnus looked over at us with irritation, although whether this was because of what Tinkler was telling him, speaking quietly in his ear, or in reaction to what his spouse was saying, was difficult to determine. He clarified the situation by striding over to us and declaring, "You'll have to forgive Emma. She's a dyed-in-the-wool anglophile."

Then he herded us out of the hotel.

We all got into Obi Van Kenobi, except for Emma. She had brought her own car, a Mini with an impressive custom Union Jack paint job. She pulled out after us as Magnus drove away from the hotel.

"I have to apologise for my wife," he said. "For her accent and vocabulary."

"Her English is excellent," said Nevada.

"But she is a little too Mockney, right? That's what you call it when someone has a phony Cockney idiom and accent, correct? Normally she isn't too bad about that. But she gets very excited when she has a chance to use it on real English people. A little overexcited, frankly." He glanced in the mirror where Emma's jaunty Union Jack Mini could be seen following the van at a safe distance, until it abruptly disappeared from sight.

"There was no need for her to bring the car, you know," he said. "She could have ridden very easily in this vehicle. And that would have saved her getting lost on the way to Christer's, which is apparently what she has now done. But she insisted on bringing our car so you could see it."

"Very nice car," said Agatha. "The Convertible Cooper S."

"But she doesn't understand, Emma simply doesn't understand, that what starts out as charming all too swiftly can become tiresome. Like this whole anglophile thing of hers. Like when she says, 'We haven't been in these ends for yonks, innit?' instead of, 'We haven't been in this part of town for ages, have we?' And anyway, we have. We are often in this part of town. We are always in this part of town. Or at least the part of the town by the hotel. Which is what she was speaking of. I apologise on her behalf. She has to try and talk like a Londoner. What she imagines a Londoner to sound like. As I said earlier, it's overexcitement. She just tends to get a little overexcited. Now…"

He slowed the van down.

In contrast to the austere, elegant uniformity of the hotel neighbourhood, the houses in this part of town were of a great variety of architectural styles, including some wacky specimens like Christer's, a mock-Spanish colonial mini villa in pastel colours that looked as if it had been airlifted from the American Southwest. It even had a cactus garden.

Magnus pulled up outside. "I'll just check that he's at home," he said. "He certainly should be." He got out of the van, went up to the front door and apparently rang the bell to no effect. After two minutes of increasingly impatient body language he came back to the van. "This is inexcusable. He is not here and he knows he is supposed to be here. And he isn't answering his phone. Which is not helpful." He started the engine. "I will drive you back to the hotel. Where is my wife? Is she still lost? Oh well, she doesn't need to find Christer's house now. Let's just hope she can find her way back to the hotel."

As it turned out, when we pulled up outside the hotel Emma was already there waiting for us. She was standing beside the Union Jack Mini.

So was someone else.

"And there is Christer," said Magnus. "What is he doing here?" He slowed the van and pulled over. "And why wasn't he answering his phone?"

I had a pretty good idea of why. Because, as it happened, I recognised Christer Vingqvist.

At first it was the ribbed black and yellow puffer jacket, but getting closer it was the man himself. The last time I had seen him, he had been standing, looking understandably pissed off, beside a burning car.

9: BOOM

"I was driving along and then the next thing I knew, flames were coming out of the engine. I was on my way to the airport to meet you guys and my car just caught fire. I was lucky to get it off the road and get out before it went up." Christer Vingqvist looked at us and added, "Boom."

"Yes, very lucky," said Magnus. "But what were you doing driving to the airport?"

"Like I say, I wanted to meet these guys off their flight." Christer glanced at us and then looked blandly back at Magnus.

"But *I* was meeting these guys off their flight," said Magnus. "I was picking them up. We'd agreed I would bring them back here to your house."

"Well, I thought it would be a surprise."

"Yes, it certainly would have been," said Magnus.

"So, your car just caught fire?" said Nevada.

"Yes, apparently so."

"And you have no idea why?"

"Well, some kind of technical fault, obviously," said Christer Vingqvist. "The insurance people will no doubt do a comprehensive examination and issue a full report."

"We saw you when we drove past…" I began.

"Yes, and I saw you," interrupted Christer. "I recognised Obi Van Kenobi."

"I didn't see you," said Magnus.

"That's because you were keeping your eyes on the road," said Agatha. Magnus didn't realise that, coming from Ms Dubois-Kanes, this was high praise.

"And I was very surprised indeed to see you there," said Christer. "Though of course I shouldn't have been. I was driving to meet you. But to be honest, having my car burst into flames before my eyes had driven all that from my mind."

"It would tend to do that," said Nevada.

"But if we saw you when we drove past you," I said, "how did you get back here to Trollesko before us?"

"Train."

"Why didn't *we* get the train?" said Tinkler.

"Because of your fucking trunk," said Agatha. Then, quickly, to Christer Vingqvist, "Sorry, we're not recording yet, are we?"

"No, not yet. Ha-ha. But we can start now." He held up his smartphone on a selfie stick and shunted his chair around so he was sitting beside Agatha at the small table.

We were sitting in the breakfast room at our hotel, where Christer Vingqvist now started filming the interview on his phone. "Okay, so we have a thriving crime fiction scene here in Trollesko. We are voracious readers, with a legion of devotees hungrily devouring every crime classic from Agatha Christie to Aurelio Zen. And speaking of the immortal Christie, today we have her namesake, Agatha DuBois-Kane. She's the young lady behind the fabulous blog *Clean Head's Crime Scene*. She has flown all the way over from London, and we are privileged to welcome her."

"I am very pleased to be here," said Agatha.

Nevada shot me a look of approval as if to say, *nice confident delivery*.

"I understand your blog, which as I say is fabulous, is focused on crime fiction in *paperback*."

"Yes, ever since I was a kid, there was something that I loved about paperbacks, something tactile about them…"

But we were doomed never to hear Agatha expound on the sensual qualities of vintage paperbacks to Christer Vingqvist, because at this point he overrode her, saying, "As it happens, *my book* is in paperback."

He held a copy of the book up in the hand that wasn't holding his phone. "And one of my spies tells me that you already have a copy."

"Uh… yes I do."

"Someone left a copy at your hotel. At this very hotel."

"Yes."

Someone left *two* copies at this hotel, I thought. And I suspected that I knew who.

Christer Vingqvist smiled a toothy smile. "What do you think so far?"

"A little early to say."

"Of course, you've only just got it. Only just got your copy. Of *Cold Angel, Dead Angel*." He held the book up higher. "The first Penumbra Snow adventure, published by Lazarus Library." He set the book down with a thud in front of Agatha. Who couldn't quite avoid glancing down at it like something nasty that had been put on her plate for breakfast.

"You only just got your copy. Naturally, take your time. No pressure." He lowered his phone. "Now for the press photos. Where is that damned photographer? He should be here by now."

As Christer went to look for the damned photographer, Agatha said, "So much for my interview." She took out her own phone.

"Oh, he'll continue it, surely," said Tinkler. "After you've *read his book*." These words were uttered with untoward ghoulish relish.

"Who knows," said Nevada, "it might turn out to be a good book." She picked up the copy Christer had left on the table and turned it over to read the back.

"The signs aren't promising," I said.

"Aren't they?"

Agatha shook her head as she put her phone away. "It turns out it's self-published. That's seldom good."

"Oh well," said Nevada. "He doesn't deserve the privilege of interviewing you. He's a pompous clown."

"He's a self-published priest," said Tinkler.

* * *

The photographer from the local paper was called Mikael. He looked about seventeen, despite his beard. He was wearing a shirt with a red and black checked pattern that made it hard to avoid thinking of the word *lumberjack*, and a brown leather jacket with a sheepskin collar.

But his equipment appeared suitably professional, and he took brisk, efficient, imaginative photographs of all of us. Then went back to Agatha and commenced a longer, more in-depth and considered photo session with her.

Christer Vingqvist, now forever—thanks to Tinkler— the self-published priest, darted in at every opportunity, interrupting Mikael's creative flow in repeated bids to get himself snapped beside Agatha, grinning that toothy grin and holding up a copy of his book.

We were relieved to see Magnus and Emma return. They'd driven off on some errand in the Mini, abandoning Obi Van Kenobi and the rest of us at the hotel. But now they joined us in the breakfast room, sitting down at our table. There was plenty of room because Tinkler had gone to the loo. Nevada took advantage of his absence to shamelessly ask Magnus what Tinkler had been talking to him about in private earlier.

And Magnus didn't hesitate to tell us. "He asked me if I could drive him somewhere."

"Of course he did," said Nevada. Despite having the money—and certainly the technical savvy—to seamlessly order unlimited rides on his phone, Tinkler would never pass up an opportunity to cadge a free lift. "And let us guess where..."

"A certain strip club that sells pizzas?" I suggested. It was a subtly, but somehow importantly, different concept to that of a pizza joint that had strippers.

"No. He asked me if I could drive him to the nicest café in town."

Nevada frowned. "Tinkler knew where the nicest café in town was?"

"No, he asked me that. He asked me what the nicest one in town was and I told him. And then he asked me if I could drive him there. Anyway, I recommended the Notre Coeur Café because he asked me for somewhere that served really good coffee and cakes."

"Coffee," I said.

"Cakes," said Tinkler, who had characteristically contrived to return just in time for that word.

"Yes," said Magnus smoothly. "We want to invite you guys for coffee and cakes."

"At my sister's place," said Emma. "She's got this banging little farmhouse just outside town."

"The farmhouse is not *banging*," said Magnus tightly. Then he recovered himself. "But it is very nice."

"And she has a well lovely cat," said Emma. Which immediately got Nevada's interest and, I have to confess, mine too. Agatha was more interested in hearing that our destination housed a large collection of vintage crime fiction.

As soon as Mikael concluded the photo shoot to his satisfaction, the rest of us drove in convoy back to Christer Vingqvist's house, that cartoon of a New Mexico dwelling that seemed to have fallen from the sky into this cold Swedish street. Christer ushered me and Magnus inside for a quick inspection of his listening room.

The quirky architecture continued inside where the front door opened onto a staircase. Instead of going up into what looked like a dining room, we went downstairs into a well-lit basement lounge. Despite the annoying nature of its self-published owner, I immediately felt this was a nice house. Something about the warm, open, well-illuminated space was inviting. The listening room was equipped to a high standard and, to quote Tinkler, clean and orderly. I was disappointed to see that the Beogram turntable had a standard pivot arm, but otherwise everything was fine.

Magnus gave me a sardonic look as I made my inspection. On the way over in the van, he had described Christer's listening room as looking like a Bang & Olufsen museum, and he wasn't far wrong. Perhaps Christer caught the look because he said, "It was my father who was the real B&O nut. This is just a small portion of his collection of equipment. He collected one example of every product they manufactured. At least one example."

"I'd love to see some of that stuff," I said. "Especially if he had any of the turntables with tangential tracking arms."

"Introduced with the original Beogram 4000 series," said Christer, a nostalgic note creeping into his voice. "Yes. I'm sure you will see one at the farmhouse."

"At the farmhouse?"

"Yes."

"Not the farmhouse where we're going next?" I glanced at Magnus, who was looking thoroughly bored. "Emma's sister's farmhouse?" The banging little farmhouse.

He nodded and Christer said, "Yes, exactly. Emma's sister Barbro is a work colleague of mine, and also a very warm and close friend. Over the years I've loaned her a lot of my father's collection. Otherwise, this stuff would just be gathering dust in a storage unit. High-end hi-fi equipment is like a high performance sports car. It's better if you run it."

"And you think there's a turntable out at the farm, with a tangential arm?" It sounded for a moment like the beginning of a moronic song. But Christer didn't seem to notice, or perhaps mind.

"At least one. Certainly an original 4000, and possibly both the 8000 and 8002. You know, the direct drive models."

The visit to the farmhouse now had more allure than the promise of coffee. Even more allure.

Magnus clapped his hands together to make sure he had our attention and said, "Anyway, are you happy? Is it agreed? You consider this…" he waved rather dismissively at Christer's hi-fi set up, "…a suitable system on which to audition the copy of Storm Dream Trooper's *Attack and Decay*, the 180-gram audiophile pressing, which I am selling to Owyn Wynter?"

Perhaps provoked by the boilerplate nature of this recapitulation, I felt a bit like the guy in the vampire movie agreeing to let a stranger cross the threshold. But I agreed.

As we were leaving the listening room, we met Nevada coming down the steps.

"You guys were gone a long time." She smiled a charming smile, but I knew she'd come braced for mayhem. I felt a warm surge of pleasure. My sweetie had my back.

We fell behind Christer and Magnus as they headed for the car. Nevada took my hand. "I was starting to get worried."

"No, everything was fine."

"How was the equipment?"

"Fine."

"Any chance they're pulling a fast one?"

"Yes," I said. "In fact, there is."

Nevada looked at me, her keen eyes wide with sudden interest. "Oh, really? How?"

"Well, Bang & Olufsen turntables are said to have an amazingly stable suspension mechanism. They can allegedly play through scratches that would be a serious issue for other turntables."

Those wide blue eyes narrowed. "So, is this potential scam a serious issue?"

"No," I said. "I'll just make sure I also audition the record on another turntable."

Magnus proceeded to drive us all out to the farmhouse. Emma followed in the Mini, the self-published priest riding along with her.

"Like Christer said, he and Emma's sister are old friends and colleagues," Magnus nodded as he peered out at the dark road unfolding in front of us. "And, of course, they are both crime fiction nuts. But Christer isn't just a crime fiction nut; he also has a serious interest in music, so he overlaps with us hi-fi nuts."

He glanced at me. I didn't resist the designation, nor did Tinkler, though he said, "We prefer the term 'discerning audiophile'."

Although the allure of coffee and cakes—and now the prospect of a turntable with tangential tracking technology—remained strong and steady, Emma's sister's farmhouse proved to be a disconcertingly lengthy drive out of town.

Finally, in the silent darkness of the back of the van, Tinkler leaned over and whispered, "Lonely murder farmhouse."

"Stop it," snapped Nevada.

"Lonely farmhouse murder," said Tinkler, varying the running order.

"Tinkler…" said Nevada. She was trying to put a note of menace in her voice, but it was a wobbling note of menace because both she and Agatha were beginning to stifle laughter.

"Murder farmhouse lonely." Tinkler uttered this as if the murder farmhouse was some kind of poor, semi-articulate creature that was declaring its loneliness.

By now I was having to suppress my own laughter. And Tinkler was trying to catch my eye and give me a mad look that would tip me over the edge.

Nevada gave a polite but uncontrolled little snort, which I recognised very well as the prelude to an eventual total collapse into hysterical mirth.

Then we saw the Mercedes.

"Black Mercedes," said Nevada.

"It's the one," said Agatha.

"Where?" said Tinkler.

"There."

It was there and gone. Because this time the Black Mercedes wasn't following us.

It was going the *other* way. It shot past us, back in the direction we'd come. Towards town. Towards Trollesko.

"Well, at least they're not going to the lonely murder farmhouse."

Despite a cold clawing at my heart at the sight of that shining, predatory vehicle, even I began to laugh at this.

Then we turned off the main road and up a gravelled lane to rendezvous with a sight sufficiently weird to curtail all laughter.

10: UFOS AND DOG POO

Obi Van Kenobi was now progressing along a narrow lane that snaked among half-glimpsed buildings and dark clumps of trees. Occasionally our headlights revealed mysterious and jagged and unidentifiable, at least to me, shapes of farm equipment lying like the skeletons of beached leviathans on this dead ocean bed.

We were slowing down. Magnus signalled a right turn and we rumbled onto a gravel access road. Another right turn brought us to a low, modern ranch-style house with inviting, brightly lit windows.

Less inviting, perhaps, were the lights weaving around in the dark field behind the house. Tinkler perhaps described it best. "Hey, miniature UFO squadron."

Magnus stopped the van and we got out. At first the lights appeared to be green, but as we got closer I could see they came from two glowing objects. The largest was a bright greenish yellow and the smaller one a bright yellowish green.

The larger object was shaped like a stubby rectangle, though it was constantly altering its shape and orientation, illuminated by a light source fixed to it. By the time we were standing beside the house, peering into the field, it was pretty clear this was someone wearing a high visibility vest, with a light attached to it, running around frantically in the dark.

The smaller shape was a glowing green ring, or more accurately a collar, on the neck of a dog—a very lively dog, who was running around and dodging the person in the high-vis vest.

This was all taking place in silence, with what would, in other circumstances, have been a commendable lack of barking from the dog. The vest chased the collar. The collar eluded the vest.

We gradually realised that there were other sources of light, out there in the darkness, but they were stationary. And they were smaller. Little insipid green glows, motionless in the long grass.

Standing beside the house, we could now see the space wasn't just open fields. It was also studded with darkened outbuildings and yet more mysterious examples of farm machinery. The glowing green person and dog continued their weaving chase around the buildings and machinery and dark clusters of trees, the person occasionally pausing and leaving another little mound of pale green in their wake.

We were still puzzling over this spectacle when headlights swept across us and the Union Jack Mini pulled up. The anglophile Valkyrie Emma Fernholm emerged, followed by Christer Vingqvist, self-published priest and heir to a sizable Bang & Olufsen collection. He took one look at the miniature UFO display and said, "Oh, that damned dog. He's back again."

"That's Barbro out there?" said Magnus.

"Yes," said Emma and Christer in unison.

"What is she doing?" said Nevada.

"Well, you see, she has this very annoying neighbour," said Christer. "Who allows their dog to come to over onto Barbro's property to defecate."

"Doesn't just allow it, the wanker positively encourages it," said Emma.

"Apparently so. At least according to Barbro. She claims this so-called 'neighbour from hell' has deliberately trained the dog to exclusively defecate on Barbro's property, instead of on its owner's property. And to do so silently at night to minimise the possibility of detection."

"Why the glowing collar, then?" I said. That did nothing to minimise the possibility of detection.

"That's a relatively recent development," said Christer. "I suppose they added that collar because winning the game— by which I mean succeeding in having the dog defecate over here undetected—was too easy otherwise, and they were just getting bored. Or perhaps they just liked the look of it. The glowing collar. It has to be said that, even with the creature wearing it, it is proving most difficult for Barbro to fend off the dog."

"Is that what she is doing now?" I said.

"Fending off the dog?" added Tinkler, unnecessarily and, as ever, open to salacious connotations.

"Well, at least keeping track of him. Of the spots where he might have paused long enough to have left a souvenir."

"So that's what the little glows are?" said Agatha, both fascinated and horrified.

"Yes, she drops glow sticks—you know the kind you break and they glow? Wherever she suspects…"

"The dog has taken a shit," said Tinkler bluntly. "So they're dog shit glow sticks."

"Potential dog shit glow sticks, yes."

"It gets on my tits," said Emma suddenly and somewhat alarmingly. "The way she throws a wobbler if there is a little dog poo on the ground. Reality check: at the end of the day, it is a farm, okay, right?"

"Barbro isn't really suited to farm life," reflected Christer. "Even on a non-working farm."

"But she really wanted this place," said Emma, a trifle bitterly I thought. "When our old dear popped off, she couldn't get her meat-hooks on it fast enough. She couldn't wait to move in. She was gagging for it."

The chase suddenly came to an end, with a final glow stick appearing and the high-vis vest remaining bent over it while the dog and its luminous collar loped happily away into the night. "Ah, the ballet concludes," said Christer. "The dog defecation ballet."

"Dog shit UFO squadron," corrected Tinkler. "The dog shit UFO squadron concludes." He wasn't pleased at having someone else labelling things.

"Somebody should do something about that terrible neighbour," said Christer.

The small yellow-green shape of the high visibility vest grew gradually closer until we could make out the person wearing it. A short, stout woman with dark hair cropped close to her head. She wore big black-framed glasses. Somehow these—and her large, beatific smile—gave her the appearance of a happy dog. Maybe I just had the happiness of that victorious defecating intruder still on my mind.

Barbro waved to us and we waved back as she came striding through the long grass. In one hand she was holding a red plastic bag, tightly knotted at the top.

"It's well weird that she's the local vicar, innit?" said Emma.

"She's a vicar?" said Nevada.

"Or you could call her a pastor," said Emma.

"Tubby female pastor," said Tinkler under his breath. "Check."

"That's right." Christer Vingqvist was nodding his big head. "Barbro and I both became deacons together in the same church. But by the time I started as the deacon at the hospital, she was already the hospital chaplain. And now she is the vicar for our entire community, and I am still just the humble deacon guy at the hospital." He sighed. "But although our careers have drawn us apart, we still share two passions—one being crime fiction."

We didn't get to hear what the other one was—though I assumed hi-fi, with special reference to the products of Bang & Olufsen—because at that moment Barbro Bok joined us. Her face was flushed, her glasses steamed up and her hair matted with perspiration. Apparently, it had been a very merry, and energetic, chase with the dog.

"You must be Agatha," she exclaimed, her English as perfect as everyone else's here, and her voice warm and welcoming. "We are big admirers of your blog." She gave Agatha a quick and awkward one-armed embrace, then repeated the process with each of the rest of us, starting with her sister, all the while holding the tightly knotted red bag at arm's length with her other arm.

"Excuse me for hugging you when I have a bag of dog poo in one hand," she said, with a self-deprecating little chuckle.

"No problem at all," said Tinkler, trying to chuckle back and not quite carrying it off. "I understand there's coffee and cakes?"

But Barbro had abruptly fallen silent. She'd caught sight of Christer Vingqvist, who'd been hanging back from the rest of us for some reason. Perhaps he was apprehensive about the dangling red bag. If so, his reticence did him no good because Barbro now gave a wrenching little sob and flung herself into his arms, embracing him fiercely.

They stood there like that for a long moment, Barbro pressing her face into his chest, right arm tightly wrapped around his waist, left hand holding the dog poo bag draped over his shoulder as she convulsed gently with silent sobs. Christer looked stiff and embarrassed. He was staring upwards at the night sky as though hoping for rescue from that direction. Even alien abduction would be better than this.

But apparently the UFO activity was over for the evening, so he was stuck with this small crying woman clinging to him. She finally lifted her face from his chest and said something in Swedish, then instantly switched to English, apparently in deference to her visitors. "I heard what happened to your car," she said.

"It just overheated."

"You were nearly killed."

"It was no problem," said Christer in a tone that hovered between boredom and irritation. "The car just overheated and so I simply steered it safely off the road and I stopped and got out. I was never in any real danger."

"You almost died. You were almost gone forever. And if you had been gone forever…"

Barbro put her face back to his chest. She now began to weep openly and frankly and audibly. Christer stared up glumly into the dark sky. Where was a flying saucer kidnapping when you needed one?

After some time, and not without struggle, Barbro stopped sobbing, regained the power of speech, and looked up at Christer again. "I saw the pictures of the car. There was nothing left."

At the mention of the pictures, Christer brightened. "Did you see the ones I posted on my socials? Weren't they amazing? I cursed myself because I didn't think to take any before it was almost too late. The fire had already died down quite a bit."

Barbro now released her grip on Christer, much to his evident relief. She stood back a little, beaming up at him, her cheeks gleaming wet with tears beneath her big glasses. If she had been a happy dog before, she was now a positively ecstatic one. She stared at Christer as if memorising his features before he set off on a long journey.

"You must be more careful," she said, stroking his arm with the hand that wasn't still clutching the bag of dog crap.

"My car just randomly burst into flames. How can I be more careful?"

Christer seemed genuinely irritated by this quandary, but Barbro was no longer paying attention to him. It appeared she'd suddenly remembered her hostly obligations. She turned to us and smiled. "No doubt my dear friend here and my beloved sister have been giving you a full account of that foolish ritual of mine. Of course, I'm aware that I look ridiculous, running around in the darkness wearing a high visibility vest. But the dog is going to be able to smell me from the other side of the farm—with dogs it's not a matter of visibility but smell-ability—so if there's no chance of concealing myself from the dog, I might as well be highly visible."

"Very sensible," said Nevada. Although, like me, I imagine it made minimal sense to her.

"That cunning dog," continued Barbro. She was trying for a light-hearted tone, but I could hear a real note of anger creeping into her voice. "He's getting very good at avoiding me and coming in here stealthily and leaving his deposit for me to perhaps step in by surprise, or eventually to be led to by my nose or by the flies."

"I don't know why you're going spare over a little dog poo," said Emma. "This is a farm. You should expect big time manure on the ground, isn't it?"

Barbro's good-natured manner vanished instantly, and I reflected on how easily siblings could push each other's buttons. "Manure, yes," snarled Barbro. "The droppings of herbivores. Which are inherently less offensive than the disgusting, stinking leavings of a creature who feeds on meat."

"August Strindberg feeds on meat," said Emma.

"August Strindberg buries his leavings."

From this exchange I gleaned that August Strindberg was a cat. The "well lovely" cat we'd been briefed about earlier. Nevada had come to the same conclusion. "Perhaps we could meet August Strindberg," she said, ever the diplomat, and now neatly putting an end to the sisters' bickering.

"Yes, of course," said Barbro. "Come inside."

August Strindberg proved to be a mound of marmalade fur, gently rising and falling, curled up and concealing all but one lazy, minatory amber eye that opened briefly to silently reprimand us for interrupting his slumbers.

"Maybe he'll be a bit more lively later on," said Barbro, without much conviction. "Please make yourself at home while I get the coffee on." She bustled into the kitchen and we wandered into the living room. Magnus and Emma elected to sit on the sofa while we explored.

The place was a rambling bungalow with verandas on three sides. These long, rectangular verandas were so effectively winter-proofed that they served as additional rooms on a permanent basis. They were filled with storage racks, oddments of furniture and… bookshelves. Bookshelves stuffed with crime novels.

Agatha immediately fell upon these, her loyal disciple Nevada at her side.

Tinkler, Christer and I went in search of hi-fi equipment. Which we found in the veranda on the side of the house facing the erstwhile UFO display and dog waste excursion.

Here, on the kind of metal shelves you'd expect in a car workshop, were numerous bulky cardboard boxes, mostly stored flat. My heart sank when I saw these. It was definitely the best way to keep your kit in good condition, in the original packaging, but from a hi-fi voyeur point of view, it was a total bust.

If I wanted to see anything, it was going to have to be unpacked and set up, at considerable inconvenience to my hosts. Christer seemed to understand my dilemma. "I'm sure there must be something she has out that you can have a look at," he said.

"What exactly is he so hot and bothered to see?" said Tinkler.

"A Beogram," said Christer.

"That's the turntable?"

"Yes, I believe there are some of the 8000 series here. They were the direct drive decks." Christer smiled a wistful, nostalgic smile. "Jacob Jensen's masterpiece."

"These are the so-called tangential decks?" said Tinkler.

"There is nothing so-called about it," said Christer curtly, his smile fading. Evidently Tinkler had managed to rile him without breaking a sweat. "They are tangential tracking and also tangential drive."

"By which you mean direct drive?" said Tinkler, rather snottily.

Before this could erupt into a full-blown train-spotter squabble over hi-fi terminology, I cut in and said, "The tangential arm tracks in the same way that records are cut."

"Okay," said Tinkler. "I concede that is interesting. But you're not cutting a lacquer when you're playing a record. It isn't the same procedure."

"Surely it is," said Christer. It was as though this was an article of faith to him.

"Well…" I said. "Actually, he's right. In one case you're creating the groove, in the other you're following it."

"Exactly," said Tinkler.

"Did you know," said Christer, changing tack somewhat, "that Bang & Olufsen are not Swedish? They're Danish."

"Sure, manufactured in Struer," I said.

Christer gave me a toothy smile of approbation. "That is right," he said. "Now let me just go and quickly check with Barbro. She must have a turntable out of its box and in operation somewhere." He left us standing in the chilly veranda, breathing the faint odour of mildew.

Tinkler looked at me. "They still make them, you know," he said. "The Beogram turntables."

I nodded. "They're reconditioning vintage examples."

"Damning evidence that the ability to manufacture them from scratch has gone forever?"

"Perhaps," I said. "If so, what a bummer."

"How much are they going for?"

"Around ten grand."

"Jesus. You could get a Xerxes for that and stick a motherfucker of an arm and cartridge on it."

"Indeed."

"And yet you're still interested?" said Tinkler.

I shrugged. There was no denying it. I was.

"This isn't serious hi-fi," said Tinkler. "You do realise that? You're just seduced by that sexy, elegant minimalist Scandinavian styling."

"That's part of the appeal, sure. But this stuff is beautifully built."

"Seduced," said Tinkler, shaking his head sadly.

Christer never returned from his turntable quest, so we went in search of the girls. And found them, as expected, avidly combing through Barbro's library. Just as we arrived, they had paused to examine a framed photograph that hung on the wall in one of the few gaps between the ever-present bookshelves.

It was a photo of Christer Vingqvist. He was standing, posing—it was a fair word—against a backdrop of mountains with a hunting rifle. The mountain mist behind him was luminous. With the rifle slung over his shoulder, Christer looked almost dashing.

It was a very good photo, perhaps worthy of Mikael, bearded boy journalist.

But that wasn't what we were thinking.

Nevada and I looked at each other. And then at Tinkler and Agatha.

Tinkler confirmed that this was another moment of group telepathy by saying, "Do you think those two were once *banging*? And I don't mean like a 'banging little farmhouse'. Although maybe they used to be banging *in* this banging little farmhouse."

"Maybe they still are," said Agatha.

Tinkler made a variety of vomiting noises and gestures, and Agatha looked progressively more impatient with each one. "You're one to talk," she said, when he had finally concluded. She glanced at me and Nevada. "He's criticising other people's sex lives while he's being fleeced by a halfwit teenage stripper."

"I challenge 'fleeced', 'halfwit' and 'teenage'," said Tinkler. "I guess that means I challenge pretty much everything except 'stripper'. Anyway, it's early days. It's just a first date. Now, I wonder when food is going to be served? That coffee certainly smells enticing."

There was indeed a promising smell wafting from the direction of the kitchen.

"First date?" said Agatha, managing to make those two lone syllables sound impressively scathing.

"What has dating got to do with any of this?" added Nevada. "You paid the little anchorite for a table dance and that's all there is to it."

"I am maintaining a dignified silence," said Tinkler. "And don't think I don't know what an anchorite is." He paused. "I don't know what an anchorite is. What is it?"

"A kind of nun," said Nevada. "A particularly reclusive nun."

"So that would be irony, right?" said Tinkler.

Before Nevada could confirm this, probably in a tone of excoriating sarcasm, Barbro called from the kitchen, "All ready."

Tinkler immediately headed in that direction. Followed, to be candid, no less eagerly by the rest of us. The long drive and the bizarre luminous hunt for dog excrement had evidently given everyone an appetite.

All of us were converging on the kitchen, including Magnus, Emma and the previously missing-in-action Christer Vingqvist. As Barbro began serving us, Christer took me aside.

"I am so sorry. I can't believe it. She has taken all the Bang & Olufsen equipment out of her system and put it into storage, except for a second-generation Beosound A1 Bluetooth speaker in pink. Apparently she is playing tunes off her phone with it. My god. She's listening to nothing but digital files off her phone. This is a woman who espouses a genuine love of music. *Listening to her phone*." He shook his big head in audiophile despair. I shared his disappointment but, to tell the truth, I was more focused on the refreshments Barbro was dishing out.

The cakes proved to be several big white plates covered with a squadron of identical little pale green marzipan cylinders filled with a chocolate-rum truffle. The things were shockingly, addictively delicious. I had to force down the urge to stuff my mouth with several handfuls of them.

"These are fabulous," said Nevada. "Did you make them yourself?"

"No," said Barbro. "I bought them at Ikea."

"Can I be buried with a pack of them in my coffin?" said Tinkler. "In fact, line the entire damned coffin with them."

The coffee was also surprisingly good. Only instant, but single estate instant. As I drank it I felt, as I often did in times of need like this, that I was pouring it directly into a hollow behind my eyes where it would refill a reservoir in my brain and allow it to start working at full capacity again, like vital oil for an intricate piece of machinery.

Barbro Bok watched with satisfaction as we stuffed our faces. But her attention was mostly elsewhere, and her eyes lit up every time she looked at Christer Vingqvist. She was so pleased to see him that it was embarrassing, at least to him.

She sat close to Vingqvist at the big kitchen table and frequently touched his arm, his shoulder and sometimes even his face. He clearly felt this was oppressive, and when she excused herself at one point and disappeared for a few minutes, he immediately started grousing.

"What's she being so fulsome about?"

"You were in a burning car, man," said Agatha. "You could have died."

"Even so."

"I think it's sweet," said Nevada.

"Do you think she'll notice if I abscond with the rest of these green marzipan things?" said Tinkler.

"Hands off, Tinkler."

"Find anything good amongst the books?" I said.

Nevada nodded. "Agatha was straight in looking for classic Penguin editions of Chandler and Hammett. And she found them."

Agatha nodded. "She has an amazing collection here. Although most of it is hardback." This last word was uttered with the thinly veiled contempt of a paperback fanatic.

"If you let me glom a bag of these marzipan things, I'll help you steal some books. Hell, I'll help you steal all the books."

"Shut up, Tinkler."

As soon as Barbro returned, Christer excused himself and went out the front door. For a moment I thought he was fleeing the scene, and on foot at that, but I glimpsed him through the kitchen window. He opened the door of the Mini and began to hunt around inside for something.

"How do you like Trollesko?" said Barbro.

"Very clean and orderly," said Tinkler.

"And pleasant," added Nevada.

"We love our hotel," said Agatha.

"There seems to be no one there," said Tinkler. "The staff are invisible."

"How fascinating," said Barbro.

"Aren't all of the hotels in Sweden like that?" said Nevada.

"Not the ones I've been in," said Barbro. "Anyway, sounds like a place for a good juicy murder, ha-ha-ha."

"*Murder at the Swedish Addams Family Hotel*," said Tinkler. "Catchy title."

"Where is this hotel?"

Barbro directed the question at Magnus and her sister, but it was Tinkler who answered. "Opposite the *vattentorn*," he said, astonishing us all. I had no idea where, or what, the vattentorn was, and I was willing to wager that a few hours ago neither did Tinkler.

"Oh, I know that part of town." Barbro nodded. "It is very pleasant there."

"Your friend is surprisingly well informed," said Magnus, looking at Tinkler with a gimlet gleam in his eye.

He turned to Barbro. "He also knew about the Red Iron Inn."

Barbro shook her head. "Under normal circumstances, the mere mention of that place would be enough to fill me with fury and disgust. But today…" She gazed out the window at Christer, who was still standing half in and half out of the Mini, bent over at the waist, absorbed in some obscure enterprise. "I am just so grateful that my friend is alive and well. Let them have their stupid little squalid striptease bistro."

"Pizza and flange," said Emma, summing up the situation with commendable brevity.

Christer finally emerged from the Mini with a white plastic shopping bag bearing the name *Hemköp* in red. The bag contained something heavy, judging by the way he carried it. He entered the house, left the bag by the front door and came to rejoin us, just as Nevada and Agatha were rising from the table. "Do you mind if we continue snooping through your books?" said Agatha.

"No, please do," said Barbro, turning on her the huge smile that had greeted Christer's return. "And 'snooping' is so appropriate to a collection heavily devoted to the noble art of sleuthing."

"I will join you," said Christer hastily, moving away from the table and hurrying ahead of us. I thought he just wanted to get out of range of Barbro and her adoring gaze. But he doubled back to the front door, picked up the bag, and headed for the veranda on the other side of the house like a man on a mission.

This veranda housed the portion of Barbro's collection that Agatha and Nevada hadn't examined yet; the other half of the library, with authors from N to Z. Or, as Agatha put it, "Magdalen Nabb to Roger Zelazny."

The mention of Zelazny led to a discussion of science fiction writers who also wrote crime, with special reference to Fredric Brown, Henry Kuttner and Leigh Brackett.

All these authors, and more, were represented among the books in Barbro's library. They were ranked on long rows of handsome rosewood shelves that stretched from floor to ceiling. It was indeed an impressive collection.

There were recessed lights in the ceiling, angled so that they provided a pale but adequate glow for reading the spines. "Museum standard lighting," said Agatha. "It won't fade the dust jackets."

Christer Vingqvist had got here ahead of us with his plastic bag and he was busy unpacking it. As we'd approached the veranda along the hallway, we had heard the thud of a considerable weight hitting the floor. We could now see that Christer had dropped a pile of books. I read the names Jack Vance—another science fiction turncoat—and Barbara

Vine on the dustjackets of the books that now lay scattered on the floor.

Christer looked at us, face sweating, trying for merriment in his eyes, but being foiled by his nervous blinking. We'd apparently caught him red-handed. He had clawed out the works of Vance and Vine from a shelf near floor level, creating a gap adjacent to the works of Charles Williams, into which he now began stuffing over a dozen examples of his own opus. We'd arrested him in the act of clumsily scooping these copies of *Cold Angel, Dead Angel* from his bag.

"Barbro will want these to give to people, as gifts," he said by way of explanation, pushing his books neatly and lovingly into place, then tidying up the volumes of Jack Vance, Barbara Vine, et al, or at least dragging them together into a disorderly knee-high pile and nudging them none too gently away from the bookshelves, to allow free access to the multiple copies of his own work.

Agatha immediately kneeled in the space he created.

But Christer's delight was short lived, as it became evident that she was less interested—much less interested, it has to be said—in the adventures of Penumbra Snow than the collected works of Charles Williams. "She's got everything by him," said Agatha. "Both in English and translation."

Nevada crouched beside her. "You know, you've got to watch out for those Serie Noire editions," she said. "The French editors rewrote some of those completely."

"I know. You told me. Sacrilege. I doubt they would have dared try that with Charles Williams, though. Very big in France, Monsieur Williams."

"*Cher Charles*," said Nevada, pronouncing the name in the French fashion, and they both giggled.

Apparently unable to endure the discussion of any literary works other than his own, Christer flounced out. A moment later Barbro came in, and fell sprawling on her face as she promptly tripped over the pile of books he'd left on the floor.

A pile of books by writers, it seemed safe to say, whose works had a greater claim to the space on the shelves of this library—indeed, any library—than the debut of Miss Snow. However hot she was.

We rushed to help Barbro, but she waved us away. She got calmly to her feet again and stood there for a moment, looking at the books on the floor and then at the slab of self-published fiction that had been crowbarred into her library in their place. Then, when she finally spoke, there was a genuine note of delight in her voice—a sort of rich undercurrent of a chuckle. "I'll put them back when he's gone."

She winked at us and shook her head in affectionate exasperation. She seemed like a woman who was finally relaxing after a long hard day.

Agatha was still inspecting the Charles Williams section, which filled almost an entire shelf by itself. "You've got the Cassell Crime Club editions," she said.

"Yes, I'm particularly proud of those. Please feel free to come over to peruse them if you like. I'd say take them back to your hotel with you to read, but as you know they are quite rare."

"That's very kind of you. But it's his paperbacks I'm into."

"Well, of course. All Williams's early books were originally paperbacks."

"Published by Gold Medal," said our girl.

Barbro nodded. "Until around 1955, I think. You know about the title changes?"

Agatha nodded. "*Scorpion Reef* into *Gulf Coast Girl*, that sort of thing?"

"Yes, exactly." Barbro smiled at us. "Your friend knows her stuff."

"Speaking of friends," I said, "where's Tinkler got to?"

"We're using the term 'friend' here loosely, you understand," said Nevada.

We went looking for the wayward Tinkler, leaving Barbro staring thoughtfully at her bookshelf. As soon as we were out of earshot, Nevada said quietly, "You didn't sound too impressed with those Cassell Crime Club editions."

"Logo's way too big," said Agatha. "Squeezes out the artwork."

"Like the title on the self-published priest's book."

"Like the self-published priest's *name* on the self-published priest's book."

There was no sign of Christer Vingqvist, though, or indeed of Tinkler. When we went into the kitchen, we found Magnus sitting alone. "Where's Emma?" said Nevada.

"She is driving Tinkler to the café. It's all right. I will drive the rest of you back to the hotel in the van."

"To hell with the hotel," said Nevada. "Let's go to the café."

11: DEVILISH DICKHEAD

When we got outside, we found that Tinkler hadn't left yet. He was still moping aimlessly, as Emma busied herself in the Mini, apparently restoring order to the interior of the vehicle after Christer had ransacked it in his search for his books. It didn't seem possible to have brought quite that much chaos to such a small car, but clearly the self-published priest had managed it.

Tinkler paused in his nervous pacing and nodded at us. He rubbed his hands together. Perhaps because they were cold—or perhaps he just wanted to put things on a brisk businesslike footing. "Well, my ride is almost ready."

"You're abandoning us?" said Nevada. "We've just arrived in Sweden and you're abandoning your oldest and closest friends on our first night here?"

"I wouldn't frame it in those terms."

"You wouldn't frame it in those terms. But you are abandoning us."

"Sorry. It's a matter of not disappointing Ida."

"Ida," said Agatha, lending considerable mirthful contempt to those two syllables.

"Ida Tistelgren. Isn't that name sheer poetry?" said Tinkler.

"Tinkler," said Nevada wearily. "What is she, seventeen?"

"Mid-twenties and wise beyond her years."

"Wise in the ways of fleecing English chumps," suggested Agatha.

"Chump-hood denied. And if you're so interested, you can come along."

"All right," said Nevada and Agatha instantly and in unison. Nevada looked at me. "Assuming that's all right with you?"

"More coffee?" I said. "Always."

"And the cake, of course," said Tinkler, "though on this occasion the presence of Ida renders that an almost secondary consideration."

Tinkler insisted on travelling in the Union Jack Mini even though we were now all headed to the same destination. "Very antisocial of him," said Nevada.

"He doesn't want to be with us because he wants to use his phone," said Agatha.

"To call the anchorite?" said Nevada.

"The dancing anchorite."

"The lap-dancing anchorite."

"Exactly," said Agatha.

Magnus, who had put up with us all day since collecting us at the airport first thing this morning, now went above and beyond the call of duty—chauffeuring us back over the dark river and past the shadowed docks into Trollesko.

First a brief return to the hotel, where the girls both made a quick pit stop, reappearing even more dolled up and ravishing than before, before he took us on to the café.

We drove there through the shopping district of Trollesko, which was pretty much deserted at this time of night. The modern glass shopfronts had posters of smiling young people in stylish bright clothes. Half the models looked like Agatha.

Magnus couldn't entirely conceal his relief—to which he was more than entitled—when he dropped us off a short distance from the café in the centre of town. "You can book a lift to take you back."

"Or we can walk," I said. I'd memorised the route from the hotel, and it wasn't far.

"Or you could walk," agreed Magnus with the patient approval of a man who wanted to encourage us in this line of thinking and never trouble him for a lift again. He drove away into the night.

"He was glad to get rid of us," said Nevada.

"Perhaps he's rushing back to his wife, innit?" said Agatha.

"Unless she's here with Tinkler, know what I mean?" said Nevada.

Then they both laughed at this rather cruel Mockney mockery of the way Emma spoke. "After all," said Nevada. "She did drive him here…"

"In her motor."

"In her well trendy motor."

"Her motor is bang on trend."

But there was no sign of the Union Jack Mini; indeed, there were no vehicles anywhere on the clean empty streets as we walked towards what declared itself, in gilt *fin de siècle* script spread across wide glass windows, as the Notre Coeur Café and Patisserie. Those windows generously spilled light out into the empty streets and there was definitely an Edward Hopper feeling to the place, just at this moment, on this night.

There were still some people inside, but the café was the last outpost of life in a street of dark and empty shops. As we drew nearer, it became clear that the café too was preparing to close. Many tables were empty and the staff, all in white shirts and black trousers, were chatting among themselves or checking receipts.

The café appeared to have once been two buildings which had been joined, with a reception area and a main entrance added in the middle. The service desk, a handsome art nouveau artefact of chrome and glass, was situated here. Its illuminated interior consisted of pale green frosted glass shelves on which were displayed the—by now much-depleted—selection of enticing cakes and pastries.

Standing awkwardly by this strikingly handsome piece of commercial furniture was the not-quite-so strikingly handsome Jordon Tinkler. He looked fretful and not much cheered by our arrival.

"Is she late?" asked Agatha solicitously.

"I thought I'd better stand here in case I missed her," said Tinkler. "I've got the two of us a table. A really nice table. I chose one through there…" He gestured vaguely to this half of the café, up a few wooden steps and through an arched doorway. "There's a great little alcove looking out on the courtyard and it has a nice sofa and table in there. But I didn't want to wait in there in case I missed her."

He looked at us, spaniel eyes beseeching us to confirm that this was the smart thing to do, or at least normal behaviour.

We all ordered beverages and chose cakes, then Agatha said, "Let's see this lovely alcove with the sofa."

"Come on, Tinkler," I said. We started up the low wooden steps, deeper into this wing of the café.

"But if we go through *there*, I might miss Ida when she comes in *here*."

"She isn't coming in here, you poor sap," said Nevada, patting him on the shoulder. We went up the steps as Tinkler gave a last anguished glance over his shoulder and sighed, evidently resigning himself to continuing celibacy and not dating any strippers, and joined us.

This half of the café had evidently once been an office building because it was a series of small rooms linked by corridors. This heritage layout created interesting little cubby holes of varying size and intimacy; thanks to the courtyard at the heart of the building, there were plenty of windows and, presumably in the daytime, lots of natural light. It was an agreeable place, the various rooms filled with oddments of curious but comfortable old furniture, some of it very ornate.

Immediately inside the arched doorway, on our right, was a kitchen area. I guessed there must be one of these on each side of the café, a relic of the twin-buildings origin. Inside this one the staff were cleaning up. We collected our coffees and cakes from them and took these deeper inside, to the alcove Tinkler had painstakingly selected.

It was, as he said, very nice. Small and cosy with a long low gilt table and a big, apple-green velvet sofa spread invitingly behind it. To our left, a window looked out into the secluded courtyard.

In it stood a lamppost, its light shining down on very antique and very worn-looking cobblestones, and a circular black marble table standing in front of a small bench of weathered pink wood with a carved love heart at the back. The bench was just big enough to seat two people.

I imagined it was a popular place for courting couples. Now, heading for closing time, it was deserted.

It was certainly a pleasant spot. But in here, on the other side of the window, Tinkler had chosen a spot that was even nicer. We sat down on the velvet apple sofa, which was as comfortable as it looked, though so low on the floor that there might be trouble climbing up out of it again later.

Tinkler sat with us and sighed.

"What a heartfelt sigh," said Nevada.

"It's the sigh of a young man thwarted in his assignation," said Agatha.

"You can't spell assignation without ass. I have no idea what I mean by that. I'm a little nervous."

"What's to be nervous about, Tinkler?" said Agatha soothingly. "Nothing is at issue here. She's just not going to turn up."

"So there you are," said a jovial female voice.

We all turned to see Ida Tistelgren standing in the corridor that led back to the front of the café. She was wearing a full-length coat in mustard-yellow suede, sleekly cut, with a long woolly red and green striped scarf curled abundantly around her throat, its ends trailing on her shoulders like a tame boa constrictor. The coat and scarf seemed a little excessive in view of the mildness of the weather, but maybe wearing next to nothing as she did all day at work, it was a novelty to put on loads of clothes when you were off duty.

"You came," said Tinkler, thankfully curtailing what was threatening to be a classic gobsmacked silence. His voice had a quaver of joyful gratitude that would have done credit to a religious visionary thirty days into a desert fast, suddenly vouchsafed a vision of the divine.

"I'm sorry I'm late." Ida began to unbutton her coat, revealing black jeans, fashionably torn at the knees, and a very expensive and soft-looking sweater in a shade of blue so pale it was almost silver. "But that wretched Bo Lugn kept me after my shift finished."

"Oh, that wretched Bo Lugn," said Tinkler. His voice was dreamily ecstatic. His stripper had turned up. "That oh-so wretched Bo Lugn."

Ida nodded as she began the lengthy business of unwinding the scarf from her throat. "It's all his fault." As she coiled her scarf in a neat red and green heap in front of her on the table, she enlarged on her opinion of this person. Ida was now speaking Swedish, but whatever she was saying was clearly not complimentary.

"Is this your boss?" said Agatha.

"Ha! He's no one's boss. He's just the guy who owns the club. Bo Lugn, *det jävla kukhuvudet*."

Nevada listened carefully enough to this phrase to be able to commit it phonetically to memory, allowing her to sketch out a rough translation the following day with help from Emma—who, it was a little surprising to remember, didn't just speak Mockney. Apparently, it literally meant "Bo Lugn, that devilish dickhead". Colloquially, it was more like the equivalent of "that fucking dickhead".

Although devilish dickhead would have been a great nickname for Ida's employer, if he hadn't already been assigned one.

"He's the Creepy Elvis guy, right?" said Tinkler.

All trace of fatigue and annoyance left Ida's face as it was transformed by honest mirth. "The Creepy Elvis guy! Your friend is very good at summing people up, isn't he?"

"I am very good," said Tinkler in the stunned voice of a farmer who just seen his house blown away by a cyclone, "at summing people up."

Ida smiled at everyone. She was forthright and friendly. In return Nevada and Agatha were entirely civil to her, though with a marked sardonic reserve, as if waiting to see in exactly what way this was going to blow up in Tinkler's face.

Ida had established herself between me and Tinkler on the sofa, setting her bag on the table to accompany the sleeping boa constrictor of her scarf. I moved aside to make room for her but could only move so far before I met an unyielding wall of female flesh. Neither Nevada nor Agatha were shifting even fractionally to make room for Ida.

As if to say, *We are not budging on behalf of this bimbo.*

I would have gallantly suggested a kinder designation, since the warm and perfumed female presence beside me had lit up some sensors in my primal canine brain that were pretty much beyond control.

But *bimbo* seemed more and more called for, and the warmth and perfume less persuasive, as Ida went on at unnecessary length complaining about her employer. "First he puts me on the day shift to punish me. Because of course the money on the day shift is shit because there are no customers. And then he tells me to work tonight, because he knows I am meeting someone."

She paused in this flow of grievance to add, philosophically, "But, on the other hand, if he hadn't made me work the day shift today, we would never have met. Myself and Jordon."

"And that would have been a shame," said Agatha.

"So, after your... dance," said Nevada, leaving a pregnant pause before the word, "you guys just struck up a conversation? You and Tinkler?"

Ida nodded. "Yes. We just started chatting. I was saying to Tinkler that I was thinking of getting my asshole bleached..."

She stopped speaking and stared into our silent faces.

"That is the correct word? Asshole?"

"Spot on," said Nevada, without blinking.

"Right, so we were just chatting and I was just saying to him I was thinking about getting it bleached, you know, and you know what he said to me?"

"No," said Nevada.

"Do tell," said Agatha.

"He said I shouldn't do it." She casually touched the sleeve of Tinkler's coat. Naturally the sleeve contained Tinkler's arm, which caused Tinkler's face to light up. "He said I shouldn't change anything. He said it was charming just the way it is. Perfectly charming the way it is."

"Well, that's our Tinkler for you," said Agatha. "The perfect gentleman."

"And chivalrous to a fault," said Nevada.

"To a fault," agreed Agatha. She was smiling and gazing at Tinkler. It was hard to read that smile.

"So I said I wouldn't," said Ida. "I decided I'd leave it as it is."

"Saved you some money then?" said Nevada, grinning. Agatha failed to entirely suppress a smile of her own, twitching at her lips.

"And also saved me some considerable discomfort," said Ida. She then commenced a brief description of the projected procedure, which wiped the smile off both the girls' faces and indeed ultimately involved some wincing all round.

"Anyway," concluded Ida. "I'm sorry for arriving so late." She stood up again, reaching for her bag.

Tinkler was instantly crestfallen. "You don't have to go already?" he blurted.

Ida smiled. "No, Jordon. I am just going to get myself a coffee, and also buy something for everybody else, to apologise for being so late and keeping you all waiting."

But Tinkler instantly leapt to his feet. "No, let me. I'll pay."

Ida shook her head, firmly, her big eyes solemn. "No. It was my fault. Let me treat you all. More of the same for everybody?"

"But I have all this currency to get rid of..." Tinkler took out a wad of banknotes.

Ida surprised us all by the sincere jollity of her laugh. "This is Sweden. No one takes cash in Sweden."

"I also have a wide array of electronic payment options," said Tinkler. "I assume they take those?"

"They do, but still you mustn't pay. You're being too kind."

"No, you're being too kind," said Tinkler as the two of them disappeared towards the service desk.

As soon as they were gone, Agatha said, "No, you're being too kind," in a tone of animated cartoon idiocy.

"No, you're being too kind," repeated Nevada, adding a high-pitched helium edge to the animated cartoon idiocy.

"Nobody takes cash in Sweden," quoted Agatha, wagging her head as though it was suddenly empty of her many brains.

"*She* does," said Nevada.

"Of course she does," said Agatha. "She takes cash."

"Up the Khyber Pass," suggested Nevada, in a Cockney rhyming slang homage to Emma, and both the girls cackled. "I hope she washes the cash before she spends it."

"Maybe she has somebody launder the money for her," I said.

And then we all laughed and I immediately felt bad because Tinkler, fool that he was, was nevertheless a friend of mine. And I'd never seen him so sincerely, simple-mindedly happy.

I said as much and Agatha said, "And all it took was…"

"A stripper," said Nevada.

"Demented stripper." Agatha and Nevada were now officially in competition.

"Demented predatory stripper."

"Demented unprincipled predatory stripper," said Agatha. "Or do we take that as read with demented already in there?"

"No, no. That's good. Let's add that."

"Anyway, the point is, despite the traditional Swedish national reluctance to take cash, our girl Ida is going to make an exception for our boy Tinkler." Agatha uttered the phrase *our boy* with some venom. "She'll be taking some cash, all right. From him. Soon."

"Yeah." Nevada nodded. "She surely will."

I said, "I don't know. She seems genuinely interested in Tinkler. And nice to him."

"It's what they call a girlfriend experience," said Nevada.

"They?" I said. I didn't know my darling was so up on stripper methodology.

"Sex workers," said Agatha.

"Religious recluse sex workers," said Nevada. And they both chuckled, and then assumed sober faces and full decorum because Tinkler and Ida the anchorite were returning, shoulder-to-shoulder, grinning and chatting. Tinkler carried a tray loaded with coffees and cakes. Ida had a steaming mug in each hand. They got to our table and started unloading.

"My god, Tinkler," said Nevada. "How much stuff did you get?"

"They were getting rid of the last of the cakes so I…"

"Helped yourself," said Nevada.

"Helped them out," said Tinkler. "We're helping them get rid of stock they can't sell tomorrow. If you think about it, it's a charitable act."

"Is it tax deductible?" said Agatha.

Ida laughed at this and sat down again with Tinkler at her side. Close at her side. "Ida insisted on paying," he said.

Nevada and Agatha exchanged a look which I read as, *She's playing the long game.*

"No one ever has enough caffeine and sugar, right?" said Ida.

"Always been my motto," said Tinkler.

Ida fell silent and sat looking at us, holding her lower lip clenched thoughtfully under her teeth for a moment. "Jordon said he wanted me to meet you guys because you'd want to check me out."

"We already had a chance to, ah, check you out," said Nevada.

"That's right," said Agatha. "We had plenty of opportunity to do so. At the pizza place."

"He meant as a person," said Ida. "Not as a body."

Which gave the girls pause.

Finally Agatha said, "So, how long have you been…"

"Stripping? Three years. Just enough time to put aside sufficient funds for soon purchasing a small house and putting myself through university in Gothenburg."

I could see that Nevada was, despite herself, impressed by this display of financial acumen, not to mention earning power, and was having trouble resisting the urge to follow up with some detailed questions about the business side of things.

Ida seemed to pick up on this interest. "Most of the girls aren't so economically astute," she said. "Mostly they throw their money away on drugs and partying."

"Those bad, bad girls," said Tinkler.

Ida giggled and blew him a kiss, which Tinkler pretended to catch with one hand in mid-air and press to his heart. I could see that, despite her earlier reprimand of Tinkler for exactly this, Agatha was now sorely pressed not to make some vomiting noises and gestures of her own.

"I adore your friend," said Ida. "He's so funny."

"Isn't he just?" said Nevada.

"What are you going to study?" I said. "At Gothenburg?"

"The cognitive anthropology of religion and ritual. I hope under the aegis of Andreas Nordin, who is the recognised expert in the field."

I could see that, again, Nevada was reluctantly impressed. This time at least in part by the use of *aegis*.

Ida now took Tinkler's hand. "Do you know why I like sitting at this table, Jordon? Do you prefer Jordon or Tinkler?"

"People also call me 'The Tingler'."

"If by people you mean my mother," said Nevada, "that's true."

"Your mother who is looking after your cats?" said Ida. Nevada and I looked at each other. How much had

Tinkler told her? "That's right," said Nevada. Naturally, at the mention of her mother and our cats, she suddenly decided she had to phone home and check on things.

I judged that things must be all right by the way Nevada began giggling almost as soon as the call connected. She held her phone so we could all see it.

The image was of Fanny and Turk, side by side, facing us. The screen was split, so apparently they were taking part on different devices. Which made sense since they could seldom be found in the same room.

"It's, like, totally awful," said Turk. She was making exaggerated mouth movements as she spoke.

"You went away and left us with, like, this old woman?" said Fanny. Her little black lips were writhing in a way never seen in real life.

"She's really old," interjected Turk. "She must be at least, like, thirty." They were both talking in the tones of needy Californian teenagers.

"When are you coming home?" begged Fanny.

"The room service around here has seriously deteriorated," added Turk.

Then they disappeared to be replaced by the smiling face of Nevada's mother. "Did you enjoy that?"

"We're still reeling," said Nevada, truthfully.

"Isn't it wonderful? The Tingler provided me with this conferencing software."

"It comes with a talking cat feature?"

"With a little tweaking it comes with a talking cat feature," said Tinkler modestly.

Persephone—never call her Percy—seemed very tickled with what she and Tinkler had cooked up together. I was a little surprised that they'd been in touch lately, but they no doubt remained in constant contact arranging consignments of Hashish Honey, destined for Tinkler's gullet. "He also helped me write their dialogue," said Persephone.

"No kidding."

"Would you like to see some genuine footage of your little beauties?"

We said we would, and she showed us our torpid, furry darlings in undignified mid-nap positions on a bed and under an armchair respectively. They didn't seem too traumatised by their conferencing debut, it has to be said, or by being looked after by Persephone in general.

"All right," said Nevada grudgingly, after grilling her mum on the details of what the cats were being fed. "It sounds like everything's all right." She said her goodbyes and hung up. Then she turned to Ida. "I'm sorry. It's like a spinal reflex. Someone mentions the cats…"

"That's fine, I understand," said Ida.

"Now, what were you saying?"

"Oh," said Ida, "just that I like sitting here because I like watching the bat." She gestured at the window, and sure enough, out there in the cone of light projecting downward from the lamppost, a tiny sharp-winged black shadow came sweeping in from the outer darkness to snap up insects.

The staff at the Notre Coeur did a remarkably fine job of not hassling us to leave, despite the fact that we were the last customers of the night. But finally guilt—not to mention satiation with coffee and cakes—got the better of us and we got up to leave. The low apple-green velvet sofa proved as difficult to wrestle our way out of as I had imagined, but we eventually succeeded.

Ida said she'd walk back in the direction of the hotel with us. "My flat is near there anyway." Strolling along beside us, she seemed less petite than I remembered from the pizza place, but she was probably wearing high-heeled boots.

As we left the Notre Coeur, I turned to see the last of the lights go out in the café.

And I also saw a man. He was standing across the street. And the way he was standing, his angle in relation to us and the light, suggested that he was watching us.

I only glimpsed him for an instant, before he was thrown into darkness as they switched out the lights.

But I was sure it was Creepy Elvis.

12: ENOUGH LOOT FOR ALL CONCERNED

Nevada rolled over in bed and kissed me; I could tell she was up to something.

"You're going to learn your first phrase in Swedish today."

"Am I?" I said. "Oh good. What is it?"

"*Secondhand-butik.*"

"I think I'm going to like this phrase."

"I think you are, too," said Nevada.

"I assume," I said, "it means 'boutique' and 'second-hand'."

"You assume right."

"High-end charity shop…" I mused as we got dressed later.

"A cheering thought," said Nevada.

It certainly cheered me, holding out as it did the promise of vintage vinyl hunting for myself and Tinkler, and vintage clothes hunting for Nevada and her willing accomplice Ms DuBois-Kanes. Always with the possible promise of finding loot. Loot all round. Enough loot for all concerned.

"Who knows what these Swedes might have lurking in their charity shops?" said Tinkler, summarising my own thoughts as we joined him for breakfast. "For all we know, maybe you'll find one of the crazy lateral tracking turntables, going for a song."

"Okay," I said. "Suddenly I want everybody to eat their breakfast really quickly so we can go and look around the charity shop."

"Shops. Plural. Apparently there are two worth hitting," said Nevada, spooning thick white yogurt from a red glass bowl.

"Hitting," gurgled Tinkler. "Now I'm getting excited. Let's *hit* the Swedish charity shops."

"*High-end* charity shops," said Nevada. "That's where the boutique or *butik* bit comes in. As opposed to the *loppis*, or *loppmarknad*—the flea markets."

"Barbro was telling us about all this last night," said Agatha. "While you men were on a forlorn search for hi-fi."

"At the lonely murder farmhouse," added Tinkler. "Never omit that cheery detail. Although I must say the coffee was surprisingly good at the lonely murder farmhouse. And those cakes, my god, those little green marzipan things…"

"Anyway," said Agatha. "She was telling us that the charity shops here in Trollesko are run by the Church."

"Who would have expected a church to be involved in the charity racket?" said Tinkler. "But nonetheless I am intrigued. Am I sufficiently intrigued to forego a lengthy breakfast? That is the question."

We were in the breakfast room of the hotel. It had three

outer walls with high windows, flooding it with daylight. Through the open doorway to a further inner room, we could even glimpse the first member of the hotel staff we'd seen.

A young woman whose duty seemed to entirely consist of replenishing the food on offer whenever it was depleted by the voracious appetites of the guests.

Who were, as far as we could tell, just the four of us.

Tinkler was disproportionately impressed by the appearance of this breakfast person. "She appears to be human enough. Even wearing jeans and a T-shirt. That could just be their cunning ploy, though. To pass amongst us."

"So the Stepford theory is still in play?" said Agatha. Nevada nodded.

"My money remains on aliens," said Tinkler. "Albeit aliens in cheerfully realistic and realistically cheerful form."

"Right," said Nevada, taking out her phone. "So, these secondhand-butiks…"

"Plural?"

"Yes, although the correct plural would be *secondhand-butiker*. Anyway…" She gave an annoyed glance at Tinkler, who had suddenly stopped paying attention and was concentrating with great enthusiasm on his own phone which clearly had just received a message. Indeed, his face had lit up. I smelled stripper action and I'm sure I was not the only one to come to this conclusion, judging by the reactions of Nevada and Agatha.

When he finished reading the message he looked up and said, "I fear I can't come to the secondhand-butiker with you guys."

"What?" I said.

"At least not today."

"Have you been summoned by Ida?" said Agatha.

"She has suggested an alternative plan of action for this morning."

"Would that 'plan of action' involve you paying for a private dance, by any chance?" said Nevada.

"Nothing of the kind. In fact, she's inviting me to go and delve in a record store." He looked at me. "Inviting *us*. A second-hand record store. All vinyl. Large jazz section. Lots of original pressings. Do you want to come?"

Whatever I might have said, the answer was written there clearly on my face. All vinyl. Large jazz section. Lots of original pressings...

Before I could even formulate a response, Nevada was getting up. Indeed, both she and Agatha were rising from our table.

"Why don't you come with us?" I said to them.

"No," said Nevada. "You boys go off to your record store. We girls will go to the secondhand-butik and look for clothes. Apparently, they have records there too, at the secondhand-butik—lots of vinyl, original pressings—but don't you worry about that. You can have a look another day. On your own. Don't give us another thought. Off you go to your record store."

Despite the sunlight flooding in, the breakfast room suddenly felt distinctly chilly.

"In fairness, *second-hand* record store," said Tinkler. "We are going to a second-hand record store."

"With a stripper," said Agatha.

"An off-duty stripper," said Tinkler. "Again, in fairness, when they have their clothes on they're just like ordinary people. And one other thing."

"What other thing could there possibly be?"

"This place is also a second-hand *book* store. And guess what? Big crime fiction section. Lots of vintage paperbacks."

The room suddenly seemed to get a lot warmer. The girls proceeded to have the silent equivalent of a conference carried out entirely by eye contact, then sat down again. We all finished breakfast in a leisurely and companionable fashion.

Then we all strolled together to the book and record store. Or, from my point of view, the record and book store. It was located across the street from us, alongside the park opposite the hotel.

The park was covered with red and yellow leaves that seemed to have fallen overnight, windblown into soggy mounds and piled up high against the unyielding face of the bandstand, a seashell shape of white stone and aluminium stationed atop a block of damp grey concrete.

Standing on the pavement at the edge of the park was Ida. She waved to us, cheery and smiling. I thought I heard Agatha cursing under her breath as we crossed the street to meet her.

It was a bright, chill morning, shining with recent rain, and Ida wore a yellow raincoat, hooded and knee length, with skinny blue jeans and yellow rubber boots showing below it. At her throat was a natty scarf in a blue and green tartan that matched the lining of the raincoat, visible inside the hood. Framed in that hood, Ida's face was pink-cheeked and merry and remarkably innocent looking.

"You all came," she said, smiling at us. "I am so glad."

She linked arms with Tinkler, much to his delight. Agatha and Nevada exchanged a look. "So, where are we going?" said Nevada.

"Over there." Ida pointed.

"To that tower?"

"Yes."

We had noticed the tower when we'd first arrived at the hotel. We could hardly have missed it, rising high above the other buildings nearby. It looked like it had once belonged to a medieval fortress, but the medieval fortress had snuck off in the night and left the poor little tower abandoned here in this clean modern town.

"It's called the vattentorn," said Tinkler. "Which means 'water tower'."

"Of course it does," said Nevada. "But how do you know that, Tinkler? You don't normally know anything about languages. Or indeed anything about anything."

"Oh, I do. I do know stuff. I know all sorts of stuff."

"Where records are concerned, you know stuff," said Agatha.

"I think it is suspicious that you know a Swedish word," said Nevada. "Deeply suspicious."

"I hope you guys find something at the store," said Ida, calling off the inquisition on Tinkler while sounding for all the world like a nervous hostess.

The water tower was a beautiful old building, a cylinder of cream brick gleaming in the morning light. A black wrought-iron spiral staircase wound around its exterior, windblown leaves heaped on its bottommost steps. The cylinder of the tower rose up from a big square base or plinth, which formed part of the building and made for a conventionally shaped ground floor. This was where we went in.

We pushed open a red wooden door with a window and a cardboard sign hanging in it with the word *Öppettider* hand-written on it, above some numbers that were clearly opening times.

A bell rang and we found ourselves in a little foyer with another windowed door leading inside—this one so plastered with posters and handbills for local bands that it took a while to determine that it too was painted red.

We pushed through this as well, into the centrally heated warmth of the shop proper.

Sitting at a desk, wrapped in a baggy orange sweater with a black and grey polka-dot kerchief tied around his neck, was a shaven-headed man with a big bushy grey beard and large ebony earrings. Keen intelligent eyes peered out from behind heavy black-rimmed glasses. Ida introduced him as Anders, the store's owner.

The walls of the several interconnected rooms in Anders's establishment were lined with bookcases. In the middle of each room, his records were housed in the traditional cardboard boxes placed on tables. Equally traditionally, low-priced dross or unsorted new arrivals resided in boxes on the floor under the tables.

The jazz records and the crime paperbacks were in adjacent but separate rooms, so Tinkler and I split from Nevada and Agatha. Ida remained chatting with Anders at the cash desk. They seemed to know each other quite well.

I soon became so engrossed in the search that I hardly noticed when Tinkler took off and left me on my own. When I finally surfaced, I had half a dozen prospects. I took the stack of records over to a window and carefully examined the playing surface of the vinyl on each in daylight. Five of the records were duly ruled out.

Happily, the one that did make the cut was a gem of a find. A jazz gem.

Tinkler, fellow crate digger, instantly sensed that I'd hit paydirt. "What have you got there? *Count Basie and the Kansas City Seven*. On Impulse… With a Van Gelder stamp in the dead wax? Yes. Of course. Wait a minute. It's a Canadian Sparton pressing and not the original US Impulse. But they used the Van Gelder metalwork…"

"So effectively it is an original. And it's the only occasion I know of when Bill Basie and Rudy Van Gelder worked together."

Tinkler checked the price on the record. "Bargain."

And it was. I was a happy bunny.

So was Agatha. She had a small but carefully chosen stack of paperbacks. "They're the Penguin 'hazard marker' editions with the Raymond Hawkey cover art," she told me happily, holding up three of Len Deighton's classic spy novels.

"I love those books," I said. "But the hero doesn't have a name."

"We never *learn* his name," said Agatha, correcting me. "And they're in exceptionally nice condition. *Horse Underwater* has the skull illustration on special high-quality paper."

Nevada had also picked up a novel to read, in its original English for a change. *The Mangan Inheritance* by Brian Moore. "I've been wanting to read this again," she said. "It's one of his best, up there with *The Doctor's Wife*."

We headed for the front of the store with our finds and paid Anders, who was frowning regretfully as he rang up each purchase, as if he was selling off his treasured personal possessions and was only now realising that he'd woefully underpriced them. Who knows, perhaps he was and perhaps he had. In any case, Ida was right about no one in Sweden taking cash. Anders didn't even seem to have provision for such an outlandish eventuality.

Speaking of Ida…

"Where's your doxie?" said Nevada to Tinkler.

"She's gone upstairs. The doxie has gone upstairs. To make us all a coffee."

"She works here? She works at the store?" Nevada and Agatha exchanged a look. A stripper with a day job in a second-hand book and record store?

"No, she just rents an apartment above it."

And so we bid farewell to Anders, who was toying thoughtfully with one of his ebony earrings and quite possibly considering repricing his entire stock, and headed upwards. The staircase was on the other side of a door in Anders's living quarters at the back of the store. Anders had unlocked the door and allowed us access with ill grace, but I imagined he was more accommodating with Ida. Indeed, I imagined she had her own key.

The staircase was a wooden spiral affair that had apparently been retrofitted to the inside walls of the gutted tower, rising around a hollow central shaft and then disappearing through a circular hole in the circular wooden ceiling far above.

"She lives up there?"

"At the top of a tower," said Tinkler with pride. "Like a princess in a fairy tale."

"This explains the staircase on the outside," I said.

Nevada nodded. "Fire escape."

As we approached the ceiling of the tower, we saw the circular opening was in fact a trapdoor skilfully cut into the dark planks. We went up through it into a small landing area. Here, I observed the round lid of the trapdoor, flipped back on its hinges and nestling in a custom-built hollow in the floor. And, rising above it, a wooden railing that circled around the open trapdoor, presumably to stop the unwary being precipitated in an abrupt and involuntary fashion through the opening, perhaps after one too many refreshing beverages.

To one side of the landing was a window in the tower wall, just a slit in the bricks that let in a cold, clean breeze and provided a narrow slice of a beautiful view of the park and the town, both looking quietly magnificent from this height in their brilliant autumn colours.

Opposite the slit window there was a whitewashed wooden wall with a red door like those downstairs. This one featured a circular porthole, fashioned of pebbled glass, transparent enough to allow light through but sufficiently opaque to maintain privacy.

All in all, it was a very funky and attractive place to live, and I was about to say as much when raised voices suddenly resounded through the door, in angry contention. Male and female voices shouting at each other—Ida and a man.

There was a yellow Post-it note stuck to the door with *Come in!* written on it and a happy face drawn below. But the savage yelling didn't encourage any of us to take up the offer, happy face or no. We all stood there, looking at each other and feeling awkward. Should we go back downstairs? Should we follow the instructions on the note and let ourselves in, calling out loudly and cheerily to announce our presence as we did so?

For all we knew, there was always shouting at Ida's place and waiting for it to end was a mug's game.

But it did end, abruptly. Followed by a rather tense and somehow ugly silence.

And then the door popped open, making all of us jump. Ida looked out at us with a rather artificial and strained smile. She was wearing jeans and a green T-shirt with cream trim and the word PIPCO on it, also in cream. I recognised it as a duplicate of the one Frank Zappa was wearing on the cover of *Lumpy Gravy*. On her feet were scruffy grey woollen socks.

"I'm sorry about that. Did you hear that? Of course you did. Come in."

"If this is a bad time…" said Nevada.

"No, come in, this is a good time. Any time that that bastard is gone is a good time."

She led us inside. The doorway led right into Ida's living room. Standing sentinel just inside was a coatrack with her yellow raincoat and tartan scarf hanging on it, and her yellow boots standing neatly in front of it, as though someone had just begun the process of building a replica Ida. On the other side of the door was a large poster. A tourist ad for a place called Skara, featuring a photo of a vattentorn just like this one and continuing the doppelganger theme.

Being in a circular tower, the walls of the apartment were curved, except for the wooden partition with the door set in it. Ida had made full use of her one flat wall by mounting an elegant skeletal wire shelving unit to the right of the door.

The fact that this was a recently achieved piece of home handiwork was indicated by the electric screwdriver lying on the floor beneath it, in the company of a couple of surplus rawl plugs. I wondered whether Ida had fitted the shelf herself—and done rather a good job—or had enlisted the assistance of a more DIY-savvy admirer.

If the latter, I devoutly hoped that she wasn't banking on Tinkler stepping into any such role.

"Please come in," said Ida. The living room was clean and cheerful, but none too tidy, mostly because there were clothes everywhere. The place smelled rather pleasantly of orange peel.

As we entered, following Ida, she marched straight through the room to the far side where there was a door with a sign above it reading *Nödutgång*. It was a heavy wooden door painted dark green with a long slim chrome bar fixed

on it vertically—a silver rod bisecting the green rectangle—
and three matching chrome hinges.

Ida grabbed the vertical bar and hauled the door open,
letting in daylight and revealing a disconcertingly empty slab
of blue sky. A bird flew lazily past as a powerful gust of cold
fresh air blew in, chasing out the orange peel fragrance.

"That's right!" yelled Ida in a voice like an air raid siren.
"Run, you bastard!"

I went and looked over her shoulder. Below us, descending
the black wrought-iron fire escape, was none other than our
old friend Creepy Elvis—Bo Lugn, strip club mogul. He'd
apparently gone out via this exit after his altercation with Ida.
He hadn't made a lot of progress in his descent, because he
was seriously encumbered with a heavy-looking black and
silver cylinder under one arm.

"What is that?" I said.

"A juicer. A Kuvings CS600 juicer. *My* Kuvings CS600
juicer. Apparently now *his* Kuvings CS600 juicer."

The juicer-encumbered Bo Lugn looked back over his
shoulder, saw Ida, and shouted, "*Hora!*" We didn't need any
translation for that.

"Jordon, come here," said Ida in a voice of peremptory
command, which Tinkler instantly obeyed, replacing me
beside her in the open doorway. She led him out onto the
black iron fire escape and began to shout at Bo.

"That's right, run away, you coward. You thief. You
cowardly thief. You cowardly thieving bastard. Run away.
My man is here." Ida wrapped her arms around Tinkler. "Run
away from my man, you coward."

"That's right," said Tinkler proudly.

"Run away or he'll kick your ass."

"That's right," said Tinkler.

"I'll send him after you."

"That's…" said Tinkler and stopped.

"He's coming after you." shouted Ida. At her side, Tinkler had now fallen profoundly silent. Luckily for him, Ida apparently had no intention of following through on her threat and actually sending him after Creepy Elvis and his juicer. Or her juicer.

Instead, Ida and Tinkler came back inside and she shut the door, sealing off the blue sky and the cold air. "I am sorry about that," she said.

"No, it's uh…" said Nevada.

"Fine," completed Agatha.

"He didn't *lend* me the juicer," said Ida savagely, striding around the room and then whirling to face us. "He took back the juicer because he said he'd lent it to me. But he didn't lend it to me. He *gave* it to me because I got stiffed on the money I was supposed to receive for a party I did at the club. A payment. Not a loan. A part payment. Not even a full payment. The bastard still owed me money and now he owes me the juicer, too. *Den jävla fittan.*"

Nevada asked for a translation of this. Ida frowned thoughtfully for a moment. "I suppose 'that fucking cunt' would be the nearest equivalent. You would say, 'fucking cunt'?"

"Oh yes," said Nevada.

"Spot on," said Tinkler with paternal pride.

"Anyway, I hope you didn't want juice," said Ida, suddenly sounding very worried that we might. "Because the juicer is gone." We reassured her that we didn't want juice. "There's plenty of coffee, then," she said. "Or tea or hot chocolate?"

"Coffee is good."

"And I have bagels," said Ida, leading us into her small galley kitchen. This was commendably neat and tidy, perhaps thanks to a house injunction against leaving clothes lying around. She did indeed have bagels—an impressive selection of them looking very golden and well presented on pale blue frosted glass plates on the counter. The upmarket bagel joint paper bags they'd apparently been purchased in earlier that morning were neatly folded and awaiting recycling. Ida smiled a dazzling though somewhat nervous hostess smile at us. "Can I toast some bagels for you?"

"We've all eaten," said Nevada. "Sorry."

"We all just ate breakfast at the hotel," I said. A very large breakfast, as it happened.

"Of course you did," said Ida, looking crestfallen. "It's all right," she said, not sounding entirely convinced that it was, as she studied the numerous and varied bagels so artfully spread before us, now all cruelly spurned.

"I'll eat them during the week…" she sounded quite forlorn. "Perhaps I'll freeze some."

"Oh, hell, I could eat one," said Tinkler gallantly, sitting down at the counter. "Perhaps more than one."

13: SECONDHAND-BUTIK

After coffee—and, thanks to Tinkler, a surprisingly large number of bagels—we parted company with Ida. Nevada and Agatha politely averted their gaze as Ida and Tinkler hungrily kissed and hugged like newlyweds being cruelly torn apart, and then we set off at last for our much-postponed pillage of the secondhand-butik.

Despite the sunshine there was a real chill in the air as we crossed the road, leaving the vattentorn, the hotel and the park behind. A couple of streets away, this residential neighbourhood turned into Trollesko's downtown area and shops began to proliferate around us. Agatha and Tinkler had fallen into a discussion about the self-published priest's self-published novel.

"Have you got to the gruesome disembowelment, yet?" said Tinkler, adding, "Gruesome disembowelment in a wintery setting, check."

"I have," allowed Agatha.

"What did you think?"

"I thought it was gruesome."

"What were its literary merits?" pursued Tinkler. "If any."

You could see Agatha was trying hard to be fair to the author. "It was vivid. It was original."

"I sense not a whole lot of enthusiasm there," said Tinkler.

"Not a whole lot," agreed Agatha.

I only heard fragments of this discussion and gleaned none of the gory details because, frankly, I was fantasising about finding a lateral tracking Beogram turntable at the secondhand-butik. I had reached the point of wondering how to pack this purely imaginary turntable so it could safely be shipped back to England, and returned to the earlier portion of my fantasy to revise it to include finding it with its original box and packing materials.

Tinkler was now saying to Agatha, "This is such a waste. Right now I could be talking to you about a whole bunch of other Scandi crime novels. Interesting, good, non-self-published, *real* Scandi crime novels. If they weren't all in that fucking trunk."

"You have to take that fucking trunk up to your room, Tinkler," said Nevada, now both provoked and, after our breakfast and the visit to Ida's, well caffeinated. Not a combination you'd ever want converging on you. "You can't leave it where it is, halfway up the stairs perched on that fucking table."

"Yeah, yeah, yeah," said Tinkler, unmoved.

This conversation might have gone on, and grown considerably more heated, but we turned a corner and found ourselves face-to-face with Christer Vingqvist—as though, like some storybook demon, our discussion of his novel had summoned him out of nowhere.

It has to be said that Christer didn't seem surprised to see us at all. Indeed, he began talking to us as if continuing a conversation he'd left off a moment before, perhaps at a party while he'd gone off to get ice for our drinks.

"You've probably been wondering about the name of my heroine, Penumbra Snow. Penumbra means—"

"We know what it means," said Nevada.

"In fact," said Tinkler, "we've taken to calling our hotel the Penumbra Inn."

Christer Vingqvist's eyes gleamed with triumph. "In honour of my character?"

"No," said Nevada. "In honour of the crepuscular nature of the accommodation on offer therein."

Luckily for us, Christer Vingqvist was hurrying to work at the local hospital where he was employed as the deacon, so the in-depth discussion of himself and his work, which he was so clearly longing for, was cut short. Though not short enough for my liking.

But we finally got rid of him and locked on to target for the secondhand-butik.

It was located near the bridge at the edge of the shopping district and occupied an entire huge stone cube of a building, visible from a remarkable distance by virtue of the fact that it was painted canary yellow. The big yellow edifice consisted of four floors of second-hand goods. "Jesus, this place is massive," said Nevada.

None of us had seen anything like it back home. This place looked either custom built or long ago renovated to purpose. It was immaculate and brightly illuminated inside, with walls painted brilliant white. "Eggshell white on the inside. And it's yolk yellow on the outside," said Agatha. "So it's like an inside-out egg."

"Clean and well lit," said Tinkler. "Check."

The ground floor of the inside-out egg was dedicated to large items of furniture. The second floor featured smaller furniture like dining chairs, all manner of kitchen paraphernalia and furnishings, electrical goods, garden implements and sporting equipment. The third floor, where the clothes, books and records were located, was where we were all headed, trying not to break into a sprint.

We emerged from the stairwell into the big open space which, as on the other levels, filled the entire floor without any dividers or barriers, just neat and orderly arrangement of items with wide aisles in between. The books and magazine section, full of publications in Swedish, hardly caused Agatha and Nevada to break stride.

They barrelled right through it, heading for the women's clothes, which were arrayed on the far side of the room, in row after row, on wooden hangers on long metal rails on wheeled frames. On the other side of the room, beyond what seemed like acres of more clothing—in this case men's and children's—in a far corner was the vinyl section. Rather a large vinyl section. Tinkler and I began to make a beeline for it while the girls went after the clothes like big supple jungle cats plunging into the undergrowth in search of prey.

Just then a voice rang out. "Bruv! Cuz! Fam!"

We turned to see Emma Fernholm standing there, wearing a knee-length silver raincoat with a hood on it and the NASA logo printed over her heart in black. Under the logo in red were the words *Nice and Safe Attitude*.

Emma's face was alight with pleasure at this surprise meeting. She hugged each of us in turn. She smelled of patchouli and cherry vape. "My days," she said. "It's so cool to bump into you lot. *Juno wham sane?*"

It took me a moment of wondering who the hell Juno was before I decoded this as "Do you know what I'm saying?" uttered with a hip street inflection emanating from the general direction of London. Possibly the general direction of North London.

Emma then joined the girls in their raid on the clothes section—as she raced off, Tinkler and I tried to outclass the distaff half of the team by maintaining a dignified and unhurried approach to the corner where the vinyl lurked. But, by the time we got there, we were virtually in a foot race. "Any first pressings of blues on Chess…" said a rather out-of-breath Tinkler.

"Should I find any such, I would be entirely open to swapping them to you for, say, any Blue Note first pressings you find."

"You bastard," said Tinkler. "That's a terrible deal."

"Take it or leave it."

"Well of course I'll take it," said Tinkler. We had now arrived at the vinyl section. Characteristically well presented, it was well-lit by both daylight from the tall windows on either side and the glow of the indoor fluorescents. The records were in wooden crates on steel shelves at waist height for easy access. Tinkler and I came to an immediate unspoken gentlemanly agreement about which section we each were checking out first, and set to work. The records were impeccably filed and it took me less than five minutes to go through them.

But in those five minutes I hit the jackpot.

"What is it?" said Tinkler, instantly realising from my stillness and absorbed silence that I'd made a discovery.

I held it up.

Owyn Wynter had described the band Storm Dream Troopers as looking like "a sort of death metal Abba". But they had apparently left that look behind by the time they'd released this album—or at least they were keeping it on the down low.

The cover art was a striking black-and-white photo of a woman—one of the women in the band—standing in a graveyard. If it was real, it was not a particularly well-kept graveyard. Indeed, it looked distinctly sad and abandoned. The woman was standing over a sad and abandoned grave, in what appeared to be a high wind, her inky hair blown back behind her in wild black streaks.

She was leaning over the elaborate, antique but now much-neglected headstone above the grave. The pose allowed—indeed, demanded—a close inspection of her exposed cleavage.

She was using one hand to support herself on the headstone.

The other held a pistol. Pointing directly and rather frighteningly at anyone who did inspect said cleavage. The frightening aspect was not so much the gun as the look in her eyes, which was genuinely wild and disturbing.

If it had been created by some later monkeying with the image, it was monkeying of genius.

It was a striking cover. The only thing that let it down was the inevitable Gothic typeface which spelled out the title in hazard-warning yellow—*Attack and Decay*.

I said, "It's the record I was hired to come here to buy."

"Holy shit, so it is."

I chuckled happily inspecting it. Too good to be true, yet here it was.

"Do you need another copy?" said Tinkler. "I mean, Magnus has already got one lined up for your client. The one you were sent here to collect."

"Nevertheless, I can still use this. I can sell it for a shitload of money."

"So it's totally surplus to the deal you came here to conclude, but it's still a good score."

"Yes."

"A side-hustle, so to speak."

I was double-checking the record. If things seem too good to be true, they generally are...

"You sure it's not a counterfeit? A bootleg?"

"It isn't. I just checked." I was pleased. This was a major find.

"Congratulations," said Tinkler.

"Thank you."

"It is the sacred, super-deluxe 180-gram audiophile pressing?"

"Oh shit," I said. "No it isn't. It's the original pressing."

"And therefore not as desirable."

"Right."

"So no longer worth a shitload of money."

"Not quite," I said. "But it's still worth at least *half* a shitload. Maybe two-thirds of a shitload."

Nevada was going to be very pleased.

"Then still cause for congratulations. So, congratulations."

"Thank you."

"What now?" said Tinkler.

I checked the time. My two plunges into record hunting this morning, combined with coffee at Ida's tower—a visit not shortened by a detailed disquisition on juicer theft—had consumed more time than I'd expected. "Now I need to meet Magnus and start doing my job."

"By doing your job, you mean checking the record Magnus is selling."

"Right," I said.

"Which is going to involve listening to it. Carefully."

"Yes," I said, looking at the woman in the graveyard with the pistol. "Unfortunately." Graveyard Woman seemed genuinely angry, though oddly not about having to stand in a graveyard holding a pistol. "In fact, unfortunately it's going to involve listening to it carefully twice."

"Twice?"

"On two different systems," I said. "Due diligence."

"So you're going to play it over at the self-published priest's house…?"

"Yes."

"And where else?"

"Over at Magnus's place," I said.

"You do realise that you're listening to that record on the two hi-fi systems in Sweden most likely to have been tampered with to make it sound better?"

"That doesn't worry me," I said.

"Because you're such a professional?"

"Partly," I said. "And partly because nothing anybody could do could make this sound better." *Was that a raven on the wing in the sky above the graveyard?*

"Very funny. You're such a music snob. You're really going to suffer having to listen to this demonic metal."

"Isn't that the point?" I said. *Or was it a crow, maybe?* It was hard to tell among all those angry grey roiling clouds. In any case the bird looked spectral, menacing, in keeping with the whole vibe of death… both long since and imminent—attack and decay indeed.

"And now you're going to have to listen to it *twice*. That will be cheery for you. Oh look. A cemetery and a handgun on the cover of the album. Do you think that might give a hint to the lyrical content and, shall we say, *general sound world* of what you have to look forward to? Look forward to listening to twice. For due diligence."

"Unfortunately," I said, yet again.

Tinkler looked at the record I was holding. "Are you going to listen to this one, too?

"Yes."

"And do a fascinating comparison with Magnus's copy?"

"Of course."

"Excellent," said Tinkler. "Original pressing versus audiophile edition in a shoot-out listening session."

"Would you like to join me?"

"Join you?"

"You claim to like this music, Tinkler. Or at least tolerate it. Why not have a listen with me?"

"Have a listen with you? Are you out of your fucking mind? I've got a date with Ida."

"Any old excuse," I said.

"You do realise that, if you are going to listen to both the original and the audiophile version, and do it on two different systems, that means you're going to have to listen to this jolly little album *four times*."

"I agree that it doesn't bear thinking about."

"*Four times*."

"Let's go," I said.

We went and found the girls. Nevada's eyes were gleaming; she was holding a sky-blue leather jacket tight to her chest as though it might suddenly try and flap its empty sleeves and fly away.

"Hey, it's the same colour as my trunk," said Tinkler.

"Even that won't put me off," said Nevada. "It's a Theory."

"Is that a fact?" said Tinkler.

"It's a highly desirable fashion label. This is their cropped biker jacket with an asymmetric front."

"I understand there's surgery for that," said Tinkler.

We paid for our finds and then I went to meet Magnus. As I left the others, Tinkler hissed at me, "*Four times,*" as if it was an ancient Sumerian curse.

I spent the rest of the afternoon first at Christer Vingqvist's little Mexican-style house near the school, and then in Magnus and Emma's penthouse at a posh apartment building overlooking the river in downtown Trollesko. It was a very nice place, and I had a pleasant and enlightening visit.

And thankfully it turned out that I didn't have to listen to *Attack and Decay* four times.

I listened to the copy Magnus was selling on the hi-fi systems at both places. Listened to it scrupulously from beginning to end. That constituted just two listenings. I merely dipped into the version I'd bought at the secondhand-butik. I didn't need to do more than that.

When we were finished for the day, Magnus drove me back to the hotel in Obi Van Kenobi and dropped me off.

I walked through the shadowy, silent lobby of the Penumbra Inn, the single eye of the skylight peering down at me, and then up the stairs, past Tinkler's trunk on the landing to our room on the next floor. As I did so I heard a thud, a door closing, then footsteps and a second and more solid door opening and closing. By the time I got to our floor, there was no one to be seen and the doors of all five guest rooms were firmly shut.

The hallway area was empty. The door to the sixth room, a pleasant little upstairs lounge, was also shut. This door had glass panels set in it. I surmised it was the less solid door I had heard closing. And the thud before that?

I opened the door into the lounge. Normally warm and cosy, it was forbiddingly cold, as if the windows had been open for a long time. Indeed, a curtain was still stirring, subsiding slowly to stillness beside the window. A window now firmly shut. So, window, lounge door, guest room door. That's what I had heard. Shut the window, shut the lounge door, get into your own room and shut that door...

Five guest rooms on this floor. Agatha, Tinkler, Nevada and I occupied three of those but all of our team were still in town...

Except me.

Someone in the upstairs lounge must have seen me coming. They would have had time to close the window—*why was the window open?*—and get back into their own room.

I shrugged. Maybe they'd been smoking a cigarette and this was behaviour strictly forbidden at the Penumbra Inn.

Actually, come to think of it, it probably was. Smoking strictly forbidden at the Penumbra Inn.

Smoking implies a smoker. It looked like there was someone else staying here now. We were no longer the only guests. I don't know why this sent a warm ripple of paranoia through me, but it did.

I unlocked the reassuringly heavy, solid and very well polished wooden door of our room and locked it again very thoroughly behind me before I switched on my phone and called Owyn Wynter.

He answered immediately. "Hello there. I'm glad you called. I was just wondering about your cats. More specifically, that mischievous little devil who sank her claws into my hand. And then she just eased them out again. And there was no trace. Almost no trace. You could train that cat to do microsurgery."

"You're welcome to try," I said. "You'd have to catch her between naps, though."

"Anyway, who is looking after those little devils while you're in Sweden? You didn't just leave food out for them?"

"No, Nevada's mother is cat sitting and house sitting."

"Ah, very sensible. So…" Small talk was now concluded. "Have you had a chance to listen to the record?"

"Yes," I said.

"And it's the real thing?"

"Absolutely."

"The limited edition audiophile pressing?"

"Yes," I said. "It's certainly that."

"And is it in mint condition?"

"Absolutely. Very good clean pressing. No factory damage at all and no wear or tear. Probably unplayed. It's in great shape."

"So everything is perfect," said Owyn Wynter. "Yet I sense that you have reservations."

"I do," I said. "For two reasons. Number one, I was over at Magnus's place and I saw something."

"He has a really nice flat, right, overlooking the river?"

"Yeah…" Another warm ripple of paranoia. Did Magnus and Owyn know each other? If so, why did they need me as an intermediary? I was entering Paranoia Heights, as Nevada and I had come to call it, courtesy of Tinkler.

Re-entering, I guess, in this case. "Have you been there?" I said. "To Magnus's flat?"

"No. He showed me pictures. He only just moved in, right?"

I relaxed a little. "Exactly right. Magnus is a very nice guy…"

"Skip all that, what do you really think of him?"

"I think he's a nerd who has recently come into money…" I remembered scruffy old Obi Van Kenobi parked beside the gleaming new Union Jack Mini. In the parking lot below their luxury penthouse. "Quite a lot of money."

"Yes," said Owyn. "He seemed to me like a guy who was in business and the business was doing well."

"Right," I said. And now I thought I knew exactly what that business was.

"You said you saw something at his place. What did you mean?"

"Well," I said, "Magnus may be a nerd who has struck it rich, but he is still a nerd. A record nut, with vinyl strewn all over his luxury flat. I mean like armchairs you can't sit in because they're full of records. And I don't say that judgementally. Because I've been there myself." In the days before Nevada. It has to be said that Fanny had quite liked napping on a pile of records in an armchair, and perhaps even missed it now. "But as a consequence of too many records and a chaotic lifestyle, Magnus let me catch a glimpse of something he didn't want me to see."

"Okay," said Owyn Wynter. "I'm intrigued."

"A crate full of *Attack and Decay*."

"A *crate* full?"

"I'd say about fifty copies."

"Of the same album that I am buying?"

"Yes," I said. "And I suspect there's even more. I think he's got a shitload of these things."

There was a pause and then Owyn Wynter said, "So you feel the situation has changed."

"It has," I said.

"And what are you proposing?" said Owyn Wynter.

"I am proposing that, since he's got lots of copies, the super rarity argument begins to fall apart and we should ruthlessly beat him down on price."

"Because there are more copies in circulation."

"Yes," I said. "Although they're not exactly in circulation."

"Which is exactly my point," said Owyn Wynter. "You may well be right, and he may well have a shitload of these things. But he may also have a plan to put them on the market very slowly over a long period of time. Drip feeding."

"Well, he almost certainly has that plan," I said. "That's precisely what I would do." And that was exactly the business I believed Magnus was in. This was how he maintained his lifestyle. With his Mockney spouse. Whom I was beginning to quite like—in fact, I had warmed to Emma more than Magnus. For all his generosity with his time and his friendliness, he ultimately seemed rather aloof and calculating. He certainly didn't have Emma's spontaneous exuberance.

"Selling them slowly to keep the price up…" mused Owyn.

"Right."

"Right. So it doesn't make that much difference if he has a lot of copies in his possession or not. Unless he dumps them all on the market at once, the market price isn't suddenly going down."

"I still say it's a psychological lever," I said. "We can use the knowledge of all these copies to negotiate him down."

"Psychological Lever," said Owyn Wynter. "Good name for a band. I wonder if it's been used?" There was a pause while he checked his phone. "Nope. I will make a note of that."

I sensed I didn't have his full committed attention to my attempt to put Magnus through the rigours of a proper negotiation of the kind that should always be taking place when a piece of highly sought-after vinyl is about to change hands for a lot of money. Really quite a lot of money.

I said as much to him.

"I'd prefer not to jeopardise this purchase," said Owyn. "It's a bird in hand, right?"

For some reason, when he uttered that trite phrase it hit me hard. I immediately pictured a bird, squirming to escape from someone's hand. Not my hand, I hastened to tell myself. And it wasn't just any bird. It was the scissor beak crow.

That crow had been on my mind for hours. Why?

I forced myself to concentrate. "A very expensive bird," I said. "A very expensive bird in hand."

"I am sure you are right. And I absolutely believe that you could save me some money—quite possibly a considerable sum of money—if you were to haggle ruthlessly with

Magnus. But I would like to ask you, as a personal favour to me, *not* to do that." Owyn was at his most sincere, friendly and persuasive. "I don't mind paying a bit over the odds because I really don't want to do anything that might even remotely jeopardise this transaction. You have said yourself it is a perfect copy. So please just pay the full asking price. I really, really want that record."

That, at least, was a sentiment I could fully sympathise with. "Okay," I said. "I just hate to let them get away with it."

"Them?"

"So, there's this guy called Christer Vingqvist…"

During my afternoon spent in the little Mexican casa, followed by the riverside penthouse, I had realised that it wasn't just Magnus who was conspicuously well off. So too was Christer Vingqvist—who was not quite the humble guy he claimed to be. Like Magnus, he seemed to live very comfortably and was not short of expensive toys, even discounting all the ones he'd inherited from his father.

"He and Magnus know each other," I said. "They're clearly not friends and there's very little love lost between them, yet equally clearly they're involved with each other somehow. I think they're in business together."

"What sort of business?"

"Okay, so in Sweden the charity shops are run by the Church."

"I didn't know that. Interesting."

"And it was the Church that was also responsible for suppressing *Attack and Decay*."

"That of course I did know," said Owyn.

"And you probably know how they went about suppressing it."

"Yes, I think I told you when I came over for supper. They bought up all the copies and destroyed them."

"Not quite," I said. "They asked all the good churchgoing people to buy the record and empty the shops of it. But then they specifically gave orders *not* to destroy them. Because they reckoned that, for example, organising a mass burning of a record in this day and age would not make for a great visual. It would have been bad publicity for the Church, making them look…"

"Oppressive and regressive. Ah yes, that makes sense," said Owyn. "Gone are the days when the good folks in the Bible Belt can put Beatles albums to the torch and expect the public to side with them." Then he hastily added, "Not that I'm suggesting that the Troopers are comparable to the Beatles."

"Heaven forbid," I said. "But the important point is that they didn't need to *destroy* these records," I said. "They just needed to take them out of circulation. They emptied the shops of the LP so nobody could buy the record and get corrupted by it. Eventually the record company caved under pressure and agreed not to manufacture any further copies. And it went out of print. Which left a situation where there were virtually no copies of *Attack and Decay* available. And it became notionally a scarce item."

"Notionally?" said Owyn.

"There may not have been copies in circulation, but there were loads squirrelled away by the good churchgoing parishioners."

"Because they'd been specifically asked not to destroy them."

"Right," I said. "So there were tons of these records, stored in attics and garages all over Sweden, bought by people at the request of their pastor. And, as the years passed, these people naturally would declutter, have a clear out, and get rid of them."

"Get rid of them," said Owyn Wynter sadly, thinking of the waste.

"But they didn't throw them away," I said. "These were thrifty, sensible people who put everything to good use. They would recycle rather than discard."

The light began to dawn on Owyn. "So they would give them to the charity shops."

"Right," I said. "With the original fuss about the record forgotten, they would simply quietly donate them to the charity shops like anything else. Because that would help raise money for the Church."

"Because the Church runs the charity shops," said Owyn.

"Right, which is where Christer Vingqvist comes in. He's a deacon with the Church and I think he's Magnus's inside man. The Church's charity shops have a centralised hub where donations are sorted and every item that is sold comes with a barcoded sticker." I was looking at the one on the back of my copy of *Attack and Decay*, thinking idly of how I would have to remove it carefully before selling it on.

"So Magnus and… what's his name? Christer? They know when copies of *Attack and Decay* are donated?"

"Yes," I said. "I think they intercept them and get them sent to the secondhand-butik here in Trollesko, where Christer creams them off and buys them at charity shop prices—in fact probably at *discounted* charity shop prices, because he's an insider—before they're even put out on sale to the public."

In the record collecting community this sort of behaviour was viewed in about the same way dynamiting fish would be viewed in the fishing community.

"But perhaps I'm doing them an injustice. Perhaps Christer just tips Magnus off that some records are on their way and Magnus goes after them pretty much fair and square, hoping to be the first one to find them when they're put out for sale.

"Either way, it's a strategy that has paid off for him handsomely. For both of them." I assumed Christer had nothing to do with selling the records on, but he was either on a percentage or a flat fee for each one sold.

There was silence on the other end of the line for a moment and then, to my surprise, Owyn Wynter laughed. "You really are the Vinyl Detective. You figured out their little scam." He sounded delighted. "Magnus and Christer." He pronounced the names affectionately, as if to say, *That pair of little scallywags*. Then he grew serious again. "But you said there were two things. Two reasons why you don't want me to buy this record…"

"Right. Letting them get away with the scam is one. The other is that today I found a copy of the original pressing. I imagined Magnus and Christer are doing exactly the same procedure with this as with the audiophile pressing—it's slightly less lucrative but still a nice little earner. Today, one of the copies slipped through their fingers."

And ended up in mine. I looked at the record happily. Magnus had been less happy when he'd seen it.

"You found a first pressing of *Attack and Decay*?" said Owyn.

"Yes," I said. "The original, non-audiophile one."

"And hence the less rare and less valuable one."

"Well, that's a judgement of the marketplace," I said. "I've had a listen to it and it's way better than the audiophile version."

"Better how?"

"It sounds more like real people playing real instruments in a real place."

"And you think it's superior to the limited edition 180-gram audiophile reissue?"

"It completely smokes it," I said.

"So you think…"

"That you should buy this record instead of the one Magnus is selling you."

"You're suggesting I just abandon buying Magnus's copy?"

"Yes." I'd discussed this with Nevada, and it would be a win for everyone if I directly sold Owyn the copy I'd found at the secondhand-butik, and we just abandoned the transaction with Magnus.

Or at least a win for everyone except Magnus. He would not, in this one instance, cash in. But I had to put the interests of my client ahead of his.

So Owyn and Nevada and I would all come out well ahead.

Which, as Nevada says, is the way we like to come out.

"All right," said Owyn. "I assume it's in near mint condition?"

"Immaculate," I said. I didn't add that it was ironic that they'd done such a great job of pressing flawlessly onto silent, virgin vinyl a grisly apocalyptic storm of industrial noise.

"Okay," said Owyn decisively. "I will buy it."

"Okay, good."

"And I will *also* buy the audiophile pressing that Magnus is selling."

"But the original has way more presence and a sense of reality," I said. "There's more air around the instruments and it times better. The bass is better defined…"

"I believe you—I absolutely believe you," said Owyn Wynter. "But I have to have *both*."

I could understand that, god help me. "Okay," I said. After all, it was his money. And it represented an even better payday for us. A very nice payday for us. "Fine."

"By the way," said Owyn. "Do you know why they suppressed the album, the Church?"

"General moral panic?" I suggested

"Not exactly. They released a statement at the time, saying that just listening to the record could unleash demonic forces." Owyn Wynter laughed. "They hastily added in a later statement that they really meant *purely in the mind of the listener*. But it is far from clear that is what they really meant."

* * *

After my phone call with Owyn I went to meet the others at the Notre Coeur Café.

"You're in a cheerful mood," said Tinkler. All of us, including Ida, were back sitting on the apple-green sofa in the alcove beside the tiny courtyard. It was true that I hadn't exactly been the heart and soul of the party since I joined them. In fact, Nevada was looking at me with an open expression of growing concern.

"It's all this demonic metal I've been listening to," I said.

The trouble with the Storm Dream Troopers was not that their music was bad. It wasn't. It was absolutely not my cup of tea, but nevertheless it was, on its own terms, very compelling. And well played—although post-recording studio hijinks was at least as important in the finished product as any actual playing of instruments.

Anyway, listening to *Attack and Decay*, very carefully, twice in one day, had left me with a number of earworms. Not the jaunty hooks of an ordinary pop song, but abstract and tortured bursts of noise that had managed to sear their way into my psyche. One distorted blast of keening guitar distortion and whining synthesiser in particular kept playing in my head. A vocal had been processed along with these other sounds, buried too deep to truly hear, but rising and falling in a hypnotic, repetitive pattern.

And the sense my mind had decided to make of that pattern was *scissor beak, scissor beak, scissor beak crow...*

That wasn't what they'd been singing, of course. Just the meaning I had imposed on the auditory chaos.

Nevada put a hand on my shoulder. "I'm glad we're charging Owyn an exorbitant fee for you having to listen to that stuff." She kissed me on the cheek. "And although I love being here, I'll be glad when this assignment is over."

"We're calling it an assignment now?" I said.

Tinkler and Ida got up and headed for the service desk in search of further caffeine and calories, hand in hand and for all the world like a happy couple. Nevada and Agatha followed, ostensibly to make their own selection of the day's cakes, but also, I suspected, to keep an eye on that happy couple.

I was left alone with the memory of the blasting music of *Attack and Decay* playing in my mind. I shook my head—as if that would help—and I turned and gazed idly out the window into the tiny courtyard.

There, sitting on the back of the weathered wooden love seat, was the scissor beak crow.

I stared at it.

There was no mistaking the distinctive deformity, or mutation, or whatever it was.

I sat and stared at it. The black bird stared back at me. The same crow had followed me a thousand miles from London. The shock of this realisation set electricity crawling across my scalp and down my spine.

It couldn't be the same crow.

It had to be the same crow.

I reached for my phone.

As soon as I did so, the crow hopped up into the air, flapped its wings, and disappeared unhurriedly into the winter sky.

I jolted to my feet, went to the window and pressed my face against the cold glass, peering up at the disappearing bird. It was now a fleeting, flapping black dot against a bank of fat grey cloud. And then it was gone.

I turned back to the table to see that my friends had all come back and were all, perhaps understandably, staring at me. Nevada had no trouble realising that something was wrong. "What is it, love?"

"The scissor beak crow."

"The one you saw in London," said Nevada.

I came and sat down at the table. They were all still staring at me. "Yes."

"You saw it just now?"

I pointed at the courtyard. "Out there. Yes."

They looked at the phone in my hand.

"Did you take a picture of it?" said Nevada.

"No. It flew away too quickly."

Nevada and Agatha looked at each other. Tinkler and Ida looked at each other.

"Are you thinking that your friend is nuts?" said Ida.

14: SNOW

"This is only until we get hold of the record for Owyn," said Nevada. "And then we can go home." She took the microwave oven out of its cardboard carton, stripped the annoying and unnecessary plastic wrapping from it, and began to set it up on the table in our hotel room. She glanced over at where I was watching glumly, sitting on the bed. "You can cook for us with a microwave, right?" she said. "It's not too terrible, is it?"

"No," I said. "It's fine for some things."

"Well, I will buy those things. I will buy those things for us from the supermarket and I will bring those things straight here and you can cook them in the room and we'll eat all our meals in here. And we'll drink all our drinks in here."

"We'll need suitable containers for cooking in the microwave," I said.

"I'll get them," said Nevada.

"And cutlery and plates."

"I'll get them."

"What about coffee?"

"I'll get a machine. I'll get all the machines. You can grind your own beans if you like. No cats here for the sound of bean-grinding to annoy! And don't worry about cost, this is all going on expenses."

I said, "Can't we just get some takeaway from Notre Coeur?"

Nevada stopped wrestling with the plug on the microwave and came over and put her hand on my chest, fingers spread over my heart. "No, love. Sorry. Not for a little while. We can't take the chance. We have to assume anything that we don't prepare right here ourselves might have been spiked with some kind of mind-altering chemical."

"Look, I saw that crow."

"I believe you," said Nevada. "But we have to also consider the possibility that someone might be trying to mess with your head, and your judgement, in relation to that record we're purchasing. Tinkler said you'd been hearing things when you're listening to it. Strange things, right?"

Good old Tinkler. "Yes."

"About this crow?"

"Yes." I had told Tinkler about the section of white noise that seemed to have a voice weaving through it chanting, *scissor beak, scissor beak…*

Nevada kissed me softly on the forehead. "So, you see, we have to make absolutely sure that no one is messing with that beautiful big brain of yours."

There was a knock on the door. Nevada unlocked it and opened it, then stood aside to let Tinkler in. He nodded at me. "How's the madman?"

* * *

Nevada went out with Tinkler to get supplies and, I had little doubt, talk about me. I watched them go, staring out the window as they headed downtown towards the shops. When they disappeared around the corner I started to turn away from the window. But something caught my eye.

A vast shimmering pointillist veil of dotted white, carried on the wind, was softening the autumn colours of the trees in the park across the road, and settling onto the ground, to blanket the heaps of fallen leaves in white.

Snow.

All of a sudden snow was falling heavily outside. I stood at the window staring out. The snow had instantly and emphatically changed the whole feeling of the day. It was beautiful. I found it soothing to watch, drifting gently down. I felt as though my troubles were settling like fat white flakes, to melt into nothing on the ground.

Though this snow was showing no signs of melting.

Instead it was beginning to clad the ground thickly, stretching in a swelling white carpet all across the park. Measuring its extent, I spotted something moving on it. Someone approaching on that white carpet, from the direction of the vattentorn, a figure in a hooded yellow raincoat, blue jeans, yellow boots.

Ida.

Swinging her arms vigorously and rhythmically as she walked, like a little soldier.

She was heading in this direction. I watched her approach,

her footsteps stretching behind her in the snow, though not very far behind her because the snow was falling so heavily now that her trail of footprints was already erased by a fresh layer of white.

As she drew closer I saw she was carrying a blue and green tartan drawstring bag slung over her shoulder.

When it became obvious that Ida was heading for the hotel, I stepped back from the window so she wouldn't see me. To be more specific, so she wouldn't see me watching her.

I went to the door of our room and opened it a fraction. I heard the front door of the hotel open downstairs. How did she know the key code? Tinkler. I heard her footsteps on the wooden staircase, pausing halfway up perhaps to admire the lethal precariousness of Tinkler's trunk, then coming all the way up to this floor. I quickly closed our door.

There was a moment of silence, during which I thought she was going to another room or perhaps continuing up the next flight of stairs to the next floor. But then there was a knock on the door. My head was so close to the door that I flinched.

Then I foolishly hesitated for a moment before answering it.

Ida stood out in the hallway, smiling at me. Snow was fringing her yellow hood, framing her pink face. She looked fresh and pretty and sunny. And there were flakes caught on her long eyelashes, tiny diamond glints. She seemed to notice their presence just as I did. She blinked them away rapidly, her eyelashes like hummingbird wings, then she scrunched her eyes shut, opened them and smiled at me again. "It's snowing," she said.

"I know," I said. I didn't say I'd watched her walk across the park, swinging her arms like a little soldier marching. What I did say was, "Tinkler's not here."

"I know, we're meeting in town. But I didn't want to see Jordon." She stared at me with her cartoon critter eyes. "I wanted to see you."

"Ah."

Ida's smile grew even bigger and brighter. "I brought you this." She unslung the tartan bag from her shoulder, opened the drawstring and then took from its dark interior a gleaming silver thermos shaped like a bullet. "It's coffee," she said. "I made it for you myself."

"I see," I said.

"You like coffee?"

"Yes I do." A considerable understatement. But…

"Because Jordon says that maybe somebody is trying to drug you so it's not safe for you to have a coffee from the café. So I made this for you myself." Ida beamed at me. "So we know it's safe."

She looked me in the eyes as she handed me the thermos. She had an unnervingly direct gaze. The thermos was warm to the touch.

"Thank you."

"The lid of the thermos unscrews and it's a cup. So it doesn't even matter if you don't have a cup. Here in your hotel room. Because you do now." Another big smile.

"Okay. Thank you."

"Well, that's all…" said Ida. "I'd better hurry or Jordon will be waiting." She leaned forward and gave me a quick and sisterly hug. Not so sisterly that my cortex didn't light up treacherously at the soft solid warmth of her body, and the proximity of her scent, a heady waft of citrus shampoo fiendishly funnelled towards me by the hood of her coat as she leaned in close.

She turned away and then turned back. "Do you know what Jordon and I are going to do tonight?"

"No," I said. My mind reeled at the question.

"He's going to help me get my juicer back from Bo Lugn." She turned and headed down to the lobby, waving happily as she disappeared down the steps. Ida hadn't been here more than a few seconds, but I was relieved that she was gone. And I think she knew it, and indeed that was why she'd departed so quickly, almost fleeing the scene.

She was accustomed to men being wary of her, especially men who were emphatically attached to other women.

I looked at the thermos in my hand.

It was not without regret that I unscrewed the top—it was indeed a cleverly designed cup—and poured the contents down the toilet. The coffee she'd served us at her place had been good and this smelled even better. As if she'd made it using only the finest ingredients, with loving care. I savoured the aroma as I flushed it to watery oblivion.

While I listened glumly to the cistern refilling, I texted Nevada to tell her what happened. Always best practice if someone might have just tried to drug you. Then I went to the window and looked out. The snow was coming down so thickly that I could see no sign of Ida. I don't know how long I stood staring out at the soft floating dance of the flakes drifting past the window, but I was brought back from my reverie by a familiar thudding sound.

It was the window in the small lounge next door, being slammed firmly shut. Then I heard the door of the lounge. I moved quickly to the door of our own room, about to open it a crack and see if I could get a glimpse of our new neighbour. But just then my phone rang. I scooped it up eagerly, thinking it was Nevada.

I'd told her about Ida and the thermos of coffee. But I hadn't told her about this hare-brained scheme she'd evidently hatched with Tinkler to get her juicer back from Creepy Elvis.

I was thinking that we might have to intervene and perhaps put the kibosh on this enterprise to prevent anyone getting hurt. "Anyone" in this case being principally Tinkler.

But it wasn't Nevada on the phone. It was Owyn Wynter.

We exchanged initial pleasantries and then he said, "It will be a few days before I pay Magnus, if that's okay."

A distant warning signal lit up in the back of my head, but I shrugged. And then, realising he couldn't see that, said, "Okay. Sure."

"You didn't want to rush back to London right away, did you?"

"No, we always planned on staying in Sweden for the rest of the week." That was how long we'd booked the hotel for. The Penumbra Inn. Come to think of it, it had been Magnus who'd recommended this place...

"Great. Sorry about the delay, but you know I'm paying for the record through the company; it seems Jaunty is embroiled in some kind of accountant's chicanery and has asked me to hold off transferring the funds for a day or two. It's all to do with how much the company spends this month as opposed to last month or next month. Or some such."

"Well, it's fine with me," I said.

"But please definitely reassure Magnus that payment is coming. It's just, like I said, that Jaunty has asked me to wait a little while. He sends his best wishes, by the way, Jaunty."

I said, "This is the corpse-faced fucker who terrorised us?"

"He'd be really appreciative if you didn't think solely of him in that light."

We said our goodbyes. I went to the window and stared out at the falling snow again, trying not to be paranoid about this delay in the payment for Magnus. I told myself that this was not a bad omen, that the whole deal was not suddenly heading south…

As I told myself this, I put my phone away and went to the door of our room. As I opened it, I revealed a man standing directly in front of it, hand raised in mid-air between us, apparently frozen in the act of knocking on our door.

The door I had just smartly swept inwards and away from him, as if to deliberately deprive him of the opportunity.

My visitor was rapidly balding, but with a blatant comb-over, strands of pale blond hair plastered horizontally across his smooth pink scalp. He wore a faded denim jacket with bits of brightly coloured cloth seemingly sewn into it at random.

In a kind of conservative counterbalance to this he also wore a white business shirt and a sober tie with diagonal stripes in beige and chocolate brown.

His trousers, however, were, or at least purported to be, snakeskin, dappled with the mottled colours of some noble but sadly no longer living reptile.

His shoes were a pair of beige desert boots—conservative—with black laces on one and purple laces on the other. Weird.

He was perhaps in his fifties.

And he was as surprised as I was.

He lowered his hand and said, "I was just about to knock. We're neighbours. I have just taken a room on this floor." He was evidently Swedish, but his accent—as usual for a Swede—was almost undetectable under his perfect English.

"Hi," I said. We shook hands.

"My name is Patrik. With a 'k'. But no 'c' like in English. I arrived at the hotel yesterday."

I repressed the urge to say that I'd noticed the arrival, in the form of a fiesta of mystery sound effects.

"And my good lady wife will be joining me shortly. We're in town on business." He smiled and winked. "You're here on business too, I understand."

A chill wariness crawled in my stomach. "How do you know that?"

"We have a Swedish expression, 'a little bird whispered in my ear'." Patrik smiled at me. His youthful face was curiously immobile despite this change of expression, as if he'd had some cosmetic surgery. Or perhaps a lot of it.

"Anyway, I just wanted to stop by and ask if you mind if I leave the window open? The window in the lounge? It won't be for long."

"No, that's fine," I said.

"I know that it's started to snow, and it's getting a little cold. But it won't be for long."

I repeated that it was fine. Then we said our goodbyes and I shut the door and went back to my own window to watch the snow come down. And, as it happened, I got there just in time to see Nevada walking up the front steps to the hotel.

She looked up and saw me and waved.

A moment later she was in the room, setting down bags of shopping and shaking moisture off her coat. "I cut the shopping expedition short when I got your text." Her hair had snowflakes in it, tiny white shapes sharply defined for a moment against those jet-black locks. They were already beginning to melt. As she kissed me, her hair seemed to have the cold outdoor air still clinging to it, the way the cats' fur brings in the weather of the day outside.

"Is this it?" She picked up Ida's silver bullet thermos.

"Yes."

Nevada shook it. "It's empty."

"I poured it down the loo."

"Did you save any of it for analysis?"

"No," I said. "I'm sorry. I didn't think."

Nevada shrugged. "Not to worry. It was probably fine anyway."

"I hope not," I said.

"Why do you say that?"

"Because if it was fine, I poured some perfectly good coffee down the loo. Instead of down my gullet." Still, there was no point crying over flushed caffeine, so to speak. Instead, I moved on and told Nevada about our new neighbour Patrik, mysterious opener and closer of windows.

"So, he's some kind of fresh air fiend?"

"Looks like it," I said. I was about to also tell her about his somewhat weird remark about a little bird whispering in his ear, but there was a knock just then at the door. "That's probably him now." I opened the door...

But it wasn't Patrik.

It was something much, much worse.

Stinky Stanmer stood there in the open doorway of our room, looking at us.

For a moment none of us seemed capable of speech. On our part at least, this was in no small measure due to Stinky not only being here but being dressed in blue-and-white striped pyjamas, blue plastic flip flops and a black leather jacket with a gold dragon painted on it.

Shamefully, it was Stinky who recovered first. "Surprised to see me, eh?"

"Stinky," I said, "what are you doing here?"

"I'm staying in this hotel. I'm on the floor upstairs. I've got a room with these girls. These two girls. They arrived last night quite late. So I was up quite late, as it happens. We all were. Because we got up to quite a lot of naughtiness, the three of us, last night and early this morning, and we only just got up. Or at least I did. They're still in bed." He smiled at us, showing blandly expensive dental work. "The two girls," he added.

"Yes," said Nevada. "We got it that you have two women who were insane enough to spend the night with you."

"And not for the first time. Not for the first time. Insane? Very good, Oregon, very good. But anyway, so I'm sharing this room upstairs with Araminta and Jocasta. You've met Araminta. At the goat festival? You remember her? And my word, you know what, by the way? These Oxbridge girls have no boundaries. No boundaries. Anyway, I hope you don't mind, I came down to ask if I could use your bathroom."

Nevada and I looked at each other. "Is your bathroom broken, Stinky?" I said.

"No. No, it's fine. In full working order. It's just that…" He glanced over his shoulder to make sure the hallway behind him was deserted and leaned forward and spoke in a lower and more conspiratorial tone of voice. "It's just that I need to do a poo, and the bathroom upstairs is right beside the bed, and it's quite a small room, and it just seems a bit rude for me to do a poo. Up there. In the room with the girls. The small room. In the bathroom beside the bedroom. Right beside it."

"So you…"

"Would like to use *your* bathroom." Stinky beamed at us expectantly.

Nevada smiled a warm and forgiving smile and I braced myself. "Stinky," she said. "You are not taking a shit in our bathroom to spare the sensibilities of your concubines."

"Concubines! Nice one, Oregon." Did he really think this was Nevada's name?

"In any case," said Nevada, "you are not taking a vile stinking shit in our bathroom. Forget it."

But now, perhaps in a face-saving move, Stinky was ignoring us and was busy slapping the pockets of his leather jacket. "Oh, it's all right," he said. "Not to worry. Jocasta has got my wet wipes anyway."

He turned to go, but before he could leave, Nevada spoke up.

"Stinky?"

"Yes?"

"Are you in a rental car, by any chance?"

"Yes."

"A black Mercedes?"

"Yes. S-Class. Lovely motor, love."

"Did you follow us?" said Nevada. "All the way to this hotel?"

"I wouldn't say *followed*," said Stinky. "Are you sure I can't use your loo?"

"Yes."

So Stinky trotted, his errand apparently now growing urgent, back to the staircase, bound for his room upstairs. As he disappeared, Nevada stopped just short of slamming the door shut behind him and instead swung it slowly open again, revealing none other than Agatha approaching us from her own room across the hall, eyes alight with interest. She came in.

"We had a visit from Stinky," said Nevada, closing the door behind her.

Agatha nodded. "I know. I just saw him going upstairs. It gave me quite a nasty turn."

"Same here," said Nevada. "I mean, what the hell is he doing here?"

"He wants to make a documentary." The women looked at me. I said, "That's my best guess. To keep his—you'll forgive the expression—*career* going, he needs to make another successful music documentary."

Agatha nodded, putting it together in her head. "And the only successful ones he's had before were the ones he got by following you around."

"That's right," I said. "His shows about Valerian and Black Dog. Those are his greatest hits."

"And now he thinks…" said Agatha.

"Apparently he thinks that the Storm Dream Troopers will do the trick again."

Nevada chuckled. "He has such faith in you." She took my hand.

"Such faith in ripping off your ideas," said Agatha disgustedly.

"That's right," said Nevada. "The detestable little wretch."

"So, Storm Dream Troopers…" said Agatha. "This is the band who did the album you came here to buy?"

"That's right," I said. I picked up the original pressing of *Attack and Decay* and showed it to her.

Nevada had already seen it and been briefed. "They were a sort of death metal Abba," she said.

"A niche aching to be filled," said Agatha, taking the album from me and inspecting the cover photo. "Amazing how your eyes go right to her…"

"*Embonpoint*," said Nevada. Which she had explained to me was essentially a classy French word for cleavage.

"Right." Agatha glanced up from the album and gave me a droll look. "So, is that where *your* eyes go first?"

"Yes," I said. "And then to the gun and then to the fucking crazy-ass look in her eyes."

"She does look pretty crazy," said Agatha.

I sat down on the bed gazing at the silver flask on the table opposite and remembered how good its contents had smelled, spiked with dangerous hallucinogens though it might have been. Perhaps sensing my despondency, Agatha handed me back the album. "I don't see these characters exactly rocking the Abba vibe," she said.

I took the record from her. "That's because, instead of the full band, this album is unusual in just having one member on the cover."

"Embonpoint girl," said Agatha.

"Her name is Gun Gylling." Both Agatha and Nevada looked at me.

"You're not serious?" said Agatha. "Really?" said Nevada.

"It really is her birthname," I said. "Which I guess led to the inspired notion of giving her, wait for it, a gun on the cover."

"Gun Gylling," said Nevada, shaking her head.

"She has a sister called Rut. She's the other woman in the band."

"Rut and Gun," said Agatha. "Now you really are making this up."

"Nope," I said. "Rut and Gun Gylling. Those are apparently pretty normal names for girls in Sweden."

"Pretty normal," said Agatha. "Okay. Excuse me a sec. I'm just going to make a quick call." She took out her phone and went to the window on the other side of the room, looking out at the heavily falling snow as she began speaking in a low voice to the person on the other end.

Nevada looked at me.

"So Ida the stripper dropped by."

"I couldn't get rid of her fast enough," I said, truthfully.

"She has a really nice body," said Nevada, conversationally.

"The main reason I got rid of her so quickly," I said, "is that her post-coital conversation proved so darned dull. After having feverish sex with her and her really nice body, I needed to kick her out right away so I could be alone and enjoy the poignant sensation of having just betrayed both my beloved life partner and my annoying best friend."

Nevada laughed. "I suppose it *would* be betraying Tinkler, too. I hadn't thought of that. I hadn't considered it from that angle. Probably because—"

"You don't actually see them as any kind of a couple."

"Do you see them as any kind of a couple?" said Nevada.

"Potentially," I said.

"You don't think they've actually done the deed? Disgusting thought."

I shook my head. "Not yet."

"Not yet and not ever," said Nevada.

"I'm not so sure," I said.

"You think, what, that they will be consummating this great romance imminently? Maybe tonight?"

"I think tonight would be contingent on a certain amount of success by Tinkler in the juicer rescue sweepstakes," I said.

Nevada's eyebrows were angled quizzically, her voice amused. "What do you mean?" I told her about what Ida had said about them being on a mission tonight to rescue her beloved Kuvings CS600 from Creepy Elvis. "Oh well," said Nevada. "Nothing could possibly go wrong with that."

"Exactly what I was thinking," I said.

"We'd better nip this stratagem in the bud."

"Again," I said, "you have read my mind."

"Unless," said Nevada thoughtfully, "we go along with them…"

"Unless we what?" I said.

"Just thinking out loud." She smiled a reassuring smile at me. I wasn't entirely reassured.

"Thinking what, exactly?" I said.

"Well, if they're planning a break-in, maybe we could assist…"

I shook my head in disbelief. "You just want some excitement."

Nevada smiled at me, eyes gleaming. "Well, it might be fun."

"Fun," I said, looking glumly at Ida's empty thermos. "I wish I had some coffee." I'd need it if we were going on some nocturnal mission of mayhem.

Nevada came and sat beside me on the bed. Our weight on the sturdy mattress caused it to yield just slightly, throwing us fractionally closer together. Nevada put her arm around me. "I'll buy you a coffee maker." She looked me in the eyes. "I'll get you one with all the trimmings."

Agatha put her phone away. "I just spoke to Sydney and she says you're absolutely right about Stinky. He thinks that the Storm Dream Troopers will be his next big discovery. Stolen from you, of course. He actually tried to hire Sydney to come to Sweden with him, as his camerawoman."

"But she refused on principle," said Nevada.

"No. When she told Stinky her day-rate, he said to forget it. Apparently, someone called Jocasta will film it with her iPhone instead."

"So Jocasta doesn't just hold the wet wipes," said Nevada.

Agatha picked up the album again. "Rut and Gun," she said, smiling a contentedly sardonic smile.

"Sums up a wide range of male activities," said Nevada.

"Exactly," said Agatha. "The Gylling sisters." She looked at me. "So are the two guys in the band brothers?"

"No. They're just married to the sisters. Or they were."

"Are their names equally absurd?"

I shook my head. "Perhaps disappointingly, they are called Oskar Hafström and…"

I fell silent. The girls were looking at me.

"What is it?" said Nevada.

"Excuse me just a minute," I said. They stared at me as I took the album and went out the door of our hotel room into the hallway and knocked on the door of the room opposite.

The fresh air fiend opened it. He had taken off his jean jacket, revealing that his white business shirt had no sleeves and that his pale skinny arms were lavishly tattooed.

"Patrik Nordenfalk?" I said.

He wasn't looking at me. He was staring down at the record I was holding. Now he looked up at me and smiled. "Busted," he said.

He reached out for the record and I handed it to him. "Would you like me to autograph this?" Before I could reply he turned it over and said, "It's not the audiophile edition. Hard luck."

15: JUICER HEIST

Patrik invited me into his room. It was a mirror image of ours, with a large four-poster bed—what Tinkler was calling the bondage beds—and two antique armchairs of dark wood with floral cushions.

"Would you like some soup?" he said. "I have a useful little device to make some soup. You can use it to make soup in hotel rooms. It is very handy."

"No thanks," I said. But I suspected I would very soon be in a position where I no longer had to routinely turn down every offer of refreshment that came my way. "This is going to sound like rather an odd question, but do you have a crow with you?"

Patrik smiled at me. "Yes, I do. Indeed, I do."

"A pet crow?"

"Well, he's more of a companion really. How did you know? Was it me opening and closing the window in the lounge?"

"Yes," I said.

"I'm sorry if that was a nuisance."

"No, it wasn't." A great feeling of relief was settling over me. "It wasn't at all."

"But he needs to come and go, you see. He's a crow. He must fly around."

"Naturally," I said. "But tell me, this crow, does he have…"

"Rather an odd beak? Yes, he does."

I felt my shoulders drop as a deep and very welcome relaxation settled over me. I could have coffee again. At Notre Coeur. "I saw him yesterday in town. Just a short distance from here."

Patrik smiled. "Very likely since it was, as you say, only a short distance from here. And he is staying here. With me. With *us* when my fine lady wife eventually alights."

"But," I said, "I also saw that crow in London. There couldn't be two with beaks like that."

"Well, there might be," said Patrik. "But I imagine it was this one you saw since Hiram recently came to visit London with me."

"The crow is called Hiram?"

"Yes. It means 'exalted brother' in Hebrew."

I said, "Okay."

"I brought him with me to London. It wasn't strictly legal to do so, true." He smiled a big smile. Like Stinky, his dental work was excellent. "But what is life without a little lawbreaking? Hence he came to London with me when I went over there to visit Owyn Wynter."

"Of course. At Whyte Ravyn Records."

"Right Raving Records. Correct."

"He said you had dinner with him."

"You are very well informed. Anyway, Hiram came with me on my trip to London to visit Owyn and, while I was there, one of Owyn's colleagues was kind enough to look after him for me."

"Look after him?"

"Yes, he took care of Hiram when I was busy with work."

"Crow sitting," I said. "You had a crow sitter."

"Yes. Effectively, yes. A chap called Jaunty."

"The corpse-faced motherfucker."

"He does look like that, doesn't he? But he's a really excellent accountant. In fact, I've hired him to look after my portfolio. And he's a first-rate crow sitter. Hiram really enjoyed spending time with him."

"Yes," I said, recalling a black fragment of shadow detaching itself from an oak tree and swooping towards me on a coppery evening. "I saw them having fun together."

This seemed to bring our conversation to a natural conclusion. Patrik filled the silence by saying, "Are you sure you don't want some soup? The turnip and sherbet is really good. The sherbet sounds unlikely, I know, but its tart sweetness brings out an almost meaty umami quality in the turnip."

Fortunately I wasn't called upon to offer a formal response to this because there was now a knock on the door. Before Patrik could answer it, it clicked open and Nevada looked in, with Agatha standing rather tensely behind her.

Patrik, who had begun to manifest a look of annoyance at somebody having the impertinence to open his door unbidden, assumed a very different expression upon seeing who it was.

"This is my girlfriend, Nevada," I said. There was a look of relief on said girlfriend's face now that she could see that I was all right, and she moved aside slightly so that she was standing more beside Agatha and less in front of her. It was no longer a situation where Nevada had to be the first through the door, to rescue me from unknown dangers.

"And our friend Agatha," I said.

"Come in ladies, please come in," said Patrik, grinning. He quickly wiped a hand across his comb-over and beckoned for them to come inside. Both the chairs in here were chaotically heaped with clothes and luggage, so the girls sat on the bed which, as if to provide an object lesson in contrast to the chairs, was neatly made up and had nothing on it except the large bolster at the back. "Would you like some soup?" said Patrik eagerly. "I have several flavours." I could sense that he was dying to push the turnip and sherbet.

"No thanks," said Nevada.

"We're good," said Agatha.

Foiled in his soup endeavours, Patrik instead held up the copy of *Attack and Decay* which he was still clutching, rather possessively. "Your friend has cleverly identified me. He just knocked on the door holding this, and I said, 'Busted!'"

He grinned at me like I was a prize student who was surpassing teacher's expectations.

"You're a member of the Storm Dream Troopers?" said Nevada.

"As it so happens, I was the founding member. Patrik Nordenfalk at your service, young lady."

"As it also so happens," I said, "Patrik has a pet crow."

"More of a companion really."

Nevada and Agatha looked at each other and then at me. Nevada now had a big smile on her face as if she, too, suddenly regarded me as a prize student.

"A scissor beak crow, in fact," said Patrik. He turned to me. "Why are you giving me that odd look?"

"That's exactly how I described him myself," I said.

"Well, how else would you describe him? The top and bottom of his beak overlap like the two blades of a pair of scissors." He crossed his forefinger and index finger and held them up as though making a promise. "Scissor beak."

"And that's what I heard on your record," I said. "Or at least, I thought I heard it."

"Ah, so you weren't sure? That's excellent. That's exactly the effect we wanted. There is a technique whereby you can put sounds into a bed of what appears to be white noise. And that's precisely what we did with the phrases *scissor beak* and *scissor beak crow* when we recorded the track 'Slipping on the Wind' on this album." He proudly held up our copy of *Attack and Decay*. He was certainly in no hurry to give it back.

I nodded, my already profound feeling of relief growing ever deeper. "I knew in principle you could do that, but I just thought this was my personal phrase…"

"Your personal phrase? We even put it in the lyric sheet."

"There's a lyric sheet?" I said.

Patrik gave the album an expert little tap with his fingernail near the top corner of its open end and a square of glossy white paper, dense with black text, came sliding neatly out. "Cost a lot of money to include this," said Patrik, frowning as if this extravagance still pissed him off a little, then he slid the sheet equally deftly back inside.

"Where did the crow come from?" said Agatha. "Originally, I mean."

"Oh, we were shooting a music video, out in the woods, and he just turned up one day. Everyone thought he looked like something out of Norse mythology, and I found he was very friendly, not to mention clever, so I adopted him. Or perhaps he adopted me. Anyway, we have been close friends ever since. He travels everywhere with me."

Nevada hopped off the bed and went to one of the armchairs. "In this?" she said, picking up what looked like a large handbag made of transparent plastic. I could now see that it had breathing holes punched in either side and a thin wooden bar that could serve as a perch, running from one side to the other.

"And in this," said Patrik, hastening to pick what looked like a large grey corduroy rucksack off the other chair. He flipped the cover open to show that this, too had a perch in its capacious interior. "This one has a sliding tray for easy cleaning. At the bottom here. Look…"

"Is that how you took him to London?" I said. Nevada shot me a quick look. I guess she'd been asking herself the obvious question.

"In something similar."

"Hiram came for a visit with Patrik," I said.

"Hiram?"

"It means 'exalted brother'," I said. "In Hebrew. Apparently, Hiram and Jaunty really hit it off."

"Jaunty the corpse-faced—"

"Crow sitter," I said.

We heard the sound of voices and laughter outside in the hallway, and then the door opened and a tall woman swept in, followed by Tinkler. The woman had blonde hair of a synthetic platinum hue worn in two big Minnie Mouse buns. In an asymmetrical splash of colour, one of the buns had a small purple and white bow in it.

The purple theme continued with her heavy purple eyeshadow and the purple and white paisley lining of her long black leather raincoat. She wore a black sweater and black leggings and high black boots laced all the way up to her knee. One set of laces was black, the other purple.

Just like Patrik's desert boots. It was sort of sweet.

The woman had evidently hit it off with Tinkler. They were both still laughing. "Oh, look," said Tinkler. "Here they are."

The woman smiled at us. "Your friend is very funny."

"Yes, everyone says that," said Agatha.

"We met on the way into the hotel," said the beaming Tinkler.

"This is my wife, Rut." Patrik went and kissed her while Nevada and Agatha did a good job of not laughing out loud at the name.

"Ah, my darling, at last," he said as he released her and held her at arm's length to look at her. But there was something ironic in the way he said it.

"Apparently this place really is called Troll's Cock," said Tinkler.

"Yes, that's correct," said Rut. "The name Trollesko or Trollsko is a corruption of the original *Trollskog*, which means Troll's Forest."

"Trollskog," said Nevada.

"Troll's Cock," said Tinkler happily.

Rut looked directly at me and I saw that her pupils were dark and enormous, suggesting use of recreational pharmaceuticals currently and perhaps generally. "Trolls do exist, you know," she said.

"I see," I said.

"And they are quite remarkable musicians."

Patrik nodded as if in agreement with this nonsense. Oh, well; he was married to her.

"Not much good on wind instruments or as singers, trolls," continued Rut. "But anything with strings they can play like a fiend. Excellent guitarists. Largely on acoustic instruments, but they're very good on electric guitar as well. They tend to prefer a slack key, open tuning."

"High or low action?" I said. Two could play at this game.

"High action. More comfortable for them to get their big gnarly claws around. Are you a guitarist yourself?"

"No, but I have a friend who is. And he explained the terminology to me. At length." At considerable length, as it happened.

Patrik chuckled. "That's musos for you."

"Our friend is Erik Make Loud," said Nevada, who was not averse to dropping names if there was any chance it might be to our advantage.

"Oh, from the band Valerian," said Patrik. "He's very good."

"If you like tinkly pop music," said Rut. Evidently Valerian wasn't heavy enough or metal enough for her.

"We also know Tom Pyewell and Jimmy Lynch from Black Dog," said Nevada hopefully.

"More tinkly pop music," said Rut. She and Nevada now exchanged a look of frank and cordial dislike.

"I thought Erik Make Loud did some good work with that Goat Aid project," said Patrik, taking an emollient tone.

"That was all to do with the women from Blue Tits," said Rut. "Nothing to do with him."

"Anyway, as Rut says, they are fine musicians, trolls," said Patrik. He was obviously eager to curtail any dispute. He struck me as a man who wanted an easy life.

"We tried to enlist one as our lead guitarist," said Rut.

"One of the Blue Tits?" said Nevada innocently.

"A *troll*. But it didn't work out."

"That's a shame," said Nevada.

"They are very tied to their homes, trolls," explained Rut patiently. "They generally stay very near their birthplace."

Patrik nodded. "As a consequence, touring would have been highly problematical."

"Remarkable musicians, though."

"Certainly."

This crazed discussion of troll musicianship was enough to break up the party, so to speak. I got my copy of *Attack and Decay* back—Patrik was markedly reluctant to hand it over—and then Nevada and I went back to our room with Tinkler and Agatha in tow.

As soon as we closed the door, Tinkler said, "I told you this place was called Troll's Cock."

"Trollskog," said Nevada. "And that was many years ago. And obviously she's completely nuts. They both are."

"Or pretending to be nuts," I said.

"Very convincingly pretending to be nuts," said Agatha.

"I think he's just humouring her," I said.

"The trouble is," said Tinkler, "you have to be nuts to humour her."

"'They generally stay very near their birthplace'," quoted Nevada.

"Remarkable musicians, though," said Agatha and they both laughed. Then Nevada turned to Tinkler and said, "Much more importantly than any troll nonsense, it turns out that Rut and Patrik have a pet—"

"Yeah, yeah, crow with a deformed beak," said Tinkler. "Rut told me all about that. Does this mean the boyfriend is sprung from microwave purgatory?"

"It certainly does mean that."

I said, "So I can have a coffee at the Notre Coeur?"

"More than one," said Nevada.

"They're on me," said Agatha.

"Ida is going to meet us there," said Tinkler, sounding even more pleased about this than about Trollskog.

* * *

We got our favourite table at the café, the one with the view of the tiny courtyard. It was already a dark winter evening. The lamp was shining down on the love seat as before, but tonight there were no bats circling. Snow covered everything.

We all squeezed onto the apple-green sofa with Ida, who was already there waiting for us. She was looking at me and smiling a warmly sardonic smile. "Welcome back to the Café Notre Coeur," she said. "I understand you poured *my* coffee down the toilet."

"I'm really sorry—"

"Don't be sorry. I'll get at least a paper out of this for my doctoral thesis. The crow as mythopoeic harbinger."

"Hiram the mythopoeic harbinger," said Agatha.

"But I'd like my thermos back," said Ida diffidently.

"Of course," I said. The loss of Ida's no-doubt-excellent coffee was considerably softened for me by a cup of the real stuff, which I soon sat savouring. I could feel its magic working on my heart, brain and elsewhere. I told Nevada about Patrik and the little bird whispering in his ear.

"So he knows who we are," she said. "And that we're here on business."

"I think Patrik Nordenfalk knows everything about us," I said. "And I think the little bird who whispered in his ear is called Magnus. Do you remember when we had dinner with our client?"

"I remember Fanny did her little trick with him."

"Yeah, he now thinks we should train her to do microsurgery."

"Do you think we should?" said Nevada. "Train her as microsurgeon?"

"No. She could never fit it into her busy schedule. Anyway, Owyn told us then he had just seen Patrik Nordenfalk…"

Nevada nodded. "That's right. And he said this record was so rare even Patrik didn't have a copy."

"Right. And I think Patrik was a little pissed off that Owyn was about to acquire an expensive trophy that he didn't own himself. After all, it was his record. His own band's record. And he didn't even have a copy. So Patrik decided to put that right. So he's buying one. And, ironically, it looks like he's buying it from the same guy as we are."

"Magnus," said Nevada.

"Right, our friend Magnus. That's why he had this crate of records out at his penthouse when I was over there. A crate full of exactly that record. He was getting it out because he's getting ready to do a deal."

"Another deal," said Nevada.

"Right. He's also selling a copy to Patrik."

"The little tart," said Nevada.

"Speaking of tarts," said Agatha. "We've confirmed that Stinky Stanmer is in town looking to make a show about the Storm Dream Troopers. Sydney Reasoner confirmed that."

"Wait a moment," said Ida. "Did you say 'Stinky Stanmer'?"

"Yes," said Agatha looking at her curiously.

"Not Stinky Stanmer the disc jockey?" said Ida, her eyes suddenly wide.

"Oh Christ," said Nevada. "You haven't heard of him, have you?"

"He's *huge* here in Sweden," said Ida. Her eyes were even wider now as a note of besotted worship crept into her voice.

"My god," said Agatha. "He isn't, is he?"

"No," said Ida, abruptly collapsing into giggles. "Of course he isn't. Jordon just told me to play a little joke on you if the name ever came up."

"Oh, for fuck's sake," said Nevada. Both she and Agatha were shaking their heads, disgusted at being taken in. But I could see they were both also mightily relieved.

"Play a little joke on you," repeated Ida.

"And you did it brilliantly," said Tinkler, gazing into her eyes.

"Really? You really think so?"

"Brilliantly, my darling."

The happy couple nuzzled each other, and then commenced smooching.

"Okay," said Nevada in her most dry and matter of fact manner. "What's all this about a juicer heist tonight?"

Ida broke off the smooch, leaving Tinkler hanging there in mid-air, pucker-lipped and shut-eyed. "Yes," she said. "Jordon and I are going to Bo Lugn's house tonight to get it back."

"Not on your own, you're not," said Nevada, in a tone that brooked no argument.

"You're going to help us? That's very kind of you. Thank you so—"

"Where exactly is this house?" said Nevada, cutting her off.

"Well actually he has two, one in town and one out of town, but since he stole the juicer from me in town and he was on foot he wouldn't have gone far. So I am entirely sure he took it to his town house, which is not far from where we are sitting now."

"Have you ever been there?" said Nevada. "Inside the house?"

"Certainly. Frequently. He has had many parties there."

"So you know the layout of the place?"

"Certainly."

"And do you know anything about the security arrangements? Alarms, dogs, that sort of thing?"

"No dogs," said Ida. "He is allergic to them. And as for alarms, he keeps forgetting the passwords and code numbers, so mostly he leaves the gates unlocked and the alarms switched off."

"Is that right?" said Nevada. My darling was leaning forward, eyes gleaming, smiling a wolfish smile.

16: BIG ANIMAL

By the time we left the Notre Coeur it had been dark for some while. A cosy winter darkness, all the hard edges of the town softened by the sudden arrival of the snow. And still more snow was settling, slowly drifting down on the four of us standing in front of the café.

Me and Nevada and Tinkler and Ida.

Agatha had remained inside because she was going to meet Christer Vingqvist. The self-published priest had apparently sworn to make good on his promise and finally give her a proper interview to publicise Agatha's crime fiction blog.

Consequently it was just the four of us walking through the clean empty streets, rendered even cleaner and emptier by the snow. Walking briskly beside me, arm linked in mine, Nevada seemed to have a spring in her step. She had been invigorated by the prospect of the juicer heist.

As we approached the vattentorn, gleaming in the night above us, we all slowed down. "Okay, we rendezvous in three hours' time," said Nevada.

"Do you want us to synchronise watches?" said Tinkler.

"We don't need sarcasm tonight, Tinkler," said Nevada. "If we are going to help you out by doing this, then we need other things. For example, punctuality."

"Okay, right, right, three hours," said Tinkler. "We rendezvous in three hours. At Creepy Elvis's pad."

"*Chez Creepy Elvis*," said Nevada. She really was in a good mood. It was the thought of sundry nefarious doings ahead.

Ida laughed. "Chez Creepy Elvis," she repeated.

Then she and Tinkler headed off to the vattentorn. Looming over them, illuminated as it was at night, it looked more than ever like something out of a fairy tale, the lonely snow-clad tower of a lost fortress.

Our hotel looked pretty good in the snow, too. With its gothic gables festooned, it appeared to belong not in a fairy tale but in an agreeably creepy kids' book—*The Penumbra Inn Stories*. Our footsteps were muffled by the snow as we approached, then rattled crisply on the stone steps as we went up to the front door. I punched the keycode and in we went.

Nevada was ahead of me, and I stopped suddenly as I came in through the door because she, too, had stopped suddenly. She was staring up at a figure standing on the landing halfway up the gleaming wooden staircase.

A figure standing holding Tinkler's trunk. Holding it in the sense of desperately grappling with it in an attempt to prevent it remorselessly crushing him.

It was Stinky Stanmer. He saw us and shouted, "Help me!"

"Stinky," said Nevada. "Well, well, well."

"Quick, before this thing falls on me. I just brushed past it. I swear I just brushed past it. This thing is fucking lethal. It's a fucking death trap."

"There was absolutely nothing wrong with that trunk," said Nevada, suddenly staunch in defence of the honour of Tinkler's trunk. "It was perfectly safe before you came along. And it could have remained safe *after* you came along. But I suspect you had to mess with it. You didn't just 'brush past it', did you, Stinky? You were messing with that trunk, weren't you? Perhaps trying to look inside?"

"I just thought it looked like such an interesting piece of luggage…"

"Was the most interesting part our friend's name on the luggage tag?"

"I never noticed that. I swear. Please help me."

"I'm sorry," said Nevada. "I didn't quite catch that."

"Help me."

"Help me what?" said Nevada.

"Help me *please*."

"No. What is my name?"

"Oregon?"

"Nope," said Nevada. "Guess again."

"I don't know the answer," wailed Stinky. "I'm sorry."

"You are allowed to call a friend."

"What?"

"Feel free to call a friend to ask them if *they* know what my name is."

"Okay, great, nice one, thank you. Can you help me hold the trunk while I make this call?"

"No."

"What?" said Stinky. He'd begun to relax fractionally in his effort to keep the trunk safely poised—as opposed to disastrously in motion with him in its path. "Sorry?"

"No. You have to make the call while you're holding the trunk."

"No. What? That's impossible."

"I'm just going upstairs to our room," I told Nevada. She nodded. "I'll be up in a minute, love," she said. "Just as soon as this business of Stinky and the trunk is resolved one way or another."

"Wait, one way or another?" said Stinky. "What does that mean?"

"See you soon," I said.

"In a minute," agreed Nevada. And then, to Stinky, "It's absolutely your choice, but I really do think calling a friend is the best option. Although I admit 'friend' is probably not the most apt description in this particular case."

"I have friends," said Stinky. "I have lots of friends. It's just impossible to call *anyone* while I also have to try and keep this thing from fucking falling on me."

"Not impossible but certainly quite difficult," said Nevada. "Quite a challenge to achieve without considerable personal injury, that's true." She was saying this with simple warm sincerity—even generosity—as I edged up the stairs past Stinky, taking care to stay out of the potential doomsday path of the trunk if he should lose his grip on it. His increasingly sweaty grip on it.

"Please," said Stinky, "mate…" as I eased past him.

"Sorry, Stinky," I said. "I couldn't possibly come between you and the wrath of Oregon."

"It's something *like* Oregon," moaned Stinky. "It *is*."

I went up to our room and used the loo, then killed some time gazing out the window at fat snowflakes falling slowly and softly from the night sky. Then I turned down the bed for use later—considerably later, since we would now wait for the quiet hours of the night before we embarked on our campaign of home invasion. Of the home of Bo Lugn, strip club mogul and all-round Creepy Elvis.

During the intervening interval Tinkler and Ida would be making good use of the time, repairing to her apartment no doubt for what Agatha had already disparagingly dubbed "pre-kitchen appliance theft sex". Agatha seemed, like Nevada, to have accepted that, whatever Ida's motives, Tinkler really was going to get the full girlfriend experience.

Personally, I thought Ida's motives were simple. Tinkler made her laugh and she liked him.

Agatha, on the other hand, who'd always been—on some level—very fond of Tinkler, had now cooled on him appreciably. Indeed, I think the fact that she didn't leave the café with us was less to do with meeting the self-published priest and more to do with her not wanting to accompany Tinkler on his magical winter walk to the fairytale location of the aforementioned pre-kitchen appliance theft sex.

I looked at the spotlighted vattentorn in the distance, snow swirling around it, and wished Tinkler well. And Ida, too.

Then, at my beloved's behest through the medium of a message on my phone, I went back into the hallway and down the stairs. Stinky was still there and still holding up the trunk. Just about.

But now he was, impressively, also making a phone call, albeit a hands-free call. "Araminta," he babbled. "What the fuck's the Vinyl Detective's girlfriend's name?" There was a pause as I walked past and nodded to his unseeing gaze. "Are you sure?" He looked down at Nevada. "Nevada?"

"Bingo," she said.

Nevada and I helped Stinky shove the trunk back to what had become its accustomed place—standing precariously erect on the small oak table on the landing halfway up the staircase to our rooms. Stinky smelled like a very scared man wearing a very expensive aftershave. After we got the trunk sorted—it would be too much to say it was secured—we went up to our individual rooms.

It seemed like Nevada and I had hardly closed our door when we were disturbed by a tentative knocking.

Nevada was in the bathroom so I went to answer it. Of the various scenarios that ran through my mind, none included Ida and Tinkler. But there they were, standing in the doorway of our hotel room—instead of being busy at the top of her fairytale tower having pre-kitchen appliance theft sex. Typical Tinkler result.

Tinkler was trying to silently mouth a word over Ida's head for my enlightenment. I eventually gleaned that Ida was here to retrieve her beloved *thermos*. He seemed to feel it was important to make this point, so I wouldn't think that Ida was really here because she was avoiding having sex with him.

Ida for her part was saying, "Jordon said that you had loads of bags of food that you bought today and you aren't going to need anymore."

Tinkler was nodding in rapid agreement here. "No more microwave purgatory, right?"

"Right," I said.

"And speaking of the microwave…" said Ida, just as Nevada emerged from the bathroom. The women looked at each other. "If you no longer have any use for this new microwave oven," said Ida, "I was wondering if I might have it?"

Nevada shrugged and looked at me. "Would you mind if we give the microwave to Ida, dear?"

"No," I said. I certainly didn't mind. I still felt bad about flushing the coffee. I was reminded to still feel bad because Ida, after being momentarily mesmerised by kitchen swag, suddenly remembered her original objective and said, casually, "Oh, and while I am here, I might as well get my thermos back." She scooped it up from the table where it was standing and hugged it to her person tightly. If we had any objection to Ida thus reclaiming it, she was clearly going to put up a fight.

And thus they prepared to take their leave, Ida clutching the thermos and Tinkler, in uncharacteristically helpful mode, carrying everything else—sundry bags of food and the now-reboxed microwave. I could see Ida was pleased with all this booty.

"The food will be stored in my refrigerator," she said. "That's one reason I'm taking it, because I know you guys don't have a big refrigerator to store it in." This was true. Our hotel room just had a small, and mercifully silent, bar fridge. "You will find the food will just be there, in my refrigerator, if you need any of it…"

"No, you use it," said Nevada.

"And if you want the microwave back…"

"We won't," said Nevada. She seemed to be warming to Ida. Or perhaps she was just in a relaxed and benign mood after tormenting Stinky on the staircase.

As the door closed on the happy couple and their loot, I said, "So pre-kitchen appliance theft sex hasn't started yet."

"And probably won't ever," said Nevada. She went to the window to watch them leave. "Our chum sure can pick them."

Personally, I held out higher hopes for Tinkler. Ida seemed to me to be a genuinely warm person, and also genuinely quite taken with our chum. But some of my benign view of her might well have been informed by what Agatha would no doubt call post-toilet disposal of coffee guilt.

We still had some hours to kill but it looked like it was going to be a fairly relaxed wait. My beloved was busy singing to herself, a happy little tuneless song. The possibility of imminent mayhem had brightened her outlook considerably.

I wish I could say the same thing. But I was considerably less sanguine about the whole enterprise, and I was wondering how best to fill the time to zero hour when there was another knock on the door. This one considerably less tentative. I opened it, Nevada protectively at my side, to find Patrik Nordenfalk.

Our neighbour was wearing a stock smile but when he saw Nevada his face genuinely lit up and his hand moved quickly across his comb-over. "Ah, hello. We thought we heard your return. My wife and I would like to invite you to join us in the lounge." He shrugged magnanimously. "Only if you have nothing better to do, of course. A healthy young couple like you, you probably have plenty of better things to do. But I should perhaps add that, besides a device to make soup, we also have one that makes rather a nice cup of coffee."

Nevada and I exchanged a look. Clearly they had been doing their research.

The coffee wasn't bad at all. Only instant, but drinkable. And I was glad of it. We were sitting in the small upstairs lounge with the window firmly shut. Apparently, Hiram wasn't due to make an appearance, which left me both relieved—however rationally explained he now was, that bird still gave me the creeps—and disappointed. I wanted Nevada to finally see him in the flesh. Or feathers.

Patrik seemed to have invited us to this little soiree with a view to talking about *Attack and Decay*. If indeed he had been fully briefed by Magnus, then he must have realised that I'd listened to his album. And, rather alarmingly, he now wanted to talk about it.

As soon as we'd sat down in the lounge, our two floral armchairs facing their two floral armchairs, Patrik had announced, "I have to say that we believe that this recording is our personal masterpiece. The band's personal masterpiece.

Wouldn't you say so, darling?" He looked over at Rut, who sat slumped in her chair with one leg hooked over the arm so her boot was jutting out in mid-air at about the same level as her platinum blonde Minnie Mouse hairdo. The jutting boot was the one with the purple laces. If anything, Rut looked more stoned than she had before.

She nodded and grunted an affirmative and Patrik turned back to me. "So, naturally, we were wondering what you thought of our little record?"

I was searching for a diplomatic way through this minefield when Nevada came to the rescue. She must have done some research online because she said, "I understand that the seven songs on the album are modelled on the seven deadly sins?"

"No," snapped Rut.

Nevada's eyebrows went up. "No?"

"No. Some idiot put that out on the internet and now everybody repeats it."

"It was a simple error, dear," said Patrik in his most mollifying tone.

"It was not the seven deadly sins," snarled Rut. "The album was based on *The Magnificent Seven*."

There was a moment of silence, during which I watched snow streaming past the window and began to long for an interruption—even if it meant the appearance of a very sinister crow called Hiram.

"*The Magnificent Seven*?" said Nevada.

"You know," said Rut, "the John Ford western."

"John Sturges," said Nevada automatically.

"In any case," continued Rut tetchily, "the album is not modelled on the seven deadly sins. It is inspired by *that movie*."

Nevada looked at me, perhaps for emotional support or perhaps just to confirm how demented this was. "Okay," she said. "Inspired how?"

"Well, for example," said Rut, "one of the songs is bald and dressed in black."

"One of the songs is bald?" I said.

"Yes."

"And dressed in black?" said Nevada.

"Yes, like Yul Brynner in *The Magnificent Seven*. And one is a smiling knife thrower, like James Coburn in that same film."

"Ah, I see," said Nevada.

"One is stone-faced and craggy like Charles Bronson. And so on."

"And so on. I see." Nevada was looking at me again. It occurred to me to ask exactly which song represented which actor in each case, but I decided that no matter how much time we had to kill, we didn't have enough time for that.

We made our excuses and got out of there as quickly as possible. Patrik took our departure affably but Rut was glaring at us, her dark eyes lambent with hostility. I suspected that at least part of her that hostility, and her general nuttiness, was attributable to the way her husband couldn't keep his eyes off Nevada.

Plus the drugs didn't help. Her perpetual obvious consumption thereof. All in all, it was a relief to get back to our room.

Where we waited until it was time to set off for our rendezvous with Ida and Tinkler, our fellow burglars. Of course, we could have collected said burglars at the vattentorn and walked to Bo Lugn's together. But we'd decided it would make our little group less conspicuous if we arrived separately. Nevada averred that potential witnesses were not as likely to remember two couples strolling by separately as four people walking together, and I defer to her in such matters.

As we put on our warmest outdoor clothes and switched off the lights one by one in our little hotel room, Nevada wandered to the window. "It's Agatha," she said, looking out.

"She's back?"

"Yes. She's been gone rather a long time."

I said, "No doubt Christer's great personal charm has a lot to do with that."

Nevada laughed and went to the door and opened it. We waited as Agatha came up the stairs. She was brushing snow off her shoulders. Then she saw us and gave us a wry smile.

"I was stood up," she said.

"No," I said.

"Yes. Stood up by the self-published priest. How low have I sunk? Where's Tinkler?"

"You don't want to know," said Nevada.

"You mean, him and the stripper...?" said Agatha. At any moment I expected rudimentary explanatory hand gestures.

"Quite possibly," I said.

"Glorious end to a glorious day," said Agatha. She said goodnight and headed to her room. As Nevada and I walked down the stairs and out through the lobby, I said, "If she was stood up, why didn't she come back earlier?"

"I'm sure she found someone to talk to," said Nevada. She might well have winked at me, but we were outside now, in the darkness and the snow and the welcome cold clean air, and I couldn't have said for sure.

Bo Lugn's house was located not far from Christer Vingqvist's place. But whereas Christer lived in a small fake Mexican casa, Bo had a large fake Roman villa. It was set in the middle of an extensive garden enclosed by a wall of honey-yellow stone, which extended up to about the height of a person's head—a fairly tall person's head—where it was topped with an unwelcoming mix of broken glass and barbed wire.

At the front of the house there was a black iron double gate big enough to admit a car. Or, in fact, a bus. It was set into the wall with faux Roman columns on either side topped with busts of ancient Roman women with fancy hairdos.

Maybe they were ancient Roman strippers.

There was a sophisticated-looking keypad system with a camera and screen set into one of the columns. And the gates appeared solid and formidable. But, as Ida had said, they weren't locked. Indeed, if you looked closely, they were slightly ajar.

We didn't go in that way. We walked straight past the gate, around the corner, and then around the next corner, which placed us in the street behind the villa. Here there was a narrower back gate set in the yellow wall for foot traffic. This too had a keypad system and intercom, but it was just audio, with no camera or screen.

And this gate was ajar as well.

We peered through the black steel bars at the distant house. There were lights on inside, and one on above the back door, but it didn't look particularly occupied.

"Routine anti-burglar lighting?" I said.

"Much good it's going to do them," said Nevada. "A pity we don't have any of the goodies we've got back in London. We don't even have our second-best housebreaking kit."

"So, you didn't bring anything with you?" I said. "That was very restrained."

"Just my birthday Swiss Army knife, which I obediently packed in our checked luggage as the law requires."

"Have you got it with you now?"

"Always," said Nevada happily. "It was a very nice present, love. And very generous. We didn't have much money at the time."

We were both thinking that our financial situation was now looking a lot more hopeful, but neither of us wanted to jinx it. So we didn't say anything, but silently enjoyed our good mood.

That good mood began to ebb as the minutes passed. Soon we started checking our phones. Nothing from Tinkler. And he wasn't taking calls.

"Where is he?" said Nevada.

"Could he be waiting around the other side of the house?" I said. "And not answering his phone?"

"He's more than capable of that," said Nevada. "Although I made it very clear to him that we'd be going in at the *back*. And I know he was listening because he made a predictably prurient remark."

We walked to the other end of the street and around to the front of the house again. Still no Tinkler and no Ida. "He is not answering," said Nevada, staring grimly at her phone.

"Of course," I said, "in true comedy fashion they might have just now arrived around the back where we were a minute ago."

I saw Nevada considering exploding with rage. No comedy here. She wanted to get started on her little housebreaking jaunt. She was all revved up and ready to go, and now she was being forced to wait by Tinkler and his stripper. But instead of exploding with rage, she calmed down and even laughed. "You know what, they just might," she said.

So we went back around the corner, then around the next corner, hand in hand, walking in the snow in the night, in a little town in Sweden. A sense of romance began to settle over our endeavours again. It did not, however, survive the discovery that Tinkler and Ida had not, in fact, comically turned up when we'd gone around the other side of the house to look for them.

They weren't here and there was still no sign of them.

Nevada began tapping her foot impatiently. Never a good sign. "Okay, we're giving them five minutes and then we're going in... Fuck it. We're not going in in five minutes. We're going in now." She looked at me and I nodded—we walked up to the back gate of Bo Lugn's Roman town house.

Nevada stopped just short of it. "Doesn't look like there's any cameras."

"According to Ida, he isn't big on security."

"Ida," said Nevada. She spoke the name with a derisive snort. Nevertheless, we went ahead and went in, pushing open the gate. It was a tall narrow grid of steel bars, black against the white of the snow. It swung open smoothly and silently, indicating that owning a strip club was at least lucrative enough to allow for frequent gate oiling.

Underfoot was a slab of black marble. It formed a semicircle around the gate area on the inside, covered with a shallow layer of slush. We squelched across it and then out onto the first of the smaller individual black slabs of marble that dotted the white snow. They were all stylishly irregular, arranged in a winding pattern, progressing in a leisurely way towards the big white colonnaded house, like the fossilised footprints of some primordial beast.

We walked carefully and exclusively on these paving stones, which allowed us to avoid leaving our own footprints in the snow. "Very bad form leaving footprints in the snow," said Nevada.

"Rookie error," I said.

"Precisely."

Every one of the black stones seemed to be damp to exactly the same degree, slick with a thin sheen of melted snow. And they were warm underfoot.

"They're heated," I said.

"Heated crazy paving," said Nevada.

"You'd have to be crazy to pay the electricity bills," I said.

"Maybe there's a windmill somewhere. Tirelessly generating energy."

"We'll have to keep an eye open for it," I said. "Very comfortable underfoot, though. Heated paving stones."

"*Very* comfortable underfoot. Or under paw. The cats would love it."

"The little devils would indeed love it. In the winter they'd never budge off these things."

The heated paving stones led us in long meandering curves towards the house. One of those curves wove through a stand of trees, all bare and black, naked branches hard to make out against the night sky. To our left, the ground fell away in a shallow oblong canyon. A swimming pool. Drained, empty and now containing snow.

And something else.

Something caught my eye at the bottom of the pool. A dark shape. Several dark shapes. Only partially covered by the snow. What was this?

We stopped, one piece of crazy paving away from the black marble apron of the swimming pool.

Down in the bottom of the drained pool there were black stains on the snow. At first, I thought it was oil and someone had drained their car here. But how had they got the car down into the pool?

Gradually the insistent realisation pressed into my awareness that it wasn't oil, it was blood.

A big animal had clearly made a kill here, and the remains of its victim—or, rather, prey—lay among the dark stains. What was left of another big animal.

My mind resisted as long as possible the realisation of just which big animal it was.

And then I saw the thing on the other side of the pool. On the marble apron at the far end, placed just above the ledge, staring at us.

It was a head. A man's head.

It was Christer Vingqvist. His dead eyes were open and he seemed to be pleading silently for me to help him.

The realisation it had been a human being was bad enough.

The fact that it was someone I knew caused the entire world to tilt one way, while my stomach tilted the other...

Nevada grasped my arm. "Careful, love," she said. "We don't want to leave any DNA here." Her voice—calm, concerned, alert—brought me back from the brink. She led me carefully back the way we had come and, in a moment or two, I was something close to fully functional again.

It helped enormously that we had turned our backs on the thing in the swimming pool.

We hurried back along the warm black slabs of crazy paving and then back through the gate. "Did we touch anything?" said Nevada.

"You pushed the gate open."

"With my elbow. Just walk nice and casual and slow." She took my arm and I forced myself to walk more slowly, but every fibre of my body was straining to run from that thing back there. We walked in slow motion, for what felt like a small but significant portion of eternity. I couldn't talk. I could hardly think.

"Just imagine," Nevada was saying. "A little north of here, we could see the northern lights. Even here, it's a very nice night for a romantic walk."

"It was," I said. "Before that…" My voice was a rusty croak. But my mind was beginning to work again. "What's happened to Tinkler and Ida?"

"I've been trying to reach them." Nevada took out her phone. "I'll keep trying."

"We don't want them going there."

"Absolutely not."

"And seeing that," I said.

"Absolutely not," said Nevada. "And we were never there ourselves."

"Okay. But someone's going to have to notify the police," I said.

The streets of Trollesko were laid out in a neat grid pattern. Now a street parallel to ours erupted with a glare of sweeping blue lights and sirens screaming back in the direction from which we'd just come.

"Looks like someone already has," said Nevada.

17: LYING TO THE POLICE KISS

When we got back to the hotel, we told Agatha what we'd seen.

She was deeply shocked, but not exactly in the way we'd expected. As illustrated by the fact that she ran into her room and came back a few moments later with her copy of the self-published priest's self-published novel and a highlighter pen.

Nevada took the book from Agatha and opened Penumbra Snow's adventures to the section now marked in bold swoops of yellow. She stared at the text, riveted in a way that would, under normal circumstances, have suggested she was mesmerised by some stroke of literary genius.

"She's right." Nevada lowered the book and offered it to me. I shook my head.

"I'll take your word for it," I said.

It wasn't just that I didn't want to have the recent sanguine extravaganza brought vividly to mind again. Of course, there was that. But also something else.

I was aware of some crucial memory trying to surface, some urgent connection that I needed to make. It was pressing and important, but it had been knocked clean out of my head by what I had seen in the bottom of that frozen swimming pool.

Who was it who'd recently been talking about how a traumatic incident could freeze your thinking, stop you making connections?

"It's just like it," said Nevada. She handed the book back to Agatha, who nodded.

"Someone has killed him in just the way it happens in his novel," she said.

"Yes."

"Gruesome disembowelment, check," said Agatha. Her voice was soft and there was imperative concern in her eyes. "You say Tinkler's still not answering?"

Nevada had wandered to the window and was staring out at the falling snow. She didn't seem to hear the question and then she suddenly spun around to look at us. "It's them." Agatha and I hurried to join her at the window.

Walking across the virgin white towards the front door were Tinkler and Ida. We rushed downstairs and reached the lobby just as the front door opened.

Tinkler came in, followed by Ida. They were both very subdued. Tinkler looked at us with such hesitancy and timidity that I was shocked. There was none of the usual fire and mischief in his eyes. "They told us to wait here at the hotel," he said, speaking so softly I had to strain to hear him. "The police. They told us to wait here."

Ida was shaking her head. "It was horrible," she said. "Jordon was really shocked." She touched his arm but Tinkler wouldn't look at her, so she looked at me instead, her big eyes locking on to mine. "It looked like the work of somebody who knows about disemboweling animals," she whispered. "Someone who knows about hunting." Ida blinked her long lashes. "Disemboweling is…?"

"The right word," said Nevada. "Exactly the right word."

I said, "We went in there too, Tinkler. We saw everything, too." It seemed important to make this point to him. That he was not alone in what he'd experienced.

"You went in there before us," said Tinkler.

"It looks like it."

"We were late. I know. I'm sorry," said Tinkler.

"That's not what I meant."

But he wasn't listening. "We were late," he said, "and so you guys went in ahead of us. I'm sorry." I tried to make eye contact but he wouldn't meet my gaze. He kept flinching as though somebody had hit him and he expected another blow at any moment.

Ida's phone rang. She answered it and spoke briefly in Swedish, and then went to the front door of the hotel and opened it.

A woman came in, shaking off snow. She was medium height, slender, wearing a grey business jacket and skinny black jeans. I saw her eyes weren't the traditional blue, but a smoky brown. Her blond hair was cut short over a pretty, elfin face that would have been very young looking but for the deep frown-line grooved across her forehead.

I imagined there was a lot to frown about if you were investigating crimes all day.

She nodded politely enough, but she was studying us quite carefully. "Kriminalinspektör Eva Lizell," she said. Perhaps because studying us carefully in total silence might have come across as creepy.

She didn't seem to expect any of us to introduce ourselves in return. And she seemed to know who Ida and Tinkler were, though you didn't have to be Sherlock Holmes to work out that, with their coats still on and their haunted faces, they were the couple who had just got back from witnessing a disembowelment.

The Kriminalinspektör took Tinkler and Ida into the breakfast room. By the time she came out again, Agatha and Nevada and I were sitting on the landing halfway up the stairs like little kids eavesdropping on their parents' party. Although, in this case, we were little kids who were sitting carefully on the side of the landing that wasn't in the path of Tinkler's potentially lethally poised trunk.

And, despite straining, we couldn't hear a word of what was being said in the breakfast room.

Now Eva Lizell looked up at us. "Ms Warren, could I possibly have a word with you for a moment. Alone, if you wouldn't mind?"

We all looked at each other. What the hell? "Of course," said Nevada, getting up and heading down the stairs, her hand passing in a brief caress across my shoulder as she went, as she might stroke one of our cats. She reached the bottom of the stairs and followed Eva Lizell into the breakfast room.

Ida and Tinkler came out immediately, as if the cop had ordered them out. They looked even more pale and drained than before.

Standing in the foyer, Ida kissed Tinkler—his lack of response spoke more strongly than anything I'd seen yet of the ordeal he'd been through. Then she went out the front door of the hotel and into the night. And Tinkler began to trudge slowly up the stairs towards us, like a man commencing a long and difficult mountain climb.

I rose to my feet, thinking I'd go to his aid, but he waved at me to sit again, and continued slogging slowly up until he was on the landing with us, as if it was something he had to do on his own.

Then he sank down wearily between me and Agatha. She promptly put her arm comfortingly around his shoulders. Again, Tinkler's lack of reaction was telling—not to mention shocking. He was like a beaten dog.

I felt bad for him, doubly so because tonight I'd been through the same thing he'd been through, but evidently weathered it better. Maybe this simply meant that Tinkler was a kinder, better person than I was, to be more deeply shocked by such a thing.

We were all sitting there together in silence, wrapped up in our own thoughts, when Nevada emerged from the breakfast room, a bemused expression on her face.

Eva Lizell came out after her a moment later. "You have my number," she said.

"Yes," said Nevada. She held up a business card in her hand.

The cop nodded and went back into the breakfast room, taking out her phone as she did so. Nevada came up the stairs and sat beside us, still looking thoughtful.

"What was that all about?" I said.

"She asked me out," said Nevada.

"She asked you out," said Agatha.

"What?" I said. Beside me, Tinkler was suddenly stirring to life.

"You mean, like on a date?" he said.

"Yes," said Nevada. "Very much like on a date."

"She just asked you out?" said Agatha.

"No, she firmly established that I was peripheral to her investigation and then she asked me out."

"Lesbian cop," said Tinkler. "Check."

"Lesbian cop with great taste," said Agatha, smiling.

"Really hot lesbian cop with great taste," said Tinkler. He'd cheered up markedly.

"Well, I wouldn't want a lesbian cop asking me out if she wasn't really hot," said Nevada diffidently.

"Naturally not."

"What did you say?" said Agatha.

"I politely declined," said Nevada.

"Did you tell her it was because you don't eat pussy?" said Tinkler. He really had rallied.

"I didn't put it quite like that."

"How did you put it?"

Nevada linked her hand with mine. "I said I was already spoken for."

"You're so boring," said Tinkler. And then we all fell

silent. But it was a cheerful, relaxed, relieved sort of silence. Our friend was back.

"Did you sleep with Ida?" said Agatha suddenly. She was looking at Tinkler, apparently with genuine interest. Her voice was low and gentle.

"Well… not sleep," said Tinkler. "We spent the evening in bed. We were pretty wide awake the whole time." He looked at me and Nevada. "That's why my phone was off. That's why I was late."

"Understandable," said Nevada. Her voice was also surprisingly gentle. And forgiving.

"I'm sorry you had to see that thing afterwards," said Agatha.

"It's all right," said Tinkler. "One thing didn't spoil the other. They're in separate compartments in my head. The death compartment and the sex compartment."

"*The Death Compartment and the Sex Compartment,*" said Agatha. "Sounds like a potential bestseller."

"Potentially by Elizabeth Kübler-Ross," said Nevada. And they both laughed. I could feel the horror that had swallowed this night, and had threatened to swallow all of us with it, begin to withdraw and release us from its grip.

We all went upstairs to our rooms. Nevada was in the bathroom brushing her teeth when someone knocked on our door. I opened it and was more than a little shocked to find Kriminalinspektör Eva Lizell standing there. I'd assumed she'd gone home, or back to the police station or wherever you went at this stage in the investigation after interviewing the suspects and hitting on the non-suspects.

"Nevada's in the bathroom," I said.

She smiled at me. "It's you I want to talk to," she said.

It was cold in the breakfast room, and not just because it was the middle of the night. Eva Lizell had opened one of the windows a little. I said a short but sincere prayer that she didn't have it open to allow for the return of a sinister pet bird.

But then I caught a faint odour of tobacco. The Kriminalinspektör had been having a sneaky cigarette.

Eva Lizell looked at me, looked at the window, and then went to close it.

I had the sudden unpleasant fantasy that she'd peered into my mind as easily as a child might peer through the glass of a terrarium, amused by the scaly little creatures climbing and tumbling inside.

She turned away from the window. "Sit down." The breakfast room was full of small circular tables with chairs inverted on them, legs in the air for the night. Ms Lizell had moved one table away from the others and placed two chairs on opposite sides of it. I sat down in one and she sat across from me in silence, looking at me thoughtfully.

I had the sense she was studying me carefully, sizing me up. There was something very familiar about this process. Indeed, I recognised precisely where it was coming from, because it had happened so many times before.

She was wondering what someone like Nevada was doing with someone like me.

It was such an accustomed process that it was almost comforting.

But there was nothing at all comforting about her next remark.

"I think that your friends are lying to me," she said.

She said like it was a casual observation. Like we were passing the time of day. I tried to strike a similar tone when I replied, after what seemed—to me at least—to be an embarrassingly protracted interval.

"Lying in what way?"

"Okay, so they are telling me that they just happened to be passing this house. Where they found the body. They just happened to be out for a romantic stroll."

"Well," I said, "the snow did make everything very beautiful tonight. It was a night for a romantic stroll."

"Granted. But that being the case, why not have a stroll in the park, which genuinely is a pretty and romantic setting and additionally is right next to where Ms Tistelgren lives? Why walk a considerable distance to what is perhaps the least pretty part of town for a romantic stroll?"

"I wouldn't know," I said. I thought for a moment of saying something about young people in love being wacky and not thinking like the rest of us. But I decided that on the whole this wouldn't go down well.

"Anyway, Mr Tinkler and Ms Tistelgren are saying that they went for a romantic stroll in this particular and somewhat unusual section of town. And once they were there, Ms Tistelgren said she happened to recognise the house of her employer and then happened to glance through the gate, to see if he was at home. And seeing lights in the house they approached it. She said she didn't try to use the entry phone because she knew that the owner of the house, one Bo Lugn, wasn't very technically minded."

She looked at me, eyes searching mine, trying to read something there.

"Does that sound plausible to you?"

"Sure," I said.

"Really? Well, personally, I think that they're lying." Her eyes were steady on mine.

"Oh, for Christ's sake," I said. And I told her about the juicer.

She listened to me so expressionlessly that her mind might have been on a meal she was planning to prepare when she got home. Finally, when I finished, she said, "So your friends were, what? Planning to break into Mr Lugn's house and steal this juicer?"

I felt a flash of alarm. "No," I said, perhaps a little too hastily. I had begun to realise how easy it would be to make a disastrous blunder when dealing with this woman. I said, "As far as I know, the plan…"

"The plan?"

"That's a grandiose name for it. As far as I know, it was their intention to call on Mr Lugn and confront him and demand the juicer back."

"But Mr Lugn wasn't at home."

"I guess they didn't know that."

"Rather odd, that they didn't know that, since Ms

Tistelgren works at his club and could be expected to know quite a lot about his comings and goings."

I could feel the hot sweat gathering all over my body. I was now wishing devoutly that I hadn't opened this line of enquiry, indeed hadn't said anything at all. "And, as it happened, he wasn't at home in his house this evening," she said. "Because Mr Lugn was at the club."

"Maybe Ida didn't know that."

"Maybe she didn't. But that still doesn't explain why they didn't just tell me what they were doing. Going there to his house to see him. To his empty house. But as I say, perhaps you are right and they didn't know that it was empty."

I shrugged. "I suppose in retrospect they wanted to have as little association with him as possible. Tonight of all nights. With the body outside his house like that. They wanted as little association as possible with Bo Lugn, the man with a dismembered body in his garden."

She nodded. "Yes, that makes sense. Although, as it happens, Mr Lugn is not under suspicion of the killing because, as I say, he was at his club tonight. And he had been there since the afternoon." She looked at me and there might have been a hint of amusement in her eyes.

"And as it also happens, your friends aren't under suspicion either. During the period when the killing and the… subsequent arrangements… took place, they were either at the Notre Coeur Café or at Ms Tistelgren's apartment in the vattentorn."

I didn't ask how she happened to know about Tinkler and Ida's movements, but I suspected it might have something to do with a chap called Anders, with ebony earrings and his own apartment at the back of a second-hand record and book store on the ground floor of said vattentorn.

"Similarly, you and Ms Warren and Ms Dubois-Kanes were at the café and then here at the hotel. So, none of you could have committed the crime and none of you are under suspicion of anything at all."

She sighed and the crease in her forehead deepened momentarily, smaller lines appearing above and below to bracket it. "Everything would be so much simpler if people just told the truth."

"I imagine so," I said.

Eva Lizell said goodnight to me and left the hotel. I walked upstairs to our room, my legs feeling like rubber, and told Nevada about the encounter as I took off my shirt, which was soaked through with sweat.

"Do you think I got Tinkler and Ida in trouble?" I said.

"By telling her about the juicer?"

"Yes."

"Of course not," said Nevada. "She doesn't give a fuck about a purely theoretical break-in that never took place in furtherance of the purely theoretical theft of a juicer that also never took place. She's a homicide cop."

She said this with such decisive conviction that I felt utterly relieved

"But, darling, in future, when you are talking to the police," said Nevada, "don't."

"Don't?"

"Don't talk to them. Say nothing."

"That's exactly what I wish I'd done."

"It sounds like she thinks you were lying about Tinkler and Ida not planning to break in and steal the juicer..."

"Yes," I said glumly.

"But on the other hand, it also sounds like you completely pulled the wool over her eyes concerning the fact that we were going to help them, or that we were there at all tonight, and in fact were the first to find the body."

"That's true," I said, cheering up.

"So well done," said Nevada, rewarding me with a kiss. A successful lying to the police kiss.

18: SRIRACHA

Not surprisingly, after what we'd been through, we slept most of the next day. Although, for my part, that sleep was far from unbroken or untroubled. During random nightmare-jangled intervals of wakefulness, I lay there in our dim, quiet hotel room, holding Nevada, clinging to her like a man fallen overboard in mid-ocean clinging to a life jacket, gnawed by the conviction that there was something vitally important that I had to remember, or to more fully understand.

Some connection I had to make.

But I could never grasp it, and I always sank back into exhausted sleep, spooning with Nevada in our big bed in the Penumbra Inn.

By the time we definitively woke up, disoriented and fuzzy headed, the sun was setting over the vattentorn. We washed and got dressed and were just wondering what we should do for supper when Tinkler and Ida turned up. Tinkler had apparently, unlike us, got up at a reasonably early hour, no doubt propelled by the prospect of Ida, and had duly spent the rest of the day with her in her tower. Well, good for him.

And good for her.

But not only did Tinkler and Ida turn up, they turned up bearing food. Food that Ida, rather sweetly, had cooked for us. Admittedly, as Nevada later pointed out, we'd given her most of the ingredients. But still… it was a kind thought. And the food was good. Though eerily familiar.

"Isn't this your cheddar and pea frittata?" said Nevada, opening one of the takeaway containers Ida had thoughtfully provided, where a bright yellow wedge of frittata was indeed nesting on a bed of red and green salad leaves. I opened my own container and I looked at my own portion. It was substantially larger than Nevada's, I noticed. Maybe to accommodate my lusty masculine appetite. Or maybe because Ida liked me better than my beloved.

"It certainly is my frittata," I said, although I had, in turn, purloined the recipe from Marks and Sparks. "Tinkler must have described it to her. He has a remarkable memory where food is concerned."

We had just begun eating with the wooden forks Ida had also thoughtfully provided when there was a knock on our door, signalling a return of the happy couple, who had been across the hallway making a similar food donation to Agatha. Tinkler was beaming with simple-minded happiness. Ida was brandishing the very familiar silver bullet of a thermos. "We forgot," she said. "We also made some coffee for you."

"She did," said Tinkler, watching proudly as Ida unscrewed the cup-lid of the thermos and poured some of the contents into it. As she handed it to me, I had a sense of being given the opportunity to put right a previous wrong. Nevada was studiously ignoring us, tucking into the frittata. Ida watched me carefully, and she gradually relaxed as I at first sipped the coffee and then drained the whole cup.

"You're not going to pour it down the toilet?" said Ida.

"Not for a few hours," I said, and she laughed.

"Jordon described your frittata recipe to me, and so I cooked it."

"I know," I said. "It's very good."

"Not as good as his," said Nevada, nodding at me. "But very good." She resumed noshing on it.

After Ida left, decanting the rest of the thermos into a large paper cup so she wouldn't have to entrust me with her treasure again, Tinkler lingered with us. "What is it, Tinkler?" said Nevada.

"What do you mean, what is it? Can't I hang out with my friends?"

"It's not so much a matter of *can't* as *won't*, when there's the alternative of a nubile stripper to cohabit with in a tower."

"Nubile," said Tinkler, distracted by the word. "I know. It's great, isn't it? Actually, it's Ida who wanted me to have a word with you."

"A word with who?" I said.

"With you," said Tinkler. "Apparently she has a theory about who is… responsible for what happened to Christer Vingqvist."

"Who?" said Nevada.

"It seems Bo Lugn, her boss—although you must *never* call him that—has these two goons he uses for security. Both are called Röd and both of them are psychopaths."

"What sort of psychopaths?" said Nevada.

"Oh, just your type, actually. Ex-army, weapons experts, that sort of thing. Dedicated hunters always out in the wintery wilderness, slaying animals. I guess the last part not so much. Anyway, Röd and Röd haven't been around lately."

"Röd and Röd," said Nevada dryly.

"Yes, both with umlauts. Ida says they've been away in distant places pursuing some kind of dodgy deal. Buying illegal firearms, she thinks. But they just got back, just before the thing happened. And she thinks they're prime suspects."

"Tell the police," I said. Nevada was nodding in agreement. Apparently her injunction to never say anything to the police didn't extend to Ida.

"That's what I told her," said Tinkler. "And she said she didn't want to tell the police. She wanted me to tell you, and that we should look into it."

"Did you explain that I am not a for-real detective?" I said.

"Yes. And I explained that I *am* a for-real coward. But she still thinks we should look into it."

"Two psychopaths called Röd," said Nevada.

"Yes. With an umlaut," said Tinkler. "With two umlauts."

"That doesn't make them any more appealing," said Nevada.

"No, but you'll love this, with your passion for foreign languages. Röd means 'red'. It's a nickname."

"Are they red-haired?"

"No, they're shaven-headed. They're the shaven-headed heavily tattooed variety of psychopaths with big bushy beards and a powerful physique."

"Are their bushy beards red?"

"Funny you should ask. But no. According to Ida, tiger striped and leopard spotted, respectively. Custom dye jobs. Röd Sill and Röd Strömming. She made me take notes. Okay, she didn't make me, but I thought I'd better. Röd Sill is a west coast Swedish psychopath and Röd Strömming is an east coast Swedish psychopath. Ida seemed to think this is important."

"You're still not exactly selling this to us, Tinkler."

"I don't want to sell it. And I definitely don't want to buy it. But Ida said that this pair of matching psychopaths were out at Bo Lugn's town house earlier that day, the day the thing happened, and incidentally she thinks they've now taken the juicer from there and brought it to Bo's place out of town. The Creepy Elvis country estate, let's call it. Or maybe it's at a third place, his office. Anyway, she thinks they moved the juicer before we went anywhere near the town house that night, so the fact that we can't get in anymore and get it—the whole place is a crime scene now—isn't a problem. Because the juicer is now at the country house. Or the office."

"Oh well, that's a relief," said Nevada.

* * *

After eating our frittata, we went out for a long walk. The night was cold and clear; the snow had stopped falling but still lay banked and heaped everywhere. When we got back to the hotel, we went straight to bed and we both slept a lot more soundly. At least, I did until I snapped awake in the middle of the night.

I remembered the thing I had to remember. Made the connection I was desperate to make.

I slipped out of bed, got my phone and found the business card Kriminalinspektör Lizell had given to Nevada.

It wasn't hard to find, because Tinkler had fixed it prominently in a corner of the mirror on our dressing table after writing "Call me baby!" on it and adding a considerable number of kisses and love hearts.

I went in the bathroom so as to not awaken Nevada and called the number. I was relieved when it went to voicemail. It was the middle of the night but you never knew—and I didn't fancy waking up a homicide cop. I left a message telling her I had to see her as soon as possible. I felt so much better that I went back to sleep immediately.

The next morning there was a message waiting for me on my phone from Eva Lizell, proposing a meeting. A very imminent meeting. I filled Nevada in and then went out to the Notre Coeur. It was early and the café had just opened. The girl on the front desk was dressed in the usual white shirt and black trousers, but a red comb in her hair added a splash of colour. She apologised for yawning as she said good morning to me. I went deeper into the building and was startled to find Eva Lizell sitting on what we'd started thinking of as our green sofa, in what we'd started thinking of as our alcove looking out on the tiny courtyard, to which we had yet to lay claim.

"This is our regular table," I told her as I sat down at the opposite end of the sofa, angling myself so I was facing her. "Nevada and I. And our friends."

"I know," she said. "The staff showed it to us when we were confirming your whereabouts during the time period in question."

"And you thought it looked nice?"

"It is nice. And the coffee here is excellent."

"You're telling me," I said. I began to launch into my explanation of why I'd phoned her, but she cut me off.

"You knew Christer Vingqvist," she said.

"A little bit. He was an associate of someone I know."

"Magnus Fernholm," she said. It seemed the Kriminalinspektör was well informed, but then that was her job.

"Yes, I met Christer through him and spent some time with Christer and visited his house."

She looked at me with those calm brown eyes. "So it must have been very shocking when you saw his body."

I very nearly fell into the trap. But I stopped myself just in time and said, "I haven't seen the body."

"Really?" She seemed casually sceptical. She picked up her phone. "There are now pictures widely available on the internet. Someone appears to have flown a drone over the crime scene and obtained photographs and then posted them. It is increasingly difficult to prevent such things."

"Well, I haven't seen them and I don't intend to see them," I said. "In my case you can consider such things prevented."

"So you are only aware of the details of what happened to Christer Vingqvist through your friends' accounts?"

"Yes. And that was plenty."

Eva Lizell sipped her coffee. I would have sipped mine but I'd already finished it. "And also," she said, "you were presumably familiar from having read that scene in his novel."

"No," I said. "I haven't read it and I don't intend to. I certainly don't need to."

"Your friend Mr Tinkler, however, *had* read it and recognised the scenario when he saw what had been done to Christer Vingqvist."

"Yes." I didn't say that this was the only part of the novel that Mr Tinkler had bothered to read.

Eva Lizell nodded. "Fortunately for our investigation, it seems that this novel didn't have a very wide readership. Only a limited number of people would have read it and known the exact details of the methodology he describes."

"That's not necessarily true," I said.

"No? Why not?"

"Because the grisly details of the murder are mentioned prominently on the back cover of the book and in all the other publicity. It's just about the first thing anybody sees."

Kriminalinspektör Lizell cursed quietly in Swedish.

"But that doesn't really matter," I said.

She gave me a hard look. "Why would you say it doesn't really matter?"

"Because that method of killing doesn't come from his book."

"What do you mean?"

I took a deep breath. "This is what I wanted to tell you. There's this Swedish band called the Storm Dream Troopers. They have an album called *Attack and Decay*."

"This is the record you came here to buy."

"Right," I said. I had given up being surprised by how much she knew. "And there's a song on it called 'Snow Angel'." This was the memory that had been trying to nudge its way into my consciousness. Fragments of ghoulish lyrics that had a hideous aptness in relation to what we'd seen in the swimming pool. "It's about the body of a murder victim left in the snow with the body parts spread around exactly the way they are in Christer Vingqvist's killing."

Those brown eyes were no longer aimed at me. They were looking up and to one side as she carefully considered things. "And in Christer Vingqvist's book."

"Yeah, but this song came out years before the book."

The Kriminalinspektör was looking at me again, with genuine interest now. "So you are saying…"

"Christer Vingqvist stole the idea from the song." I imagine in his long and profitable association with Magnus, selling copies of the record, Christer had had a chance to either listen to it or at least scan the lyric sheet. In any case, it was clear where his inspiration had come from. If that was the word.

"Stole the idea," said Eva Lizell. There was a note of amusement in her voice.

"Yes. Which opens up a whole new area of possibilities."

"By possibilities, you mean potential suspects?" More amusement.

"Yes," I said.

"I understand what you're implying," said Eva Lizell. "It's clear from the way you keep saying how the idea of the song was *stolen*. You're suggesting that perhaps the members of this band somehow learned of Christer Vingqvist's book, and this 'theft', and didn't like it. And perhaps they took revenge."

I shrugged. "It's possible."

"Yes, it is possible. It is also, if you don't mind me saying so, an extremely far-fetched hypothesis. And besides, regarding this band, who knows where any of these people are now?"

"Two of them are staying at my hotel," I said.

My rendezvous with the Kriminalinspektör had taken place so early that, when I got back to the hotel, Nevada and Agatha were still in the breakfast room. First, though, I had to run the gauntlet of the table occupied by Stinky.

He was sitting with a young woman wearing a pink blazer with big silver buttons. She was generically pretty, had straight blond hair, very pale skin and an upturned button nose. I didn't recognise her, and I'd met Araminta, so by process of elimination this was Jocasta, the third point in

Stinky's much boasted-about triangle. One of those Oxbridge girls who knows no boundaries.

Stinky confirmed this by looking up from his avocado on toast and saying, "I don't believe you've met Jocasta. Jocasta, this is the famous Vinyl Detective." Stinky gave quite a rich and sincere laugh at this designation which, despite me trying hard to rise above it, got my back up. Jocasta also laughed, but I could see she was just doing this to toady to her boss. So, in a qualified sense, I forgave her.

"Where's Araminta?" I said.

"Oh, Araminta." Stinky shook his head gravely. "She started to get very sulky. She doesn't like sharing me, you see. Started to get very sulky and moody, and I can't abide a sulky, moody girl. That's one thing I can't abide."

Jocasta was staring intently at Stinky while he said this, as though she was mentally taking note of what he did and didn't like so she could be at pains not to do anything to displease this man. So, I do mean mentally.

"Well, if you'll excuse me," I said, moving towards the table where Nevada and Agatha waited.

But Stinky said, "Now Araminta has been replaced, with another old pal of yours."

I stopped. "What do you mean?"

"Your old pal Alicia," said Stinky. "From that mad time on that island when you guys had that funeral for that car. On the beach. That beach funeral. Beach car funeral."

"Alicia Foxcroft?" said Agatha at the next table. "Foxy Foxcroft?" said Nevada. They'd stopped pretending to not be listening to what Stinky was saying—always the preferred default, along with the even more popular option of actually not listening to what Stinky was saying.

"That's right. Foxy? Ha, ha. That's right… love," said Stinky to Nevada. "And she'll be bringing her Zoom H1N with her."

Since Alicia Foxcroft was a sound engineer, I assumed this was a piece of recording equipment. Stinky was looking at Jocasta, who was nodding at him as he expounded. "She'll also bring the specially designed fixing so I can fit it to my phone," added Jocasta.

"And then we can start shooting," said Stinky. He looked at me. "We're going to shoot this guerrilla style. Down and dirty. It's the same sort of rig Spielberg used when he shot *Unsane*."

"Soderbergh," said Nevada loudly.

Stinky stared at her blankly for a moment and then looked at the table on the far end of the room with the large and varied spread of breakfast foods arrayed on it and said, helpfully. "Sorry, love, I don't think they have any soda bread."

His second use of the word *love* instead of Nevada's name suggested that he'd forgotten it already. I didn't fancy his chances if he got caught by Tinkler's trunk again.

Jocasta showed Stinky something on her phone. He glanced at it, then at me. "Mate, did you hear about that murder? Found this bloke at the bottom of an old swimming pool in the snow. And his entrails and stuff and his lungs and organs and all that were spread out in, like, a pattern around his body so they sort of made like wings around him. Like an angel in the snow sort of vibe."

Memories came flooding back. Very specific visual memories. "Stinky," I said. "Just shut up."

Jocasta and Stinky were both staring at me. He said to her, "This could be some useful local colour. Can we get some shots of his reaction when he hears about the body and all that?" And then, to me, "Would you mind signing a release?" He looked over at Nevada and Agatha. "Can you guys all sign a release so we can film you?"

Nevada lifted one of the condiment bottles off her table. It was the sriracha bottle and it was sizable and made of glass. She hefted it thoughtfully in her hand and said, "If a bottle of hot sauce was smashed in half, Stinky, and the jagged glass fragments shoved into your…"

"No need to be aggressive," said Stinky primly.

"Would that constitute a clear refusal to sign a release?" concluded Nevada, putting the bottle down again.

"Naturally we'll respect your wish for privacy," said Stinky even more primly. Then he huddled with Jocasta and whispered something to her. Meanwhile, I finally joined Nevada and Agatha, sitting down with them.

"So, how's the lesbian cop?" said Agatha, spreading sweet butter on a croissant.

"Still hot?" said Nevada.

"Cool as a cucumber, actually," I said.

"She's not a woman I'd want on my case," said Nevada. "If Tinkler was here I would add, 'in any sense'."

"Because 'on your case' could have a Sapphic connotation?" said Agatha.

"It would if Tinkler was here," said Nevada.

"And Tinkler is…" I asked. Although I had a pretty good idea.

"Tower," said Nevada.

"Stripper," said Agatha. Then, after a pause, she added, "She actually makes a pretty good omelette."

"You got some too?" said Nevada.

"Yes. If only good ol' Tinkler was here to also wring some innuendo out of that."

"Do you miss him?"

"I do, sort of," said Agatha.

"Frittata," I said. The womenfolk looked at me. "Not omelette. Frittata."

"I stand corrected," said Agatha, then she yawned into her fist. "Excuse me. I didn't sleep too well."

"Nightmares?" said Nevada.

"You might say that. I keep having the same dream, over and over. Like when you have a fever."

"What is it?" said Nevada. "The dream?"

Agatha hesitated, looking at us, and then said in a carefully neutral voice, "It's about Christer Vingqvist."

"Really?"

"Or rather, just a part of him," said Agatha.

"Dare I ask which part?" said Nevada.

"His severed head."

"Holy shit."

"Yeah. And his severed head started talking. And once it started it wouldn't sht up. It kept asking me if I've read his book."

"Jesus," said Nevada. "Death didn't stop him."

"No," said Agatha. Then, evidently to change the subject, "So Foxy Foxcroft is on her way here."

"Another of Tinkler's conquests," said Nevada. And they both laughed, as well they might, because Tinkler had signally failed to sleep with Alicia Foxcroft when they'd first met on Halig Island.

"But maybe he'll have a threesome with her and the stripper." Agatha said this with a detached, sociological sort of amusement.

At the next table, Stinky had his phone out and I suddenly became aware that he was saying, "Can you believe it? In a little piss-hole like this. Two. Two in two days." I started listening attentively, even more so when he said, "My god. Did you read what he did to her? My god, do you see that golf club?"

I turned around in my chair and said, "What's that, Stinky?"

"Another murder. Can you believe it? In this tiny little Swedish town? They reckon it must be this woman's ex-husband. Not an amicable divorce, ha-ha-ha. She got his golf clubs. In more ways than one. Ha-ha. Apparently, all that was left of her head was this sort of mashed pink jelly."

"Stinky…" said Nevada with a warning note in her voice.

"No, apparently he really went to town with that golf club. It was a four iron. Honma Beres. I recognised it right away. Lovely irons, those. Designed in Sakata, Japan. I can't believe her ex-husband left that behind, even if it was a bit mucky. They have optimal face flexion. I wonder if he left the whole set? And I wonder if after the police have finished using them in evidence they'll, you know… sell them off at an auction or something. Possibility of a bargain there. Make a note, Jocasta."

I quickly excused myself, giving Nevada an *I'll explain later* look, and went up to our room. I took the lyric sheet out from *Attack and Decay*, and confirmed what I already knew. And then I rang Eva Lizell. She answered immediately but sounded impatient. "Yes?"

"There's been another murder," I said.

"We are aware of that. We are also aware that it appears to be in no way related to the incident of Christer Vingqvist. Since this information is, or shortly will be, in the public domain, I can tell you that the woman who died last night was a retired advertising executive and as far as we can determine she and Mr Vingqvist didn't know each other and never met. What is more, this woman recently went through an acrimonious divorce and one of the points of contention was the ownership of a set of expensive golf clubs. The clubs which furnished the killer with their weapon. So, as you might imagine, we are eager to speak to the ex-husband."

"I don't think it was him," I said.

Eva Lizell's voice was amused but nevertheless politely interested. "Why do you say that?"

"Because there's another song on *Attack and Decay*. It's called 'The First Golf War'."

"Gulf as in Arabian Gulf?"

"Golf as in game of golf. And it's about people being beaten to death with golf clubs."

Eva Lizell fell silent now.

I said, "And did you know that Christer Vingqvist's car burst into flames a few days ago?"

"Yes," she said, a trifle impatiently. Evidently, this was a dumb question, or implied that I had insulted the efficiency of not just her, but the Swedish police, and indeed perhaps the Swedish population in general. "We are waiting for the insurance people to hand the wreckage over to our people so we can do our own checks on it." Suddenly all trace of impatience vanished as a thought occurred to her. "Do they also have a song about a burning car?" she asked.

"Well," I said, "there's one here called 'Fire'."

She cursed briefly in Swedish, then said, "How many songs are there on this album?"

"Seven."

19: WITH AN UMLAUT

Nevada said, "So we think that some psychopathic serial killer type may be on a murder spree?"

"Unfortunately," I said. "Yes."

"A murder spree based on songs from this album?"

"Yes," I said. "Again, unfortunately."

"And in addition to the murder songs there's also a song about a crow?"

"Yes."

"And that has come true, too?"

"It hasn't come true," I said. "It just so happens that we have met the guy who wrote the song about the crow, and he happens to have the crow with him." We were walking around the park arm in arm, passing the bandstand at this point.

"In fact, he carries that crow around with him in a variety of natty custom made luggage."

"Right," I said.

"And he happens to be staying with his crow—"

"And the natty luggage," I said.

"And the natty luggage," allowed Nevada, "in the room right next to us in our hotel."

"Exactly."

"With his rather unpleasant wife."

I said, "I think she's only unpleasant because he's treating her like crap."

"Anyway," said Nevada, "there is a song about the crow."

"Yes, there is. There certainly is."

"And there is that song about what happened to Christer Vingqvist…"

"Yes, there is that, too." The bandstand was behind us now and we were walking back towards the hotel. It was a bright afternoon. The snow still spread across the park, crunching underfoot and glittering in the sunlight. Only here and there had it begun to melt, exposing heaps of sodden yellow and red leaves.

"What else?" said Nevada. "What did you say was the other murder song?"

Murder song? I guessed that was what we were going to call them. It was as good a name as any.

I summarised for Nevada 'The First Golf War', a graphic account of an outbreak of homicidal impulse on a golf course with use of golf terminology in relation to gruesome vignettes of mayhem.

As I summarised, she said it had a David Cronenberg vibe to it.

Then there was 'Gallows Pole'. A rather bleak but compelling folk song made widely known through the Led

Zeppelin version, which this one closely followed. You might almost have said slavishly.

There were two more cover versions. "One, believe it or not, is a noise-core reinterpretation of 'Candle in the Wind'."

"By Elton John?"

"By Elton John and Bernie Taupin."

"What is noise-core?" said Nevada.

"You don't want to know."

"Is it noisy and hardcore?"

"Exactly right."

The other cover version was 'Fire' by Arthur Brown. "Which may or may not have some bearing on the near immolation of Christer's car," I said.

"My money is on 'may'," said Nevada. "But that's only six songs."

"Oh yeah," I said. I wasn't surprised I'd left this one out. I was trying to forget that it existed… "There's also one called 'Active Shooter'."

"As in…?"

"Yes," I said. We walked the rest of the way back to our hotel in silence.

As we let ourselves in and stepped into the lobby, Nevada went in ahead of me, as was her habit. She stopped abruptly just inside and took my arm. Standing in front of us, at the foot of the staircase, blocking any attempt to go up to our room, were two men.

They were a pair of shaven-headed giants dressed in tracksuits, wearing heavy duty combat boots and thickly ribbed sleeveless thermal jackets of the sort called gilets or body warmers. One giant had an army-green tracksuit, the other one a powder-blue tracksuit. Their boots were black, as were their gilets—which both had the little Ralph Lauren red polo player emblem on them.

They stood, powerful arms folded, silently massive.

It was immediately obvious this was the famed Röd and Röd, the bodyguards of Creepy Elvis.

Tinkler had told us about the custom dye jobs on the beards—leopard and tiger, respectively—but he hadn't told us about the elaborate braiding. The leopard beard was divided into two big fat braids which were tied together again at the bottom. The tiger beard was in three thick braids, which were united with a more elaborate knot.

I sensed a beard braiding war about to break out here; I was willing to wager that, at some point soon, the leopard beard would respond with four braids. And a *very* elaborate knot.

There was a heavy smell of cheap aftershave hanging in the lobby, which was ironic because it had clearly been a long time since either of these jokers had shaved, unless it was their heads. The four of us looked at each other for a moment, then Nevada and I started for the staircase.

The Röd on the left held up his hand, palm outwards. "Could you wait for just a moment, please?" His tone was so mild and polite that it disarmed us. I could feel Nevada, who had been tensing herself for a confrontation, relax beside me.

"We're guests at this hotel," she said, though. She was still more than ready for a scrap.

Röd on the left—leopard beard—nodded and made an understanding sympathetic expression which you wouldn't have thought a face like that was capable of and said, "This should only take a moment." Meanwhile Röd on the right—tiger beard—moved to the lectern which served as a check-in desk. Admittedly, a permanently uninhabited check-in desk.

I hadn't noticed before that a bright yellow case had been placed on this, the sort of thing that might contain a heavy duty professional electric drill and its accessories. Tiger Röd went to this and opened it.

"Why exactly..." said Nevada, but before she could finish framing what was shaping up to be a sarcastic enquiry, the door opened behind us and we turned to see Magnus and Emma come in.

Emma grinned happily when she spotted us. Magnus seemed somewhat less pleased. Particularly with me, for some reason.

Nevertheless, we all exchanged civil greetings. Magnus and I shook hands while everyone else hugged. I didn't think surly Magnus deserved a hug from Nevada, but there you go. "So, what's with these guys?" said Magnus pugnaciously, looking at the two Röds. "Are they friends of yours?"

Before Nevada or I could state the obvious and deny this, Leopard Röd surprised us by turning to us and saying, "You can go up to your rooms now. Thank you for your patience." He had just glanced at Tiger Röd, who was looking up from whatever was inside the yellow case and nodding at him as if confirming something.

Leopard Röd moved aside and stood at the lectern with Tiger Röd, leaving us free access to the staircase.

As Nevada and I went up the stairs with Emma and Magnus, Emma looked back over her shoulder at the two Röds standing below and then looked at me and said, under her breath, "Those muppets are off their crust. Juno wham sane, bruv?"

I didn't realise that Magnus had overheard this until we reached the top of the stairs and he hissed furiously, in Emma's ear, but loud enough to be heard by the rest of us, "Why don't you just say, 'Those fellows are crazy, don't you agree'?"

"Cos that would be pants, innit," said Emma.

I didn't hear any more of this contretemps—I particularly regretted missing Magnus's translation of "pants"—because the door of the lounge clicked open and Tinkler hurried out to join us. He'd evidently been lying in wait for our arrival. Which begged a number of questions. Nevada waded right in by saying, "What the fuck is going on here, Tinkler?"

Magnus and Emma tactfully went into the now-vacated lounge, leaving us in the hallway to conduct our private conversation. "That's Röd and Röd," said Tinkler, in a low voice, nodding towards the staircase and the lobby below.

"We know," said Nevada.

"We guessed from your description," I said. Who else could it have been?

"But what are they doing here?" said Nevada.

"Well, Ida is here just at the moment, in my room..."

"Oh great," said Nevada. "Ida, the source of all things safe and bountiful."

"I have no idea what you mean by that," said Tinkler. "Anyway, Bo is in there right now, talking to her."

"Bo Lugn," I said.

"Creepy Elvis. Yes. Do you want to know what they're talking about?"

"Yes, Tinkler," said Nevada. "We do want to know. Tell us."

"What they're *arguing* about, actually. He is offering Ida protection. And she doesn't want it."

"Protection?"

"He said he's going to go to the mattresses. It's a phrase from *The Godfather* and it means—well, you know what it means. You've seen that movie more times than I have. You probably know exactly what it means." Tinkler looked at her hopefully with his doggie eyes. "You could probably tell me what it means."

Nevada sighed and said, "It means during a gang war you dig in somewhere safe and secure, where you can defend yourself. And you prepare to weather the storm."

"Right. That's exactly what I thought it meant."

I said, "And Creepy Elvis wants Ida on his mattress with him?"

Tinkler did a very good animated-cartoon-character shudder. "Despicable, isn't it?"

"What exactly does Bo Lugn think she needs protection from anyway?" said Nevada. "Who is this war supposed to be with?"

"He thinks Christer Vingqvist's mutilated body was left outside his house as a warning," said Tinkler.

"A warning?" said Nevada.

"Some warning," I said.

"Ida says Bo thinks that a lot of deeply moral, deeply religious people around here were very upset when he opened a strip club on their doorstep. So they took revenge on him."

"These deeply moral and religious people took revenge by disembowelling a deacon?"

"Hey, the disembowelled deacon... No, I think we'll stick with self-published priest. The poor guy. Anyway, Ida says that Bo thinks they'd been planning to take revenge on him for a long time, and this is just the beginning."

"Just the beginning," I said.

"Yes."

"Do you believe that?" said Nevada.

"No, of course not," said Tinkler.

"Does Ida believe that?"

"No," said Tinkler. "Nobody in their right mind believes that. And, as I told you, Ida is very strongly promulgating the theory of Röd and Röd being behind everything."

"But if she's right," said Agatha, "then Bo Lugn is about to go to the mattresses with them."

"Yup," said Tinkler.

"He's going to snuggle up with the psycho killers."

"I couldn't have put it better myself. I'm going to tell Ida exactly that and steal your turn of phrase and give you no credit. Snuggle up with the psycho killers."

"There's something not right with Röd and Röd," said Nevada, thoughtfully.

"No shit," said Tinkler.

"No, I'm saying if they're here for security it's surprising they didn't try and frisk us. Which could have turned out badly. For them, I mean," said Nevada. "But they didn't even try. And yet they let us come upstairs, where their boss is."

We all glanced at the closed door of Tinkler's room, where the boss in question was currently sequestered with Ida. I wondered how Tinkler felt about that.

"Which meant they were running the risk of letting someone into the building with a weapon," said Nevada. "Someone who could assassinate their boss."

"If only," sighed Tinkler, staring at the closed door of the room. Personally, the only thing I could imagine going on on the other side was a strongly worded reprimand from Ida, directed at the man who had stolen her juicer.

"But you said they were militarily trained?" said Nevada.

"Yes," said Tinkler. "Röd and Röd are allegedly from some elite unit. Essentially, he was boasting about how safe Ida would be with his two bodyguards and therefore with him."

"Has this guy got a thing about Ida?" said Nevada.

"Who hasn't?" said Tinkler. "Anyway, he was doing this big sales pitch about the supposed action hero pedigree of the two Röds in lots of detail. Considerable detail. Ample detail. It would have tranquilised an elephant."

"Well, in any case," said Nevada, "they must be sufficiently professional to know better than to let someone up here with a weapon."

I said, "And yet, as you said, they didn't frisk us."

"I don't think they needed to. I think they *scanned* us."

"The thing in the yellow case," I said.

Nevada nodded. "I think it was some kind of scanning device."

"You mean like they have in airports?" said Tinkler.

"On a smaller scale, yes," said Nevada.

"Does that mean they saw what you guys look like under your clothes?"

Nevada shrugged. "Maybe."

"Definitely a mixed blessing," said Tinkler. This was clearly directed at me.

"Tinkler," said Nevada. "Don't underestimate these guys."

"What, these guys with their very cool beards?"

"They could be dangerous," said Nevada. "They could be very dangerous." She didn't sound overly worried, it has to be said.

"They probably are, if they're your bodyguard," said Tinkler. "In that case, your life expectancy is probably approximately that of a fruit fly. With anyone else, I think they're about as dangerous as a couple of fantasists who have watched a lot of instructional videos can be. I mean, look at those beards. Don't get me wrong. I'm still *scared* of them. But I'm scared of everyone."

At that moment the door of Tinkler's room opened and Bo Lugn came out, followed by Ida. Bo hardly glanced at us before heading down the stairs. Ida nodded at us but was obviously preoccupied with being angry about something. She addressed Tinkler. "He says he wants Röd and Röd with him at all times. As if *he* is in danger."

"But they could be the killers," said Tinkler. "The two Röds."

"I know, hilarious, isn't it? Perhaps not so hilarious for him." Ida smiled a malicious smile.

Downstairs we heard the voices of the two Röds and Bo Lugn, and then the sound of them leaving the hotel through the front door.

"So you're not taking Creepy Elvis up on his kind offer?" said Nevada.

"What, staying with him?" said Ida. "Of course not. I'm staying with my man," she took Tinkler's arm.

"That's me, right?" said Tinkler. And Ida giggled.

"Would you like to go back to my place now?" she said, looking up into his eyes.

"Does the pope shit in the woods?" said Tinkler.

"Does the pope…?"

"He means yes," said Nevada wearily.

As soon as Tinkler and Ida said their farewells and left the hotel, Agatha came out of her room. Indeed, she came out with suspicious promptness, as if she'd watched their departure from her window.

"Okay, what was all that about?" she said.

As we filled her in, Magnus and Emma came back out of the upstairs lounge. Magnus was looking increasingly disagreeable and impatient. Emma, by contrast, was excited as a puppy to see Agatha. "Cuz!" she cried and ran to embrace her.

Agatha suffered the hug good humouredly. We'd all come to be quite fond of Emma, Mockney nutcase though she was. The three women went into Agatha's room no doubt to discuss clothes, with specific reference to the obtaining cheaply of further high-end specimens locally, while Emma's husband waved me impatiently into the upstairs lounge. I felt absurdly like I was being summoned into the headmaster's study.

As I came into the lounge, Magnus had his back to me, staring out the window—the window that Patrik liked to leave open for his crow—and then he turned around suddenly, as though he was going to surprise me and catch me out with a trick question.

"Who are those guys? Those thugs in the lobby?"

"They're the strip club owner's bodyguards," I said. "They're gone now."

Magnus was shaking his head. "Your friend was very ill advised to get involved with these people."

"There's only one of these people Tinkler wants to be involved with."

"You mean that dancer?" said Magnus. "She's as bad as the others. They're all cut from the same cloth." Magnus had stopped shaking his head, but now he started again. There was no love lost between him and Tinkler, and indeed there hadn't been since our detour for pizza during the drive to Trollesko on that first day.

Magnus might well have been right in this instance, but I felt compelled to stand up for my old friend. "She seems perfectly nice," I said.

"All of the people who work at that place are very dubious types. They are most of them criminals and on drugs and unstable personalities. And I have no doubt she is just looking for some way to take advantage of your friend."

Despite the fact that this had been very much my own original assessment, I now bristled at the suggestion. Perhaps he read the anger on my face because Magnus immediately changed the subject. "Anyway, that is not what I came here to discuss with you."

"What did you come here to discuss with me?"

Magnus gave me a hard look, or what he hoped was a hard look. "What's going on with my payment?"

"You mean…"

"I mean not paying me for this record. I mean this sudden delay in paying me."

I resisted the urge to ask if a delay could be considered sudden and said, "You know as much as I do. But Owyn assures me that the money will be here soon."

"Can you define soon?" said Magnus, rather snottily, I thought.

"No," I said.

"Well, my patience is wearing thin. I have another buyer for this record." Magnus tried to maintain a poker face while staring me down, but his eyes flickered in the direction of Patrik Nordenfalk's room.

I nodded. "You have another buyer, all right, and you also have about another hundred copies of the record."

Magnus started to deny this, and then changed his mind. "So what if I have? You had no right to spy on me and search my flat."

"I didn't spy on you or search your flat," I said. "I didn't have to. You left that crate of records right out in the open."

Magnus dismissed this with a gesture, as if throwing away a handful of invisible waste paper. "In any case, it doesn't matter how many copies I have. Only I decide when I sell them. And if I conclude that my analysis of this situation is correct and Mr Wynter is indeed wasting my time, then his opportunity to buy this exemplary copy of this very rare record will simply vanish. He will have missed the opportunity."

"No problem," I said.

Magnus stared at me. "What do you mean, no problem? Do you know how upset Owyn Wynter will be if he doesn't get this record?"

"Doesn't matter," I said. "He's better off without it."

"What are you talking about? Are you suggesting this isn't the genuine audiophile pressing?"

"Oh no, it's that," I said. "It's that, all right. Which is exactly the problem."

"How is it a problem?"

"Well, I've heard the original."

"Oh yes," said Magnus. "You found a copy the other day, didn't you, at the secondhand-butik? Good for you. Congratulations." He said this last word tightly and ironically.

"I've heard it," I said. "And, to be frank, it pisses all over the audiophile version."

"What do you mean?" said Magnus.

"I mean it sounds way better," I said.

"I know that's what you mean," said Magnus. "But how can you say that?"

"It's easy."

"You can't hear the superiority of the audiophile pressing?"

"I can't hear it because it's not there," I said.

"What are you talking about? This is the half-speed mastered, 180-gram—"

"It's all of those things, and yet it's not as good as the original."

"You're crazy," he said. And he said it like it was a dangerous kind of craziness. Magnus was starting to get angry, and an angry nerd is never a pretty sight. I was trying not to get angry myself—who needs two angry nerds?—when a bell rang.

"The front door," said Magnus.

We both went to the window and stared out. The figure ringing the bell was concealed in the doorway below and would have remained so if he hadn't stepped back impatiently into view and stared up at us. It was Anders, who ran the book and record store in the vattentorn. Or rather, the record and book store. Looking up, he saw us and waved.

We went down and let him in. He seemed a little out of breath, as though he'd run over here. Anders started speaking in Swedish then switched to English. He looked at me. "I think you have met Barbro Bok?"

His polite inclusion of me was all of a piece with his speaking in English. It was typical of the classy behaviour we'd received from everybody since we'd arrived in Sweden.

I nodded, thinking of Barbro running around in a high-vis vest in the farmyard darkness, chasing a luminous canine collar in an anti-defecation quest. I had indeed met her.

"She came into my shop today," said Anders. "Just now, in fact, to collect some books I'd obtained for her. And... I suppose what happened next was my fault. In a sense it was my fault. But I simply offered my sympathies to her because of the passing of Christer Vingqvist. Simply offered my sympathies. I knew that she knew him, that he was a work colleague."

They were closer than that, I thought. It was heart-breaking to remember Barbro's primitive, pure joy when she saw him that night—the night of the dog poo glow sticks—after he'd survived his burning car. And then to think how cruel it must be for her to have had him snatched from her, after all...

"Anyway," said Anders, "maybe I shouldn't even have brought up the matter. Because now Barbro has become very upset indeed." He sounded genuinely worried.

I said, "You left her back at your store?"

He nodded, his head going up and down quickly, like a nervous bird. "I had to. I had to come here to ask for your assistance." This was directed at Magnus, rather than me.

Magnus was unmoved. Indeed, he seemed quite irritated. Christer Vingqvist had never been a close friend of his while alive, and now in death he was proving to still be something of a nuisance. He said, "What do you want me to do about it?" This was less a request for specifics than a petulant remonstration.

"You're Emma's husband," said Anders.

"Yes," said Magnus. "And Emma is upstairs somewhere. So why don't you locate *her* and ask *her* to go to over to your store to help you with *her* sister?"

"She isn't upstairs," said Anders.

"What?"

"She's over at my store."

"I thought she was upstairs," said Magnus, thoroughly taken off guard now.

"She is over at my store. She is currently there, with her sister. That is the problem. That is exactly the problem."

"She is with her sister?"

"Yes," said Anders.

"Are they…?"

"Yes. They are having one hell of an argument," said Anders. "Please come over and see if you can stop them."

Magnus sighed. He wasn't going to be able to get out of this one.

I said, "So, I will be up in my room…"

"Oh, I almost forgot," said Anders, turning to me. "I have obtained a new batch of records. Old records, you understand. Originals. I wondered if you would like to look through them before I put them out in the shop?"

"Okay," I said. "So, I won't be up in my room."

We walked over to the vattentorn, Nevada and Agatha accompanying us. We were walking briskly but we all slowed down as we walked past a slightly eccentric vehicle parked in the street near the building. It was a jaunty little pink van. On the side of it in big happy dark purple lettering was printed *Jesus vill vara din BFF!* The dot on the exclamation mark was a smiling cartoon fish.

"Does that mean Jesus is your best friend?" said Nevada.

"*Wants to be*," said Anders helpfully. "Wants to be your BFF. '*Is* your BFF' would be *Är din BFF*."

"Är din," repeated Nevada.

"Yes."

"It's Barbro Bok's van," said Anders.

"So we surmised," said Agatha. She and Nevada were tagging along with us frankly out of car-crash curiosity. I had gone up to our room to let Nevada know what was happening and the women had immediately grabbed their coats and come with.

If this was just a simple human hunger for shoddy soap-opera spectacle, it was one certainly shared by Tinkler and Ida, who had come hurrying down from her fairytale redoubt at the top of the tower to witness proceedings.

Now the gang was all here in the front room of Anders's little shop. Personally, I was only passing through on my way to the *back* room where the batch of mystery vinyl awaited my close and eager scrutiny, but even I was here long enough to receive the full brunt.

There is nothing quite as ugly as family ugliness.

Barbro was standing beside the till, her right hand on a stack of books, as though they were Bibles she was about to swear on. In fact, they later proved to be religious texts of various sorts: theological history, theology and philosophy. And not, as Tinkler had theorised, pornography.

So perhaps there was indeed a Bible among them.

Behind the big lenses of her glasses, Barbro Bok's eyes were hot with anger. She turned those hot eyes on

Magnus as we came in. Magnus almost did a U-turn and went right back out again, and I didn't blame him. But, to his credit, he didn't flee and instead slowly edged into the room, trying to move towards his wife and more-or-less avoid Barbro, but while looking in her direction occasionally and even trying to smile. Not at her, but just generally smile.

"And Magnus would agree with me," she said.

"Would I, Barbro? Hello, by the way. How are you?"

"I am fine, Magnus."

"Good, good."

"And I am very glad to see you, Magnus, because I was just saying I am sure you will agree with me."

"Were you? I see. About what?"

"Well, a little while ago Emma joined me here and the talk turned to Christer—"

"That was my fault," said Anders, eager to do a *mea culpa*. "Entirely my fault. I just wished to extend my sympathies."

"Which you did very simply and with real sincerity and which I appreciated very deeply, Anders. Thank you."

"You're welcome."

"What I did *not* appreciate very much was when Emma—when my sister continued speaking in that ridiculous affected way she has adopted of late. Continuing to speak in that absurd patois. While I was talking about my dead friend." Barbro's angry gaze swept across all of us. "While *we* were talking about my dead friend."

"It's my fault," said Anders. "I brought it up."

"And I said," said Barbro, ignoring him, "'Why are you talking in that stupid voice, Emma? Why are you pretending to be someone you're not?'"

Magnus abruptly stopped edging across the room. He'd been making a beeline for Emma and trying not to even make eye contact with Barbro. But now he relaxed visibly and smiled at her and said, "Exactly."

He said it with a note of happy triumph.

"You see," said Barbro. "Your husband and I both agree. It's time to drop this ridiculous pretentious façade."

"It is very much time," said Magnus.

"Emma," said Barbro, "your problem is that you don't have any true personality of your own."

"Exactly," said Magnus.

"You have never quite developed one," said Barbro. "So instead, you take these shortcuts—"

"Stupid childish shortcuts," said Magnus.

"You take these stupid childish shortcuts," said Barbro. "Like speaking in English but in this ridiculous accent in a desperate attempt to make yourself interesting because you know you are not interesting because you have no real personality of your own."

"Exactly," said Magnus. "I'm sorry darling, but exactly."

He and Barbro were both gazing at Emma, grinning. She looked back and forth between them, for a moment seeming like a cornered animal hunting for a way out. Then she came out of her corner fighting. She strode quickly past Magnus. "Go and piss up a rope, wanker," she said.

Then she turned to her sister and said, "Fuck you and fuck your dead friend."

And then she headed for the door. But before she got there, Barbro managed to get out the following summary: "She's just showing off. Silly little girl has learned a dirty little word."

I was standing nearest the door as Emma went out. She didn't look at me, but she didn't have to. I could see the raw hatred in her eyes. Then she slammed through the door and out into the daylight and the snow.

Anders winced a bit at the gunshot loudness of the door slamming behind her, but I could see that he felt he'd got off lightly. Barbro paid for her books—not in cash of course—and nodded to us politely as she left, presumably to be reunited with her jaunty pink BFF van. She appeared perfectly calm.

But after she left, we all looked at each other with a shared sense of having witnessed something brutally ugly. Perhaps what we had seen was a family finally and irreparably tearing itself apart.

On the other hand, when I finally went through that batch of records Anders had acquired, I found a masterpiece of Italian jazz. *Afrodite* on the Vedette label. So that was a major jackpot.

20: HELL BREAKS LOOSE

When Nevada, Agatha and I got back to the hotel, we found a party in progress in the upstairs lounge. It was a small party in a small lounge, admittedly, but it was intent on growing. The glass door was flung open and Patrik Nordenfalk emerged, smiling. "Please, come in and join us for a drink."

"Well, actually we were…" said Nevada, beginning to smoothly roll out an excuse.

"Champagne," said Patrik quickly. "Non-vintage but still very good." His eyes swivelled between the women. Agatha's presence meant that at least his creepy attention didn't fall entirely on Nevada. Patrik caressed his comb-over as his gaze roved from one young woman to the other, never looking at me.

But the next person who came out of the lounge was very much looking at me. And I was instantly staring at her. All of us were staring at her. It was the woman from the cover of *Attack and Decay*. Gun Gylling. Sans handgun. At least as far as I could see.

She was wearing black boots, black jeans and a black raincoat with a long scarf of high-vis yellow, reminiscent of the colour scheme of the lettering on the album cover.

And her face and hair were exactly the same as they were in the graveyard photograph. She didn't seem to have aged a day; an illusion that, it turned out, she could maintain until one got remarkably close.

Right now, she was smiling at all of us. And all of us would have been staring at her boobs—sorry, her *embonpoint*—if her raincoat hadn't been firmly buttoned up to just below her chin where the scarf formed a contorted soft cushion, a splash of yellow colour, on which her face seemed to float. Her eyes held bright yellow highlights from the scarf. Was that why she was wearing it? She was, after all, a woman who seemed to have given some consideration to the impression she was going to make.

"Are these the fascinating people you mentioned, Patrik?" she said. Her voice was soft and slightly rasping. Her English held no discernible trace of an accent.

"Yes. Our good neighbours." He beckoned to us. With Gun as his wingman, so to speak, his blandishments were more difficult to resist. "Come in. Have a drink."

"Yes, we've just opened the champagne," said Gun.

Nevada gave me a *What can you do?* look. We filed obediently into the lounge, where we found Gun's sister had undergone a transformation. The cheerful, relaxed person before us bore so little resemblance to the sullen woman we'd become accustomed to that it felt like some kind of trick.

The new Rut was laughing as a man poured champagne for her.

The champagne pourer was a big fellow. Probably the first thing about him that a dispassionate observer would notice was that he was wearing a kilt. A black leather kilt of narrow interlocking panels that were not entirely silent. Indeed, they creaked alarmingly every time he moved. The garment was vaguely reminiscent of something an ancient Roman legionnaire might have worn—perhaps while listening to thunderous music in a very sketchy discotheque.

But this champagne-dispensing fellow had somewhat chickened out of the full kilt experience; instead of his stocky and rather short legs being bare and exposed to the elements, they were clothed in black thermal leggings that disappeared into shiny black Doc Marten boots. Above the kilt he wore a chunky black fisherman's sweater and chunky silver bracelets and necklaces.

His wild and disarrayed hair was also black and the black smudges under his eyes could either have been make-up or, just as easily, the well-earned marks of a dissipated life. For such a big burly guy he had a surprisingly lean, sensitive-looking face.

We were way ahead of him when he introduced himself as Oskar Hafström. "The founding member of the Storm Dream Troopers."

"You weren't the founding member, were you?" said Rut, sipping her champagne. "Patrik always says he is."

"Well, I'm the one who named the band," said Oskar. "Do you remember when Patrik and your sister wanted

to call us Storm Trooper's Dream?" He winked at us—
Nevada and Agatha and I—as he poured our champagne. I
saw Nevada check the label. She gave me a look that said
it wasn't Veuve Clicquot, but it sure as hell wasn't bad.
Oskar chuckled a self-deprecating chuckle. "The Storm
Trooper's Dream. I thought that might have been just a tad
too controversial."

"Were you worried about the *Star Wars* lawyers?" I said.

To my surprise Rut giggled happily and helplessly at this,
and then set her glass down and went to Gun and threw her
arms around her and dug her face happily into her sister's
neck and nuzzled her contentedly. I didn't know if it was
the presence of Champagne Oskar and his creaking kilt, or
being reunited with the aforementioned sister, but Rut was
a woman transformed.

Maybe it was just that, for once, we were seeing her when
she wasn't stoned. Merely drunk.

Oskar was busy chuckling some more, but now in warm
and generous appreciation of what I'd just said. "No, I was
thinking more of the World War Two sort of storm troopers.
The SS. Memories of the Nazis are still very alive in this
part of the world, you know. So I told the others we had to
change the name of the band."

"If nothing else," said Nevada, "because your initials
would have been STD."

Oskar gave a snort that threatened to send champagne out
his nose. "I hadn't realised that! Excellent point. I wish I'd
had it as an additional line of argument at the time. Anyway,
when I said the name must change, Gun was fine with it but

Rut and Patrik disagreed. They disagreed fiercely. It was the first of our ferocious disagreements. But far from the last. Life with the Troopers was never dull."

"And now the band is back together," I said. We looked around the room. Patrik was sipping his champagne and starting moodily out the window, perhaps waiting for Hiram to come flapping back out of the grim slate-grey winter sky. Behind him the Gylling sisters had ceased hugging and were chatting with Nevada and Agatha.

Nevada was saying, "It has a David Cronenberg vibe to it."

Gun was staring at her. "That is exactly right."

Rut was nodding eagerly. "That is exactly what we had in mind when we wrote it."

Nevada basked modestly in their astonished approval, proud as a praised cat despite never having heard the song in her life and acting entirely upon my brief summary of its content. She slipped me a wink to let me know that she knew I knew she was—as Emma might have put it—totally blagging it.

Oskar was nodding, too, as he resumed topping up our glasses, waiting for the foam to subside and then fitting in as much champagne as he could. Nevada watched with approval. He said, "Yes, indeed, the band is back together for the first time in years. We don't see each other as much as we should. But we came immediately as soon as we heard; as soon as Patrik and Rut told us what was going on here, we came immediately. It is terrible to come together under such tragic circumstances." He had assumed a serious expression as he said this but then permitted his smile to come back, tentatively. "But it is good to be back together."

"And what exactly brings you here?" I said. "Right now?"

"I think I just told you. These terrible events…"

I shrugged. "I guess it makes sense to have the whole band together when the shit hits the fan."

"When the shit hits the fan?" said Oskar. Patrik leaned in grinning, delighted to have a chance to weasel into the conversation, and said, "In Swedish we might say *När helvetet brakar loss*."

"Breaker loss," said Nevada, phonetically paralleling and free associating to arrive at a rough-sketch translation. "Break loose… When all hell breaks loose?"

"Precisely," said Oskar. "Very clever of you to work that out."

"Not just beauty but brains, too," said Patrik.

We all ignored him. "Okay," said Oskar. "But exactly what sort of shit or hell are you talking about?"

"Publicity," I said.

Oskar's eyes glittered with humour. He turned and looked at Nevada. "Your friend here…"

"Lover, actually," said Nevada.

"Really?" Oskar looked at me again, in a reappraising way. "Lucky man. And as well as lucky he is astute. For it is indeed publicity that has brought us here and brought us together. Although perhaps not in the way you imagine."

I imagined it was exactly in the way I imagined. For all the talk of tragic circumstances, I sensed that a sensational string of killings based on their songs was going to translate into the sort of publicity that money couldn't buy for the previously forgotten Storm Dream Troopers.

"You see," said Oskar, "what we need is a defensive strategy." He suddenly threw one arm over Patrik's skinny shoulders and reached out with his other hand to grab his wife's hand. Gun seized it with reciprocal fierceness while keeping one hand on her sister's knee as they sat talking, close together, on the sofa. It was quite touching. The entire personnel of the Troopers were now in personal contact, skin on skin, like a circuit closing. I had a sense of them as a composite unit instead of merely individual people. Oskar looked at me, sincere and serious. "We have to be ready to protect ourselves."

"Protect yourselves from whom?" said Nevada, who could always be relied on for a good *whom*.

Oskar leaned forward and lowered his voice and at that moment, by coincidence or—if you prefer—synchronicity, all conversation naturally came to a pause and the entire room fell silent, so he might as well have shouted. "The Church."

"You need protection from the Church?" I said.

"From, as you say, the shit hitting the fan. Or as we would say, hell breaking loose. I don't think you can begin to imagine the storm of negative publicity that will be coming our way from the... let us say... more enthusiastically religious community in this country, not to mention the more conservative press."

"We still haven't recovered from last time," said Rut. It was almost reassuring to hear a note of familiar petulance surfacing in her voice.

"Indeed," said Patrik.

"By last time," said Agatha, "you mean…"

"When *Attack and Decay* came out," said Gun.

"You would be hard pressed," said Oskar, "to imagine the campaign of vilification directed against us. Just for daring to create our music. Music which we believed in, and which they so hated. So how are they going to react now, when they can legitimately link that music to some concrete social harm in the form of these horrible, tragic…"

I could see he was searching for a word. "Brutal," I said.

"Yes, these horrible, tragic and brutal and very real killings."

They were very real all right. I remembered the drained cavity of a swimming pool on a snowy night. Drained but not empty. Not empty enough for me.

"They will now claim that everything they said about our record in the first place was right. That it exerts a demonic influence on people. We needed to get the band back together, as you say, so we could be ready to address those kinds of accusations. Be ready with a united front for that onslaught. Work out a defensive strategy. Work out what to say to the media."

"Okay," I said. "You want something to say to the media? How about this? The record does *not* exert a demonic influence. That might be a good place to start."

Oskar laughed and topped up my glass. "Ah, a rationalist. Yes, that might be a very good place to start. That will certainly be a central plank of our strategy. Where are the rest of your friends, by the way?"

Nevada and Agatha and I looked at each other. "Well, there was one more of us," said Agatha. "But he's shacked up with a stripper at the top of the vattentorn across the road."

"Well," said Oskar, grinning. "When this colourful character emerges from the vattentorn, with the stripper, you must introduce us to both of them." I could see that Agatha wasn't much pleased with Tinkler being promoted to the status of colourful character.

"Is this Tinkler we're talking about?" said Rut. She was standing up now, so it was easier to detect that she had begun to sway under the impact of the champagne. "He's a delight."

"He certainly is," said Agatha.

Oskar suddenly seized my arm. He was strong, or at least he worked out, and although this grip was apparently intended to convey his ferocious pleasure in my company, it was mostly just unnecessarily uncomfortable. "I am so glad you could drop in," he said. His kilt creaking as he moved, he guided me towards the window, which was free for the moment of crows and crow owners, for a semi-private conversation. "I wanted a word with you about business."

"Business?" Nevada, who had been casually shadowing us, now officially joined the conversation.

"Meet my business manager," I said.

Oskar chuckled and nodded. "Very sensible man. Very lucky to have such a manager. Okay, so Patrik outlined what you do for a living…"

"I find records," I said. Just in case what Patrik had outlined was at variance with what I actually do.

"Yes, so we're hoping you can find some records for us."

Nevada took a deep, joyful breath which she disguised as inhaling the bouquet of the champagne.

"What records?" I said.

At that moment Gun joined us. She squeezed her husband's arm in an echo of the gesture he'd employed on me. "Darling, you mustn't monopolise these lovely people."

"We were just talking business, darling."

"Exactly what I was afraid of," said Gun. "We certainly can't have that." She smiled at Nevada. She smiled at me. She seemed to genuinely believe that she was saving us from a dreary, boring situation rather than depriving us of a potential and much desired payday. "Now, what were you saying about having a friend who is travelling with you, but who isn't here today?"

Agatha had also drifted over to join us, since the confidential business negotiations had obviously gone up in smoke. She said, "I said he's shacked up with a stripper at the top of the vattentorn across the road."

"Ah yes, of course. He's the amusing character who has my sister so charmed—and it's no small thing to have charmed Rut, so I look forward to meeting him. But I believe that there is also another Englishman staying here, at this hotel…"

"There is," said Agatha. "But he is no friend of ours."

The shadow of Stinky had fallen across the conversation.

"His name is Stuart Stanmer?" said Gun.

"Yes," said Agatha. "He's very tiresome. He thinks he's famous."

Oskar smiled a knowing smile. "Oh, one of those. And why does he think that?"

"Oh, I suppose he does have some small fame," allowed Nevada reluctantly.

"How so?"

"He was the last man in England to be diagnosed with leprosy," said Agatha.

"How fascinating," said Gun. "Will you excuse me for a moment?" She went over to Rut, who had begun to weave around drunkenly in the centre of the small lounge, as if she was about to break into a highly inventive and cutting-edge interpretative dance. But she pulled herself together as Gun drew near and resumed peacefully hugging her sister, a move which had the additional merit of allowing Gun to hold her up.

As soon as Gun left us for sister-holding duties, Agatha wandered away too, sensing that it would give us a much-needed chance to finish talking business. Unfortunately, this meant Patrik had the opportunity to swoop on her. But Agatha took one for the team.

Oskar turned to us and said, "Now, what were we saying before?"

Nevada nodded briskly. "You were just about to offer us vast sums of money to find some records for you."

Oskar laughed. "I can see why you're the business manager."

"You're after copies of *Attack and Decay*," I said.

He looked at me with surprised approval. "Yes, we are. As ridiculous as it sounds, none of us have a copy. None of us has a copy of our own album. Not an original. Not on vinyl."

"And that's where he comes in," said Nevada, smiling at me proudly.

"I hope so," said Oskar. "It seems that, through forces beyond our control, we are about to be thrust into the spotlight, along with this record we created. At the very least we should have some copies of the record in question."

Useful for visuals, as props when you're being filmed, I thought. And probably for later resale, once the notoriety of the record increased and the market value skyrocketed. But none of that was any of my concern. I would just look for the records. "So, we'd like to hire you," said Oskar.

"Sure," I said.

"And I understand you are already in possession of one copy."

No prizes for guessing who'd told him that. Patrik had barely been able to let go of it. "That's true."

Oskar shrugged. "Okay. Fine. I want to hire you to find more copies for us. As many as you can. We'll pay top market value for them…"

Nevada almost broke into a happy little dance.

"I'll have to talk to Magnus," I said.

"Why?" said Oskar.

"Why?" said Nevada, little happy dance now a forgotten thing of the distant past.

"I'm operating on his home turf," I said. "It would be a professional courtesy."

"Well, I'll leave that up to you." said Oskar. "But frankly, my understanding is that Magnus is something of a pain in the ass and that he has had the monopoly on selling copies of our record for far too long."

I couldn't fault any of this assessment.

However, I said, "I may not be able to find any copies of your record."

"Oh, come on, if this Magnus person has managed to obtain more than one copy…"

"Quite a lot more than one," I said.

"Well, there you go," said Oskar. "If he has managed to find copies then surely the Vinyl Detective will be able to find some?" I could see Nevada happily buying into this pep talk.

Actually, I was fairly confident that I *could* locate some copies locally and I had a pretty good idea where to look. But, among other things, this involved calibrating such small matters of etiquette as how long you should give someone to mourn the death of a close friend before approaching them to ask if they had any records to sell.

"In any case, you have one," said Oskar. "You have one already."

"That I have," I said.

"And I assume you don't need to talk to Magnus before you sell that one to me?"

"You would be assuming right," I said. "But unfortunately, that particular copy is spoken for." By Owyn Wynter.

"Well, let's assume you find another one. How much would you want for it?"

I set about haggling with Oskar, purely theoretically, over the next copy of *Attack and Decay* I found. Nevada stood nearby, listening happily. She enjoyed it when I haggled, in much the same way the cats enjoyed it when I prepared food. There was the same happy, respectful observation of me as I pursued a matter of some obvious importance.

Nevada was an excellent haggler in her own field — the second-hand clothing hustle. But she deferred to me entirely in matters related to record pricing.

Oskar and I settled on a fair price—fair, but nevertheless one that could make our visit very profitable indeed. Nevada was back in happy dance mode.

She took my arm and we headed quickly for the door. Agatha broke off her conversation with the Gylling sisters to come over to us. "We're going back to our room," said Nevada.

Agatha's eyes widened with concern. "Is something wrong?"

"On the contrary. Team Vinyl Detective has just scored big and we are going to reward ourselves with a little private celebration."

Agatha winked at us. "You kids have fun."

But before we made it through the door, Rut blocked our way. She was apparently more steady on her feet now, although somehow even drunker than before. "We must all be on our guard," she said. On the other side of the room, Gun saw us and started to our rescue.

"Okay," said Nevada.

Rut peered at us with deeply inebriated owlish seriousness. You could smell the champagne coming out of her pores like an expensive yeasty *eau de cologne*. "The trolls might not be happy about any unauthorised killings in their town."

"Right. The trolls. Unauthorised."

Gun arrived and led her sister away and Nevada and I went back to our room. It has to be said that there was something rather comforting about Rut having reverted to type, even if that type was raving lunatic.

The next morning, we made the unfortunate error of going to the breakfast room while Stinky was still nourishing himself there. Jocasta shot us an apologetic glance. She and Stinky were the only people present, although a member of the hotel staff may well have been hiding in the back room. Stinky was holding forth at volume.

The volume went up a notch when he saw us. "There's been another killing," he said. "This time it's really got weird. The victim's face had been sort of *deformed* to make it look like a bird's face. Like a giant bird's face. And, for the bird's beak, the killer has split the guy's face open and inserted *scissors...*"

"Fucking button it, Stinky," I said.

"Okay, dude." Stinky recoiled as if I'd actually moved to hit him instead of merely doting on the notion. "Chill."

21: BENSINDUNK

"Creepy crow song," said Tinkler when we told him about it. "Check."

He and Ida had met us outside the Notre Coeur, where we'd decided to relocate for breakfast after being propelled away from the hotel by our close encounter with Stinky.

Kisses were exchanged—did Nevada and Agatha seem marginally less silently malevolent towards Ida?—and we were just about to go into the café when a car pulled up beside us.

A Union Jack Mini. Emma scrambled out quickly and hurried happily towards us for more hugging and kissing, this time accompanied by cries of "Nice one!" and "Oh, my days!" Meanwhile Magnus climbed out of the Mini slowly and did not hurry happily towards us. Instead, he stopped some distance off and summoned me towards him with a curt gesture.

When I responded to this with spontaneous good-natured laughter, he angrily strode up to me and said, "We have to talk."

"Agreed," I said.

"Apparently you think you are going to start dealing vinyl in my town?"

"Magnus, I'm going to be gone from your town in a few days…"

"But not before you see how much damage you can do?"

"No," I said. "It's not like that."

"No? And yet it seems you are now suddenly officially in charge of finding copies of *Attack and Decay* for the Storm Dream Troopers. Officially in charge of finding records for the band. Well, good luck." This last was uttered with very little sincerity.

"I was going to talk to you about this, Magnus," I said.

"Oskar Hafström has already talked to me about it. How did you insinuate yourself with these people? What did you say about me behind my back?"

"Nothing," I said.

"What makes you think you'll find anything for them?"

"Maybe I won't," I said. "But I'll take a shot."

Magnus had been avoiding eye contact but now he looked right at me, a gaze of roiling rage. "Okay, if it's war you want," said Magnus, "it's war you've got."

"Great way to put a positive spin on things."

"Be as sarcastic as you like, and as smug as you like. You will regret the day you crossed swords with Magnus Fernholm. Come along, Emma." He took Emma by the arm.

She shook herself free. "Laters," she said.

"What do you mean, 'laters'?"

"Right now I am having brekkie with me mates."

Magnus sighed a sigh of exhaustion and disgust. "You stupid girl," he said. He gave me one last hate-filled look, then got into the Union Jack Mini and drove off.

"Passive aggression gone pyroclastic," said Agatha, who had caught the look.

"Hell has no fury like a vengeful nerd," said Tinkler. "That may not be the exact quote from Shakespeare, but you get the picture."

We were all sitting down at our regular table when I got a text from Kriminalinspektör Eva Lizell. "She wants to meet me," I told Nevada.

"When and where?" said Nevada

"Now," I said... I was reading another text from Eva Lizell which simply said, *Look up*.

I looked up.

She was standing on the other side of the window.

"And here," I said.

I joined her in the tiny courtyard placed, like a jewel in a brooch, at the heart of the café. She was dressed in jeans and a pale blue leather jacket, standing by the little love seat. I had a funny feeling the Kriminalinspektör had not chosen this location because she was planning on making a romantic declaration to me.

This was swiftly confirmed as she lifted a crafty cigarette to her lips. A roll-up, by the look and smell of it. She blew pale blue smoke up into the chill winter air, setting it spooling towards the snow-clad lamppost above us. This was why we were meeting outdoors.

"You wanted to talk to me?" she said.

"You might already know this," I said, "but the remaining members of the band are now here in town."

Her brown eyes became still and thoughtful. "I did not know that."

"Yup. Full line-up of the Troopers. Currently residing in our hotel."

"Oskar Hafström and Gun Gylling are the newcomers." Eva Lizell was now looking at her phone, held in the same hand as her cigarette.

"Yes."

"Well, thank you for letting me know. Did they happen to say why they have come here?"

"To do damage limitation on the negative publicity that is about to erupt."

"Yes. I imagine a considerable amount of such publicity is indeed about to erupt. Have you heard of the latest incident? Of course you have. It seems to also match a song."

Scissor beak crow.

"Yes," I said. "I'm not clear if Oskar and Gun knew about that one or if they were already on their way here when it happened."

"On their way here to do damage limitation," said Eva Lizell.

"So they say."

"It sounds like you think they're here to do something else."

"Yes," I said. "To cash in. Big time. On the principle that there's no such thing as bad publicity."

"And also presumably on the principle that the suspect pool is never large enough." Eva Lizell sighed. "Have you learned anything else that might be relevant?"

"No," I said.

"You are sure?"

"Well…" I said.

"Well, what?"

"Unless you want to consider that the trolls might not be happy about any unauthorised killing in their town."

There was a pause while Eva Lizell stared up into the winter sky, watching the slow ascent of her cigarette smoke as it curled, dispersed and ultimately vanished into the high emptiness of the world. "The trolls?" she said.

"Yes," I said.

Now the Kriminalinspektör's eyes met mine. "Well, you know what? That actually is quite an interesting theory."

"Is it?" I said.

"No." Eva Lizell spoke with meticulous patience. "It is shit. And you know it is shit."

She smiled and put out her cigarette by pinching it between thumb and forefinger and then slipped the dead stub into the pocket of her jacket. I hoped she hadn't burned the lining. It was a very nice jacket. And rather familiar.

Nevada grinned at me. "I was wondering if you'd notice."

I was back inside sitting with our friends at the table,

and the Kriminalinspektör had returned to her investigation, now with the benefit of nicotine in her system.

"She got in touch via the website." This was Nevada's vintage clothes website. "Obviously she'd been profiling me..."

"Checking you out," said Agatha.

"Stalking you," said Tinkler.

"...and she stumbled on my website and saw that jacket I found at the secondhand-butik and she liked it and bought it."

"A woman who knows what she wants," said Agatha. "Speaking of which, do you think it was a stratagem to meet with you?"

"I think it was a stratagem to get a really great jacket at a terrific price," said Nevada. "But in all modesty, I think meeting with me was a bit of a bonus."

"Did she go in for a kiss?" said Tinkler.

"No," said Nevada. "But it was odd. When she was standing near me, I could actually feel the heat coming off her, as if it was directed at me, seeking me out—her body heat. I could actually feel it."

"So the lesbian cop really *is* hot," said Agatha.

"Was it pleasant?" said Tinkler. "Her body heat seeking you out?"

"It certainly wasn't unpleasant," said Nevada.

"Not exactly a ringing endorsement," said Tinkler. "'It certainly wasn't unpleasant.' On the basis of such a TripAdvisor review, I don't predict any muff diving for the good inspector in this vicinity any time soon."

When Tinkler had finished with this line of discourse, I filled the others in on my own meeting with the good inspector. "She didn't much like the troll theory," I said.

"Rut will be disappointed," said Nevada.

Ida was looking raptly at her phone. She suddenly put it away and whispered something in Tinkler's ear. Tinkler in turn said something in a low voice to Agatha, then he and Ida got up from the table and slipped past her.

I was taking all this in only peripherally while I discussed with Nevada what I assumed would be the ramifications of our recent chat with Magnus, our pyroclastic nerd. "I don't think we can count on completing our purchase for Owyn Wynter," I said. "Magnus sounds like he's washed his hands of me."

"More fool he," said Nevada.

"But it does mean we lose our commission on the sale." Not to mention having to pay back large swathes of expenses, I reflected, rather glumly.

"On the other hand," said Nevada, intent on cheering me out of any glumness, "Oskar has guaranteed to buy every copy of the record you can find."

"Do you think you can find any?" said Agatha.

"Well," I said, "over the last few years Magnus, in association with Christer, has picked the carcass fairly clean. But even if there's only a few copies left, that will be a major payday for us. And I have a pretty good idea of where we might find some."

"Where?" said Agatha.

Before I could reply, Emma said, "Oh my god." She was

looking at her phone—clad in a Union Jack case, of course—with her eyes wide. "Tinkler and Ida…"

"What about them?" said Nevada.

"I thought they had gone to look at the cakes," said Agatha.

"That's what they wanted you to think," said Emma, staring at her phone. "That's what Tinkler says. He apologises for misleading you."

"He apologises for misleading us?"

"Yes. He has just messaged me. With a message for you."

"Why didn't he just message us directly?" said Nevada

"Because he says he is afraid that you will be angry with him."

"Shit," said Nevada. "What has he done now?"

"He says he and Ida have gone to rescue the juicer."

"Not the fucking juicer again."

"I guess he was right that it was going to make you angry."

"Where is the juicer?" I said.

"They think either at Bo Lugn's office or his country estate."

"There's a killer on the loose," said Agatha, "and Tinkler's going on a quest with his stripper to rescue a juicer? From Creepy Elvis's country estate?"

"Or his office. They said they were going to the office first."

"In the middle of a killing spree?" said Nevada. "With a criminal investigation in full swing?"

"He's cunt-struck," said Emma simply.

We all paused to briefly consider the justice of this

observation and then Nevada said, "Once again we're moved to commend your command of colloquial English, Emma."

"Cheers."

"Because that's exactly what he is," said Agatha.

"Cheers, me dears."

"But it doesn't change anything," said Nevada. "We still have to go to the poor fool's rescue."

Going to the poor fool's rescue was expedited by the fact that Agatha had already been scoping out the car hire situation in Trollesko. "After a few days anywhere, I start to get itchy feet," she said.

"Itchy to start driving again?" said Nevada.

"Yes."

"So, it would be the foot that goes down on the accelerator that gets itchy."

"Mostly that one, yes."

Agatha drove us—myself and Nevada; Emma wisely elected not to get involved—out of town at a high but legal speed in a Volkswagen Tiguan. "I've never driven one," said Agatha. "And I wanted to compare it to the Toyota RAV4."

"You don't have to justify your addiction to us."

We reached the Red Iron Inn in record time. In fact, the car that was leaving the parking lot as we pulled in— we were the only two vehicles in a wasteland of tarmac— was the one that had just dropped off Tinkler and Ida. They looked at us like they'd been expecting us, although perhaps not so soon.

"Look, darling," said Tinkler. "My annoying friends."

"Mine too now, I hope," said Ida.

"How come you guys only just got here?" said Nevada. "You texted us ages ago."

"That's all my fault, I'm afraid," said Ida. "I had to change into my burglary garb."

"Burglary garb?" said Nevada.

"I think that's the word for costume or clothing, isn't it?"

"Yes."

"It's all Jordon's fault, actually," said Ida.

"How is it Jordon's fault?"

"Well, he told me how *you* always dress up specially for a break-in." Ida smiled at us. The smile was mostly directed at Nevada but didn't make any inroads with her.

"I do normally," said Nevada. "I didn't have a chance to today."

"Well, I did," said Ida happily. She was wearing a black raincoat that would have done credit to a woman in a graveyard with a gun. Now she opened it for me, displaying black Converse high tops, skin-tight black jeggings and a black roll neck sweater that clung to her closely enough to reveal that she wasn't wearing a bra. The sweater looked very soft and expensive and the idle thought that it was cashmere triggered in me a startlingly powerful desire to reach out and touch it, an endeavour that could only end badly.

The black theme concluded in a black slouch beanie worn over her blond hair.

"Do you like it?" said Ida.

"I couldn't possibly comment," I said, and everyone laughed and I heaved a silent sigh of relief.

"All right," said Nevada. "So you think that this fucking juicer is here?" She was looking at the square concrete building in front of us.

"I know you are very fed up with this affair," said Ida. She sounded genuinely contrite. "Which is why I said to Jordon that we shouldn't bother you with it."

"No bother," said Nevada, though with detectible weariness. "So, is it here?"

"Either here or at Bo's country place. Almost certainly."

Nevada's weariness did not diminish much at the multivalent imprecision of this reply. "If it is here, where is it? Your best guess?"

"In Bo's office. Almost certainly."

"I take it that Bo himself isn't in his office," said Nevada. "At the moment."

"There's no one here," said Ida, waving at the empty parking lot. "No Bo. No Röd or Röd. Not for about two hours yet. Until two hours from now, the place is deserted."

"Okay," said Nevada. "And I take it we're not going in through the front door?"

"No," said Ida. "Let me show you." She led us around the back of the building into a semi-enclosed space with a variety of dark green recycling containers and dumpsters. There was also a small private parking area.

The rear of the club, least likely to be seen by the public, was ironically the most strikingly decorated. Whereas elsewhere blank white brick walls covered the concrete, here a brilliantly coloured mural covered the white brick. It echoed and continued the garish pop art decor of the bar inside.

"It's your favourite French comic," said Agatha.

"That's right," said Tinkler. "*The Adventures of Jodelle.*"

"That's when I knew Jordon was special," said Ida. "Most idiots think that mural's supposed to be Lichtenstein or Warhol. But Jordon knew it was *Jodelle.*"

The section of the mural that enlivened our immediate vicinity depicted a young woman with red hair. Against a background of lurid blue sky—it made me think of a hot beach somewhere—her enormous pink face was happily and blithely chatting in the direction of her enormous pink hand, which clutched with bright red fingernails a big black rectangle of cell phone that, on closer inspection, turned out to be the big black back door of the club.

Between the face and the "phone" a white speech balloon hung against the hot blue sky. It read *Bla bla bla*. No translation necessary.

"Isn't there an alarm on this door?" said Nevada.

"In theory," said Ida. "But the girls often come out here for a smoke and leave it wedged open with the alarm off. And I made sure that's what happened last night." She swung the black door open, and we all went in. We walked down a short echoing corridor of cold concrete and turned right into another one and then a moment later turned left into a third.

Nevada and Ida were walking in front of me and Tinkler and Agatha. So, when they stopped, we all stopped. I heard Ida say, "That's a... *bensindunk*..." For once she was at a loss for the English word.

"Benzene tank…" said Nevada, whittling out a phonetic translation. "Petrol can?"

"Right, gas can or petrol can," said Ida, getting her full command of English back.

By now I was standing beside them, or rather between them, looking over their shoulders.

There on the floor in front of us, arrayed neatly along the wall, were a number of red plastic fuel cans of the sort that you keep in your vehicle in rustic places. Sitting on top of them was a package about the size of a paperback book wrapped in several layers of transparent plastic that had been fixed in place with adhesive tape. All I could make out inside the package was a greyish smudge with some coppery lines across it.

A soft grey shape with wires attached to it.

"Okay," said Nevada. "Everybody get out of here right now."

The black giant-phone door slammed behind us as we retreated into the parking lot and then hurried around to the front of the building. "Back inside there," said Tinkler. "That was a…"

"An explosive device," said Nevada. "With a lot of accelerant. A firebomb."

22: EAGLE

When she was satisfied that we were a safe distance from the strip club—and all that explosive and accelerant—Nevada turned to Ida. "You need to call the fire department."

"And the police," I said. I started to give Ida the number for Kriminalinspektör Eva Lizell but of course she already had it. "Call her too," I said.

"Make sure they understand that it's an incendiary device," said Nevada. "They'll need someone who can disarm it." She looked at me and I was pretty sure I knew what she was thinking. *Assuming they get here before it goes off.*

Ida was nodding in a businesslike way. "Okay. Do you guys want to get out of here?"

"Yes, please," said Nevada.

"Okay." Ida took out her phone. "I'll make the call as soon as you are gone."

"And I will rule out the other place, honey," said Tinkler. He and Ida kissed, and then we all left her standing there in the parking lot, a small lone figure all dressed in black, as we piled into Agatha's hired car and got away at speed.

"What was that about the other place, Tinkler?" said Nevada. "About ruling it out?"

"Well, the juicer might be at Bo Lugn's country house."

"This fucking juicer is going to get somebody fucking killed," said Nevada in a thin, angry voice. But Agatha took directions from Tinkler and we set off for chez Creepy Elvis, country style. As we sped away from the strip club, we heard sirens rising in the distance. Ida had clearly got through on the phone.

Bo Lugn's country house proved to be like his town house, but on a larger scale. A faux Roman villa with columns, set on a hilltop in a big spread of grounds which had apparently once been farmland. There were no heated paving stones here, though, and thankfully no enclosing wall. I found myself praying that there also wouldn't be a swimming pool.

As far as I could see, there wasn't. There was, however, some Roman statuary dotted around the grounds and a winding tarmac driveway leading all the way up to the house. We contented ourselves with parking in the road and walking from there.

The snow of recent days had largely melted away and there were now only occasional patches of white left on the expanse of wet yellow grass. We avoided these, and therefore leaving footprints, as we left the driveway and made our way towards the house. There were no vehicles parked outside and no lights on inside.

"Our intel is that the place is currently empty," said Tinkler.

"Intel?" said Nevada.

"Okay, Ida heard that Bo and the two Röds went out of town last night and aren't due back until lunchtime, when they'll head straight for the club."

"If it hasn't been blown to hell," said Nevada.

"Or burned to the ground," said Agatha.

We were now approaching the largest piece of statuary outside the house. At first, from a distance, I thought it was a horse.

Albeit a horse that was wearing a cape. And rearing up on its hind legs, while for some reason still wearing that damn cape. That was all I could think of that might justify the scale of the thing.

But it wasn't a caped horse. It was an eagle.

A Roman eagle just like the ones on the gateposts of his town house. Except, as Tinkler put it, "This motherfucker is huge." We were all now standing in the shadow of the statue, sheltered from the wind by the wings curving in on each side. It was a strangely comforting feeling of sanctuary. The big bird was wrapping us in its protective wings. It was an insane piece of statuary of the oligarch folly school. And I fervently doubted any real ancient Roman had ever had a monstrosity such as this stationed outside his country villa.

But it was a friendly monstrosity and made a good place for us to wait while Nevada did the dirty work. "Okay, so there's a door on the side of the house, Tinkler..."

"Right."

"And Ida thinks it's unlocked?"

"Ida is super-sure it's unlocked."

"I'm glad she's super-sure," said Nevada. "And it leads directly into the kitchen?"

"Right," said Tinkler. "Directly into the kitchen. And that's the most likely place for the juicer to be."

"No shit," said Nevada. Then she went into the house through the side door while, as she'd insisted—"No one is getting killed over this fucking juicer"—the rest of us waited outside. She seemed to be gone for an eternity. But if my phone was to be believed, it was less than fifteen minutes before she came out empty-handed.

"Where is it?" said Tinkler.

"Not in that house," said Nevada with certainty.

We started walking back to the car. We were about halfway there when someone started shooting at us.

We didn't realise it at first, or at least I didn't. I thought it was firecrackers exploding rather inexplicably—perhaps it was a Swedish holiday—somewhere nearby, echoing loudly off the front of Bo Lugn's house.

Then Nevada pulled me down, and I found myself lying on the cold wet ground beside her and Agatha and Tinkler, breathing the intimate primal and comforting smell of mud and grass. The noise—what I now understood to be gunfire—suddenly ceased.

"Someone is shooting at us," said Agatha.

"Afraid so," said Nevada. "Automatic weapon. Over there by the road. Downhill, so we'll be relatively safe as long as we stay down."

There was a long moment of strange, tense silence and then Tinkler said, "Maybe they're gone," and began to get to his feet.

The gunfire instantly started up again and Tinkler quickly dropped back onto the ground. "Tinkler, for fuck's sake, *stay down*," said Nevada.

"I'm sorry," said Tinkler with enormous sincerity.

The gunfire stopped.

"As I was saying," said Nevada. "We'll be relatively safe as long as we stay down. Anyone who stands up is an excellent target."

"I don't want to be an excellent target," said Tinkler. "I want to be a really bad target."

"I don't want to be a target at all," said Agatha.

"Right," agreed Tinkler fervently. "What she said. I'm with her."

"Okay," said Nevada. "Let's head back to the big eagle. And when I say head back, I mean crawl on our bellies staying as flat as we possibly can. And keep your bum down. Unless you want it shot off. I'm looking at you when I say this, Tinkler."

"Bum down, got it," said Tinkler.

We crawled back across the cold damp grass. It felt like we spent a substantial slab of eternity crawling like that. And doing so in perfect silence. At first, we took sustenance from this silence. After all, we weren't being shot at.

But then, about halfway to the big eagle, the silence seemed to change. Now it didn't seem to be so much that we weren't being shot at as that we were *about* to be shot at. Imminently. At any second.

And waiting for the appointed second was emphatically not a pleasant experience. There was a cold area of my lower back that felt very vulnerable indeed as I crawled along the ground, as though it was a glowing target for the unseen marksman.

Suddenly there was a sound. A vehicle starting up.

We heard it pull away, moving quickly, accelerating and disappearing.

"Not a small vehicle," said Agatha. "An SUV, maybe. Diesel."

"Bu they've gone?" said Tinkler.

"We cannot make any assumptions at all," said Nevada. "Keep crawling towards the eagle." We kept crawling, but now my lower back was feeling a lot more comfortable. Once we were in the shelter of those big stone wings, Nevada said, "Okay. Everybody wait here."

"No," I said. "You're not going back out there."

"I have to. Someone has to."

"No, stay here with us."

"He's right," said Agatha. "Stay here with us."

Nevada stood there, looking at us. Agatha nudged Tinkler. He said, "You can guess my vote. I think anyone is completely nuts to risk their skin at any time for any reason. So get with the program and stay here with us."

Nevada smiled and shook her head. "I love you all." She looked at me. "Particularly you. But someone has to make sure they're actually gone, instead of waiting out there with a nasty surprise for us. And I'm the one to do it, because I'm the only one who's been trained for this sort of thing."

"Well, after this," I said, "you can't be the only one."

"Okay," she said, "I'll train you."

"And me too," said Agatha. "Train me, too."

"Don't look at me," said Tinkler. "I think you're all fucking nuts. Don't you dare try and train me."

Nevada seemed to be gone for even longer than when she went into the house. But, according to my phone, it was less than five minutes. "All clear," she said when she returned. We left the stone embrace of the giant eagle, not without reluctance, and walked back to Agatha's hired car, trying not to break into a run.

Because that would have been undignified.

"I have looked into the matter," said Kriminalinspektör Lizell. "Although it is not strictly my area of responsibility."

"Why isn't it your area of responsibility?" I said. We were both sitting at our regular table in the Notre Coeur, looking out at the little courtyard where we'd last met. It was a little weird thinking of me and Eva Lizell having a regular table, but it had come to that.

It was just the two of us. I could have asked Nevada to join our little meeting, but to be honest I didn't particularly want the Kriminalinspektör emanating body heat at her.

"It's not clear that the incident is part of my investigation."

"Someone shooting at us isn't part of your investigation?" I said.

"Of course, if someone was shooting at you, then it was. And as it happens, I personally believe that someone *was* shooting at you. But at the moment, all I have is effectively a complaint about unknown parties discharging a firearm. An unsubstantiated complaint."

I said, "No one else heard the shooting?"

"No one that we have interviewed so far."

"Bo Lugn had two bodyguards called Röd," I said.

"I am aware of those gentlemen."

"So perhaps you know those gentlemen are supposed to have recently concluded an illegal weapons deal. Don't you think they might know something about someone discharging firearms?"

"Enquires are underway." This didn't sound promising.

"And still no luck," I said, "finding any of the considerable number of bullets someone was shooting at us?"

"It is the middle of the countryside," said Eva Lizell. "On the top of a hill amongst farmland. Not many things for bullets to hit."

"Except for us," I said.

"We have nevertheless searched as large an area as we can without further resources being allocated. I am afraid there is not a great deal more I can do."

"Would it help if we had bullets in us?" I said.

"*Help* is not the word I would use in that context," said Eva Lizell. "However, at least it would decisively constitute evidence. But assuming that whoever was firing at you is the same person responsible for the killings…" To her credit, it did indeed sound like she was assuming that.

She leaned forward, looking at me, the elfin youth of her face contradicted by that deep line grooved across her forehead. "And working on the assumption that this was based on one of the songs…"

"'Active Shooter'," I said. "It would have to be that one."

"Yes, I think so. Let's summarise these songs…"

"There's 'Snow Angel'," I said.

"Which corresponds with the death of Christer Vingqvist."

"Right. Then there's 'The First Golf War'."

"Malin Rozelle," she said.

"The retired advertising executive," I said.

"Correct. And then there would be 'Slipping on the Wind'."

The one about the scissor beak crow. "Right."

"The victim of that particularly vicious mutilation is one Filip Over. He is—was—a very successful and affluent local businessman with no apparent links to either Vingqvist or Rozelle. Like Malin Rozelle, he was killed in his home where he lived alone." She looked at me. "Actually, he lived quite near your hotel, in the same street."

"Well, it wasn't me," I said.

"I didn't think it was." The amusement in her eyes faded. "However, it would be entirely possible, logistically speaking, for someone else from your hotel to have gone to Mr Over's house, committed the crime, and returned to the hotel during the night in question."

"Okay," I said. I had no idea what to do with this information.

"Which means in total that's three," she said. It was three, all right. Three song-based murders. "What songs are left?"

"Okay," I said, "so there's 'Fire'..."

"And that could apply to what happened to Christer Vingqvist's car."

"Yes," I said. "And also apply to what almost happened at Bo Lugn's strip club."

"Yes," she said. "What almost happened. It was tremendously lucky that Ms Tistelgren happened to find the device there and notify us about it." The amusement was back in the Kriminalinspektör's eyes. "She chanced to find it when she just happened to be visiting there early in the morning. All by herself."

I had the distinct feeling that Ida's attempt to keep us out of that business had achieved very little. I altered the course of the conversation by saying, "You see the implications of that?"

"The implications of what?"

"Two attempts to do the 'Fire' song."

"Yes." The frown line deepened, causing me—very much to my surprise—to want to reach out and brush her forehead with my fingertips, and erase it, the way you'd wipe away a child's cares. "The implications are: if a crime is attempted based on a song, and the crime fails..."

"The song goes back into rotation," I said. "So to speak. Until it can be used again."

"Yes," said Eva Lizell. "It isn't considered used up if the attempt was a failure."

"Unfortunately," I said.

"Very much unfortunately. The device at Bo Lugn's establishment was attached to a timer that would have detonated it at noon. Lunchtime. There is every chance that a number of people would have been seriously hurt and there might well have been some fatalities. Not as many as would have occurred if it was set to go off later. But the later they left it, the greater the chance of the device being discovered." She sighed. "So anyway, the song 'Fire' can be considered, to use your phrase, still in rotation. What else is in rotation?"

"'Candle in the Wind'," I said.

"Do we feel that either of those attempts at arson could actually be connected with *that* song?"

"Well," I said, "as far as I know neither of them involved a candle or the wind."

"All right, so we'll assume that song is also still in rotation and that we have yet to see any attempt to use it."

"Which leaves two others," I said.

"Yes. There's 'Gallows Pole'…"

"And then there's 'Active Shooter'," I said, because I couldn't stand waiting for her to say it. "Which is also still in rotation. And even less promising."

"Yes," said Eva Lizell curtly. She was staring out the window at the tiny courtyard and I sensed that she was longing for a cigarette.

I said, "Have you…"

She turned angry brown eyes on me. "What?"

"Taken any measures…"

"Measures?"

"Made any preparations…" I said.

"What kind of preparations?"

"In case they try 'Active Shooter' again," I said.

The anger in those eyes was now sardonic. "You think, perhaps, I should have a special tactical unit on standby ready to prevent mass fatalities as the result of someone going on the rampage with an automatic weapon?"

"Yes," I said.

"And you think that this unit should be available full time and ready at a moment's notice when we have no idea of exactly when or where it might be needed? Or, indeed, if it will be needed?"

"Yes," I said. "I do think that."

Eva Lizell sighed again and her shoulders sagged. "Well, so do I. And I have made my thoughts known and made requests for exactly those kinds of resources. But I am afraid my superiors aren't entirely convinced that they can justify the commitment of such resources on the basis of what they feel is a rather tenuous hypothesis."

"Tenuous?" I said.

"They don't fully believe in the connection between the killings and the songs."

"Well, they've had three out of seven," I said. "How many do you think they want?"

23: THE SHELF-FITTING PERSUASION

As I walked back from the café my phone rang. To my surprise it was Magnus. Without preamble, he said, "I am still awaiting payment from Owyn Wynter. When do you think I might expect it?"

I felt a spreading, rising warmth that was not solely to do with all the coffee I'd just drunk, and I said I'd get onto it right away. Then we bid each other goodbye, really quite civilly, and hung up. I was jubilant. It seemed the deal hadn't gone south after all.

And I was as good as my word, I did get on it right away. I called Owyn.

"I know, I know," he said. "As it happens, Jaunty has just given me the go-ahead, so I will send payment now. There. I've done it. Check with Magnus. He should have the money now."

I did. And he had. As soon as I put my phone away, in a very good mood, it rang again. It was Nevada. I filled her in on my conversation with the Kriminalinspektör and then I told her about the deal. "I think Magnus came to his senses. He was furious because the band wants to do business with me instead of him. But then he realised the implications of this."

"No more money coming in," said Nevada.

"Exactly," I said. "At least from this direction. At least for now. So that reminded him keenly he had a deal in place, one that guaranteed him a healthy payday. He couldn't turn his nose up at that."

"If he did," said Nevada, "he would be cutting off his nose to spite his face. You notice how his nose keeps coming into this?"

"It's not much of a nose," I said.

"It isn't," she agreed. "Yours is much nicer. So the deal is going ahead?"

"It's *gone* ahead."

"Already?"

"Yes," I said. "The money has been transferred and Magnus has received it."

I could tell Nevada was doing something else for an instant. And then she said, "And so have we. *Woohoo*. I just checked and we've been paid our commission."

Perhaps a little premature, I thought. I didn't actually have this piece of vinyl in my hands yet. And I wouldn't relax until I did. "I'll collect the record from Magnus tomorrow," I said.

"No, my love," said Nevada. "*We'll* collect the record from Magnus tomorrow. Are you coming back to the hotel now?"

"Yes, by way of the vattentorn, where I'm meeting Tinkler."

"Ah, at the record shop. Of course. Don't let him lead you astray."

"When you say 'lead me astray', do you mean by helping me talk myself into buying expensive vinyl?"

"Chiefly that, yes."

"I won't."

When I got to the record and book shop, Anders said, "Your friend was just here."

"Tinkler was just here?"

"Literally just standing right here. But he suddenly thought he might have missed you."

"How could he have missed me?" I said.

Anders shrugged, continuing to go through an enormous box of paperbacks, pricing them. "He thought you might have gone up to Ida's apartment."

"Without walking past him standing right here?" I said.

"He thought you might have used the outside staircase. You see, they—Jordon and Ida—have a habit of leaving the door open up there, or at least unlocked. I have warned them about it on several occasions. I mean, I have warned Ida already and now I have warned Jordon, too. But they are incorrigible. They are both incorrigible. They both leave it unlocked or even open. I know categorically that on many occasions they have done so."

"So Tinkler's what…" I said. "Gone upstairs?"

"Yes, to meet up with you, he thought. You having gone upstairs by the outdoor staircase. As he surmised. Wrongly as it happens. But if you *had* gone up by the outdoor staircase, you probably would have had no problem getting into the apartment. They constantly leave it unlocked."

This was clearly a bone of contention between the lovebirds and Anders, who now, however, shrugged a philosophical shrug and returned to his Sisyphean project of pricing paperbacks. "It's perhaps not as much of a hazard as you may think. This is quite a peaceable town. Not much crime here, not much crime here at all."

A trio of recent grisly murders might have put a dent in that statistic, I thought. But I did not feel compelled to say as much.

"Also," said Anders, "it's a long way up the steps to the apartment at the top of the tower. I don't imagine many people would go all the way up all those steps purely speculatively."

"Tinkler just did."

"No, he used the *indoor* staircase."

"Okay, well I will too. Use the indoor staircase. If you see him before I do, tell him I've gone upstairs."

"I will."

As I wound my way up the wooden spiral of the stairway, I began to detect the welcome smell of coffee drifting down from above. It grew steadily more tantalising as I progressed up the seemingly endless green-carpeted steps and finally through the circular trapdoor and onto the landing.

I noticed once again how cleverly crafted the trapdoor was—when open, the lid hinged back and lay flat in a neatly carved hollow in the floorboards, flush at floor level so you could walk across it. Indeed, I *did* walk across it, and past the thin slice of beautiful blue sky in the slit window in the stone wall.

Through that window you could see a splendid view of Trollesko spread below. A bird's-eye view.

But I didn't have time to admire it now. The door to Ida's flat was open.

I called through it, "Tinkler." I waited for a moment. There was silence except for the cold high whistle of the breeze blowing up through the tower. I went in.

The apartment seemed empty. I admired the shelf unit that had been recently fitted. It hadn't fallen off the wall, and that was always commendable in any DIY project. And it was now full of books and magazines. Taking a closer look, I was surprised to see that it was Frank Zappa fan literature. I suppose I shouldn't have been surprised. It certainly explained Ida's *Lumpy Gravy* T-shirt.

I would have to ask her if she had any Zappa on vinyl. The pre-digital stuff, of course.

I also took a look—a considerably closer look—at the floor under the shelf unit. The rawl plugs were gone, as was the electric screwdriver.

This interested me because I was wondering who had put up the shelf for Ida. Because it might have implications for Tinkler's carnal idyl.

Just then Ida herself came trotting into view. She made a tragic face. "Tinkler was just here. He just went down the stairs, to look for you. Only just now."

"Oh, for fuck's sake," I said.

"Down the outside stairs."

"Of course he did." We walked into the small kitchen together, from which the convincingly coffee-like smell was drifting. Ida was minus her sneakers and her slouch hat, but otherwise was wearing the same ensemble as the last time I'd seen her. "Are you planning another burglary?" I said.

"No need," she said. She proudly showed me a substantial black and silver appliance prominently displayed on the counter. I assumed it was the infamous juicer.

"You got it back?" I said.

"Bo returned it to me."

"He *returned* it?"

"Yes. To thank me for saving the club from being firebombed."

"Well… that was good of him." I couldn't believe that we'd finally got the fucking juicer back. Or that I was thinking of it in terms of "we".

Ida smiled as she poured me a cup of coffee— commendably, without asking or being asked. "Regarding what I'm wearing, Tinkler just likes me dressing up like this. Do you call him Tinkler, not Jordon? Tinkler?"

"Mostly, yes."

"It feels a little odd. Rude. I mean, it would for me. I think I will resume calling him Jordon and continue to call him Jordon." She handed me the coffee. As I sipped it and reflected that it tasted almost as good as it smelled, Ida gave me a knowing smile. A caffeine-addict gotcha.

With her standing there, her body all soft contours in black, her face happy and open and smiling, we were close enough that I was glad of the open doors, and the cool breeze blowing away any treacherous body heat that might have been emanating from anyone in any direction.

Given all this, it might seem odd where my gaze had just fallen—the object on which it fell. The electric screwdriver. It was here on the counter, happily plugged into its docking unit, which I hadn't spotted amongst the other kitchen tech on our first visit.

I was lavishly pleased to see it. Perhaps foolishly so.

But I'd been bracing myself, expecting to find evidence of someone else in Ida's life, someone of the shelf-fitting persuasion. Someone who might ruin things for Tinkler. A knuckle-dragging boyfriend in the shape of a murderous biker would have been my top bet, if I'd been forced to make one.

But now it was looking like there was no such person. Plus full marks to Ida for keeping a power tool properly charged.

I looked at her, seeing her in a new and more positive light. But also not failing to notice, as perhaps I should have, the softly clinging black sweater that revealed every detail of what Nevada had called her 'really nice body'.

Ida was looking me squarely in the eye, possibly reading every thought in my head. She leaned back, elbows on the counter and thereby probably not entirely coincidentally causing the sweater to grow more snug over her breasts and said, "You never told me what you thought of this outfit."

"I'm with Jordon," I said.

She laughed and then she gave me a shrewd, assessing look. "Tell me what you are thinking. At this moment. Exactly you are thinking. The truth, please."

"I was thinking how impressed I am that you put up your own shelves," I said.

She laughed again. And the thankful cool breeze kept blowing over us.

It was a constant in the building, and seemed to add to the atmosphere of ancient time that the place possessed. The breeze came from below, flowing up the tower, presumably entering through the open slit windows. It then rushed through the cleverly carpentered circular trapdoor, into this room then out again through the green fire exit—green was an odd choice for a fire exit, come to think of it—that led to the exterior staircase.

The latter was, as Anders had prophesied, wide open.

Just then the door to the landing also opened and Tinkler came in, looking exhausted but contented. He had about him what, on anyone else, I would have called the healthy glow of exercise. He heard Ida happily laughing and started happily laughing himself.

And so did I. It was good to see my old friend, debauched fool though he was. "Where the hell have you been, Tinkler?" I said, eventually.

"Well, I have to say it was worthy subject matter for a nursery rhyme. When you were upstairs, I was downstairs, and vice versa."

"So you've been running up and down the staircase. Staircases, plural."

"Yes. Inside and out. This is a really cool place. Those twin spiral staircases are almost like strands of DNA. Sort of."

"Tinkler, are you stoned?"

"Of course."

"Well, for Christ's sake be careful you don't have a heart attack, running up and down the stairs. The twin staircases."

"I don't think I will. I really don't think I will."

"I don't think he will, either." Ida went to him, they kissed and then she patted him on the ass as she might a healthy horse. Tinkler's face was that of a man in rapture.

"Jordon has been losing fat and putting on muscle," said Ida.

"I've been losing fat and putting on muscle," said Tinkler. "She did say it that way around, didn't she?"

By the time I eventually disentangled myself from the happy couple and concluded a quick survey of the vinyl in the shop below, Nevada had become worried enough to call me. "What's going on?" she said.

"Jordon has been losing fat and putting on muscle."

"He has, has he? Are you sure it's not the other way around?"

"We went into that, and apparently not."

"You must tell me more."

I was crossing the road between the vattentorn and the hotel.

"Back home in a second," I said.

"Well, be ready for a circus," said Nevada.

24: CIRCUS

When I got back to the hotel, a circus was indeed in progress.

For a start, as soon as I stepped through the door, I found a young woman blocking me from going any further, equipped with an official-looking silver clipboard and an ingratiating grin. It was the grin as much as the red hair and freckles that made her name come immediately to mind. Alicia Foxcroft—known as Foxy.

"Hello, Alicia." She was mostly known as Foxy behind her back.

"Oh, it's you," she said. "You can go right in. I don't even need to check my clipboard." She waved me in. As I went up the stairs, I met Nevada coming down, presumably to greet me, possibly to warn me.

"Why is Foxy Foxcroft brandishing a clipboard?" I said.

"She is 'controlling the location'," said Nevada, making gestures in the air to clarify that this was a direct quotation.

"The location for…"

"The filming," said a voice from above us. We looked up

to see Oskar Hafström's smiling face. More of him emerged into view as we walked upstairs. He was wearing his black sweater but, as we were able to thankfully confirm when we reached the upper landing, not his kilt. Just a pair of fairly ordinary leather biker trousers. No boots this time.

Indeed, he seemed to be scampering around in a pair of white socks with yellow Simpsons characters on the ankles—presumably because this footwear option was quieter than boots.

His quest for silence didn't prevent him greeting us loudly, however. "You were rather naughty," he said, wagging a finger at us, a finger so covered with silver rings that only the tip of it was visible—a segment of pale digit tipped with glossy black nail varnish. "You guys were rather naughty, telling us that your friend Stinky Stanmer had leprosy."

"He's not our friend," said Nevada. "And he does. Moral leprosy."

"Ha-ha, yes. Very true. I know exactly what you mean. He is a slippery little shit. But nevertheless, he may prove useful to us."

"Is he something to do with this filming that's happening?" I said.

"Oh, yes." Oskar nodded vigorously, setting the assorted jewellery around his neck in motion. "Very much so." I realised that a viewfinder of the kind used by movie directors was swaying among the silver necklaces. "We—which is to say the Troopers—are giving him an exclusive interview on the understanding that we retain ownership of the footage and exercise full editorial control."

"Very sensible," I said.

"Very," said Nevada.

"Effectively what we are doing is filming ourselves talking without Stinky. Meanwhile Stinky quite separately films himself asking us questions related to the stuff we are talking about. And then we can cut it together later. This way we don't have to interact much."

"Again, very sensible," I said.

"Of course, we'll do a few shots of us together with Stinky, to tie things together, perhaps with him nodding seriously as we say something. He seems to be particularly fond of nodding seriously. Anyway, to help create the illusion it's an actual interview, we'll need to do a few shots together."

"As few as possible," suggested Nevada.

"So, Stinky is in there," Oskar nodded at Patrik's room, "filming some pickups, while Rut and Gun are in *there*," he nodded at the lounge, "filming their bits. Or at least they will be when the director joins them." He puffed out his chest and his viewfinder glinted. "By which I mean myself. Did you know that in addition to being a musician, which undeniably is my first love, I'm also a filmmaker? I know what you are going to say. You are going to say that for a man named Oskar, it was an inevitable calling. In any case, what I am saying is that I am currently being unfaithful to my musical muse by consorting with my filmmaking muse. So to speak. I got into filmmaking through still photography. Did you know that? I did the cover photography for *Attack and Decay*."

"I did not know that," I said. And I was intrigued. It was an excellent cover.

"The graveyard?" said Nevada. "And the boobs?"

Oskar laughed. "Yes, exactly."

"Very striking photo," I said. Quite sincerely.

"Very striking," concurred Nevada. "Especially those boobs."

Oskar laughed again. "Yes, well I am married to them, so I have had a lot of experience getting the best out of them."

There seemed no answer to this. To fill the silence, Oskar went on. "I'm glad you like the photograph. We had a huge argument over whether the cover could be in black and white. The idiots at the record company wanted it to be in colour. I didn't even want the *title* to be in colour. But the idiots got their way in that one instance."

Oskar seemed to sense that he might be boring us with reminiscences, so he changed the subject. If continuing to talk about yourself, only in a different context, can be regarded as changing the subject. "Why don't you come in and watch us at work?" He gestured towards the lounge where Rut and Gun could be seen through the glass door, sitting on the sofa, chatting companionably. "Myself directing the girls. You'll enjoy that. Come and watch."

Before we could reply to this kind offer, the door to Patrik's room swung open and Agatha, of all people, peered out. When she saw us, her face lit up. "You're just in time," she said.

Nevada asked the obvious question. "For what?"

"To watch Stinky filming," said Agatha.

Again, it was left to Nevada to do the honours. "You've got to be kidding," she said. "Why would we want to watch Stinky do anything, let alone filming?"

"Because of *who* he is filming."

"Who is he filming?

"Hiram."

Nevada looked at me, eyes alight with mischief. "At last. My chance to meet the mystery crow."

"I hope he doesn't disappoint," I said. Somehow, I didn't think he would. Nevada followed Agatha back into the room. I was right at Nevada's side but perhaps, if I'm to be honest, I was a little reluctant to get up close and personal with that spooky crow again.

However, I instantly stopped thinking *spooky* and started thinking *smart* when I beheld the spectacle.

There were three people in the room besides us: Stinky, Jocasta and Patrik. Jocasta was holding her iPhone and acting as camera person. Stinky was acting—and acting is the right word—as director. Meanwhile Patrik looked on as a kind of referee.

Stinky was saying, in the voice of a child well on his way to a tantrum, "We have to get this shot, Jocasta."

"Well, if I could use a mirror…"

"A mirror?"

"For example…" her voice trembled. Jocasta was close to tears.

"We are not using a mirror," said Stinky.

"I mean, to get a reflection…"

"I know what you mean, Jocasta," said Stinky, now at

his most nasty and sarcastic, and evidently quite prepared to push Jocasta the rest of the way to tears. "But we don't need to get the shot by way of a fucking mirror. By means of a fucking reflection. We need to get it clean."

The object of everyone's attention was on one of the small bedside tables, which had been moved to the window, presumably to take advantage of the winter daylight.

On this table was the large transparent handbag we'd seen before. The one with a perch in it.

Only this time, perched on the perch was Hiram, who glanced at me as we entered the room. Stinky was bent down, leaning towards the crow on his perch, the vile Stanmer countenance veritably pressed to the transparent plastic like a child peering into a goldfish bowl. Hiram looked at him and then looked at me again. Was it fanciful to think that the crow was giving me an ironic look? Perhaps. But not as fanciful as it was to think this look conveyed the question, related unequivocally to Stinky, *Who is this cunt?*

Nevertheless, that is exactly what I thought. And all credit to Hiram for the perspicacity of his analysis.

"We need this shot," said Stinky, "because we are going to go from a shot of the mutilated face of the murder victim—as gory a pic as they'll let us use—to a matching shot of the crow. We may do it as a dissolve. I haven't decided yet. But to do it at all, we have to get the fucking shot of the fucking crow."

"I know," said Jocasta tremulously. "I'm trying."

"Well, try harder. No, in fact, *I'll* try. Give it to me." Stinky seized the phone from her. Jocasta clearly interpreted this as having now completely failed in her duty. She looked utterly bereft. Stinky leaned in towards Hiram again, taking aim with the iPhone, trying to record.

But as soon as Stinky pointed the phone at him, Hiram shuffled around on his perch so that his *back* was to the camera. Stinky moved, and Hiram also moved, perpetually keeping his back to the camera.

Agatha leaned over and whispered, "That's exactly what he's been doing whenever they try and film him."

"Fucking crow," hissed Stinky, giving up. He handed the iPhone back to Jocasta who apparently took this as a reprieve, smiling gratefully and blinking back tears. "Fucking stupid fucking crow," said Stinky.

"Please," said Patrik. "He can hear you. And he understands English at least as well as he understands Swedish." In its own way, this was probably an irrefutable truth.

But Stinky ignored it and ignored him and instead directed all his attention, and his petulant rage, at Jocasta. "We need that shot, Jocasta. We need that crow to look into the camera."

"If we could take him out of the bag and if someone could hold him…"

"No one is holding him, or handling him," said Patrik with such equable firmness that my regard for him shot up. He wasn't letting anyone mess with his crow. "If you can't get your shot, then I'm afraid you can't get your shot."

"But he won't cooperate," said Stinky, pointing an accusing finger at Hiram but only after first waving his tensely clenched fist at the crow for some considerable time. Hiram watched all this with cool, alert interest.

"If he won't cooperate, he won't cooperate," said Patrik.

"Can't you do something?" said Stinky. I realised that he was probably as close to tears as Jocasta.

Patrik shrugged a debonair continental shrug. "What can I do? He is a free agent. If for whatever reason you have failed to elicit his creative cooperation then I'm afraid you're not going to get the shot you want."

"Fucking stupid crow," said Stinky.

"I warned you that he can hear you. And he is not stupid. He is far from stupid. Corvids are extremely intelligent."

"Evidently," said Nevada. I could see that, on the basis of this brief acquaintance, Hiram had already become her favourite crow.

"We've got to get this shot," said Stinky, edging a little closer towards tantrum.

Agatha and Nevada and I made our excuses and left, not least because when Stinky eventually blew he was bound to take it out on Jocasta, and we couldn't stomach seeing that.

We went out into the hallway and closed the door of Patrik's room behind us. If nothing else, the experience had left us with warm memories of Stinky Stanmer being driven to despair by a feisty corvid. Before I could remark along these lines, my phone rang. It was Owyn Wynter.

"There was one other thing I wanted to say to you," he said. "It's fairly important."

"Okay," I said.

"I understand that all the members of the Troopers have now converged on Trollesko."

"Yes," I said. "That's right."

"In fact, they're staying in the same hotel as you."

"That's right."

"Okay, so I don't want you to take this the wrong way, because they are all nice people. Rut and Gun and Oskar and Patrik. All very nice, fine people. Individually. And in various combinations. However…"

"However?"

"When they are all together, all four of them together in the same place at the same time, be careful."

"Be careful," I said.

"Yes. Individually they are fine, they are nice people. But when they come together as a unit, they can be… dangerous. So, watch out. Just watch out. Look, I've got to go. Please don't take anything I've said the wrong way."

"The wrong way?" I said. But he was already gone. What the hell was the *right* way to take something like that? I told Nevada and Agatha what he'd said. To our surprise, this seemed to confirm something to Agatha. "I have this theory…" she said.

Just then the door of the lounge opened and Oskar stood there smiling blandly at us. "Are you coming in?" We looked at each other. There was nothing for it. Agatha and Nevada and I filed obediently into the lounge. Rut and Gun were sitting on the sofa, both dolled up and dressed immaculately within the terms of the band's usual sensibility. Which embraced a lot of black and a lot of leather.

In front of them, on a tripod set squarely at the centre of a small red rug, a camera peered in their direction. On another tripod there was a microphone positioned to hang above the sisters' heads, high enough to be out of shot.

Oskar smiled at us and then hurried to peer through the camera. "Okay, you bewitching temptress, whenever you are ready." Gun nodded and assumed a serious expression that Stinky Stanmer would have been proud of and started talking, directly into the camera.

"Obviously these murders are a tragedy," she said. "But many people will want more context on this tragedy. Indeed, *need* more context. To help them to understand. To grieve, to move on, but above all to understand."

"Okay, pause there," said Oskar, looking up from the camera. "This is where we will insert a graphic of *Attack and Decay*." He grinned at me. "We'll use a shot of the album cover. Of the record we will buy from you. Vinyl cred!" He turned back to Gun. "Now, you enchantress, whenever you are ready. Pick up from where you left off."

Gun resumed talking. "To get a better understanding, you should definitely get a copy of the album that the killer seems—and I stress, nothing is for certain here, but it *appears* the killer might be somehow responding to at least some of the songs on our highly regarded album *Attack and Decay*. You should pick up a copy right now, available on vinyl in all good record stores and also in a limited edition digipack CD—which is also available free with every copy of the vinyl. Downloads are available as well, of course. Exclusively at the band's home page. As I say, a highly regarded collection of songs that really will help you with valuable context for the thing that is going on here in Trollesko." Gun paused here

THE VINYL DETECTIVE

to look even more serious than before. "The terrible human tragedy that appears to be unfolding here."

"Great," said Oskar. "That is absolutely marvellous." He turned to me. "We don't actually have any LPs for sale, yet. Or indeed even CDs. But we've placed orders at the pressing plants."

"The downloads are ready to go," said Gun.

"Yes, and they are selling like hot cakes," said Oskar cheerfully. "Now, Rut. It is your turn, my darling." He adjusted the angle of the camera slightly and then waved his hand in a flamboyant starting signal.

Rut leaned forward and smiled. When she smiled she had a very pleasant face. She said, in the usual perfect English, "My name is Rut Gylling. I just wanted to add that my autobiography *Rut Me* is now available." She held up a book.

On the cover, she was younger and wearing only what appeared to be a modest number of bondage accoutrements and an intriguing selection of tattoos. Gun leaned in so her head was beside Rut's and she abandoned her serious face now to smile, too. A rather impish smile, or as impish as the cosmetic surgery still allowed.

She said, "If I wasn't her sister and it wouldn't be sort of weird, I would tell you that this book of hers is *really hot*."

"And with every copy you get a free download of our *new* album," said Rut.

Big smiles from both sisters. As Oskar stopped filming and declared himself more than satisfied, in the most florid terms, Agatha and Nevada and I made our excuses and got the hell out of the lounge.

To make sure we couldn't be overheard, we then went into our room and finished our conversation with Agatha behind a closed door. "Tell us about your theory," said Nevada.

"Well, when I heard Owyn Wynter had said that…"

"That the Troopers are dangerous when they're together?"

"Yes," said Agatha. She looked at me. "That is what he said, isn't it?"

"Yes," I said. "He told us to watch out."

Agatha bit her lip. "Well, I have this theory about them. I've started checking and it looks as though none of them could be responsible for the murders…"

"Okay," said Nevada.

"But when I say none of them, I mean no *one* of them could be responsible. If we look at any of the four and try and match them against the murder, inevitably each one is in the wrong place at the wrong time for one of them. But…"

"But?" I said.

"But the four of them working together, taking turns, could have done all the killings."

25: RED HALO

I slept badly that night. Theoretically everything was going swimmingly for us. For all of us—Tinkler and his mad stripper romance included. The juicer had been retrieved, our deal had gone through, and we had been paid in full…

I should have been jubilant.

But all I felt was a growing sense of dread. Lying in a creepy old hotel in a country far from home, you might say this was to be expected. Mere insecurity and homesickness. Yet I felt entirely at home in the creepy old hotel, and very much welcome and at home in Sweden generally.

No, the seeds of dread were sprouting elsewhere. And, in my head at least, were spreading fast.

The next morning I resolved to talk to Nevada about this. We breakfasted late—in the breakfast room at the hotel, which was mercifully Stinky-free. There was also no sign of Jocasta. Perhaps they were both still in exhausted oblivious slumber after their harrowing ordeal trying to film Hiram.

Tinkler ambled in to join us. "There you are," he said.

"There *you* are," said Nevada. "We've lost track of when you're at the hotel and when you're staying inside Ida's tower. So to speak."

"Oh man," said Tinkler, "being inside Ida's tower is so nice."

"We don't want to hear about it."

"It's just a bit drafty. She likes to keep the doors open."

"Oh, okay," said Nevada. "Maybe we *can* hear about it."

"You were interpreting her tower as a sort of sexual reference?" said Tinkler.

"I'm not entirely sure," said Nevada. "I somewhat lost track. Stupid smutty innuendo really is more your line."

"Damned right."

"Anyway," said Nevada. "It's a pleasant surprise to see you, which isn't something we can often say about you, Tinkler."

"No, ma'am," said Tinkler. He went up to the buffet table and rejoined us, heavily laden, and started shovelling down food.

"I thought you were replacing fat with muscle, Tinkler," said Nevada.

"To achieve that one first needs fat," said Tinkler. Polishing off his fried eggs, he wiped up the spilled yolk with a fragment of sweet pastry in true Tinkler fashion. It was a rather enticing pastry, I had to concede—soft, golden and topped with apricots, dusted sugar and crushed almonds. And now a fair quantity of egg yolk.

"I don't think you're in danger of running out," said Nevada. "Of fat, I mean."

"I got it."

Agatha joined us even later than Tinkler, bringing her plate of food over to the table where we were now lingering over our coffee. Seeing Agatha's selection of bounty caused Tinkler to go scurrying back for more for himself.

"So, are you going to tell us what your mysterious errand was?" said Nevada.

"Who said I was on a mysterious errand?" said Agatha, neatly slicing the top off a hardboiled egg. "Oh, all right. I was. I was eavesdropping. On Oskar and Patrik."

"Eavesdropping?" said Nevada. "Do you realise how dangerous that can be?"

"It's all right. If I sneak out of my room to a certain spot in the hallway, I can hear what someone is saying in the lounge and they can't see me."

"I repeat, dangerous. Your own theory is that these two guys are half of a…"

"Murder squad," I supplied. It was a relief to finally name and pin down one scenario of the many that swirled around me in a generalised cloud of dread. A cloud of dread that indeed I had resolved to discuss with my beloved this very morning at this very table. And apparently now with additional input from our beloved friends.

"Half of a murder squad," agreed Nevada.

"A music-making murder squad," said Tinkler.

Nevada refused to be amused. She ignored him and continued to address Agatha. "Did it not cross your mind that it might be dangerous if these guys found you eavesdropping on them?"

"I'm sorry," said Agatha. "I knew you wouldn't approve. But I was pretty sure I could pull it off. And I did. I got away with it."

"Well, for Christ's sake don't make a habit of it," said Nevada. "So, what did you learn?"

"Okay, so yesterday when I was watching Stinky trying to film Hiram—"

"You mean watching Hiram refuse to be filmed by Stinky."

"Yes," said Agatha. "To be honest I couldn't get enough of that. My only regret was that you guys weren't there to see it. And then you turned up! Anyway, it went on for quite a while before you got there, and Patrik and I fell to chatting with each other while we watched Stinky and Jocasta fail to film Hiram."

"I really do love that crow," said Nevada.

"I know. So do I. And he's also showing great good taste. Because apparently he's not usually camera shy."

Indeed, and this is where I really began to pay attention, Hiram had collaborated with them on a film project. With Oskar and Patrick. "He said they made a music video together, the three of them. He spoke of Hiram like he was an equal. Like they were three equal partners, the crow included."

"I think that's rather sweet of him," said Nevada. "I like the way he treats Hiram like a person."

"Just so long as he doesn't start talking about fucking trolls again," said Agatha. "Anyway, Patrik said, far from being camera shy with them, he not only cooperated flawlessly when being filmed, they'd also actually got Hiram to *wear* a camera for them. To fly around wearing a camera. So they could get these amazing sweeping shots, this vista of landscape passing below Hiram. Which they could then process in intense unreal colours."

"Cool," said Tinkler.

"Of course you think it's cool. You're always stoned."

"So are most of the people watching music videos."

"You may well be right," said Agatha. "I defer to your superior knowledge in this instance. In this one instance. But the point is, this music video they shot using Hiram turned out so well that they started using him to do all sorts of aerial photography. He became highly proficient. And then they devised a way of telling him *where* to fly, so they could guide the camera."

"Okay," said Tinkler. "So, we're talking about a remote-controlled crow."

"Yes. They added this little device to Hiram's camera rig. It emits a noise. Four noises, actually. One indicates that Hiram should fly to the left, another to the right…"

"And the others are for up and down," said Nevada.

"Right. Apparently, with just these four sounds played at different volumes, Hiram learned to be steered with a remarkable degree of accuracy. Although Patrik would object strongly to the word *steered*."

"Of course he would," I said.

"I knew all that," said Agatha, "before I even did my eavesdropping this morning. What I learned that's new to me—though it shouldn't have been, I should have put two and two together—was that *they're* the people who got the shots of poor Christer Vingqvist and put them online. Of his body at the crime scene. Patrik and Oskar. And I suppose we have to include Hiram too. They couldn't have done it without him…"

"Holy shit," said Tinkler.

I said, "Kriminalinspektör Lizell said she thought someone took those pictures using a drone."

"It wasn't a drone," said Agatha. "It was a crow."

"A crow-drone," said Tinkler. "A 'crone', if you will."

"We won't," said Nevada. "Thank you all the same. So, Hiram flew over the crime scene and they got a picture of the mutilated body and then put it online?"

"Yes," said Agatha.

"Why?" said Tinkler. "To drum up publicity?"

I nodded. "After all, it is a murder based on their song. The Troopers want to stage a major comeback. And publicity like this is priceless."

Nevada was deep in thought. Now she looked at Agatha. "Your theory is that the Troopers, working together, did the killings?"

"Yes," said Agatha. Then she suddenly paused. "Oh shit…"

"What's wrong?" said Tinkler.

I said, "Ms Warren is just implying to Ms Dubois-Kanes that if the Troopers are indeed the killers, they wouldn't need to be resorting to crow drones to get pictures of the crime scene."

"Because if they'd actually been there, committing that atrocity," said Nevada, "they would have had plenty of opportunities to photograph the whole grisly smorgasbord."

"Maybe they just forgot," said Tinkler. "And then afterwards they were like, *Damn, we should have got some pictures…*"

It was perhaps squalid and sordid of us, but we all laughed at this.

Although Nevada and Agatha had already rampaged all over the district, I had yet to visit the second of Trollesko's secondhand-butiks, or rather, *secondhand-butiker*. The one I had already been to—the yellow and white building that Agatha had dubbed the inside-out egg—was about ten minutes' walk from the Notre Coeur Café, near the bridge at the edge of the shopping district. The other was further in the same direction, just over the bridge, in the industrial area near the docks.

That was where we headed after breakfast, strolling over the river by means of the big white bridge, then down the steps to the paved footpath and mercifully away from the road traffic.

This secondhand-butik was quite different from the inside-out egg. It was more grubby, rough-and-ready, and was housed in what had once been some sort of school or civic centre. Most of the interesting stuff—in other words, records and clothes—was spread out in a former gymnasium.

"This one is more like a *loppmarknad*, a flea market," said Nevada knowledgably as she arrowed towards the vintage clothing.

Our morning was well spent searching through this place. I found a terrific late-period Chet Baker album on the Artists House label, complete with the booklet.

And Nevada purchased an impressive selection of hats.

It was fun and satisfying. But the whole time at the back of my mind, like the sound of a smoke alarm going off in the house next door, walled off but still maddeningly audible, was a nagging warning signal.

I couldn't forget the fact that someone had tried to kill us.

Or forget about those songs that were still in rotation.

I just wanted to collect the record from Magnus, complete our mission and get the hell out of Trollesko, as lovely as it was.

Which is why I felt such a great sense of relief as we left the secondhand-butik and walked back towards the river, glittering grey-green in the winter sunlight. Rising up on the other side of the water, we could see the apartment building where Magnus and Emma lived.

It was a sleek rectangle of glass lying across six cylindrical columns like stubby fat legs. The columns, seen from a distance, were pink. But when you got close, you could see that they were inlaid with tiny tiles, red and white rectangles alternating across their considerable surface.

The area between the columns, in the shadow of the building's underbelly, served as its car park. It was reassuring to see both the Union Jack Mini and Obi Van Kenobi sheltering here. At least someone was at home.

In the centre of the car park was a glass cubicle containing a staircase and an elevator leading up into the building. The glass door of this cubicle was locked, but we pushed the button for Magnus and Emma's flat and were immediately buzzed in.

We took the elevator up to the penthouse.

Nevada hadn't been here before, and I could see that she was impressed; the floor-to-ceiling windows and gleaming parquet flooring began as soon as we stepped out of the lift. The door to the penthouse was at the end of the short corridor, full of sunlight. It was open.

Magnus called from inside. "In here." His voice sounded strange.

We stepped into the flat and the first thing we saw was Emma lying unmoving on the floor. Her eyes were shut and her face was that of a child in sickly sleep. Her skin was as white as the deep white rug on which she lay sprawled. Spread out around her head was a puddle of blood, a red halo.

She was wearing her coat with the words *Nice and Safe Attitude* on it.

Standing beyond her, by the floor-to-ceiling window with its panoramic view of the glittering river, was Magnus. He was holding a phone, staring at us. "I thought you were the paramedics," he said.

"What happened to her?" said Nevada.

Magnus was now avoiding our gaze. "I don't know. I found her like this. I have called for the police and called for an ambulance. I thought you were them." He suddenly looked at me. "You came for your record. If you don't want to be involved in this, just take it and leave."

We took it and left, just as the ambulance was pulling in.

"I'm sorry about your friend," said Kriminalinspektör Eva Lizell.

"So am I," I said. "How is she?"

"She remains in critical condition. The doctors are doing everything they can." She paused. "What are you looking at behind me?"

"The sofa's free now."

We were in Notre Coeur and, for once, our table had been taken when we arrived. But the middle-aged couple and young child who'd so inconsiderately occupied it were now rising to leave, gathering up their shopping.

"You want to move to your favourite spot?" said Eva Lizell sardonically. But she followed me with commendable alacrity, gathering her up own belongings and coffee and transferring them to the other table. I sensed, sarcastic or not, it was her favourite spot, too.

As she seated herself, I was gazing out on the little courtyard and thinking of the scissor beak crow. Had Hiram been wearing a camera that day?

Eva Lizell took a sip of her coffee then put it aside. Down to business. "I asked if you could meet me, because I wanted to ask you a question."

My threat level went up to high. "Okay," I said.

"Was Emma Fernholm with you and your friends that day you went to the striptease club and discovered the explosive device?"

I started to deny that we'd ever been there—the official story was that it had all been Ida on her own. But then I just gave up. "No," I said. "She stayed here in Trollesko."

At the time I'd thought she'd been very sensible. But much good it did her. I saw once more the red halo, the milk-white sickly-child's face.

"I see," said Eva Lizell.

"Why do you ask?" I said.

I didn't expect her to tell me. But she said, "I thought someone might have attacked her for the same reason they shot at you." I noticed that our being shot at was no longer in question.

"And what was that reason?" I said.

"I was considering that it might be revenge."

"Revenge?" What had we ever done to anyone?

"For finding that device before it went off. You ruined someone's meticulous plan to destroy the striptease club. But since Emma wasn't with you when you found it, my revenge theory is clearly wrong. In any case, it doesn't seem that what happened to her is connected with the other crimes."

"Why?" I said. "Because she's still alive?" If Emma wasn't dead, it wasn't for lack of someone trying.

"No," said Eva Lizell. "And she may yet die."

I winced. "Sorry," she said. "But this was another reason I wanted to speak to you." She took out her phone and showed me a picture. It was an irregular yet somehow elegant lump of crystal, photographed against a black background with a white ruler beside it.

I leaned close, trying to read the markings on the ruler.

"It's about the size of your fist," said Eva Lizell. "It's made of what we call ice glass. Possibly manufactured by

Iittala in the 1970s. It's a paperweight. Miss Fernholm was hit on the head with this, repeatedly." I winced again but she didn't apologise this time. "Can you think of any songs on the album that might be associated with an object like this, or behaviour like that?"

I considered carefully. "No," I said, finally. "Not really."

"No. Neither can I." She switched off her phone.

I ran through the songs in my mind again. 'Fire', 'Active Shooter', 'Candle in the Wind'…

"Hang on," I said.

"What?"

"Do you have a photograph of the other side?"

"Of the paperweight?" she said. She'd switched the phone back on and was shuffling through pictures. "Here," she said.

The other side of the lump of the crystal looked much the same—except it had a shallow cylindrical hole bored in it.

"It's not a paperweight," I said. "It's a candle holder."

26: TAVERNA

The next morning Nevada and I found ourselves in the hotel breakfast room once more, staring at the usual generous spread of high quality food, but quite without appetite. Memories of Emma were still too raw.

We were about to sit down and just have coffee. But then we realised if we were going to just have coffee, we might as well have the best in town... "Notre Coeur?" I said.

"Right," said Nevada. We fetched our coats and left the hotel, texting Agatha and Tinkler and Ida to meet us there.

We got to the café before the others and indulged a long-cherished whim to sit out in the tiny courtyard, on that little pink two-seater bench with the love heart carved in it.

The bench creaked under our weight as Nevada and I settled into it, after brushing off the snow. Following a fresh fall last night, it lay heavy on the flagstones and thickly coated the little marble table that stood by the bench, like white icing on a dark cake.

We'd hardly sat down when Tinkler and Ida joined us.

It was good to see them. They were a lot less subdued than we were. Indeed, they were clearly enjoying each other's company. But then they hadn't seen Emma lying there like a child, deeply asleep and very ill, bloody halo on the thick white rug. And I was dismayed to find that I rather resented them having been spared that sight.

We got up and let Tinkler and Ida try the little lovers' bench—it creaked rather more under Tinkler and Ida's weight (chiefly Tinkler's, it has to be said) than it had under ours—and then we all went inside the café to our usual table. As we were sitting down, my phone rang. It was Eva Lizell. I showed Nevada. Her eyebrows went up and she made a show of moving closer to Tinkler and Ida so I could take the call in relative privacy.

If I'd wanted real privacy I would have gone back out into the courtyard, but I had no intention of doing that.

"I would like to check some details with you," said Eva Lizell. "If that's all right."

"Of course," I said.

"Several people have reported that Emma and her husband Magnus had at least one very heated argument in public."

I suspected that those "several people" were all actually a single Anders. But I simply said, "Yes."

"You have heard this was the case?"

"More than that, I actually witnessed one of those arguments." Was it only one? It seemed in retrospect that the couple's bickering had been habitual.

"And yet, you seem sure Magnus is not the one who assaulted Emma?" Tried to smash her head in, she didn't say. With a paperweight that turned out to be a candle holder, she didn't add –perhaps a somewhat tenuous connection with the song in question, but clearly sufficient.

"I didn't say that," I said.

"You didn't need to," she said. "That was obviously your attitude."

"Well, it's true," I said. "I don't believe Magnus did it."

"Why not?"

I thought of the luxurious deep white pile rug, Emma with her crimson nimbus vivid around her head. I hesitated. "This will sound silly."

"So what?" said the Kriminalinspektör.

"Well, Magnus is very proud of his new flat. It's so beautiful and clean and shiny... If he had been going to... *hurt* Emma, I don't think he would have done it in a way that would have ruined his rug."

"Okay." She sounded amused. "Interesting. Thank you." She hung up and I put my phone away.

Ida said, "So you are getting phone calls from Kriminalinspektör Lizell?"

"Yes," I said.

Ida chuckled. "Why is that funny?" I said.

"I'll let Jordon tell you while I go to the toilet." Ida got up and left the table. I looked expectantly at Tinkler. He smiled.

"Ida has this theory about you and the lesbian cop," he said. "It's rather sweet really."

"Is it?" I said.

"Basically, what it boils down to is, she's wondering, should Nevada be jealous?"

"Hmm," said Nevada. "*Should* Nevada be jealous?"

"Of me talking to the Kriminalinspektör?" I said.

"Yes," said Tinkler. "When you did so just now, did you find that it 'certainly wasn't unpleasant'? Because, if so, you're definitely in the danger zone."

"Speaking of danger," said Nevada. "We've been wanting to have a little talk."

"A little talk with who," said Tinkler. "Or do I mean 'whom'?"

"With all of us," said Nevada, "including Ms DuBois-Kanes." We looked up to see Agatha approaching the table. She was smiling like she had something to tell us. But she didn't get a chance to because, as Nevada had said, it was time for a talk.

"I was waiting for all of us to be together," said Nevada.

"What about Ida?" said Tinkler.

"It helps that she's in the loo," said Nevada.

"This doesn't sound good," said Tinkler.

"Just listen, Tinkler," said Agatha. And he shut up.

"Okay," said Nevada, "so we came here to get a rare piece of vinyl…"

"And to see beautiful Sweden," said Tinkler. He hadn't shut up for long.

"That, also, absolutely," said Nevada. "But now we've got the rare piece of vinyl. And things have become rather dangerous for us here in beautiful Sweden."

"I noticed," said Tinkler. "They were shooting at me, too."

"In fact, you more than the rest of us," said Agatha.

"That's right," said Tinkler.

"Because you kept standing up."

"That's right," said Tinkler.

"So we're going to get out of here," said Nevada.

"Of course," said Tinkler.

"Good. We'll leave tomorrow."

"*What?*" Tinkler looked up from the generous slab of chocolate cake, with a dollop of sour cream and a dusting of cinnamon, that until now had been receiving at least half of his attention. "We're booked here until next week."

"I know, Tinkler, sorry. But a booking isn't worth dying for."

"What about Ida?"

"Ida isn't worth dying for," said Nevada. But she said it gently. "Tinkler, this place is getting very dangerous."

I said, "We want to get out of here before they try to do 'Active Shooter' again."

"Shit," said Tinkler. He morosely speared a piece of chocolate cake with his fork. "I hate this whole fucking murders-based-on-songs business."

"Amen to that," said Agatha.

"It's just so creepy."

"It is."

"So we're going tomorrow, Tinkler, right?"

"I don't know. Ida…" He looked off in the direction Ida had disappeared in. The toilets were on the other side of the café, just past the service desk. There was no sign of her. Nevada followed his gaze and politely cleared her throat. But he kept staring in that direction. So, she spoke to the back of his head.

"We want you with us, Tinkler. It's not safe for you here."

"Well, maybe it's not safe for Ida." He stopped looking for her and turned to us again.

"We have no reason to think that," said Agatha.

"No reason to think that?"

"We don't think anybody wants her dead," said Agatha. "Not the way they clearly want *us* dead. For example, she wasn't with us when they were shooting at us."

"What are you trying to say?"

"We're not trying to say anything," said Agatha. "She wasn't with us when someone was shooting at us. It's a fact."

"So what?" said Tinkler. He seemed to be getting genuinely angry at Agatha, an emotional scenario I'd never witnessed before. Or even envisioned. Judging by her rapt attention, neither had Nevada. "It was *her* strip club that was going to be blown up," said Tinkler. "Someone was going to firebomb the place where *she* works."

"At a time when *she* wasn't on shift," said Agatha.

"How do you know that?" said Tinkler.

"Look," said Nevada. "We're going back to London tomorrow, Tinkler, and we want you with us."

"Please come with us, Tinkler," I said.

His anger—a rare Tinkler phenomenon—faded away and he sighed. "Maybe Ida will come with me. She'd like London. And stripping is a transferable skill."

"Here she is now," said Agatha. Ida was making her way back to our table. She smiled at us as she sat down. If she was aware we'd been talking about her, she gave no indication.

"Hello Agatha," said Ida. "You look even more slender and gorgeous than usual."

"I haven't been sleeping."

"Oh, I'm sorry," said Ida. "Post-traumatic stress?"

"Sort of," said Agatha. "Manifesting as bad dreams about Christer Vingqvist's severed head."

"Oh dear," said Ida.

"It opens its eyes and talks."

"Good heavens."

Agatha smiled. It was a tight smile. "It keeps asking me if I've read his book."

"It could be worse," said Tinkler. "He could be asking what you thought of it."

On the way back to the hotel we took a detour through the park, which looked freshly beautiful in the new snow. As we strolled towards the bandstand a familiar figure came into view. Two familiar figures, Oskar and Gun. It was a continuing relief, though perversely also a bit of a disappointment, that Oskar hadn't braved the cold weather wearing his kilt.

In fact, he was dressed relatively normally, in jeans, heavy boots and a sheepskin coat. Though the sheepskin coat did have some wacky patterns of multicoloured beads on it. Gun wore a matching coat and boots, but also a black miniskirt and stockings. Which made Oskar seem even more of a wimp for chickening out with his kilt.

They were standing in front of the bandstand as we

approached. Oskar smiled then assumed a sober expression. "We're sorry about your friend."

"Her condition has stabilised," said Nevada, "but she's still critical."

Gun shook her head. "It was terrible what happened. The poor girl."

"Have they arrested Magnus yet?" said Oskar.

"Magnus didn't do it," I said.

Oskar and Gun looked at each other. "You seem pretty sure of that," she said.

"I am pretty sure of that."

"Who do you think is responsible, then?" said Oskar.

"I have no idea," I said. I was being polite. I certainly had at least one idea. Or rather, Agatha had—and it involved these two...

Plus Patrik and Rut—"A pair of murder couples," as Agatha put it—working together in a highly organised homicidal cooperative. But I didn't feel the need to go into that.

Luckily, Gun changed the subject. "We are thinking about doing a concert," she said.

"Maybe not a full concert," said Oskar.

"A gig," said Gun.

"Yes, certainly a gig."

"You and the rest of the Troopers?" I said.

"Yes," said Oskar. "You were right about the band getting back together."

"And we're thinking of playing our first gig here." Gun nodded at the bandstand.

"We need to get clearance from the local authorities of course," said Patrik. "But we are very hopeful. And all proceeds will go to charity. Of course."

"Of course."

As part of our new policy of keeping a low profile until we left town, Nevada and I spent the afternoon in our hotel room quietly reading while the sunlight faded in the high windows. Then, when night fell, we yawned and stretched, very much like the cats we were missing, and put our books aside with our places carefully noted to resume reading later, very much not like the cats we were missing. Then we bundled up in our warm clothes and went out walking in the winter darkness.

In search of supper.

For our evening meals we'd narrowed our options down to the good old Notre Coeur, where they served an excellent selection of quiches, savoury tarts and salads, or a little Greek taverna nearby where, in addition to admirable Hellenic dishes, they also had some terrific pizzas.

That was where we headed tonight, collecting Agatha from her room and walking together across the dark snowy park, past the vattentorn. Ida and Tinkler had already gone ahead to the taverna.

"They went early?" said Agatha.

"Couldn't wait," I said. "Tinkler is a hungry chow hound at the best of times."

"But now he's what… also worked up an appetite?"

said Agatha. She mimed a shudder. "That doesn't bear thinking about."

"It certainly doesn't," said Nevada loyally.

Personally, I wished the lovers well, atop their snowy tower above this small town in their winter's idyll, working up an appetite.

An appetite they were quelling with garlic bread as we arrived. They waved to us from their table in the back room as we came through the steamed-up glass door, out of the snowy streets into the warmth and cooking smells.

The taverna was a bustling, friendly place. The front room had white and blue tiled walls and a red tiled floor, with white wooden picnic tables and benches situated in front of a serving area dispensing takeaway food.

Theoretically you could sit and eat a meal here, but the plentiful tiles guaranteed that it was too noisy for conversation—perhaps a deliberate move to encourage a quick turnover—*collect your takeaway and off with you*.

But the back room, where Tinkler and Ida were installed with their garlic bread, was much more inviting. It had wooden walls painted blue and soft furnishings: old-fashioned velvet armchairs around small spindly Victorian wooden tables with blue-and-white-check tablecloths. Tinkler and Ida were well established at the largest of these, both in armchairs, with one more armchair and two wooden dining chairs squeezed around the table.

"We thoughtfully provided seating for you," said Tinkler as we came in.

"So we see," said Nevada, taking one of the wooden

chairs. I took the other one and Agatha settled into the armchair.

"We also took the liberty of ordering for you," said Tinkler.

"Wait until you see how quickly the pizzas sell out here," said Ida.

The pizzas in question arrived at the table soon after we did. We divided up the spoils, having trouble finding sufficient room on our small table for all this food.

"It could be warmer," said Agatha, munching on a triangular slice of seafood pizza.

"It's because it's travelled such a long way from the kitchen," said Ida.

Nevada gave a muffled snort—an unmuffled one while devouring pizza might have been deemed unladylike. "Right. A long way."

"About five metres," said Agatha.

Ida looked at Tinkler. "Should I tell them?" He nodded and Ida smiled and said, "The pizzas they serve here come from the strip club."

"What?" said Nevada. "Seriously?"

"Yes. They just place a large takeaway order every evening and send a kid on a moped—we call it a *moppe*—to go out to get them. The poor kid, there's hardly room for him on his moppe with all those pizzas. But they're too cheap to send a car. And then he brings them back here and they resell them."

Agatha was staring at her. In fact, we all were, except Tinkler, who'd obviously already been briefed on this. I was reflecting, with the benefit of hindsight, that the pizzas did indeed look familiar. "You're kidding," said Agatha.

"No. It allows the good people of the town to enjoy the excellent food from the sinful and abhorrent place where I work without feeling they are directly partaking of the sin and abhorrence of that place. The pizzas have been decontaminated, so to speak, by being resold through this restaurant."

"Plus the price has gone up," said Nevada. "Considerably."

"I'm considering writing a paper on the topic," said Ida.

"On the pricing?"

"No."

"The moral decontamination of the strip club pizzas for the good people of the town?" suggested Agatha.

"Yes," said Ida.

"I thought you were writing a paper about the crow as mythopoeic harbinger," said Agatha.

Ida nodded. "I was indeed. But I abandoned that notion. Do you know why?"

"No," said Nevada. "Tell us why, Ida."

"To be completely honest, and I like it when people are completely honest, and I try to be completely honest myself, so I will be completely honest with you now and tell you that I gave up the notion of writing that paper because it scared me."

"Scared you?" I said.

"The notion of writing the paper scared you?" said Agatha.

"No. That *crow* scared me," said Ida. "And I know this

is terribly insensitive of me, but Hiram gives me the creeps. I understand this is a terrible character defect in myself to feel that way." She looked into my eyes, as if for corroboration of this character failing.

I said, "I once would have said the same myself. But no more. You just need to see him making a film with Stinky Stanmer."

"That's right," said Agatha. "It would transform your view of Hiram."

"You'd be amazed how quickly you can fall in love with a crow," said Nevada. Tinkler summarised for Ida the redoubtable corvid's antics with Stinky and Jocasta.

Then crow talk ceased and we all ate in contented silence for a while. Finally Nevada spoke up.

"So are you going to tell us?" she said, looking at Agatha.

"What?" said Agatha.

"You've been itching to tell us something all day." I'd been aware of this too, ever since we'd seen her at the café.

"Okay," said Agatha. She smiled and leaned forward, and we all leaned with her, our heads coming together in a conspiratorial cluster. "All right," she said. "So, I've been continuing my surveillance campaign on Oskar and Patrik…"

"By which you mean standing in the hallway listening to them?" said Tinkler.

"Don't spoil the magic," said Agatha.

"It won't be very magical if they catch you," said Nevada. "I thought I told you not to do that again."

"You told me not to make a *habit* of it. And I won't. It was just this one last time."

But Nevada wasn't buying this. She was shaking her head. "This is a genuinely worrying tendency," she said.

"What is?" said Agatha.

"Risk-taking that doesn't involve driving at very high speeds," said Nevada. "Something at which, might I say, you're supremely proficient. But you're not supremely proficient at this. Eavesdropping on dangerous people. Maybe not proficient at all."

"Proficient enough to have learned something."

"I am serious about this, Agatha," said Nevada. "If you're not behind the wheel of a car, I don't want you taking big chances. Life-risking chances."

Agatha smiled a Cheshire Cat smile. "Does this mean you're not interested in hearing what I found out?"

"No. Of course we're *very* interested in hearing what you found out."

27: COMB-OVER BASTARD

What Agatha had found out included something she didn't think Ida would like. "But it's what I've heard, and she needs to hear it, too…"

"Why may I not like it?" said Ida.

"Because it involves Hiram," said Agatha.

"Oh, I won't mind that," said Ida. "Now that I know how this crow behaved towards Stinky Stanmer, I do indeed view him in a more favourable light. Jordon was right about how obnoxious he is, the fucker. Stinky Stanmer, I mean."

"Hear, hear," said Nevada.

"Okay," said Agatha, "so Oskar and Patrik spend a lot of time in the upstairs lounge at the hotel drinking champagne and waiting for everybody's favourite crow to come back from his filming missions."

"The crow drone," said Tinkler. "Or 'crone' if you will."

"Nobody's buying it, Tinkler," said Nevada.

"Sometimes," said Agatha, "they follow Hiram's progress on a laptop. But a lot of the time they wait until he comes back to see what he's got—the camera rig transmits but it also records onto a memory card. You will see the significance of that in a moment. Anyway, when they're not looking at the laptop, Oskar and Patrik drink champagne and reminisce about Hiram, boasting about their accomplishments and the way they can steer him—they never call it that, their preferred term is 'guide'—so he will film whatever they want. But Hiram, it seems, has a mind of his own."

"Of course he does," said Nevada, who was now solidly a big fan of this bird.

"So sometimes he gets fed up with filming and he removes the rig."

"What, he takes off the camera?"

"Yes," said Agatha.

"He just… removes it in mid-air?" said Nevada. "And it drops to the ground?" I could see her wincing at the expense this would incur. Not to mention the inconvenience.

"No, he always lands first and takes it off and carefully places it somewhere for retrieval later."

"Smart crow."

"And Patrik goes out and finds the camera and brings it back."

"Does it have a GPS tracker in it?"

"Quite possibly," said Agatha. "But they don't need that."

"Why not?" said Nevada, and then answered her own question. "Because the camera keeps filming."

"Right. The camera doesn't switch off when Hiram ditches it. It's possible to work backwards, to review the transmitted footage and work out where he left it." Agatha could no longer repress a triumphant smile. "Anyway, he did it again."

"Ditched the camera?" said Nevada.

"Yes. This morning."

"Where?"

Agatha turned to Ida. "In your tower."

This startled Ida considerably. "What?"

"He left it in the window outside your flat." I recalled the slit in the stone wall of the tower. The high narrow window that afforded a bird's-eye view, ironically enough, of the fair municipality of Trollesko spread below. Ida was frowning at this information.

"That crow has been there," she said, "outside my flat?"

"Right."

"When?"

"Apparently a number of times. He likes it there."

"He *likes* it there?" said Ida. It was clear that Hiram hadn't been entirely rehabilitated in her view, despite his behaviour with Stinky.

"Yes," said Agatha. "He likes perching there and looking down at the town, according to Patrik and Oskar. He does it mostly at night."

"At night?" said Ida. "So, when I'm asleep that creepy crow is hanging around outside my flat?"

"Afraid so."

"Thank god Jordon is there to protect me."

"Well, I think we'll just let that pass without comment," said Nevada.

"And get back to Hiram in that window," said Agatha. "Apparently this is the second time he's left the camera there. The last time it happened, Patrik traced the location and retrieved it."

"What do you mean retrieved it?" said Ida. "He was in the vattentorn?"

"Yes."

"How did he get in? Did Anders let him in?"

"No," said Agatha. "That's why you need to know about it. He went up the fire escape and in through your flat."

"He went in through my flat? He went into my place?"

"Yes. Sorry to give you the bad news. Apparently, you left the door open."

Ida was cursing swiftly in Swedish. She caught herself and switched back to English in deference to us. "He's been in my flat? Patrik broke into my flat?"

"Technically," said Nevada, "breaking in would entail the door being locked."

But Ida wasn't interested in technicalities. She was furious. "Wait. Which one is Patrik? Is he the one with the kilt? Or the one with the *överkamning*—the comb-over?"

"The comb-over."

"Fucking bastard. Fucking comb-over bastard has been in my flat."

"Fucking comb-over bastard," said Tinkler, as though offering a response in church. A lively evangelical church. With a liberal policy on swearing.

The last time I'd seen Ida so angry was when Bo Lugn

had been making off with a certain appliance that dare not speak its name.

"How did he know I wouldn't be at home," said Ida, "when he went through my flat?"

"The same way that I found out," said Agatha. She looked at Tinkler. "It's easy to know when Ida's working. Just check her schedule on the strip club website."

"Fucking comb-over bastard. That schedule isn't always accurate."

"I guess it was this time, though," said Agatha tactfully.

"That bastard... If he touched my coin collection..." said Ida.

"I think all he was concerned about was the camera," said Agatha.

"The crone camera," said Tinkler.

"Still nobody buying, Tinkler," said Nevada. "You have no takers."

"And now the camera is there," said Ida. "On the windowsill where the crow left it."

"Yes," said Agatha. "And he plans to collect it tomorrow."

"Why not tonight?" I said.

"Because tonight the Troopers are busy working on their interviews with Stinky, god help them. So Patrik plans to collect the camera tomorrow."

Agatha grinned. "But I'm going to collect it tonight."

28: EYE OF THE BEAST

As we left the taverna, two men who had been looking in the window, as if trying to make up their mind about eating, suddenly turned and walked off into the night. They moved swiftly, disappearing around a corner. But no amount of speed could conceal their very familiar hulking silhouettes.

I looked at Nevada. She nodded. "Röd and Röd," she said.

"Those muppets are off their crust," I quoted.

"Juno wham sane," added Nevada. She said it softly and rather forlornly.

We walked along, lost in thoughts of Emma, until Agatha said, "Look, her sister is here." The pink BFF van was parked outside the vattentorn. Prominently and somewhat incongruously stationed behind it was a large and rather wicked-looking black motorcycle.

We let ourselves into Anders's shop, which was open late tonight. Once again, we found the owner in the middle of a transaction with Barbro Bok.

She turned to look at us as we came in. She was holding

a stack of books with sober typographical covers; Anders was standing at what elsewhere would have been a cash desk and was here an emphatically non-cash desk, busy processing a payment.

"We are so sorry," I said, to Barbro.

"About Emma," said Nevada.

"We really like her," said Agatha. "She's a wonderful person."

"Thank you," said Barbro. "She certainly is." There was a note of genuine pride in her voice. "I am just sorry that last time you saw the two of us together, in this very room—"

"Oh, no," said Nevada. "Don't worry about that."

"It's just that between sisters, things can become—"

"We understand."

"I am so sorry you saw us behaving like that. We really aren't like that."

"Of course not."

"I was being horrible to Emma. Now my every waking moment is full of thoughts of her. Thoughts of how I wish I could apologise to her. How I desperately long for that opportunity. So, to stay sane, I am throwing myself into my work." She lifted the stack of theological texts, as if offering them to us.

Tinkler gave me a droll look which I took to mean, *There has to be some porn in there*. I suspected there wasn't.

"You were not the only one being horrible to Emma that day," said Anders. "Her so-called loving husband Magnus was being equally vicious."

"Oh, now…" said Barbro.

"And I am convinced that Magnus is the man who attacked her."

"Oh, now," said Barbro. "Poor Magnus. He loves Emma. He genuinely loves her. I am sure he's suffering as much as I am. I'm sure it's not him."

"And who will be next?" said Anders suddenly, and rather portentously.

"Well," said Barbro, looking at him with some alarm, "I had best be going." I could hardly blame her. It seemed like we were in for a full-blown anti-pep talk about the current murder spree from Anders, a man who had so recently been extolling the virtues of crime-free Trollesko.

So Barbro said her goodbyes and left. "I must be going now, too," announced Anders as soon as she was gone. So, no anti-pep talk. That was a plus. As he put on a leather jacket and began zipping up its numerous zippers, Anders looked rather pointedly at Tinkler and Ida. "Is there any use in me mentioning again that you should keep the tower door locked?"

Much to his surprise, Ida kissed him on the cheek. "Anders, we have been very remiss in this regard. But going forward I think you'll find us to be exemplary."

"Exemplary? Okay."

"We are certainly going to keep everything locked."

Anders smiled. "Okay. I'll believe it when I see it." He reached behind the non-cash desk and took out an electric-blue motorcycle helmet with a skull, an elaborately floral skull, painted on it in red and white and yellow. "You can start by locking up behind me."

"I will," said Ida. "Have a wonderful evening."

"I will, thank you." Anders put his motorcycle helmet on, slipping it over his shaved head. I imagined he was glad of it in this icy weather. "You guys, too. Goodnight, everyone. Ida, thank you for the coupon." Then he went swiftly out the door into the winter night.

Ida stared after him for a moment and then made a great show of locking up the store. As she did so, I drifted to join Nevada at the window. She was watching Anders getting onto his big black motorcycle under a streetlight and Barbro getting into her little pink BFF van under an adjacent one. They paused and waved to each other and then drove off in opposite directions.

The street was now empty, and snow lay smoothly over everything except a lone dark patch of tarmac that was being erased by the white flakes drifting steadily down under the streetlights.

Nevada turned to me. "Moody winter street scene, check."

As I was turning from the window, I thought I saw a hulking figure step out of the shadows. Two hulking figures, actually. But Ida, who had now finished locking up, distracted me by saying, thoughtfully, "What the fuck did Anders mean about a coupon?"

"If you don't know," said Tinkler, "no one does."

Ida shrugged. "Come on everybody. Let's go upstairs." She led us through the store. "Then you can find the crow camera and fuck over that comb-over bastard Patrik." Ida was still very angry with Patrik for violating the sanctity of her home. And quite rightly so.

Still, if nothing else, the incident was at least going to trigger a strict regime of keeping the door to the tower locked up tight in future. A long overdue regime.

"You know what?" said Ida. She was leading us through the door in the back of the shop that gave access to Anders's living suite. "I think I know what he must have meant about a *coupon*. They have coupons at the strip club. They can be given as gifts…"

As usual, we went through Anders's suite as quickly as possible, to minimise the sense of intruding in someone's personal space. "Maybe somebody gave Anders a coupon as a gift and he thought it was from me." Ida led us out through the door at the back.

"A strip club coupon?" said Agatha.

"Yup," said Tinkler, nodding knowledgably.

We were now in the shadowed alcove where the staircase began its long ascent to the top of the fairytale tower. There was a dry, spicy smell of sawdust in here. "So, you buy a coupon for a…" said Agatha.

"A private dance," said Ida, switching on the lights in the alcove. "And there's this girl at the club that Anders likes."

"Anders is a dark horse," said Nevada.

"What does that mean?" said Ida.

"It means he likes to fuck horses after dark," said Tinkler.

"Really?" said Ida.

"Yeah, he sneaks into stables, wearing a special outfit, and—"

"*Tinkler*," said Nevada.

"It does *not* mean that," said Agatha.

377

"Well, anyway," said Ida. "As it happens, this girl Anders fancies does look a little like a horse." We began our long ascent of the impressively crafted but really rather extensive staircase.

I had admired this staircase on earlier visits. It was a spiral of pale polished wood with a narrow tongue of dark green carpet that wound a slow corkscrew path up inside the tower, clinging tight to the walls of the high stone shaft. Now and then we passed a slit window as we ascended, footsteps muffled on the carpet. With the world fallen dark outside, we felt these windows more than saw them, the cold air flowing in across our backs.

To our right, beyond the highly polished wooden handrail that curved elegantly upwards, and not incidentally helped us avoid plunging to our doom, a small wind whistled up the shaft. A djinn conjured by the local conditions of air flow and the design of the building.

Above us was the circle of wood that represented our roof and the floor of Ida's flat. There were white fluorescent tubes fitted on this radially, like spokes in a wheel, providing plentiful light in the stairwell—which needed a lot of light since it ran virtually the entire height of the gutted tower. Ida had switched the lights on at the bottom and would switch them off again at the top. If she didn't remember, a timer would remember for her.

Between a pair of those tube lights was the dark circle that indicated the open trapdoor that led up to Ida's apartment. We were about halfway up to it when we heard a loud sound from below.

Whoomf.

To me it sounded like an enormous piece of furniture being suddenly moved, dragged across the floor with explosive suddenness.

Explosive...

"Oh shit," said Nevada. She looked at me.

"What was that?" said Ida.

"*Shit,*" repeated Nevada, in a searing whisper. I was wondering if she was seeing what I was seeing. In my mind, I now beheld the murderous little pile of arson-related goodies that had been waiting for us at the strip club. *Bensindunk.*

But this time it had gone off.

This time they had got us.

Down below us, the dark circular roof of Anders's flat began to glow strangely in several places, blistering patches of bright orange. There was a sudden keen smell of scorching...

"Okay," said Nevada. "Everybody keep moving upwards, as fast as we can."

"Somebody has bombed my tower?" said Ida.

A hot wave of air floated up past us, an invisible elevator of heat rising and then passing the point where we stood on the staircase. The smell of it reminded me of someone trying to start a barbecue with lighter fluid, but on a gigantic scale.

"Yes," Nevada. "Sorry."

"Shit, shit, shit," said Tinkler.

"Keep moving up," said Nevada. As she said it, the lights went out, shrouding us in darkness.

Complete darkness.

We all froze for a moment, temporarily blinded.

Trapped in a burning tower, in total darkness.

"Shit," said Tinkler again. I felt he could be forgiven for that. Burning tower. Total darkness.

Then a light came on. Nevada had her phone out, in torch mode, a bucket of light pouring out onto the steps ahead of us. "Everybody stick together, don't get disorientated, and keep moving up," she said.

As we moved upwards Nevada said, "Call the fire brigade. Someone, please."

"I can't get a signal," said Agatha.

"I can," said Ida. "I am calling them now."

"Keep moving," said Nevada. Below us, the orange blisters on the roof of Anders's flat had turned an intense, wrathful red and begun to split open, collapsing inwards with a small dry crumbling sound, releasing a sudden angry surge of yellow flame.

The flame rushed out, lashing upwards, stretching in the racing updraft until it touched the staircase and all at once engulfed it, the big wooden structure catching fire instantly.

The staircase was now burning.

The staircase we were on.

I turned away from this cheerless spectacle and resumed moving briskly upwards, as quickly and calmly as I could, although in the current situation, "calmly" was a relative term. I was aware of my friends hurrying all around me, all of us breathing rapidly and raggedly. Except Ida, who was speaking on her phone swiftly in Swedish. She hung up and said, "Someone has already reported the fire. The emergency services are on their way. But they say they won't be here immediately."

"They won't be here immediately," repeated Tinkler. He didn't sound pleased. I wasn't very pleased myself. We kept moving up as fast as we could, no need for our phones to guide our way now.

The light all around us was golden, festive, ten thousand candles glowing to illuminate a ballroom. And the heat was increasing steadily, ballooning up in the column of air that rose inexorably and endlessly through the tower.

This was the same flow of air that fed the flames, I realised. We had to shut off that flow. I looked up at the circular trapdoor and remembered with a surge of satisfaction its beautifully engineered lid, hinged back flush into the floor.

Get up there and slam that lid, I thought. Choke off the fire.

The trapdoor was near to us now, almost within reach, a circular opening dark within the disk of wood that formed the ceiling above. The disk itself was brightly illuminated in the glare of the flames. These were streaming up the staircase below us at a businesslike and productive clip, eating everything in their path in a fury of incineration and flying sparks.

The fire. Now we could *hear* it too.

A growing roar at our back, a swelling commotion— the unholy enthusiasm of a mob that wanted us, so badly, to join it, that couldn't comprehend why we wouldn't want to. It pursued us with a mindless lust to unite with us, this blindly roaring multitude. One embrace is all it would take…

I looked back down and saw with sinking horror that the speed of the fire had altered massively and terribly. It was coming so much more swiftly now, flying up the staircase in pursuit…

We were racing up the final length of the burning staircase, as fast as we could move, the fire swelling and hot at our backs.

We went up through the trapdoor and onto the landing beside Ida's flat. A cold breeze flowed in through the slit window and chilled the sweat on my face. That window, high in the brick wall, a slit of open space, too narrow for any human to escape through.

There was something we were supposed to do in connection with that window…

But that had been in a plan formulated a thousand years ago. I had other things on my mind now. One thing, actually. Just one thing.

Choke off the fire.

I looked down and saw that, where there had been the hinged-back lid of the trapdoor, lying so neatly flush and beautifully carpentered, there was now just an empty hollow in the floor.

"Shut the trapdoor," said Nevada.

"There is no trapdoor," I said. "It's gone."

"Fuck."

Just an empty hollow in the floor, and two big black iron hinges, attached to nothing. Someone had removed the trapdoor. That was unhelpful.

"Everyone," said Ida. "Come in here, quickly." She was holding open the door of her apartment. "Through here and out the fire exit."

We should have known then. At the moment we saw that the trapdoor had been removed, we should have known...

But we had no time to stop and ponder implications. Through the circular hole in the floor—a hole we now couldn't shut—we glimpsed the inferno flooding up from below, coming inexorably after us.

Then Nevada and I followed the others, fleeing into Ida's apartment. I was the last one in and I slammed the door shut. This at least seemed fully present and fully functional, a reassuringly heavy slab of wood. But through the pebbled glass of its porthole window I beheld an unwelcome glow, swiftly rising.

Agatha, Ida and Tinkler were standing at the green door on the far side of the room. Tinkler was looking on helplessly, which is something he was good at, as the result of long and diligent practice. Ida was holding up a key in one hand. Agatha was pulling with both hands on the long chrome bar fixed to the door. I had the immediate impression that she wasn't the first to try pulling on it. Tinkler turned to me.

"It won't open."

"Have you unlocked it?" said Nevada.

Ida didn't even dignify this with an answer. She just passed Nevada the key and let her try it, which she did. Nevada twisted the key in the lock and then pulled on the bar, which Agatha had now abandoned.

"It won't open," said Tinkler. "It's unlocked but it's stuck."

"Because somebody has stuck it," said Nevada.

"We're trapped," said Agatha.

"Because someone's trapped us," said Nevada.

From below we heard a rattling, slipping, thudding sound. It was what was left of the staircase collapsing. I suddenly realised that the wooden floor was getting hot underfoot. Noticeably hot.

Between the planks, tiny ghosts of smoke were rising.

"Can we smash the door open?" said Ida.

Nevada shook her head. "There's no point trying. It opens inwards…"

Great fucking design for a fire exit, I thought savagely. And then I thought of something else. I went into the kitchen. The floor was even hotter here. It didn't matter. All that mattered was that the electric screwdriver was still there, in its place on the counter, and still fully charged.

I took it and went back into the sitting room where the others were standing by the green door. As I moved towards them, they got out of my way. Because of the eccentric design of the putative fire exit—opening inwards—the hinges were on the inside. And exposed.

I said a fervent prayer that was answered when I saw that the screws on the hinges were cross heads—Phillips—matching the screwdriver.

"We'll take the hinges off," said Nevada, getting it immediately and grinning as I set to work. Ida began to run around the apartment, grabbing things. Tinkler began to help her, and then Agatha joined them. But I was only peripherally aware of all this. Instead my attention was focused on the three hinge plates fixed in the door frame, silver rectangles in the dark green wood.

There were three chrome screws in each plate. Nine screws. I started at the top.

It was very hot in Ida's flat now. Sauna hot. I realised there were no windows in here. Just that slit in the wall on the landing outside. It dawned on me that this was why Ida kept the door open for ventilation. It wasn't so silly after all. What do you know?

I had slotted the screwdriver into the head of the top screw on the top hinge plate. It was seated firmly and I had thumbed the button on the screwdriver's handle. And now it was buzzing and jumping in my hand, growing warm with the blade trying to spin, nothing happening, everything jammed... the screw resisting utterly for a heart-stopping instant.

And then it began to move.

The first screw came out. I pulled it clear of its hole and it came out in a small cloud of sawdust and fell, clattering, to the floor. That floor was getting seriously hot now. I ignored this realisation as I seated the screwdriver into the second screw, set it buzzing, pulled it out and dropped it on the floor. Then the third.

That was the top plate done.

Ida's apartment was slowly filling with smoke, but I'd scarcely registered the fact.

My concentration had narrowed down to nine chrome screws in three chrome plates.

Six now, in two plates...

As a reward for reaching this milestone, I let my universe expand again for an instant and chanced a quick look over my shoulder...

This was a mistake.

At the other door of the room, the one that was holding the fire at bay, the round pebble-glass window was now glowing an angry smoky orange like a giant baleful demonic eye.

In the brief flash of an instant as I looked at it, this was the specific notion that lodged very firmly in my head.

As though it had found itself agreeably at home there.

I tried to shake this thought back out of my head, as I returned to the hinge plates. But I couldn't help following the logic of my own vision. A great beast with one huge smoky orange eye aimed towards us.

Just one eye. So that meant the monstrous head must be in *profile*, looking at us sidelong...

And so, it followed that at any moment the huge demonic head would turn and look at us full on with *both* eyes.

This little fancy did nothing to steady my hand.

But nevertheless, I was now down on my knees and labouring diligently on the bottom hinge plate—I had decided to work inwards towards the middle because that would allow us to get the door open in a controlled way, removing it in a stable fashion on its centre of gravity.

Though removing it in any fashion would be a very welcome result.

The odour of burning was all around us now, a hellish smell.

I had been aware of Nevada standing above me as I kneeled on the floor working—she literally had my back. Now I sensed she was gone. I looked up to see that she had joined Tinkler, Ida and Agatha in their efforts—their efforts to do *what* exactly, I didn't really know because I was no longer looking at them. And, to be honest, I no longer cared.

Because all my attention was back on the door with the glowing orange eye in it. Or, rather, the wall beside that door.

The one with the poster of the vattentorn, a big photograph of a tower that was a mirror image of the one we were in. The poster began to char and smoulder, the mirror image tower burning, vanishing into flames just like its doppelganger...

Which also did nothing to improve my concentration.

I got the last of the screws out of the bottom hinge plate and stood up to work on the middle one. And that was where our luck ran out. I stood frozen. Nevada immediately realised something was wrong and came over to me. "What is it?"

There were three screws left. Two of them were fine—they were Phillips heads, like the screwdriver. But the third one, in the centre, was a flat head. Why the hell was that? Was it a little stylistic flourish by whatever eccentric had built the door?

Or had they just run out of screws? It didn't matter. The reason didn't matter...

What mattered was the screwdriver I had in my hand. There was no way it could remove that screw. Ida had joined us, also aware that something wasn't right. I said, "Do you have a flat head screwdriver?" I showed her the screw in question.

"No. I always use star screws—*stjärnskruv*."

Shit. Nevertheless, I went ahead and removed the last two screws that I could.

Smoke was now beginning to make itself noticeably felt in the room. What had been a ghostly vapour had become a visible pall, and the air was getting difficult to breathe, an acrid catching at the back of the throat.

"Can we force the door now?" said Nevada, as I removed the last of the Phillips screws. "I'll try." She grabbed the bar and twisted. Ida joined her in the effort. Nothing budged. "It's just one screw," snarled Nevada. "You took out the other eight."

"It's right in the middle," I said. "In the worst possible position." The centre of gravity all right. Any other screw would have given us a better chance of forcing the hinges off and getting the door open. This one was going to stop us, at least for some time.

And time was what we didn't have.

We had to get that screw out. "Does anyone have any coins?" I said. A coin of the right thickness would serve as an improvised screwdriver.

"This is fucking Sweden," said Tinkler, who had now joined us, along with Agatha. "No one uses cash."

"Wait, my coin collection," said Ida. She ran and grabbed something and came back with it. When she had mentioned her coin collection earlier, I'd envisaged something in display cases at the very least.

However, what she was holding was a big glass jar that, according to the picture on the lid, had once contained pickled cucumbers and was now filled with random coins. She proffered it to me eagerly.

But Nevada said, "Keep the change."

My sweetheart had remembered something that I should have remembered myself. She took out her Swiss Army knife and passed it to me. It was the limited-edition model with the cool black handle that I'd given her for her birthday.

Much more importantly, one of its numerous blades was a flat head screwdriver.

So I got the screw out.

Then everyone grabbed the bar and wrenched the door inwards and it gave way at the hinge plates, popping out of the wood on our right. On our left there was a splintering, cracking sound as it came loose from whatever had been keeping it stuck so firmly and unhelpfully shut.

Nevada and Agatha and Ida were working as a perfect team keeping the heavy door upright, all three women holding the length of the chrome bar, and slowly walking the dead slab of the door into the room. Tinkler watched with admiration, always excited to see women at work. Or indeed anyone, so long as it wasn't him.

Winter air blasted into the room, dispersing the smoke, icy and biting and clean, chilling the sweat on me. Behind me, cinders were rising. In front of me, snow was falling. I stood on this liminal boundary of two worlds, giddy. Then I looked back at the door where the women had set it down. It was like a drunken party guest, laid flat on its back on the sofa…

And then I turned back to find what had been keeping the door shut. A hefty thickness of plank that had been industriously nailed—or more likely screwed; we weren't the only ones who knew how to use power tools—to the outside frame.

So the door had been sealed on the outside.

Like a coffin lid, I thought.

Just then the gust of icy air pouring in through the open door hit the fire rising in the tower under us and began to *feed* it. I heard the blaze increasing, erupting, like a deep-throated roar of approval from a demonic multitude.

"Come on," said Nevada. "Everybody grab two bags."

I finally saw what Ida and the others had been doing. Rather optimistically, they'd been packing bags. Those big blue Ikea bags. Filling them with Ida's belongings. Ten of them—two each. "Do you mind?" said Ida, looking at me now with her big eyes as the tower burned around us, with the infernal legions baying and roaring at our feet.

"No," I said. "I don't mind."

We grabbed the bags and got the hell out of there.

29: ENOUGH NOT TO BE INSIDE

We watched the vattentorn burn down from the window of our hotel room.

And then we went to bed. We were strangely untroubled by the tower continuing to burn across the street, or the emergency efforts to quell it.

It was enough for us just to not be inside it.

We slept surprisingly well, the sleep of deep exhaustion. And I dreamed only intermittently and fleetingly of the great head turning to look fully upon us, both those baleful orange eyes coming to bear...

Upon awakening on our last day in Trollesko, we found that the weather had changed yet again. The snow had turned to rain. The blackened stump of the tower across the street looked even more desolate on this grey morning of dismal, wind-whipped rainfall.

"Miserable day," I said, standing at the window looking out.

"Come back to bed," said Nevada. I was on my way to

comply with my darling's wishes when there was a knock on the door. I opened it to find Kriminalinspektör Eva Lizell standing there holding a brown paper bag.

I stared at her.

She was also staring at me, possibly because I was wearing only an oversized T-shirt with the image of a tearful blonde printed on it in primitive comic book style and the caption *Nuclear War? There Goes My Career!*

"Forgive me," she said. "I listened at the door."

"You listened at the door?" I said.

"Just to make sure that you guys were awake. I wouldn't have knocked if I hadn't heard that you were awake."

"Do you want to come in?" I said. Not least because I had realised—or, to be more accurate, had *smelled*—that the paper bag she was holding contained coffee.

Three coffees in paper cups, to be specific. She unpacked them as she came in. "They're not from the Notre Coeur. The Notre Coeur is not open yet. But these aren't bad." She handed me a coffee. I tried it. It wasn't bad. It wasn't hot as it might have been, but given our recent experiences, a little heat deficit here and there in the universe was quite welcome.

The Kriminalinspektör handed the other cup to Nevada, who accepted it and sipped it using a limited range of motion, because she was in bed and not wearing anything. Like me, she'd been sleeping in the nude.

Unlike me, she hadn't been first into the big silly T-shirt.

"I know it's early," said Eva Lizell, settling into one of the armchairs, "but people react differently to trauma. Some want to sleep all day. Others have to get up the instant they see daylight. You seem more that sort."

I sat on the bed beside Nevada. Eva Lizell sipped her coffee and made a point of not looking directly at us as she said, "These also tend to be the type of people who are more accustomed to being in extreme situations."

"Last night was an extreme situation, all right," I said.

"So I understand. I have received a very vivid account from Mr Tinkler."

"Already?" I said. This was rather early in the day for Mr Tinkler. But then, he'd been having a lot of excitement lately and his routine was probably shot.

"Yes," said Eva Lizell.

"Did you take Mr Tinkler a coffee?" said Nevada

The inspector smiled. "No. Nor Ms Tistelgren, who I also spoke to. She is now staying with Mr Tinkler in his room at this hotel."

"Because she is now homeless," I said.

"Although we did we manage to rescue most of her possessions," said Nevada.

"So I saw," said Eva Lizell. I had a vision of Tinkler and Ida surrounded by ten big blue Ikea bags in a small hotel room. But very much alive and blissful.

"Her landlord Anders Lind was not so fortunate," said Eva Lizell.

"He was fortunate he wasn't there," I said. "When his place went up in flames."

"Someone gave him a coupon for the strip club," said Nevada. "To make sure he wasn't there, we think. To make sure he was out of the way when the place went up in flames."

"Yes, that is an interesting possibility," said Eva Lizell. "And we are looking into tracing who sent it to him. But, by their very nature, these striptease coupons are designed to be given anonymously."

"I would imagine so," said Nevada drily.

"He could even have sent it to himself," I said.

"Exactly," said the women in unison. They looked at each other, then at me.

"So we are no closer to working out who is doing this," I said.

"We are proceeding with enquiries," said the Kriminalinspektör.

"Good luck with that," said Nevada.

"We saw the two Röds last night," I said.

"That's right," said Nevada. "We saw them outside the taverna and then you saw them later, didn't you love, outside the vattentorn, just before it went up?"

"Yes," I said, "I think so."

I expected the Kriminalinspektör to pounce on my lack of absolute certainty here. But instead, she said, "We are talking to them."

"The two Röds?" said Nevada. We were both completely taken aback. And this seemed to provide some much-needed amusement for Eva Lizell.

"Yes. Mr Sill and Mr Strömming. We are talking to those two gentlemen at this very moment and have been for some hours now."

"Wow," said Nevada.

"Excellent," I said, feeling myself relax perceptibly.

"And, incidentally, regarding the fire in the vattentorn…"

"It was arson," I said.

Eva Lizell gave me an ironic smile. "I believe you are right."

"We heard the device go off," said Nevada.

"What I was going to say," said Kriminalinspektör Lizell. "Regarding the fire. I just wanted to say… I am so glad you got out safely."

She said it very simply and she was looking at us both when she said it, and she seemed to mean it for us both. It was a rather moving moment of quiet emotion.

And not in the body-heat-seeking-you-out kind of way.

"And I can assure you," said Eva Lizell, breaking a fairly long silence, "that whoever was responsible for installing a fire exit of that design in that tower is going to find his life enlivened by prosecution by the state."

"Don't knock that design," I said.

"Opening inwards? With no crash bar? Locked with a key? It was non-standard, to say the least."

"It may have been non-standard, but it saved our lives," I said. "That may be *why* it saved our lives."

"Saved your lives after almost killing you," said the Kriminalinspektör.

Well, that was true.

"Is Anders in trouble?" said Nevada.

"No, he is not the owner, he is not the landlord, he did not install the fire exit. Anders is just a tenant in the building.

Or was. He is now temporarily homeless, without a business, and very few of his possessions have survived the fire. What's more, the poor fellow's misfortunes don't end there. He had his motorcycle stolen last night."

"What?" I said.

"Yes, from the car park at the striptease club," said Eva Lizell. "Which leads to the interesting speculation that perhaps he was sent the private dance coupon not to make sure he avoided the fire, but…"

"So somebody could steal his motorcycle," said Nevada.

"Yes." Eva Lizell nodded. "Yes, they would know exactly where he was going to be at a certain time with his motorcycle and also know he'd be quite preoccupied. Which would therefore make it very easy to steal. That is certainly a possibility." The Kriminalinspektör finished her coffee and stood up to go. We all looked at each other. For some reason, I realised we were all acutely aware of the fact that Nevada was nude under the covers.

"Well, as I said, I am glad you are both safe. I am sorry about the poor coffee."

"No, it was good," I lied.

"No, it wasn't. But now I am on way to the Notre Coeur to get some good stuff."

"I'll come with you," I said on impulse. "Just let me pull some clothes on."

"All right, I'll wait in the hallway." Eva Lizell went out, closing the door carefully behind her.

I looked at Nevada. She smiled at me. "Ida thinks the Kriminalinspektör has a thing for you."

"Just so long as Ida doesn't think I reciprocate," I said, and Nevada laughed.

"Enjoy your coffee."

"I'll bring back some breakfast for you."

"Would you?" said Nevada, holding up her face to be kissed. I kissed her. Despite a very thorough shampooing, the smell of burning vattentorn still lingered in her hair. And, no doubt, in mine.

"Meanwhile you can go back to sleep," I said.

"That sounds like a plan."

Such a good plan that by the time I'd dressed and left—less than two minutes later—she was asleep again.

Kriminalinspektör Lizell and I walked through the lobby under the high blind eye of the skylight, the sound of rain steady on it, and let ourselves out of the sleeping hotel into the wet grey morning.

The inspector had thoughtfully brought an umbrella that she put up for both of us. The rain beat a comforting tattoo on the gold and maroon striped fabric as we walked along, snugly dry beneath it. We were walking so close together that I could smell the cigarette smoke on her. Not as intense as the aftermath of tower arson on me, though, I imagined.

"What did you want to talk about?" said Eva Lizell.

"What makes you think I wanted to talk about anything?"

"You very clearly wanted to walk to the café with me," she said.

"That's true," I said. "But that's not because I need to talk to you."

"No?"

"No. It's because I really want to walk to the café and I feel a hell of a lot safer walking there with a cop."

"Very sensible," she said. She sounded amused again. I was glad I'd provided some further welcome entertainment for the Kriminalinspektör, but I was deadly serious.

I just wanted to get out of this town with my beloved girl...

And my beloved friends...

And my beloved self...

All in one piece.

Meanwhile, militating against this, the songs 'Gallows Pole' and, most worryingly, 'Active Shooter' were still in rotation.

Come to think of it, 'Fire' was probably still in rotation, too, since even that most recent and high-spirited third attempt at murder by conflagration could not be said to have been an unqualified success.

From the killer's point of view, that is.

This was a dispiriting reflection. But my mood lifted when we reached the café. They weren't open yet, but I recognised the young woman at the service desk, elegant in white shirt and black apron, black hair scraped back in a bun, fixed in place with that bright red comb.

She immediately came and unlocked the door for us. She recognised us, both in the sense of being regular customers, and also in the sense of knowing who Eva Lizell was and what she did.

I let the Kriminalinspektör purchase our early coffee with the authority of a member of the emergency services in urgent need of caffeine, while I went to our regular table—an action I regretted almost immediately.

Outside the window in the tiny courtyard the rain had washed away the snow on the cobbles. The last melting remnant was dripping off the little marble table and the pink two-seater bench and the lamppost. And something else.

Something hanging from the lamppost.

Or, rather, someone.

Bo Lugn.

My first reaction was that it must be terribly uncomfortable, cold and damp, hanging out there in the cheerless drizzle. But he was long past discomfort.

I suddenly felt terrible for all the times we had called him Creepy Elvis. He was a person. Or he had been. And now he was an adornment on a lamppost in the rain. I turned and walked back to the front of the café. I met Eva Lizell coming the other way, carrying our coffees.

She took one look at my face and then set the coffees down and hurried past me. I walked back to the front of the café and stood tensely by the service desk. The young woman who had let us in was sneaking looks at me, trying to work out what was wrong.

The Kriminalinspektör came back and started speaking to her rapidly in Swedish. I saw the young woman's head snap back in shock so abruptly that the red comb almost sprang out of her hair. She immediately started making a phone call.

Eva Lizell turned to me and handed me my coffee. The fact that she'd remembered it—and her own—raised her further in my esteem. I badly needed to drink this.

But not in here.

"I'm stepping outside," I said.

"Of course." She came with me. We stood outside the Notre Coeur, sipping our coffee. It seemed insanely casual and commonplace, with Bo Lugn hanging there in the courtyard of the building behind us. I hated myself for being able to take it in my stride, but I was relieved as well.

I said, "There's no chance it was suicide?"

"Not unless he was showing off by hanging himself with his hands tied behind his back."

Ask a silly question… "Do you mind if I go back to the hotel?" I said.

"Of course not," said the inspector. "Be careful."

"Thank you. I will."

"And please don't leave town."

"What?"

"Please do not leave Trollesko."

I turned to look at her. I was shocked and a little upset because leaving Trollesko was exactly what I had had in mind. "You want us to stay here?" I said.

"Yes."

"For how long?"

"Until further notice," said Eva Lizell.

"We're due to fly back to London tonight," I said.

"I'm sorry."

To hell with it, I thought. She can't stop us. I would lie to her face now and say, *Yes, of course we're staying*. But we'd just leave tonight as planned. The train to Gothenburg was fast, and then we'd be at the airport, and once we were in the air...

Eva Lizell was looking at me. "Please don't force me to impose this request officially, for example in response to you doing something foolish. Like trying to leave Trollesko."

"Look," I said. "Please. Just let us go."

"I can't."

"You can interview us by phone or online or something, once we're back in London. We can answer any questions you have. We can come into the Swedish embassy to be interviewed by the police if you want. But it's not safe for us here."

"I know and I am sorry."

"There's still 'Active Shooter' to go," I said.

"I know."

"Or 'Fire' again. That's still in rotation. Another fucking fire." I looked in the direction of the vattentorn, and then found my gaze dragged inexorably the other way, towards the courtyard, where poor Bo Lugn's body was hanging like a heavy, still pendulum. At least 'Gallows Pole' wasn't still in rotation.

"I know," said Eva Lizell. "I'm sorry. If I could put you and Ms Warren and your friends into some kind of protective custody, I would do that. But it's a question of resources. Of willingness to commit them."

"Is it?" I said. "I'll be at the hotel. We won't leave town."

I turned to go. "Wait," she said. I stopped.

"I know you are angry," she said. "And you are scared. But I am doing everything I can to stop whoever is behind these killings. And think of this. That man in there was hanged because he didn't have his bodyguards to protect him."

"So what?" I said.

"So, who do you think took his bodyguards away from him?"

I stared at her, remembering how she'd told us that the two Röds were being questioned by the police.

She was looking at me, eyes cold under that deep crease in her forehead. There would be no erasing that with a caress now, I thought.

"Yes," she said. "That is my responsibility."

30: THE RAIN DOESN'T READ

"Rain is better than snow," said Oskar Hafström. "The snow is a continuity nightmare, whereas the rain doesn't read. It doesn't read on screen. You don't even know it's happening." We were getting a lecture on guerrilla film-making from Oskar, but at least he wasn't wearing the kilt.

We were increasingly torn between a growing sense of relief concerning the absence from public view of this item of his wardrobe, and a foreboding that it might make a dramatic reappearance sometime soon.

Tinkler's insistence that there was a perch for the crow concealed inside said kilt, and that sometimes the crow was actually there, concealed while Oskar was wearing it, swinging on his hidden perch under the stylish kilt, had been firmly rejected by all of us.

"It doesn't make sense," said Nevada. "It isn't even his crow."

"I know," I said. "Exactly."

"Tinkler is slipping in his ability to conjure pornographic conjectures."

"Conjure *convincing* pornographic conjectures."

"Exactly," said Nevada.

It was difficult to chat with Oskar now, standing in the park opposite our hotel in a thin persistent drizzle, without memories of such conversations coming to mind. They were certainly more entertaining than the bulk of the bombast he was currently inflicting on us.

"In fact, if anyone watching the film *is* aware of the rain," said Oskar, "it will simply contribute to the effectiveness of this segment. Enhance the mood of sadness."

"Enhance the mood of sadness," said Nevada.

"Yes, in this scene where we find Patrik sitting on the bench." He nodded at a wet green wooden park bench halfway between us and the bandstand.

His wife Gun was standing beside it, holding an umbrella. A black umbrella, admittedly, but a large and sensible one. Not large enough to keep the bench dry, though, if that was what she was trying to do. Which would not have been sensible.

"We find Patrik on the bench," said Oskar, "and he hears about the killing, the first one, the one based on 'Snow Angel'—*allegedly* based on 'Snow Angel'…"

Christer Vingqvist, eviscerated in the empty swimming pool, in the snow.

"Patrik is going to hear about that killing," said Oskar. "And when he hears about it, we are going to get his reaction."

"But he heard about it days ago, right?" said Nevada.

"Precisely. That is precisely why we need to restage the

scene where he hears the news. We missed it the first time because of course we didn't know it was going to happen." Oskar was looking at us, rather closely now, I thought.

"Right?" he said.

"Plus, it gives you a chance to enhance the mood of sadness," I said.

"Precisely. So now we can stage it on the park bench, which is a great visual. Patrik can hear the sad news while he is sitting on the bench. And when he hears the terrible news of the killing, he is going to cry."

"Cry?" said Nevada.

"Yes, to express his sorrow. To express the entire band's sorrow, about this awful atrocity, this human tragedy, that is being associated with *our* song. He is going to be so upset about this he is going to start crying. It will be a deeply human moment." His gaze flickered to Gun, who had left the bench and was wandering in our direction, and then back to us. "Patrik is very convincing when he cries, and he can cry at the drop of a hat. And speaking of hats…" said Oskar.

"We owe you a huge thank you," said Gun, who had now joined us, thankfully bringing her big umbrella with her. She thoughtfully angled it to give all of us the benefit of its cover, the thin endless shower spattering softly on the other side. "For finding all those wonderful stylish hats for us," said Gun.

These were the hats Nevada had picked up at the secondhand-butik and immediately sold on—at a smart mark-up—to the potential murderers in the hotel room across from ours.

"Always happy to separate customers from their money," said Nevada. Oskar and Gun laughed. My darling had charmed both husband and wife.

"And thanks to those hats," said Gun, "we've managed to get Patrik to conceal his egregious comb-over," said Gun.

"It really is egregious," agreed Nevada, who always loved apt use of language.

"He normally flatly refuses to wear hats. It's as if he has a perverse pride in those absurd wisps of hair on his patently bald head. As if he has to show off this pitiful display. Under normal circumstances, it is impossible to get him to wear any kind of hat. But your selection of hats was so well chosen: they were all stylish in their own right, and what's more they all *suited* him."

My guileful darling was absorbing this praise as if she was about to start purring.

"Believe me," said Gun. "I've art-directed quite a number of photo shoots, so I know when someone really delivers the goods in the props or costume departments. And thanks to you on this occasion, we finally get that vile comb-over concealed. I don't know how my sister puts up with it, her husband having something like that on his head. But I asked her once and do you know what she said? She said, 'You can get used to anything.' And I suppose that's true. You can get used to anything."

On this philosophical note she and Oskar took their leave of us to join Patrik, owner of the comb-over, and Rut, tolerator of it, who had just arrived at the park bench.

It seemed filming was finally about to commence. And Patrik was indeed wearing one of the hats Nevada had sold them. Perhaps the delay had been occasioned by Patrik having to approve this headwear from among the rich and exciting range on offer.

Nevada and I missed Gun's umbrella almost immediately. We had to tough it out just in our coats and own silly hats—although Nevada's, which had a strawberry on it, was nice and richly nostalgic rather than silly. But mine was definitely silly—standing there in the middle of the park, in the rain, while we waited for our friends.

We could have been waiting indoors at any number of locations, but the grisly possibilities of the song 'Active Shooter' was a powerful disincentive to stay in any one place for long. Nowhere seemed safe.

We saw Agatha from a long away off, viz our hotel, as she left it, crossed the street and came over to join us. She had an umbrella, luckily. It wasn't as large as Gun's, true, but we were grateful to have anything.

As we huddled together under her umbrella, Agatha was looking at Patrik and Oskar and Rut and Gun clustered around their bench. "Do you think still they're prospective killers?"

"Surely that's your own thesis?" said Nevada. "And besides, don't you think it looks like Patrik and Oskar lured us into a trap last night? Lured us into the tower with all that crap about Hiram leaving a camera on the windowsill?"

"You're assuming that they knew I was eavesdropping," said Agatha.

"That is indeed what I'm assuming," said Nevada.

"And that they thereby used me as a catspaw to try and lure us to our doom," said Agatha.

"Yes, precisely," said Nevada. "Though I'm a little uncomfortable with the term *catspaw*, because I think cats already have enough bad press."

"In other words, you think they baited me," said Agatha.

"Baited us," I said.

"With a crow camera."

"There never was a crow camera," said Nevada conclusively. "At least, not in the tower. Not that night."

"There was," said Agatha.

I said, "What?"

"Really?" said Nevada.

"And I duly obtained it." Agatha smiled at us. "While you were looking for the trapdoor. I scooped up the crow camera. I guess you didn't notice."

"No," I said. "I think it's fair to say we were too preoccupied with the notion that someone had stolen the trapdoor."

"In an attempt to burn us to a crisp," said Nevada.

"Exactly," I said.

"So you pluckily obtained the camera?" said Nevada.

"Yes," said Agatha.

"With the memory card?" I said. I waved at Tinkler and Ida, who had now left the hotel and were heading in our direction. "With the memory card recording all the details of Hiram's flight?"

"That's right," said Agatha.

"We should watch it," said Nevada.

"I have," said Agatha.

I was keeping an eye on Tinkler and Ida as they waited for traffic to pass by before they crossed the road. I couldn't help seeing every one of those vehicles as a potential threat to my friends.

"You have?" said Nevada. "You've watched it?"

"Well," said Agatha, "fast-forwarded through most of it, actually."

Tinkler and Ida crossed the road unscathed and ambled towards us.

"Nothing interesting on it?" said Nevada.

"Crow camera footage," I explained to Tinkler and Ida as they joined us. I was delighted to see that Ida also had an umbrella with her, a large one, at least as big as Gun's, but bright red with white love hearts. She now opened it to share it with us.

Agatha still had her own umbrella open; I fully expected brolly wars to break out and for us—by which I mean me—to have to choose sides. Instead, to my astonishment, Agatha immediately closed her umbrella. She and Nevada crowded in with me and Tinkler to take shelter, all pressed close together under Ida's more capacious apparatus.

I guess there's nothing like being in a burning tower to promote bonding and team building.

"Crow camera footage," said Tinkler. We could all see him straining to conflate the words into some kind of abbreviation—he was still smarting from the rejection of "crone".

"A lot of boring blurry aerial footage," said Agatha. "And lots of stuff that would probably be of interest to other crows, involving other crows. Social stuff."

"Any crow fucking?" asked Tinkler immediately. Ida chuckled. It seemed that he genuinely amused her. Tinkler was a very happy man and I was happy for him. And Nevada and Agatha had changed their attitude. They now seemed entirely benevolently inclined towards the happy couple as we stood here in the shelter of Ida's big red umbrella with its silly white love hearts.

"Sadly not," said Agatha. "No crow carnality. Nothing that interesting. Eventually I finished watching the footage, which was a whole load of nothing, and I gave the memory card and the whole camera rig back to Oskar."

"You returned it to Oskar?" said Nevada.

"Yes. He's less creepy than Patrik."

"Well, that's true," said Ida.

"What did you tell him," I said, "when you gave him the camera?"

"Yes," said Nevada. "How did you account for having it?"

"I said I just happened to see it on the windowsill in the tower and I recognised it from chatting about it with them, so I rescued it from the fire and brought it back for them."

"And did they believe that?" said Nevada.

"They certainly did," said Agatha. "And they were absolutely delighted that I'd saved their crow camera. Very grateful. Apparently, I'm going to receive a case of champagne to say thank you."

"I hope you didn't give them your address to send it to," said Nevada.

"No, I gave them Tinkler's," said Agatha.

"Really?" said Tinkler.

"No, of course not. They're not sending anybody a case of champagne. Not physically. They're giving me a gift voucher so I can buy my own champagne."

"Well, that's good," said Tinkler. "Because it always pays to be careful when accepting champagne from potential killers."

I said, "Actually we were just discussing if they *are* potential killers." We all looked over to the four members of Storm Dream Troopers, standing by the bench in the rain, apparently arguing. No doubt about some deeper artistic aspect of what they were about to film. Perhaps they were trying to enhance the mood of sadness.

"What do you think?" said Ida. She was looking closely at me. As, disconcertingly, she so often was. "Do *you* think they're the killers?"

"I don't know," I said. "At first I was really struck by the argument that if they were the killers, they wouldn't have needed Hiram to photograph their crime scene."

"Because they would have been there."

"Right," I said. "I thought it was a very telling point."

"But then you realised," said Agatha, who had clearly also given this a lot of thought, "that even if they had been there, they couldn't use any pictures they took."

"Right," I said. "Because they'd clearly be too..."

"Up close and personal," said Nevada.

"Yuck," said Tinkler.

"The police wouldn't throw a lot of resources into pursuing someone who merely filmed a crime scene with a drone," I said. Then I realised I was talking about police resources just like the Kriminalinspektör. "But…"

"But if it was a picture that was clearly taken at the crime scene," said Ida, "taken by one of the killers…"

"That's right," said Agatha.

"Then the police would throw everything at it," I said. "And go after them."

"So, even if they are the killers," said Agatha, "they'd still need to get their crime scene pictures from Hiram."

"The crow drone," said Nevada. "Don't say 'crone', Tinkler."

"I wouldn't dream of it," said Tinkler.

Ida turned to me. "Jordon keeps talking about your sonic screwdriver abilities," she said. She was giving me a sardonic look.

"His term, not mine," I said.

"He said this isn't the first time a screwdriver saved your life."

"Jordon is exaggerating," said Nevada. "The other occasion simply involved a domestic repair job that impressed my mother." She looked at me and smiled. "Won her over, in fact."

"So, *almost* as important as saving your life," said Ida, also smiling.

The mention of her mother prompted Nevada to phone our place in London and check that our cats were okay. They were, although Fanny had disappointed our cat sitter by not doing her trick of drinking from the tap and instead, perversely, insisting on drinking from a cat bowl like any normal cat. Other than that, all was quiet on the feline front. When we concluded the call, Tinkler said, "So, what now?"

"Well, the good inspector has ordered us all not to leave town," said Nevada.

"We know," said Ida. "We heard."

"Bummer from the potential mass murder point of view," said Tinkler.

"Anyway," I said, "we thought, if we can't leave town then I might as well do what I'm good at..."

"Drink coffee?" said Tinkler.

"Track down rare vinyl," said Nevada. "If there is an upside to being caught up in a murder spree, it's that we can sell as many copies of *Attack and Decay* as we can find. At a premium price."

"To reprise my earlier scepticism," said Tinkler, "what makes you think you're going to find any?"

"I made a phone call," I said, "and I confirmed a hunch I had. Barbro Bok has several copies of the LP."

"Barbro?" said Tinkler.

"Emma's sister?" said Ida.

"Yes."

"But she and Christer were friends," said Tinkler. "Maybe even more than friends, though obviously that doesn't bear thinking about. Right?"

"Right," I said.

"And Christer was helping Magnus sell every copy of that pestiferous record they could get their hands on," said Tinkler. I could see Nevada giving him extra points for *pestiferous*.

"Right," I said again.

"But therefore wouldn't he have long ago strip-mined any copies of the record that Barbro had? Surely she would have been the first person he asked when he was looking for that record?"

"No," I said. "She would have been the *last* person he would have asked, because he didn't want to give the game away."

"The game?" said Ida.

"That he was exploiting the Church's charity business for his personal profit," said Nevada. "In a series of nefarious, underhanded deals."

"Ah, I see," said Tinkler. "Who would have imagined the Church might frown on nefarious, underhanded business deals? But if so, good for them."

Ida was looking at me. "So you rang up Barbro to ask if she had some records to sell?"

"Sure," I said.

"You didn't think that was a little callous?" said Ida. "Considering her sister is in a coma?"

"Oh now, honey," said Tinkler. "This is *vinyl* we're talking about here. Anyway, I've been in a coma, and it wasn't so bad."

"Actually, I did think it was a little callous," I said. "But not then. Earlier, when Christer was killed. I never would have called her then. I never would have intruded on her grief. But then when Emma was... hospitalised... that somehow made it easier."

"Easier?"

"Easier to approach her."

"Her double tragedy made it easier to approach her." Ida didn't sound convinced.

"Ironically, yes," I said. "You see, I realised that someone who was going through that much hell would probably welcome a distraction."

"And she did," said Nevada.

"And she did," I said.

"She welcomed it," said Nevada. "In fact, she's eager for us to go over to her place and pick up the records."

"What now? You're going to the lonely murder farmhouse?" said Tinkler.

"Farmhouse with nice cat," said Nevada, who was running a campaign to rebrand this dwelling.

"Same place," said Tinkler. "What was that cat's name? Ludwig Wittgenstein?"

"There's a cat called Wittgenstein?" said Ida, suddenly taking an interest.

"No," said Agatha scornfully, but her scorn was directed at Tinkler. "The cat is called August Strindberg."

"I was close," said Tinkler.

"You were not close."

Recognising a lost cause when he saw one, Tinkler turned to me and said, "So your crazed lust for rare vinyl has driven you back to the lonely murder farmhouse?"

"We are *not* calling it that," said Nevada. "We're calling it the nice farmhouse with the lovely cat. And I am going, too. So, I'll have his back."

"And I'll be doing the driving to the nice farmhouse with the lovely cat," said Agatha. "And if anything looks dubious, I'll just put my foot down and get us the hell out of there."

"Reassuring," said Tinkler.

"In fact, I'll get the car now," said Agatha, and walked purposefully off across the park towards the side street where she'd left her rental car. Luckily, she still had her own umbrella, which she briskly reopened as she left the shelter of Ida's.

"Why is it reassuring?" said Ida. "Is Agatha a good driver?"

"Yes, really good," said Tinkler.

"Would you guys like to come along, Tinkler?" I said.

"On your jaunt to the lonely—"

"Tinkler…" said Nevada.

"—farmhouse," concluded Tinkler.

"Yes," I said.

"Love to," said Tinkler. "But we're going shopping." He took Ida's hand.

"Yes," said Ida. "Jordon is taking me shopping in the charity shops to replace items I lost in the fire."

"Well, be careful," said Nevada.

"Don't worry," said Tinkler. "We've got the lesbian cop on speed dial."

"We really do," said Ida. "Do you mind if we take the umbrella away?"

"No," said Nevada. "We're going to the car now anyway. I meant what I said about being careful, by the way."

"We know. Thank you."

Tinkler and Ida went their way, and we went ours, to join Agatha in the side street where the car was parked. When we got there, we found Ms Dubois-Kanes wiping her hands on a greasy rag.

"Have you been doing maintenance on a rental car?"

"No, I've been checking it for bombs."

"Holy fuck. Thank you for that."

"You're very welcome."

We got in the car and drove out of town, past the park and the bandstand and the bench where the Troopers all stood.

I was a little sad that we were going to miss Patrik's big crying scene.

31: LONELY MURDER FARMHOUSE

On our way to Barbro's farm, we passed the strip club where there had been a firebomb waiting for us, and then the side road that led to poor Bo Lugn's country house where we had been fired upon, repeatedly, by someone with a deadly weapon.

So perhaps it was understandable that we were on high alert.

Like Nevada, I alternated between fixating on the traffic approaching us and the traffic following us. We frequently twisted around in our seats to look back at the latter. Agatha used her mirrors to do the same with substantially less effort.

"Do you see that SUV following us?" she said.

"Yes," said Nevada.

I said, "It looks just like Obi Van Kenobi."

"Right," said Agatha. "Except it doesn't have the sticker at the top of the windscreen that says *Obi Van Kenobi*."

"Right," said Nevada.

"In other words," I said, "it looks like Obi Van Kenobi with the sticker removed."

"In a futile attempt to disguise a distinctive vehicle," said Nevada.

"Exactly right," said Agatha.

"Is that Magnus at the wheel?"

"I don't know. I can't see. He isn't close enough and he isn't *getting* close enough."

Nevada glanced back at the road behind us. "I think it's him."

I glanced back, too. The indistinct figure at the wheel could well have been Magnus. It could equally well have been someone else entirely.

"I've tried slowing down, to get a look at him," said Agatha. "But then he slows down, too." She demonstrated by smoothly decelerating and, sure enough, the vehicle following us slowed to maintain a constant distance between us.

"If it is Magnus," said Agatha, "what the hell is he up to?"

"I have no idea," said Nevada. "And there's little point speculating about that, or indeed about why he apparently thinks he's rendered himself invisible by removing the Obi Van Kenobi sticker."

"If it is him," I said.

"Could there be another vehicle that looks just like Obi Van Kenobi?" said Nevada, leaning forward, towards Agatha, to whom she was directing the question. Agatha stirred slightly in her seat, suggesting a shrug. "There's no shortage of beat-up ten-year-old Toyota Siennas in a shade of silver grey. So, yes, sure, it could be someone else."

Nevertheless, we all agreed that the sooner we got to our destination, the better. Because, despite Tinkler's attempts to impose a scary lonely-murder nomenclature on it, Barbro's farmhouse had so far subjected us to nothing worse than a nocturnal hunt for dog shit.

And there was no chance of even that now, because it was still the middle of the day and, as Nevada observed, those particular protagonists only came out at night. "Like the creatures in Richard Matheson's masterpiece," said Nevada.

"You're talking about *I Am Legend*," said Agatha, overtaking a slow driver, which is one of the things she liked doing best. "And you're talking about vampires."

"I prefer not to use the term. I don't like to think I'm guilty of actually having read a vampire novel," said Nevada.

"Then you should try Matheson's straight-up suspense fiction," said Agatha. "*Ride the Nightmare* is really good."

"Maybe Barbro will have a copy," said Nevada.

"Quite possibly. But she's unlikely to part with it."

"Oh, I don't know," said Nevada. "She's very generously letting me have her duplicate copies of Charles Williams novels in the French Serie Noir."

"Letting you have?" said Agatha, with a little chuckle.

"All right, selling them to me for a pretty penny. But I'm glad to get them. I'm looking forward to comparing them to the English originals. It's going to make for a very interesting exercise in textual comparison. Thank you for introducing me to Charles Williams, by the way."

"He's amazing, isn't he?" said Agatha. "I believe this is where we turn." It was indeed where we turned. She signalled a right and we pulled off the main road onto a long, curving lane bordered with tidily planted shrubs and flowers. To either side of us were farmhouses and outbuildings among clusters of trees. Agatha signalled another right turn and we exited onto a gravel road leading to Barbro Bok's place.

Barbro was standing outside waiting for us, with a fat marmalade cat—the famed August Strindberg—nestled comfortably in the crook of one arm. In her free hand she held a glass of red wine. "I know it's immorally early," she said, "but I'm having a glass of Bordeaux. Would you care to join me?"

Nevada indicated enthusiastically that she did indeed care to, though I knew secretly she would rather have had something from the Rhône. Or, indeed, anything from the Rhône.

I declined because I didn't want to interfere with my coffee buzz, and also because I was doing a record deal and needed my wits about me. Agatha declined because she was driving.

Barbro bent forward to carefully spill the orange-furred bulk of August Strindberg to the ground. In so doing, she also managed to spill a little wine. The cat trotted a few paces, sat down on the grass and began grooming himself. Agatha crouched to stroke him, which August did nothing much to resist.

Barbro led us into the house and poured Nevada her glass of wine and then gave her a pile of paperbacks featuring black covers with yellow trim, and yellow and white lettering—the famed Serie Noir Charles Williams novels. Nevada looked through them and I saw the titles, *Le Pigeon* and *Un Quidam Explosif*, whatever that might mean.

Nevada contentedly inspected her swag and then took the books, and her glass of wine, back out of the farmhouse, ostensibly because she wanted to put the books safely in the car, but actually because she wanted to join Agatha in fawning over August Strindberg. The glass of wine was the giveaway here—the fawning was likely to be a protracted business, and refreshment would be required along the way.

Barbro led me into the living room where the records awaited my scrutiny. They were neatly stacked in an armchair, not coming anywhere close to fully occupying it in the way they would in any self-respecting vinyl nut's abode. Then Barbro politely left me alone to inspect them and retired once more to the kitchen.

There were six copies of *Attack and Decay* here—one was the original pressing and five were the considerably more valuable but also considerably more shitty-sounding audiophile version. This represented a substantial payday for us. I checked the records. It didn't take long. They were all authentic. And the original pressing was still sealed, as were four of the audiophile ones.

I singled out the one unsealed audiophile copy for inspection. I slid the record out of the inner sleeve and went over to the window to inspect it in daylight. It was immaculate: near mint, as a hardnosed record grader would put it. I slipped the record back in the inner sleeve and then into the outer cover. The fact that it wasn't sealed would drop the price a fraction, but I could still accurately describe it as unplayed. It was worth virtually the same as the others. Nice result.

Then something occurred to me. I felt around inside the cover and found the lyric sheet, teasing it out. I hadn't perfected Patrik's natty little trick of getting it to slide out with the snap of a finger. I carried the lyric sheet into the light and studied it. I was glad I did.

Because, unlike the vinyl, this had seen some use.

It would still have been pristine, except for one ghostly semicircle of pink at the edge of the paper. It almost looked like it was meant to be there, a contrived little design detail. But I'd seen other copies of the lyric sheet, and I knew it wasn't.

Plus, as half of a couple who'd been known to enjoy the occasional bottle of red wine, I recognised exactly what it was. The mark of a wine glass that been overfilled at some point and had left the ghostly red imprint of its damp base on the paper.

This would definitely drop the price of the record among those record collectors who were annoyingly anal-retentive perfectionists. Which was virtually all record collectors, so it would take another small bite out of our profits.

It certainly provided a case for beating Barbro down a little on the price. But my instinct in this instance was to be magnanimous and just forget about haggling. Indeed, my instinct would have been to do this even if the seller hadn't recently experienced a concatenation of tragedies.

So I paid Barbro's full asking price for the six records. She was aware that the album was valuable, and I was paying her a significant sum. But I would sell them on for many times what I'd paid, so we were all winners—

including the Church charity Barbro had nominated to receive her fee.

I paid, both for the records and for Nevada's books, on my phone, transferring the money from our account.

Barbro must have had access to the charity account and been keeping an eye on it, because almost immediately she called, "Thank you," from the kitchen. I went in to tell her she was very welcome. She was smiling up at me from the table where she was sitting, a stack of books and a bottle of wine in front of her. They were the theological texts she'd bought from Anders. I took all this in only at the periphery of my attention.

Because what I was really looking at was the stretch of road visible from the kitchen window. Moving along it, in a leisurely manner, was the SUV that had been following us. "What is it?" said Barbro. I pointed at the window.

"Is that Magnus's van?"

With maddening slowness Barbro put on her glasses and turned to look. She chuckled. "No," she said. "Magnus's van has a silly name on it."

"I know," I said, trying hard not to lose my cool. "I know that. But he could have removed it. He could have removed the silly name."

"No." Barbro turned away from the window, shaking her head. "I know that vehicle. It just happens to resemble Magnus's. But this one belongs to the brother of Malin Rozelle."

"Malin Rozelle…" I said. My memory helpfully retrieved this name. The woman who'd had her head bashed in with a golf club. The retired advertising executive.

"She was my neighbour." Barbro took off her glasses. "Her brother must have made an arrangement with the police to visit her house. They allowed him in once before, when he collected the dog."

The dog. The dog that Malin Rozelle had trained to shit on Barbro's property.

That was when I knew.

I made a conscious effort not to let it show on my face. But I knew then.

Actually, I realised, I'd known before. When I found the lyric sheet with the stain of a wine glass on it.

I hadn't been able to accept the knowledge, but I'd known.

Someone had perused that lyric sheet at their leisure over a nice glass of red. As if to reinforce this point, I saw now that one of the books on the table had a similar mark on the cover.

Apparently Barbro was careless about such things.

It didn't have to be true, of course.

She might just have been curious after she'd heard about the killings. What could be more normal than to take an interest, take out the lyric sheet? Study it over—or, rather, under—a glass of wine.

But I *knew*.

I knew and I couldn't let it show.

Barbro was studying me as she sipped her red wine. "Are you all right?"

I said, "I was just trying to remember something Christer said. That night we came over. He was telling me that you and he shared two passions. One of them was crime fiction. But he never got around to saying what the other one was. At the time I assumed it was hi-fi equipment."

Barbro chuckled. "No. It was hunting."

Hunting. I tried desperately to say something suitably casual while my mind filled with an image of Christer Vingqvist in the swimming pool, eviscerated by an expert. "So," I said, "that photograph of him in the mountains…" The one hanging between her bookshelves.

"Yes. That was taken on one of our hunting trips."

"You took it."

"Yes."

"Great photo," I said, on my principle of always offering sincere praise when given the chance. Even to a crazed killer.

"Thank you." The crazed killer sounded pleased.

The door opened and Nevada came in, smiling, with her empty wine glass. "August Strindberg is the best cat in Sweden."

"Well, certainly in this part of Sweden," said Barbro happily. Everyone likes to have their pet praised. "Would you like another glass of wine?"

Before Nevada could reply I said, "Actually we have to be going."

Nevada looked at me, instantly realised that something was wrong, and said, "That's right. We're so sorry but we need to be getting along. Have you paid for the records, darling?"

"Yes, I have, honey. And for your books."

"Oh, I'd forgotten about those. Ha-ha."

"Ha-ha."

We said our goodbyes and got out of the house. I could feel Barbro's eyes on us as we joined Agatha and pried her away from August Strindberg. She realised that something was wrong almost as quickly as Nevada had.

"What is it?" said Agatha, as we walked towards the car.

"Is it *her*?" said Nevada.

"Yes," I said.

32: ANSWERING SHADE

Agatha put her foot down and we rocketed back to town. We were no longer worried about the speed limit—in fact, if the police did stop us, that would be a plus. Meanwhile I rang Kriminalinspektör Lizell. Or tried to.

"Isn't she answering?" said Nevada.

"No. But I've texted her."

"What did you say?"

"*Barbro Bok is the killer. We just left her at her home.*"

Nevada nodded. "That's pretty unambiguous."

"That's what I thought," I said.

"Where are Tinkler and Ida?" said Agatha.

"At the secondhand-butik," said Nevada. "I don't know which one, though."

I had never seen Agatha use her phone while driving before, but now she took it out and stuck it upright in a docking station on the dashboard and made a call. It was on speaker, so we all heard the phone ring an infuriating number of times. Then Tinkler answered. "How's everything? Everybody still alive?"

"Where are you, Tinkler?" said Agatha.

"At the inside-out egg. That's what Ida calls the secondhand-butik with the yellow walls on the outside and the white on the inside. The inside-out egg. She dreamed that up. Isn't it cute?"

"Tinkler," said Agatha, "I came up with that fucking name."

"Wait a minute. So you did. That's right. I beg your pardon. Ida calls it the *upside-down* egg. Isn't that cute? She gets everything mixed up. Come to think of it, so do I. I just got that mixed up."

"Tinkler, are you high?" said Nevada.

"Of course."

"There is a killer on the loose and you're potentially in their sights…"

"Surely being high is the best and indeed only way to deal with such a situation?"

"Tinkler," I said, breaking in, not wanting to, reassured by the familiar rhythm of their bickering. "Barbro Bok is the killer."

There was silence, but not for long. "I never trusted her," said Tinkler. "Too much theological literature and not enough pornography."

"Tinkler," said Nevada. "Are you indoors at the moment?"

"Yes. We're on the top floor of the butik."

"Well, get down to the ground floor and stay inside but stay near the exit. We'll come and get you."

"We're on our way, Tinkler," confirmed Agatha. "We should be with you in about—" she checked something on the dashboard, "—three minutes."

"Okay, but what are we going to do about this Barbro Bok thing?" said Tinkler.

"I think we should all stick together," said Nevada.

"Don't you think we should also call the cops?"

"We've *called* the fucking cops," said Nevada.

"Sorry. I didn't mean to impugn your badass crime-busting credentials."

"Relax, Tinkler," I said. "I've called the inspector."

"The lesbian cop."

"Yes."

"Good. I trust her. Her, I trust. What did she say?"

"I didn't speak to her," I said. "I left a message."

"You left a message?"

"Sent a text actually," I said.

"Well, for Christ's sake," said Tinkler, "that's not good enough. Speak to her in person."

"I've tried. She's not picking up."

"Why isn't she picking up?"

"I imagine she has other things to do," I said.

"Well, if she doesn't get your message, she really will have other things to do."

We picked up Tinkler and Ida and then sped back to the hotel. Agatha parked considerably nearer this time, in fact right outside. As she pulled up, we saw a familiar vehicle parked across the road by the scorched ruins of the vattentorn.

"Looks like Anders got his bike back," said Nevada.

"That's not all that's back," said Agatha.

Standing in front of the hotel, out of the now-returned rain and smoking a cigarette, was Oskar. And his kilt had also now returned.

"Guys, I swear the crow has a perch under there."

"Tinkler," said Nevada, genuinely exasperated. "He isn't even the one with the crow."

"What?" said Tinkler. "This guy isn't the crow guy?

"No, darling," said Ida, "it is the comb-over cunt who has the crow."

"*That* guy?"

"Yes.

"In that case," said Tinkler, "you know what that makes him? The comb-over crow-owning cunt. That's not necessarily easy to say."

Oskar politely extinguished his cigarette on our arrival. Nevada told him, "We've got something important to say to everyone."

"Yes, I can see by your faces," said Oskar.

"Do you mind coming inside?"

"Not at all."

He put the snuffed-out cigarette butt carefully in his pocket and followed us up the steps and into the hotel.

We were inside. Finally. With the door closed behind us.

Instantly I felt safer. I had no idea if the keypad on that door, or the door itself, would keep anyone out. But this place, with its high ceiling and pale skylight gazing benignly down on us, had begun to feel like home.

And now we all paused in the lobby, gathered under that benign gaze. Oskar turned and looked at us, or rather looked at me, and said, "By the way, I've been meaning to say, virtually since we first met, I've been meaning to tell you, to let you know that *Attack and Decay* may not mean what you think it means. It's actually—"

"It's actually a sound engineering term," I said. I was damned if I was going to be lectured to by a guy wearing a kilt, particularly if he didn't have a crow under there.

I said, "It means the beginning of a sound, like the leading edge of a note. That's the attack. And the way the sound, the note, fades away at the end, that's the decay."

As I was saying this, someone was coming down the gleaming wooden staircase to join us. This person all too swiftly proved to be Stinky Stanmer.

"Stinky," said Nevada.

Stinky flinched at the mere mention of his name by my honey, not least because he'd no doubt once again forgotten hers and could expect her full and well-earned retribution if a suitable situation arose. Diligently keen to avoid such a situation—who knows, the call-a-friend option might not be open next time—he came down the steps carefully on the opposite side to Tinkler's trunk and joined us in the lobby.

"Stinky," said Nevada, "we know who is doing the killings." This definitely got Oskar's attention, as well as Stinky's.

"Great," said Stinky. "Can I record this?"

"No. Shut up."

"Who is the killer?" said Oskar impatiently.

"Barbro Bok."

There was a moment's silence. "So, wait," said Oskar. "Okay. So, who is that?"

"Emma's sister," I said.

"The girl who speaks in English slang?"

"Yes."

"That's Emma?"

"Yes," I said.

"Okay. So, we met Emma, but we never met her, the sister, but I guess this is welcome news. I mean that her identity has been exposed."

"Wait, did I meet this Emma?" said Stinky. "What does she look like?"

"Not up to your standard," said Nevada. "What are you doing?"

"Just a bit of *cinéma vérité*," said Stinky. He held up his phone and filmed himself saying in his serious voice, "Attack and decay. It's a sound engineering term. It means the beginning or the leading edge of a note. That's the attack. And the way the sound fades away at the end. That's the decay."

He stopped filming.

"You really are a despicable little shit," said Oskar. But he said it almost admiringly and Stinky winked at him.

Nevada was saving her rage for another day. "I think we're all safest on the ground floor," she said. "We can all get out most easily at ground level. And I think maybe we should. Get out, I mean. But we'll see… Everybody stay down here while I get everybody else from upstairs and bring them down. And then I think we should go outside. Like a fire drill."

"We're not going to have to stand out in the middle of the fucking park again?" said Tinkler.

"We have my umbrella, darling," said Ida.

"That's true." Tinkler brightened up, and Ida in turn was clearly pleased that her umbrella was getting the approbation it was due.

"And if Gun brings hers," said Agatha, "there'll be enough rain cover for everybody."

"Good thinking," said Oskar.

"I'll do that," said Nevada, "I'll get Gun's umbrella." She started up the stairs on her urgent mission to collect a big umbrella and round up all the other people. Also, no doubt she was just plain eager to be out of the company of Stinky.

Who was currently saying, "She isn't likely to turn up, is she?" Stinky looked around apprehensively and then at me with pleading eyes. "This Emma's sister, the killer? She isn't about to show up, is she?"

On the staircase, Nevada paused in her ascent.

"That is a very good question," said Oskar, now fully alert and also looking at me.

I shrugged. "We just left her at her farmhouse, apparently none the wiser, and Agatha drove here like a bat out of hell…"

"I did, indeed, drive like the proverbial bat out of hell," said Agatha, with a well-earned note of pride. "In all modesty. And even allowing for picking up Tinkler and Ida…"

"We were all prepared and ready to go as soon as you arrived," said Ida.

"You were," said Agatha. "And even allowing for picking you up, in all modesty, the only thing that could have beaten us here is…"

She fell silent. And then looked at me. I was looking at Nevada. It was a fair bet we were all thinking the same thing. As was Ida.

"Anders's motorcycle," said Ida. "He didn't get it back. He wasn't the one who put it there…"

"No, that was myself."

We turned to see Barbro Bok coming in from the breakfast room. She was wearing a leather jacket, combat trousers and boots—presumably a hunting outfit that was also good for riding a motorcycle. She had a green, white and grey camouflage pattern motorcycle helmet, probably military surplus. She carried it cradled in the crook of one arm the way she'd carried the cat.

She set her helmet down just as carefully, but on the lectern not the ground. And the hand that had recently held the glass of wine, and spilled some, now held the gun.

Some kind of machine gun.

Unlike the glass of wine earlier, this did not dip or waver. The weapon was gravely steady.

Barbro left the helmet on the lectern. Now holding the gun in a businesslike grip with both hands, she moved to a central position in the lobby where she could watch all of us. Her gaze settled on me.

"It's so easy to read your face," she said, smiling.

"I've warned you about that, love," said Nevada from above us, almost absent-mindedly.

"I took the motorcycle last night," said Barbro. "I took it from the striptease club. I knew it would be useful. I am familiar with motorcycles, quite familiar."

"She's a dark horse," said Ida, her voice tiny and quiet under the high roof, under the now evidently uncaring gaze of the skylight. Tinkler made no attempt at a joke.

Barbro Bok didn't seem to hear her. "And as I suspected, it *was* useful, very useful. So I am here now. Thanks to Anders's bike, I arrived before you. I came in through the back of the hotel through the service entrance. And I waited, just in there. You couldn't see me, but I was sitting in the darkness listening. I could hear you all when you came in. I was listening to see if any of you were worth saving. But I can't in all conscience say any of you are."

She lifted the gun. "So you're all about to take part in a great experiment. A great ontological experiment."

"I'd rather not," said Tinkler.

I agreed with Tinkler. So did everyone. 'Keep the crazed killer talking' was very much a unanimous and instantly and silently agreed-on policy. And she seemed happy enough to talk.

"In a sense, this whole thing has been exactly such an experiment," she said, as if the concept had just struck her.

"From the terrible day when Christer's car caught fire…" She fell silent.

Silent was not what we wanted.

"That's what I didn't understand," I said. I remembered her on the night of the dog poo glow sticks. "You were so clearly glad to see that he had survived."

She looked at me, her friendly intelligent eyes gleaming behind her spectacles. "Yes, I was. I was *so* glad."

"And yet you…" I didn't feel I needed to go into detail on what had befallen Mr Vingqvist in that empty swimming pool, on that night, with the snow falling steadily, softly and endlessly.

"Yes, I did," she agreed.

We needed longer answers than that. "Was it just an accident," I said, "that his car caught fire?"

"Oh, no. I set a device."

"You put a bomb in his car."

"Yes, and I put a timer on it."

"You built all this yourself?" I said. Encourage her. Encourage her.

And she seemed eager enough to talk. Quite proud really. "Oh yes, the internet was immeasurably helpful in that regard, but I imagine I could have managed without it. Both of my brothers served in the military. I felt it was wasted on them. Military service. But I learned about motorcycles from them. And other things. So building the device was straightforward enough."

She paused then. She seemed finished.

"How did you source the explosive?" said Nevada.

"I bought it from the same gentlemen who sold me this gun."

Gentlemen, I thought. Plural. Röd and Röd were said to have recently concluded an arms deal...

She looked at the gun in her hands. "I told them I didn't feel safe at the farm. Alone. At night." She was looking at her purchase as if she was suddenly remembering she'd acquired it for a quite different reason.

I immediately said, "So you built the bomb to kill Christer?"

She looked at me and nodded, the gun mercifully forgotten for the moment. "I knew he was taking the long drive to Gothenburg to the airport to meet you. And I could estimate when he would be driving through a long stretch of largely deserted road in the countryside. In fact, that describes most of his route. And I set the timer accordingly, so as to minimise any chance of other casualties."

This was more like it. This was much more like it. We wanted nice long answers like this. But how to elicit another one?

Nevada spoke from above us. "You set the bomb, yet you were glad he'd survived?"

This proved to be a jackpot question because, taking a step closer to the foot of the stairs, Barbro Bok began to speak thoughtfully and at length. "How to describe that day? How to describe the suffering of one human mind, one human soul, during those endless hours? I placed the device in his car with the timer set and he left exactly on schedule, and everything was going exactly to plan, and I was very pleased, very pleased with myself. If you regard pride as a sin, I was bursting with sin. So proud and pleased and happy with what I had done. And then, suddenly, it was as simple as this—as simple as grace—I had a change of heart. I realised how terrible and wicked was this thing I had done. I suddenly saw clearly. It was like waking from a sickbed dream. This person who had placed the bomb in the car was not me. Could not be me. I was a person who desperately wanted no harm to come to anyone, and most of all no harm to come to my friend. I tried desperately to ring him, but he very sensibly had his phone switched off, to be safe and maintain concentration on his long drive, so my calls kept going to voicemail. I thought about notifying the emergency services. I looked at the clock and I saw it was too late. My change of heart had arrived too late. No one could reach him in time. I fell to my knees and prayed with a desperation and a fervour unmatched in a lifetime of prayer."

She fell suddenly silent. We didn't like sudden silences. I searched my mind for something to say…

"And it worked," said Nevada.

Barbro drifted closer to the foot of the stairs and looked up at her. "Yes, I suppose you could say it did. In fact, you could say it was a miracle. And I did. I said it was a miracle. I believed it was, when I saw that he had survived. When I saw the pictures he had posted, I believed it was a miracle. I was so grateful. I had been given a second chance. He was alive. And then you guys came over to my place bringing him with you, and there he was in the flesh. It was the happiest moment of my life. I was in rapture."

She sighed. It was a relaxed sigh and we all relaxed with her.

Barbro Bok wandered back to the centre of the lobby, standing directly under the grey ellipse of the skylight.

"I was in bliss," she said. "Life was perfect and my friend Christer Vingqvist was alive and there had been this miracle and he had been spared and everything was perfect. And then something happened, something later that evening. You were there when it happened. I was floating along, on a cloud of bliss, full of love for my friend, full of love for everyone. And then I tripped over that pile of books in my hallway. The pile of books he had left there. He had just pulled my books off the shelf so he could fill it with copies of his own stupid self-published novel. He had left all the other books lying there in the hallway, all my beloved books, and I tripped on them and I fell—I fell on my face—and you ran over to try and help me up and I waved you away, *Thank you very much but I am fine*. And I *was* fine. Because when I tripped over that pile of books, all my love for him just turned to hate. In an instant. In a split second. It was like water turning into wine. In a way, it was my only true experience of the miraculous, of the divine. It easily eclipsed the feeling I'd had earlier that day when I learned he was alive. Now I felt peace, true peace at last. Because I knew I was going to kill him after all. And if he was so fond of his novel, then let the novel be the means of his undoing. Consequently, I did to him exactly what he did to the character in his stupid Penumbra Snow story."

She paused, lost in thought. Where might that thought end up? Was this a silence that we shouldn't interrupt or that we should interrupt at all costs?

Barbro sighed. This sigh definitely did not sound so good. So I said, "You had no idea about the song?"

"The song he copied the murder method from? I had no idea at all—at first. I only learned of it when Christer told me about it. He became very talkative towards the end. Essentially, he was confessing, for stealing that idea and putting it in his novel, confessing for all sorts of things. Or apologising, if you want to use less loaded language. But it was too late for that. Too late for apologies."

Now, a sudden and very unpromising silence. The expression on Barbro's face was changing and we could all feel this going to a very bad place.

I said, "And then you discovered there were other songs?"

Barbro nodded and smiled, her dark chain of thought evidently and thankfully broken. "Yes, certainly. That was ironic. I thought I had imitated a murder in a book but then I discovered the murder wasn't even original to that stupid book. It was from a song. So my imitation was now an imitation of something else. Something I had never intended. And I remembered I actually had a copy of this record that he'd been talking about, *Attack and Decay*, so I went and found it."

She smiled her happy dog smile. "I had no intention of doing anything, of course. I was just curious what the other songs might be about. I read the lyric sheet…" She looked at me. "And I imagine I must have left a wine stain on it, judging by the way you were looking at a wine stain on that book on the table in my kitchen."

Having her gaze fixed on me like this was like standing in front of an open door with a cold wind blowing through it—a cold wind coming straight at me.

"And you found something in the lyrics," said Agatha. Barbro's gaze shifted to her, away from me, and the door closed and the cold wind stopped.

"Yes," said Barbro. She was now addressing Agatha like one crime fiction fan to another, discussing a favourite plot. "As it so happened, one of the songs was called 'The First Golf War'. I knew that Malin Rozelle's husband had been an avid golfer. And he'd left much of his equipment in her house. He'd certainly left his clubs. Thus when I learned that there was this song about killing people with golf clubs, it was like a sign." Barbro gave a self-conscious little chuckle. "But even then, I was not going to do anything about it. It was just a notion. Purely theoretical. And then I stepped out of my front door on a beautiful morning for a walk on my beautiful farm, and I step right into a big fat soft squishy dog turd. It immediately went deep into the grid pattern of the soles of my walking boots." She indicated the boots she was wearing and we all nodded in immediate comprehension and absolute sympathy.

"It took me an hour, even with the assistance of a hose, to get my boots properly clean, and by the end of that hour…" She shrugged. "That was that for Malin Rozelle.

"Anyway, once I'd dealt with her I still had five songs left. Five opportunities to improve the world. By removing people like Bo Lugn, who opened that detestable venue outside of town—outside of *my* town. He told everyone it was going be a pizza place with a difference. At least he didn't lie about that, the contemptible vermin. And there was Filip Over…"

Scissor beak crow, I thought.

"He was the gluttonous entrepreneur who had sold Bo Lugn the land in the first place. Sold him the land for his despicable striptease club despite the protestations of decent people in this town. He lived in this town, too. Indeed, he lived on this street. Filip Over had a house as big as this entire hotel."

She suddenly looked at us in an odd new way, as if awakening from a trance, like someone realising how late it is and how much they have to do. Like someone about to wrap things up…

We did not want that. "So, it was just a coincidence," I said. "About one of the songs being 'Fire' and you burning Christer's car?"

"Oh yes," she said, her interest suddenly caught by her tale again. "That was indeed entirely felicitous. I mean, if you plant a device in the car, the car is going to burn, but it was entirely coincidental that it could be interpreted as the song 'Fire'. Entirely coincidental and very useful. But now, of course, we have a different song…"

She lifted her gun and I realised with a thrill of horror that she was about to get started.

"What about Emma?" said Nevada from above us.

Barbro lowered her gun, and every one of us wilted with relief as she became caught up in her narrative.

"Emma? You would like to know what happened to my sister? I went to see my sister. To talk to her. Talk to her very seriously. About the future of our farm. Our parents' farm. I still believe it could be a working farm. That we could give to the soil and take from the soil. But to proceed with my plans I needed Emma to give her consent, because we have shared ownership of the property."

As she spoke, Barbro drifted slowly back towards the foot of the staircase.

"But not only did she not give her consent, she laughed at my dream. My dream of a working farm. She told me I should forget about it. Told me I should 'knock it on the head'. She was speaking in that ridiculous British slang she uses. And that was the final straw. So, she got 'knocked on the head' herself. She got knocked on the head, all right."

Barbro was standing at the foot of the staircase, addressing Nevada. Now she looked away from Nevada, sighed a getting-down-to-business sigh, and raised her gun.

In the doorway of the dimly lit breakfast room, emerging from the darkness, there was a flash of colour—pale blue—as Eva Lizell came out of the shadows in the leather jacket Nevada had sold her.

She had a gun in her hand.

She must have come in through the service entrance, I thought.

Barbro saw her and began to turn her own weapon towards her.

Then, halfway up the stairs, Nevada made the smallest of movements. Perhaps she just brushed her hip against the table where Tinkler's trunk stood.

And down it came, a blur of pale blue, an answering shade to the inspector's jacket. Thundering and bouncing off the steps, a tumbling juggernaut. Barbro swung her gun around and fired at the trunk as if it was a living creature and she could stop it.

She couldn't.

The trunk hit Barbro squarely in the face and upper chest. Smashed her to the floor, falling like a slab on top of a grave. Barbro lay unmoving, her limbs splayed out, her bright red blood making a striking contrast on Tinkler's sky-blue luggage.

Her machine gun lay on the floor.

Eva Lizell moved quickly into the lobby.

The Kriminalinspektör came to where the weapon was lying, put one foot firmly down on it and stood on it. In one hand she held her own gun, in the other hand her phone.

She spoke into the phone now, quietly, calmly, quickly.

33: FAREWELL, TROLLESKO

"As our time in Sweden draws to a close," said Tinkler, "can I just voice my disappointment at how relatively few Scandinavian and Scandi noir stereotypes were confirmed? I mean, where was the oafish, overweight computer hacker? Wait a minute... that's *me*. Check."

We were standing outside the remains of the vattentorn with our luggage—now much diminished since Tinkler's trunk had been impounded a few days earlier as evidence in a complex murder investigation.

The woman at the centre of that investigation, who had been flattened by said trunk, was in hospital and doing well in terms of recovery and would soon be fed into the Swedish justice system, ultimately bound for trial, sentencing and whatever program of rehabilitation was deemed most suitable. Enlightened penal system, check.

Agatha brought the car around.

As we got in with our much-diminished luggage, there was a thunderous chord from the bandstand in the park.

Spotlights were stabbing the dimming winter sky as daylight began to fade. The Storm Dream Troopers were doing a sound check.

They had, surprisingly, secured permission for a concert and were playing a charity gig tonight—a benefit for Anders, who had lost everything in the fire.

The fact that it was great publicity for the Troopers, and that the scorched ruin of the tower made a terrific visual in the background, would only have occurred to the most cynical.

We would later hear that it was a very successful fundraiser and Anders bought a house on the proceeds. Not just any house, either: Christer Vingqvist's Mexican casa. It needed a new owner.

At least it wasn't the fake Roman monstrosity where we'd found Christer's body.

Anders moved into his new house with a new girlfriend, the lady Ida had pronounced horse-faced.

Around that time Barbro Bok, the cause of so much carnage, left hospital to go into custody, and her sister was also discharged. Emma had come out of her coma largely recovered and intact in the wake of what had been a fearsome head injury.

"She just has some very particular trouble with language skills," Magnus told us when he called us to give us the good news. Then, speaking in a low voice, apparently so she wouldn't overhear him, he explained that—for the time being at least—Emma couldn't speak Swedish. "She can only speak Mockney."

Thus warned, we were then allowed to speak directly to Emma. But since we'd pretty much never heard her speak Swedish anyway, she sounded and seemed completely normal when she appeared on screen, apart from a wearing a Union Jack beanie indoors—which she might have done anyway, although in this case it was to conceal evidence of a repaired but still terrible head wound.

After talking to her, we did speculate that perhaps this inability to speak anything but Mockney was payback for Magnus, who did deserve a bit of payback.

But he and Emma seemed tight as a couple; they moved into the family farmhouse and adopted the farmhouse cat, August Strindberg. Or rather, he adopted them, and proceeded to assist Emma with her rehabilitation and recovery by sleeping in her lap at every opportunity.

Owyn Wynter got his two copies of *Attack and Decay*, the original pressing and the crap audiophile one. We'd already been handsomely paid for these. But when I went to see him and deliver them, I took the opportunity to ask him why he'd felt obliged to warn us to watch out for the Troopers—saying they were dangerous when they were all together as a unit.

"Well," said Owyn, "you and Nevada seem like a nice couple. And those four... They're pretty intense swingers. Couples who get drawn into their orbit, who get too close to them, end up torn apart. And I wouldn't want that little devil who sank her claws into me to be a child of divorce."

Fair enough.

But I knew none of this the day we left Trollesko. Agatha drove us to the station and left her rental car there. We carried our minimal luggage onto the train and made the journey to Gothenburg and then to the airport where we were to meet up with Ida, who had come to Gothenburg ahead of us because she wanted to visit the university in connection with her proposed PhD.

Then she would rendezvous with Tinkler at the airport. That was the plan.

"She's going to live with me in London," said Tinkler. His face suddenly assumed a haunted look. "Oh, Christ, I'm going to have to clean the toilet. And the bathtub. And the sink."

Nevada and Agatha exchanged a look but said nothing. We were waiting at the security gates at the airport. We hadn't gone through yet because we were waiting for Ida to join us.

It reminded me poignantly of that first time in the Notre Coeur, waiting for this nutty exotic dancer to turn up. And nobody actually expecting her to, except Tinkler.

We waited. She didn't come. While we waited, the talk turned to Barbro Bok.

"She was very disparaging about that killing in the Penumbra Snow novel that turned out to be a rip-off of a song," said Agatha. "But with her string of killings, she herself was doing a rip-off. She was ripping off a golden age classic of crime fiction."

"How so?" said Nevada.

"She was bumping people off for reasons of her personal agenda," said Agatha, "but disguising it as a serial killer

choosing random victims following a specific pattern for
the murders. In this case, an album of songs. In the case of
the golden age classic, it was a quite different pattern."

"But would Barbro have known about this golden age
classic of crime fiction?" said Nevada.

"Oh yes. I saw a copy on her shelf. It would be on the
shelf of any lover of classic crime novels."

"What is this book?" said Tinkler.

"I won't tell you because it would be a spoiler. But she
pinched the plot."

"So, she isn't just a killer," said Tinkler, "she's a
plagiarist."

Even Tinkler had begun to think that Ida wasn't going to
turn up when Ida turned up.

She was wearing a red coat with black lining. It was cut
off at about hip level, revealing tight black leggings and red
boots. Over one shoulder she had slung a black drawstring
bag. She looked chic, but for a girl with ten blue Ikea bags
full of personal items, who'd recently been shopping for
more, she was travelling remarkably light.

She hurried over to us, smiling, whispered in Tinkler's
ear, and smiled at us again as she led Tinkler away out of
earshot, where they stood and began to talk.

Nevada and Agatha and I looked at each other. Nobody
thought this looked good. In its own modest way, it was
an unbearable moment. So, to distract everyone, including
myself, I said, "She didn't set out to be a plagiarist."

"Barbro Bok?" said Agatha.

"That's right," I said. "She only intended to bump off one poor self-published priest."

"But as soon as she realised that there was the possibility of expanding the body count, she went for it," said Nevada. "She *liked* what she was doing."

On this uncheerful note, Tinkler came back to us from where he'd been standing with Ida. Ida remained where she was, watching us. Her gaze was unreadable at this distance.

"Tinkler, what's happening?" said Agatha.

Tinkler looked at us, blinking slowly, then looked down at the floor. "Ida said she can't come to London with me. She's been thinking, and she's decided not to come to London. She said, 'I'm sorry, but after everything that happened to me, I just think it's too dangerous to be hanging out with you.' Except she said it in a cute Swedish accent."

Tinkler looked up now, and to our amazement, he was smiling. "It's just too dangerous hanging out with me," he said, apparently savouring the words. I realised we were witnessing his transformation, in his own mind at least, and to be honest probably at most, into Jordon Tinkler: International Man of Intrigue.

None of us pointed out the obvious…

That the danger to Ida, which had been real and plentiful, had mostly arisen out of her own connection with a certain strip club pizza joint and was little to do with our Tinkler. But perhaps Ida had shrewdly chosen exactly this way of dumping him as the method least likely to break Tinkler's heart.

As for Tinkler, was he perhaps even a little relieved? After all, this way he wouldn't have to clean the bathroom. "Why is she still standing there, Tinkler?" said Agatha.

"She sent me over here to see if she could come and say goodbye."

Nevada said, "She did what?"

"She's worried you might be angry at her."

We beckoned to Ida and she hastened over eagerly to join us for a series of florid hugging and kissing farewells. Saying goodbye to me last of all, Ida leaned forward and whispered into my ear, her breath hot and ticklish, "I am going to give you a screw."

As she said this, she pressed something clandestinely into my hand and at the same time kissed me under my ear. Her lips were soft and warm, and she'd chosen a remarkably sensitive spot.

All of which undermined my attempt to collect my wits. What did any of that mean? How was I supposed to respond?

This problem, at least, was solved because Ida turned and started walking away, turned back and waved and then turned away again, disappearing into the airport crowd.

I didn't actually see her go. I was looking at what she'd pressed into my hand.

It was a screw.

I started to chuckle.

Then I looked at it a little more closely and saw it was a more profound message than just a reminder of that evening, when the face of a dismayingly oversized hell-beast seemed about to swing its full regard on us in a burning tower in a snow-clad town...

Because it was a special kind of screw.

It combined both what she called the star head and what we call a flat head. It was universal. Any screwdriver would work with it.

I showed it to the others, and they got it right away.

"She's a bright girl," said Nevada, handing the screw to Agatha. "Profound message suggesting a subtle and interesting intelligence?" she suggested.

"We certainly can't discount that possibility," said Agatha.

"Okay," said Tinkler. "But what does it *mean*?"

I said, "I take it to mean she's wishing us safe. Because we'd have been safe in the fire if we'd had these to deal with. So, she's wishing us well and wishing us safety in the future."

Nevada nodded. "That's what I read into it, too." She looked at Agatha.

"Sure," said Agatha. "But what does the Tingler think?"

"I just thought it meant she was bisexual," said Tinkler. "Like, you know, she works both ways..."

"Don't you already know whether she is bisexual or not? From your exciting time together?"

"It seemed rude to ask during our first few weeks," said Tinkler. "It seemed somehow unromantic. So I was waiting..."

"But it turns out your first few weeks were also your last few weeks," said Nevada.

"Ouch," said Agatha.

"That's true," said Tinkler. "There aren't going to be any more weeks." His head had begun drooping. His voice was forlorn. "Dang it."

"Now, Tinkler," said Nevada very firmly. "I think we've established that your friends expect proper swearing from you."

Tinkler perked up. "That's true. Fucking well fuck it."

"That's more like it," said Nevada. "Much more like it." We began moving towards the departure gates. A woman in an oyster-coloured raincoat stood up from the bench where she was sitting as we approached.

It was Kriminalinspektör Eva Lizell.

"I thought I'd come and see you off."

"That's very decent of you," I said.

"I also felt you might have some questions and I might be in a position to answer some of them." She looked at us with level brown eyes. Was the worry line across her forehead carved a little less deeply now?

"Actually, as it happens," I said, "we do have a question."

"What was Barbro's beef with the self-published priest?" said Tinkler.

"That's right," said Nevada. "This all began with her wanting to blow up Christer Vingqvist in his car. But she never explained *why*."

"Although we did get the distinct impression that she was angry with him," said Agatha.

"Out of patience," said Eva Lizell. "That is how I would describe it, more than angry. Out of patience after a long, long dispute over some detail of Church policy."

"You mean," I said, "someone got killed because of a doctrinal dispute within a Church?"

"Yes," said Eva Lizell.

I said, "If only there was some kind of historical precedent for such a thing."

It was the first time I'd ever head the Kriminalinspektör laugh out loud.

"What about Röd and Röd?" said Nevada.

"What about them?" said Eva Lizell, something in her manner shutting down. She was suddenly cagey.

I said, "We think they sold Barbro her gun."

"For her 'Active Shooter' spree," said Tinkler.

"And the C4 she used to make her bombs," added Nevada.

"We think you should arrest the two Röds," concluded Tinkler.

"I cannot comment on an ongoing investigation," said Eva Lizell. But it sounded a lot like confirmation.

Certainly to Tinkler, who said, "Don't put them in the same cell. They might start braiding each other's beards."

Then we said our goodbyes. She embraced each of us in turn, not lingering notably longer with Nevada.

And then she waved a quick final farewell, and as she did so, perhaps because she was feeling warm or perhaps to make a point, she unbuttoned her raincoat to reveal underneath the sky-blue leather jacket she'd bought from Nevada.

The flight back to London was swift and uneventful, except briefly on our arrival at Heathrow, when we paused in horror to watch a news report unfold on a large screen in Arrivals.

A revered and beloved broadcaster was saying, "You just seem to have the knack of being in the right place at the right time, right before a story breaks."

The horror began when the camera revealed Stinky Stanmer nodding seriously, and replying modestly, "I suppose one just develops an instinct for this sort of thing."

Agatha, being Agatha, had arranged a paying gig in the form of collecting a luxury vehicle at the airport's short-term car park and returning it safely to the home of its owner while they were off on a foreign jaunt. This meant she could drop us at our own home in comfort and style, but couldn't linger with us because she had to deliver the car.

So it was just me, Nevada and Tinkler walking the familiar path to our front door. On the little row of houses where we lived, there was a vine-shrouded corner we would pass on our way home—an unruly, towering, flowering vine in whose shadowed recesses our cat Fanny would often lurk. She liked to pop out and ambush us as we walked past, getting the drop on us.

It was now fully night, and the only light was some minimal estate lighting, so Fanny found it very easy to appear out of nowhere, a trick she could perform even in broad daylight given some half-decent cover.

She darted out of hiding now, proudly squeaking and full of herself. "You have some explaining to do, young lady," said Nevada, as Fanny fell into step with us. "I mean, not doing your sink-drinking trick for my mum. She was *so* looking forward to it…"

"I've got a sink-drinking trick I could do," said Tinkler. "Do you want to hear about it?"

"No thank you, Tinkler."

Tinkler was tagging along with us on the assumption that he could score a home-cooked meal, which would be of a surprisingly high standard given how quickly it was going to be assembled, and also quite possibly receive some commiseration about the stripper that got away into the bargain.

And he was right on both counts.

We reached our front gate and began to open it. Normally this would have elicited a response from our other cat Turk if she, like her sister, was anywhere in the vicinity.

Usually that response would consist of racing to join us and then charging hell-for-leather through the now-open front gate as if this was the only way she could ever possibly gain access to our lodgings, despite the fact that she could not only easily jump over the aforementioned gate at any time, but she could also easily slip under it, as supple as a mongoose.

On this occasion, though, Turk's response was very different. Instead of racing to join us, she was evidently staying put wherever she was, and giving voice to the most pissed-off yowl I'd heard from her since—

We looked over to the source of the sound and saw the corpse-faced motherfucker standing beside a large concrete planter full of shrubs in front of one of the buildings opposite. As soon as he saw us looking at him, he fled into the night.

"That was the corpse-faced motherfucker," said Tinkler.

"Right," said Nevada.

"What's his name?"

"Jaunty," I said, not very happily. Even though he'd been demoted in our minds from fiend of the night to financial comptroller, this was not a welcome visitation.

"What the hell is he doing hanging around here?"

Before anyone could propose an answer to that question, Turk finally emerged from hiding among the shrubs in the planter and raced to join us.

We unlocked the front door while the cats, who could have both gone in through the cat flap several times and been waiting comfortably for us inside, instead waited patiently for us to open the door for them. Nevada finally held it open, and the little geniuses scooted in. We all followed.

There was music coming quietly from the sitting room. Edith Piaf on vinyl, it sounded like. Penny had been briefed on the use of the turntable, so that was fine. I idly wondered where she'd picked up a vintage record, which is what this sounded like. No doubt in one of the charity shops which, like her daughter, she regularly plundered for high-end clothing and masterpieces of world cinema.

Penny herself appeared as we sat down in the sitting room, while Piaf sang about love and loss. Nevada and I and the cats sat on the sofa, Tinkler in an armchair. Penny was wearing a silk dressing gown I recognised as belonging to Nevada. She looked flushed with rude health, as if she'd just emerged from a sauna after a brisk round of tennis.

"Hello everyone," she said. "So lovely to see you all."

"So you didn't manage to kill the cats, then?" said Tinkler. He was making small gestures of enticement to try and lure Fanny from the sofa, where she lay snugly tucked between Nevada and myself, watching him with silent contempt.

"No, they're fine," said Penny. "Everything is fine. I was just a bit wrong-footed because I wasn't expecting you until tomorrow…"

"Mum," said Nevada, "I sent you a message."

"I know, I just checked and you did and it's all my fault. Sorry, the place is a bit of a mess, the bed is a bit of a mess."

"Oh, we'll sort it out," said Nevada. She slumped over on the sofa, abandoning all pretence of sitting upright, instead lying down, curled up, her head in my lap. The cats immediately divided the spoils from the opulent new range of places available to snuggle in comfort.

"And I opened one of your good bottles of wine," said Penny. "The Domaine de Thalabert. But I've ordered a replacement from the Wine Society."

"Same vintage or younger?"

"Younger," said Penny.

"Good," said Nevada. "I think it's better and fruitier when it's younger." The discussion of wine had caused her to lift her head from my lap and look at the bottle of wine in question, now empty, standing on the dining room table.

Suddenly Nevada sat bolt upright. The cats launched off the sofa like a pair of affronted, hairy sprites. Nevada was staring at the bottle on the table. "Has someone been here?" She was right. There were two glasses with the empty bottle.

"Well, yes, there was," said Penny, a mite defensively. "He just left, in fact. He's very nice. His name is Jaunty."

A silence ensued that was so total we could hear one of cats exhaling breathily as she yawned. "Jaunty?" said Nevada.

"Yes," said her mother. "He's very nice. And he's been paying visits while I've been here... in fact, he's been staying the night now and then. He stayed last night and in fact he only just left. I'm sorry the place is in a state. But as I say, I wasn't expecting you back until tomorrow."

"Staying the night?" said Nevada.

"I'm a grown-up," said Penny, rather indignantly. "We're both grown-ups."

"Jaunty has been staying the night?"

"Yes," said Penny.

Tinkler chortled. "The corpse-faced motherfucker," he said. "Quite literally."

ACKNOWLEDGEMENTS

I'd like to thank the following people.

Anna-Maja Oléhn provided invaluable help with details about life and language in Sweden, as did Jonas Tistelgren (who also provided a surname for Ida!) Joel De'ath (yes, his real name) was a rich source of background information about the Scandinavian extreme metal music scene.

Matt West organised our trip to Sweden and talked me into going in the first place. Heartfelt thanks to Cherry Koivula and Jonas Anderson, Kristina Rudbjer, Johan Ingebäck and Lee W Lundin for making us so welcome. Also Barbro Bornsäter, who provided the first name of another character.

I hope the inhabitants of Lidköping won't mind me transmuting their lovely town into the purely imaginary Trollesko. I should also hasten to add that there is no pizza strip club there or indeed, to my knowledge, anywhere in the fair nation of Sweden.

Big thanks to Ken Kessler for reading the books and for

chatting hi-fi with me. And to Carol and Martin Piper for suggesting a novel murder weapon. Not to mention Gordon Larkin, for suggesting troll malarkey.

Last but not least, many thanks to Jerome Lewis and, most recently, his brother Nico for their continuing support and help with the Vinyl Detective series.

ABOUT THE AUTHOR

Andrew Cartmel is a novelist and playwright. He is the author of the Vinyl Detective series, which was hailed as "marvellously inventive and endlessly fascinating" by *Publishers Weekly*. His work for television includes commissions for *Midsomer Murders* and *Torchwood*, and a legendary stint as script editor on *Doctor Who*. He has also written plays for the London Fringe, toured as a stand-up comedian, and currently has a play entitled Glacier Lake scheduled to open this spring. He lives in London with too much vinyl and just enough cats. You can find Andrew on Twitter at @andrewcartmel.

For more fantastic fiction, author events,
exclusive excerpts, competitions, limited editions and more

VISIT OUR WEBSITE
titanbooks.com

LIKE US ON FACEBOOK
facebook.com/titanbooks

FOLLOW US ON TWITTER AND INSTAGRAM
@TitanBooks

EMAIL US
readerfeedback@titanemail.com